MW01701699

KIRSTEN G. SCHUDER

INSIDE DWELLER GENESIS

INSIDE DWELLER SERIES

BOOK ONE

Black Rose Writing | Texas

This book contains scenes and subjects with sexual assault, suicide, violence, and death. Reader discretion is advised.

The author grants the final approval for this literary material.

First printing

ISBN: 978-1-68513-275-0
PUBLISHED BY BLACK ROSE WRITING
www.blackrosewriting.com

Printed in the United States of America
Suggested Retail Price (SRP) $23.95

Inside Dweller is printed in Gentium Book Basic

*As a planet-friendly publisher, Black Rose Writing does its best to eliminate unnecessary waste to reduce paper usage and energy costs, while never compromising the reading experience. As a result, the final word count vs. page count may not meet common expectations.

I would like to thank, first and always/ my family.

To my husband, best friend, soulmate, and the bravest and best person I have ever met.

To my children, also my best friends, and two of the loveliest people I have ever known.

I could not have achieved what I have without you.

You have helped me become the best version of myself.

You have advised me and encouraged me.

I dedicate everything to you.

Also, I would like to thank the countless beta readers who have provided me with feedback. I can only hope that our exchanges were as meaningful for you as they were for me.

Last, but not least, I would like to thank the readers who picked up this book. I hope the adventure we go on together will be a memorable and fun one, as dark and twisted as it may be.

List of Characters (in order of appearance)

Miranda Sheppard: A twenty-nine year old accountant; experiences difficulties of known and unknown origins.

Alison Sheppard: Miranda's sister, surrogate mother, and retired skydiver.

Dr. Daniel Foreman: Neurosurgeon.

Dark Stranger: A mysterious enigma.

Janice: Nurse.

Alistair and Ester Foreman: Daniel and Steven Foreman's father and mother.

Steven Foreman: Daniel Foreman's brother; Miranda's boyfriend.

Dr. Gerald Fine: Psychiatrist: Dr. Gallagher's business partner.

Dr. Jack Gallagher: Clinical psychologist.

Harry: Home security technician.

Mike and Joe Cavanaugh: Paranormal researchers.

Bill and Rita: Emergency medical technicians.

Tim: Mike and Joe's cousin; paranormal computer guru and technician.

Tara: Infrared camera technician.

Dr. Abraham Tetenbaum: Head scientist of world's most powerful MRI; Dr. Gallagher's friend.

Mrs. Berkshire: Family friend to the Sheppards: Local business woman.

Heather: Drs. Gallagher and Fine's secretary.

Frank: Restaurant owner.

Dr. Grace Kelly: Dr. Gallagher's mentor.

Dr. Favian Widener: Teacher and bibliophile; Dr. Grace Kelly's friend.

Mrs. Jack Gallagher: Jack Gallagher's wife.

Dr. Svoboda: Psychiatrist.

Dr. John O'Connor: Psychologist; author of Id Speak.

Dark Stranger's Friends

All Fiction Is Real in the Land of Possibilities.

"The greatest trick the devil ever pulled was convincing the world that he doesn't exist."

—*The Usual Suspects*, 1989

INSIDE DWELLER
GENESIS

1
MIRANDA

Miranda Sheppard had crossed a line, unable to turn back time to extract her from the set of circumstances placing her at the intersection of Wilson Street and Marten's Place in Davenport. A scream evolved from a deep, primal urge she didn't know existed until the moment her life was in peril. Miranda's seventeen-year war with God stopped dead. Using her last conscious seconds, she begged a faceless, callous entity for her life with all she could muster, an enervated, "Please..."

Miranda braced herself for the ruinous impact. A million pins stung Miranda's arms and hands as she clutched the steering wheel and slammed both feet on the brakes. The nose of Miranda's 2007 custom-painted, candy-apple-red Corvette convertible collided with the flank of the crimson Shop-n-Bag box truck and crumpled inward. The cancer scare, the constant state of exhaustion from the last six months, the horrible dreams and images lurking every time she closed her eyes, and the last image, her sister, flashed across her mind and then liquesced as she plummeted into darkness.

Trapped. A pair of eyes glimmered from a vast expanse of blackness. Loud buzzing filled her ears, the noise tormenting her for the last six months. Darkness enveloped her entire being. Dark vines exploded from Miranda's core and smothered her from the inside out, choking her. They smelled like sewage, burned matches, and rotting flesh.

The entire scene dissolved and morphed into a darkened room. With Miranda's wrists bound to the arms of a chair and her ankles to the legs, she could not escape. She could not look away, her head strapped to the high-backed chair. She could not blink, forceps forcing her eyes to remain open. She could not scream, a ball gag stifling her cries. A movie screen played bloody images, skinned alive, dismembered, disemboweled, charred bodies in the wake of atomic bombs, children crying next to their parents' motionless corpses, blight, sores weeping pus and blood. Storms, earthquakes, walls of water ravaged the landscape until our beautiful, blue globe acquiesced...

For months, these images had shocked her awake, making sleep impossible, but in waking, she had been able to avoid the images. Forced to witness, Miranda screamed through her ball gag before succumbing to the darkness.

• • •

The mixture of misery and antiseptic cleanser and the sight of the I.C.U. at Morningside Hospital in Davenport made Alison's eyes sting with tears. The image of Miranda, head bandaged, the left upper side of Miranda's gaunt face engorged with different colors, and breathing with the help of a respirator, shocked Alison back into the worst day of her life. The blood rushed to her head. Alison doubled over at the prospect of having to bury her last living family member, her sister.

"Whoa, easy." A pair of hands caught her under her arms.

"Thanks." Alison gulped in air to keep herself from crying. Her eyes met Dr. Foreman's. The last seventeen years had been kind to him. Bits of white intermingling with his black hair at the sides of his head and little crow's feet around his brown eyes were the only detectable differences. If Dr. Foreman's face had not become synonymous with the darkest days of her life, Alison would have considered dating him, preferring men with a swarthy complexion since her teenage years.

"Here, Ms. Sheppard." Dr. Foreman steered Alison to an empty examination room and sat her down on a stool with wheels.

"You remember me."

"It's difficult to forget the extraordinary. I remember the strength you had for Miranda."

Yeah, sure. If I were that strong, I would have dragged Miranda to the doctor myself. No force of nature, though, was as resilient as Miranda's will. Alison's lunch with Miranda earlier that day haunted her. Miranda's copper-kissed, red-brown hair, usually shiny and straight, looked like a pile of orange straw, her face gaunt, and her green eyes dull, almost lifeless. She didn't eat her lunch, and she kept swatting at imaginary insects swarming her ears. Alison could see why Miranda had been avoiding her. The entire day disrupted her sense of reality. On her way home, she considered staging an intervention to save Miranda's life. *Could she really be losing her sanity? Was it just the lack of sleep?* Tears blurred her vision. "I don't know if I have any strength left if I... if I..."

The loudspeaker of the hospital's public announcement system squawked about someone bringing something somewhere.

In anticipation of the end of Alison's fragmented sentence, Dr. Foreman offered, "Miranda sustained an injury to her head, but she is very lucky. We did an MRI and a CT, and we didn't find any damage. She incurred severe external injuries. Her brain is intact, thankfully, and the skull was not fractured. She is not in a coma, but she has a concussion."

"Oh, thank God." *Shoot.* Alison hated it when her eyes and nose leaked.

Dr. Foreman reached over to the end table, took a tissue, and handed it to Alison.

"It's not just like Mom, when she..." Alison gulped, dabbed her eyes, and pinched her nose with the tissue. "Why isn't Miranda awake, then? And why is she on a ventilator?"

"With head injuries and a loss of consciousness, it's a precaution we use to guarantee her brain receives oxygen, which aids the recovery process. The next forty-eight hours are crucial. We will be monitoring her to ensure her brain doesn't swell. If that does happen, we will insert a catheter to normalize the pressure. Now, we manage her injuries and wait."

"She is going to wake up, right, Dr. Foreman?" Alison drew in a shaky breath.

"She's critical, but we're optimistic at the moment. It could be worse." After a pause, Dr. Foreman asked, "Was Miranda having any medical issues? She shows signs of malnutrition."

Alison shrugged. After all, she didn't have any proof that Miranda was mentally unstable. After her extreme concern, she convinced herself that it had to be the lack of sleep, explaining her lack of intervention she would live to regret. "Miranda couldn't sleep or eat for the last six months. She always has some small issues around the anniversary of our parent's death, but this year was different. It's almost like something vexed her." *Now this. I knew something was really wrong. It's my fault. I should have stopped her.* Alison's sobbing became involuntary. She stood up and hugged Dr. Foreman.

For the first time in Dr. Foreman's history at Morningside Hospital, which included becoming the youngest doctor to run the Neurosurgery Department, he hugged the family member of a patient until Alison's sobs subsided, allowing himself to feel attraction without acting upon it. "Your sister is a fighter. She'll come through."

Alison laughed, stepped back, and wiped her eyes. "Yeah, she's too stubborn to die."

Dr. Foreman nodded. "I will make my rounds and be back in a little while to check on her. Okay?"

Alison nodded. Dr. Foreman opened the door for her. She made her way to the nurse's station surrounded by a circle of I.C.U. beds. Nine of the beds remained empty, and patients on respirators and heart rate monitors occupied three others. Alison walked on the outside of the circle and took her place next to Miranda's bedside.

Alison made eye contact with a woman approximately in her seventies sitting at the bedside of a gentleman, most likely the woman's husband. Through their generational differences, Alison understood the woman's look of hope intermingled with desperation. No one sees it until the moment a loved one lies in a hospital bed, struggling for just one more breath. If she had seen this woman in passing, she wouldn't have felt any connection with her at all.

Alison wouldn't have taken any moment for granted had she known that at the young age of eighteen, she would have to pull the plug on her mother's respirator and the intubation tube from her esophagus while her father lay on the silver, cold table in the morgue.

2
AWAKE

An encasement of pain gripped Miranda's head. Through her one open eye, she could make out blurred, misshapen colors and light. *What the hell is this thing in my mouth?* She couldn't scream for help. *What the hell is on my hand?* She pulled on the lump and winced, withdrawing something sharp from her skin. She heard the footsteps of the aliens. They blocked her vision with complete blackness and despair. Their black tendrils seized her wrists.

• • •

Alison had only left for a moment to use the bathroom. When she spotted Miranda, she had already pulled out her I. V. The blood from the back of Miranda's hand spotted the crisp white hospital sheets, her olive-green hospital gown, and smeared her cheeks and forehead. Miranda felt the respirator tube in her mouth, and her arms flailed. Her heart rate monitor beeped in response to her distress. Alison grabbed the nurse walking back to the nurse's station in the middle of the circle of beds. "Hey, over there." The nurse ran to the phone and called for help. A doctor ran to Miranda's bedside.

• • •

A male voice trickled into Miranda's ears: "Stop pulling on the respirator tube..." She yielded, too weak to struggle against the tentacles holding her wrists in place. They reminded her of tar.

• • •

The next time Miranda opened her eyes, she lay in a hospital room, the curtains drawn on the windows. Alison's blond hair hung in front of her eyes as she dozed in the chair next to her bed. *I wonder how long she's been sitting there...*

• • •

Miranda awoke to the sunrise, the brown-beige curtains unable to conceal its brilliance, outlining the figure of a man with his face darkened, like a photograph lit from the back. She could only see his dark hair, eyes blacker than a cloudy night with no moon, and his seven-foot stature, taller than any person she had ever seen. A pungent smell invaded her nostrils, and she coughed. *I wonder who he is.*

• • •

Miranda awoke again to the stream of sunlight peeking through the curtains, insufficient in their ability to block the warm, yellow rays invading the dim light of the room.

"Heeeey. How are you feeling?" Alison stood up from the chair, sat on the bed, and took Miranda's hands in hers, mindful not to unrest the IV Miranda pulled out ten days earlier. "You scared the crap out of me. You can't imagine how happy I am to see those green eyes of yours."

"What..." Miranda whispered, but coughed because of the dryness in her throat. Her tongue was slow and thick, like it was getting in its own way. "Water?"

"I'll ask the nurse if it's okay." Alison pressed the buzzer. "You were in an accident."

The question sat on Miranda's face. Her Cherry Red, her Corvette, her baby.

"No, I'm sorry, hon. Your car didn't make it."

A car. It wasn't just a car. After all, Alison had never owned a Corvette, so she wouldn't understand. A Corvette is an expression of beauty, and when one has been decimated and could no longer participate in the world, its lack of presence must be mourned.

"Well! You're awake. And how are you feeling, Ms. Sheppard?"

"Janice. I remember you," Miranda croaked. Janice, an I.C.U. nurse, had cared for her mother before her death. Janice had gained at least seventy pounds. Her hair had taken on a dyed strawberry-blonde hue, a change from the jet-black she wore seventeen years ago. Janice's ample hips and legs swayed as she made her way to the end of the bed to check Miranda's I. V. Miranda wouldn't have recognized her if it weren't for her unmistakable southern drawl. Even though she had transplanted from Alabama decades ago, her voice sounded like she carried her hometown with her. "Like I got sat on by an elephant."

Janice and Alison laughed. "Yeah, a car accident can do that to a person."

"And thirsty," Miranda added.

"Is it okay for her to have a drink?" Alison asked.

Janice checked Miranda's chart. "Yes, of course it is! Would you like some ice?"

Miranda tried to nod and smile, but winced at the pain in her head.

"All right, I'll go get it. Welcome back to the world, Ms. Sheppard."

"Thank you, Janice," Alison said.

Janice returned with the pitcher of water and poured Miranda a cup. "Here you go," Janice handed the cup to Alison. "I'll let Dr. Foreman know you're awake. He'll come in to see you in a few hours. I'll return to check on you in a little while."

"Thanks again, Janice," Alison smiled. "Nice and cold. Sip it slowly." She held the plastic straw to Miranda's mouth while Miranda took in the cool liquid bit by bit.

Miranda leaned back. She reached up and touched the bandages on her forehead making her face feel heavy.

"Yeah, you're pretty banged up there." Alison placed the cup on the bedside table. "You are crazy lucky, though. No broken bones. You have a concussion."

"How long have I been out?"

"You've been in and out of it for ten days."

Miranda groaned. "I must not have a business left."

"Oh, don't worry. I asked Mrs. Berkshire to help you out. She went through your appointment book and called all of your clients for you, claiming to be your new secretary. I also called the accounting program at the local college and arranged for you to have an intern. You can start interviewing as soon as you get out of here."

Miranda paused. She didn't need to ask how Alison's week had been: hair disheveled, clothes wrinkled, and eyes puffy with dark circles. She looked just like Mom with that blond hair and her blue eyes. So pretty, as messy as she was, like one of those Hummel statues of the kids with perfect features and the little dirndls. "Wow, that's incredible. Thank you so much."

Alison nodded. "I'm happy you're back."

"How do you manage it?" asked Miranda.

"What?"

"After Mom and Dad died, I cried, I screamed, I sulked, carried on, I went Goth and stuck my ears full of holes and pins, and I didn't listen to a word you said. And somehow, you always kept your cool, just like now. How do you do it?"

A trace of a smile traversed across Alison's lips. "What you see doesn't match what you don't. But, I focus on what's going right, and I get myself back on track. Right now, for instance, you're alive and awake. You conquered half the battle. Maybe you were catching up on sleep."

"What are you talking about?" Miranda yawned. "Owww," Miranda moaned. She couldn't even yawn without pain. So tired. The bed drew her head down onto her pillow.

Alison paused for a moment. Could her sister be putting her on even in this condition? She was just the type of person to do it if she could pull it off. "Don't you remember, all those doctors you saw? You went for months with only a bit of sleep every night."

"I don't remember the crash."

"Dr. Foreman told me that it is common."

"I had trouble sleeping? I can tell you, I don't think that will be a problem anymore." Miranda closed her eyes and drifted off to sleep.

Alison sat back down on the chair next to the bed. "So, what exactly do you remember?" she whispered.

3
RECOVERY

"What about the fact that she doesn't remember the last six months?" Alison had pulled Dr. Foreman outside Miranda's hospital room while the nurse had her busy signing forms and listening to instructions for her release.

"Sometimes, memories come back a little at a time. It's only a six-month period. Some people lose a majority of their childhood memories or can barely remember anything at all. It could have something to do with the sleep deprivation, which can also affect memory and not have much to do with the trauma. It's best not to push her on it. Just be there to listen if the memories return."

"But, isn't it strange that she's forgotten everything, including visiting all those doctors, the insomnia, the malnutrition?" Alison didn't know why this unsettled her, but she couldn't deny it, like something trying to scratch through a wall in her head or pick away at a scab.

Dr. Foreman waved his hand. "Well, we don't know everything about how the mind works, but it's not so strange when you think about it. If the memory of the accident was traumatic for her, all the other memories might have been buried or forgotten only because of how close they were to the event."

Alison wondered if he erred, and if he did, would he be as confident?

While Miranda's lack of recall concerned Alison, relief flooded through her at the return of Miranda's mouth.

"You should go to your bed, you know." Alison opened the side door leading into the kitchen of Miranda's house. "Dr. Foreman said..."

"I'm sick of staying in bed. Don't you think I've already spent enough time in bed?" She hobbled through her little galley kitchen. "I want to lie on the couch for a little while so I can feel more like a normal person, not an invalid," Miranda argued. "Besides, you can keep a better eye on me on the couch because you won't have to run up and down the stairs to go to the bedroom."

Alison sighed, although Miranda's obstinacy promised signs of her recovery. The alternative was much worse. "Remember, Dr. Foreman said for you to take it easy. I've already called the physical therapist and set up your first appointment, and you have your appointment with Da... um, Dr. Foreman too."

Even through her pain, Miranda caught the slip-up. "With who?" Miranda's lips curled upward.

Alison could only shake her head and put their bags on the floor. "Here. Let's get you over to the couch." She took Miranda's arm.

"Yes, and you can tell me all about Daaah."

She's always been too smart for her own good. When Miranda was three, their dad lost the tiniest screw while fixing his glasses, and after almost an hour of the family searching for it, Miranda found it in the shag carpet. Her parents had commented on her sharp mind and intellect even then. Alison learned that her sister's uncanny eye for detail meant she noticed *everything,* as if she could see right through her. Now, not even a concussion and an exorbitant amount of pain could distract her from observing Alison and Dr. Foreman's new first-name status.

Alison knew better than to try and bypass the subject. She hoped Miranda had forgotten after she established her in the living room with pillows, a blanket, and chicken noodle soup she had made at home, but Miranda never forgot anything. Miranda's crossed arms and expectant look worked better than her usual verbal pestering.

"Okay, okay. Dr. Foreman, Dan, took me to the cafeteria for a cup of coffee a couple of times while you were under. Of course, I couldn't even think of him that way, since getting you better was my total focus, but we spent a lot of time talking. I always had thought of him as attractive, but I never acted on it, because, you know." Alison paused and looked down at her hands. "Well, on the way out, he asked me if we could go out for coffee again."

"So, did you guys fuck yet?"

"Miranda!"

Alison's shock produced a smile on Miranda's lips.

Why was Miranda always so happy when she annoyed Alison? "Infant." Alison rolled her eyes and turned away to walk into the kitchen but stuck her middle finger in the air on her way.

Miranda laughed, wincing from the pain it caused in her head.

Alison turned back. "Why do you do that?"

"What?"

"Laugh when I stick my middle finger up at you?"

Miranda smiled. "'Cuz I know I got to you."

"Yeah, well..." Alison turned and stuck her middle finger up behind her as she walked to the kitchen to start the dishes. Miranda chuckled. "Hey, guess what?"

"Yeah, what?"

"*The Davenport* did a story on your accident."

"Really? Why?"

"Do you want to see?" Alison brought the newspaper over and placed it on the coffee table. "Here's your mail and your magazines. I figured I should tell you before you found out another way." Alison walked back to the kitchen to clean the dishes. “I found out myself a day or two ago,” Alison called from the kitchen. “I went to the newsstand right outside the hospital, and I looked down and saw your picture. The reporter didn’t even contact your office, or me, or anything. I have no idea how they even found out.”

Miranda took the paper and saw the portrait she had of herself on her website. *Local Business Woman Survives Devastating Auto Collision.* “See, this is proof, me on the front page, why my friends and I almost died of boredom throughout high school. Nothing exciting happens in this town. Ever.”

Alison laughed. “As a rule, I would agree with you if you weren’t selling yourself short, Miranda. You underestimate your importance. You have accomplished so much, and you’re not even thirty.”

The heat rose to Miranda’s cheeks. She didn’t usually think of herself in terms of accomplishments. Sure, she provided accounting and tax services to most of the businesses in the community, and she had a turkey drive for Thanksgiving, a coat drive for the winter, and a toy drive for the kids every Christmas, but it simply constituted part of what she did with her time. She didn’t find anything extraordinary in it.

She tried to read beyond the first sentence of the article, but focusing her eyes hurt her head, although she did catch Mrs. Berkshire’s name as she scanned down the page. That would explain it. Mrs. Berkshire came off as a dowdy old woman, but the girls had learned over the years that she was a lot shrewder than she let on, as if she enjoyed other people’s underestimation of her abilities and intellect. “It’s like they’re talking about a stranger.” Miranda put the paper down on the coffee table, leaned back on the couch, put her feet up, and closed her eyes. She couldn’t even think, like someone beat her head from the inside with a hammer.

Alison finished washing up, dried her hands, and sat on the black leather easy chair next to the matching couch. “Tired from the trip home?”

"Yeah. I still ache from head to toe, but mostly from head. Oh, who was that really tall doctor at the hospital? You must have met nearly everyone. They all told me you practically lived there."

"I didn't meet a really tall doctor. The tallest one I saw was Dr. Foreman. Maybe the guy was part of the night shift."

Miranda shook her head. "Can't be. Strange. The sunlight poured into the room, but I couldn't see him, sort of like a shadow hid his face. I figured you saw him. And I smelled something awful."

"A smell like what?" Alison put out the feet of the recliner, sighed, and closed her eyes. Maybe she should get some new furniture like this chair. She could fall asleep in it.

"Like rotten eggs."

"Huh." *What could smell like that in a hospital?* "Maybe it was iodine or something."

"No, it definitely had a rotten egg smell."

Alison waved her hand as if she could make it disappear with magic. "It was probably a dream. You were pretty out of it. They had you on pain killers too."

"I guess. It seemed pretty real to me, though."

"Sometimes dreams will do that. Besides, you also thought aliens experimented on you." Dan had explained many intubated patients experience hallucinations of undergoing medical experiments conducted by aliens.

Miranda laughed. "Yeah, I guess I was out of it."

Alison hopped out of the chair, sat next to Miranda on the couch, and patted her own lap. "Here."

Miranda smiled and laid her head on Alison's lap, just like she did as a teenager. Alison was good at being there when she needed her.

Alison smoothed her hand over Miranda's coarse hair: still so pale, so thin. She resumed eating and sleeping in the hospital but still had a long way to go. Alison rubbed Miranda's uninjured cheek until her green eyes closed.

• • •

A few minutes faded into the darkness of the evening. Alison woke with a start. Miranda's feet rested on her thigh. She looked to the side to find Miranda's sleeping face on the other end of the couch. She grabbed the back of her neck and winced, appreciating the fact that her pain couldn't possibly surpass Miranda's.

Miranda's accident was just one incident in a long line of life trials for the sisters. Losing their parents eradicated their former existence with an ideal family to a troubling childhood for Miranda and a shaky start for Alison's adulthood.

Her parents had visited her aunt and uncle a mere ten miles away from their house on August 28th, seventeen years ago. When Alison awoke the next morning and found her parents absent, she called her Aunt Cheri and Uncle Dave. A sickening feeling settled into the pit of her stomach when she heard the worry Aunt Cheri tried to conceal in her voice.

Aunt Cheri convinced the police that they needed to drive along the ten-mile route from their house to her sister's house as soon as possible, an easy sell due to the fact that her brother-in-law worked with the police chief on a group of ritualistic mass murders. This prompted a drive-through of the route from Aunt Cheri's to the Sheppard home.

Officer McGloughlin discovered the unfortunate evidence that Aunt Cheri's instincts possessed more than worried imaginings. At 6.8 miles from Aunt Cheri and Uncle David's door, at mile marker 15 on County Road 25, he discovered the skid marks leading down the side of the mountain. He followed the tracks to where the silver 1998 Oldsmobile Cutlass and its victims lay and the tree responsible for its haphazard part in their demise.

Dr. Allen Sheppard had passed on impact. Upon examining Dr. Joy Sheppard, Officer McGloughlin discovered a faint pulse when he placed his ungloved finger on the side of her neck. His quick response allowed her to survive another 24 hours in the I.C.U. at Morningside Hospital, where Aunt Cheri, Uncle Dave, and Joy's two girls, Alison and Miranda, kept vigil and waited.

The following day, after Alison authorized the tests needed to determine the condition of her mother, Dr. Foreman showed Alison the extent of the injuries her mother sustained to her cranium and the pictures of the parts of her brain destroyed in the crash.

Even though the chances of her mother having any type of recovery were null, it did nothing to ease Alison's conscience or to quell the reoccurring nightmares she still had of taking her mother off life support. She needed to be the one to send her mother into the afterlife, her way of honoring the greatest woman she ever knew.

An autopsy revealed two healthy, 48-year-old adults with no evidence of drugs or alcohol in their system, passing from the injuries sustained in the crash. The weather had been clear that night. The police presumed Dr. Sheppard swerved to avoid something in the road, maybe a deer. Her aunt accepted this explanation more readily than Alison, but Alison's certainty of foul play led her to ask the chief of police, Mr. Joseph Halenbecker, to investigate.

Halenbecker entertained the conversation out of respect of his former colleague but did not pursue it any further. He assured Alison that his investigation revealed no signs of murder. Alison later resolved that her parents most likely swerved the car to avoid hitting a deer, and her feelings, something insidious surrounded the circumstances of her parents' death, arose due to the shock of her parents' sudden death.

Besides, she had enough problems with Miranda. Her parents would have wanted her to focus on her sister rather than their demise.

Aunt Cheri and Uncle Dave offered to take them in, but Miranda wanted to stay in her parents' house, unwilling to lose any more of her mother and father than she already had. Miranda could not bear the thought of moving from the home where her mother and father's presence could still be felt, seen, and smelled, the place they had lived all their lives. After the accident, she fell asleep every night in her parent's bed where she grew up feeling safe and comforted, sleeping on her mother's pillow still enveloped with a hint of lavender, the scent of her mother's favorite shampoo.

Alison couldn't force Miranda to leave their house and rip her from her home after her parents' departure ruptured her entire childhood. She would have to plan their finances carefully, but she could make it work thanks to the life insurance policies her parents had left them in their will. Alison tried her best to fill both her mother's and father's shoes, but when Miranda hit thirteen, dyed her hair black to match her clothes and makeup, stuck her face full of metal rings, her usual self-confidence faded into a worry so profound for Miranda, it made her stomach churn day and night.

Aunt Cheri, though, kept a watchful eye over them, serving as an advisor for Alison. "She's a teenager. Uncle David and I don't have children of our own, but you know I have been working with eighth graders for fifteen years now. Even children who don't lose their parents go through this. Keep trying to communicate with her. She'll get it." Aunt Cheri's blue eyes gleamed. She looked so much like Alison's mother, with the fair complexion and blond hair. It should have given Alison some solace, but at times, it caused her more pain, a reminder of the absence in her life.

"Yeah, but I'm not Mom. That's who she really needs, and there's no way I can give it to her. It's all my fault." Alison's voice faltered as she tried to swallow the impulse to cry.

"Hey, hey, look at me." Aunt Cheri laid her hand on Alison's cheek to assure eye contact. "They died in a car accident. Not your fault."

"Yeah, but I killed... I killed Mom." Alison couldn't stop the steady flow of tears trickling down from the corners of her eyes.

"No, honey, you didn't. She had already passed."

"I know all that, but it doesn't help the nightmares I have every night. Miranda's mad at everyone and everything, and she has every right to be. Yes, I feel guilty for taking Mom off of life support and because I had a normal childhood and she doesn't. It's not fair that she doesn't have Mom and Dad the way I had them. I know Miranda blames me too, so why shouldn't I blame myself?" Alison collapsed in a deluge of tears.

Aunt Cheri took both of Alison's hands in hers. "You know, I admire you."

Alison couldn't help laughing, choking at the same time as she rubbed the tears on her cheek. "Yeah, right." She grabbed a handful of tissues. Maybe she should invest in a tissue company. She probably kept them in business, especially lately.

"No, really, I'm so proud of you. You are so young, and you did what most young women your age couldn't even fathom. You have shown such strength through impossible circumstances."

"I don't feel strong."

"But you are. You handled your parent's funeral with a grace I haven't seen from most adults. You stayed to take care of your sister. I don't know many people who would have handled these things the way you have, regardless of their age."

"So, what do I do with Miranda? I can't seem to do anything right. If I agree with what she says, she gets even madder. If I try to put my foot down, she yells that I'm not her mother, so she doesn't have to listen to me. It's like watching a train wreck that I can't prevent, or like I'm stuck in an alternate universe called Opposite Land where my parents are dead and my sister hates me. I hate me too. She used to follow me everywhere and cry when I had to go to my room to do my homework."

"Oh, no, please don't talk like that," said Aunt Cheri, patting her niece's hand. "I wish I worked in your school system, but I do know the guidance counselor there. I'll speak with her to see if we can get her an appointment."

Miranda hated seeing the school counselor more than having to wake up every day and pretend as if her parents weren't dead. Her friends and she had drifted apart. She supposed they got tired of her crying all the time. Still, she detested the idea of talking to anyone about how horrible it had been to live life without her parents. Her sister and Aunt Cheri convinced her to go with the veiled threat of dragging her to a psychiatrist instead.

Ms. Krishner, the school counselor, wasn't a bad person, per se. She would sit there and say nothing at all. Sure, she seemed to be listening on the surface, nodding and um-humming at the appropriate times, but her eyes focused on something else in the room, most likely on a mental vacation to a tropical island with a hunk named Jacques rather than listening to the tortured soul of a teenage girl.

Since Miranda's precociousness and her intolerance for boredom often prompted the trouble she elicited, she decided that since she didn't want to attend the meetings in the first place, she would make up stories to pass the time. At first, she tested the waters and threw in something a little strange, such as running around her room in her underwear, to see if it registered a response, but none came. Miranda's conclusion: Ms. Krishner was either comatose or hard of hearing.

As a source of amusement, Miranda challenged herself to make up outrageous stories, each week topping the previous to see if she could make the dead rise from her chair.

"So, Miranda, how has your week been so far?"

"I had a better week. My ritualistic sex club cheers me up."

"I see."

"Yeah. You know, orgies are really fun. A great distraction. I got to have sex with at least eight different guys. Girls, too. We had orgies every night this week so far."

"Uh humm."

Miranda used the orgy conversation as proof that her attendance at these weekly sessions was as useful as Congress has been in balancing the national budget, something they read about in their government class.

"How do you know what an orgy is?" Alison asked.

"Alison, really? I'm not five any more you know." Miranda's tone dripped with sarcasm.

"How long has this been going on?"

"Three months. I've made up every kind of story imaginable. I even told her I was kidnapped and ravaged by pirates over the weekend, and it was a lot of fun. Great party." A fake smile accompanied her upward-turned thumbs.

"Mir-an-da!"

"You would think I would have gotten some sort of reaction. It's like talking to a giant mushroom." Miranda folded her arms, her smile conveying a sense of satisfaction for making a well-argued point and a clever simile comparing the shape of the counselor's curly hair with her level of responsiveness all at the same time.

Alison sighed. If her parents had survived, she wouldn't have to sit with the angry, sullen version of her sister. Alison would have join her friends at Boston University instead of holding down two part-time jobs and attending the community college, and her parents would know what to do. Her mother would employ her superior listening skills, say all the right things, and work out whatever issue Miranda brought to her. Her father would offer a few more things to make Miranda feel all better and happy. After all, they spent their lives helping others feel better.

Besides, Alison remained convinced that she could not provide any more comfort to Miranda other than the fact that she would stay with her no matter what, but even this was offered on a shaky foundation. Alison could die tomorrow as well. If it happened to her parents, who seemed indomitable in almost every sense, it could happen to her. *Come on, Alison. It's not like you didn't learn anything at all from your parents. Try and think of what they would do.*

"All right, listen. You can see the doctor Aunt Cheri found for you, Dr. Gallagher..."

"Yeah, right," Miranda snorted. If they weren't her parents, she didn't want to speak to anyone else.

"You can see our pastor at church and speak with him..."

"Why? He's consorting with the God who snatched our parents away," Miranda snapped.

Alison rolled her eyes and blew out a sigh. *We'll work on that.* "Or, you can start talking to me or Aunt Cheri."

For a moment, Alison saw the true Miranda for the first time since her parents' passing. "I don't know if I can," Miranda whispered, tears welling up in her eyes.

"I'm sorry life has been so hard, Miranda." Alison folded her hands over Miranda's pale, slender hands. "We'll get through this together somehow. I won't leave you. I promise. I didn't go to Boston and dump you off at Aunt Cheri's house. I'll keep trying. Even when you're a pain in the ass." Alison and Miranda laughed with tears in their eyes. "Okay?"

"Okay. I guess I can try too. It hurts."

"I know. Let's figure it out together."

Things changed, for the most part. Miranda's outlandish behavior subsided, but she couldn't bring herself to speak about her inner turmoil. She decided to take the pins out of her face, dye her hair back to red, and wear colors other than black. It was time for her to move on and figure out what she wanted out of life. Her parents would have wanted that.

Alison smiled at her slumbering sister through the darkness, grateful that at least she lived through the accident, but also at the memory of what Miranda did in her sessions with Ms. Krishner. She commended herself for keeping a straight face when Miranda told her the first time. If it weren't for the circumstances, it would have sent her into a giggling fit.

Alison slid Miranda's feet onto the couch and pulled the blanket over her. She picked up her bag she left in front of the kitchen door and padded over to the bathroom down the hallway on the other side of the wall of the kitchen, appreciative of the location of the first floor bathroom, a decent distance from the living room so she didn't have to worry about waking Miranda up. Dan said Miranda would probably sleep a lot, which would promote her recovery.

As Alison brushed her teeth, she heard a noise. She paused, the toothbrush still in her mouth. She narrowed her eyes and listened, but attributed it to her unfamiliarity with her sister's house noises. Her father used to say that houses had creaks and moans because of the way they settle over the years. Her mother would counter that it is a spirit. Alison used to hope her mother was joking.

She finished washing her face. Another noise, this time louder, like the footfall of heavy boots? *That couldn't be Miranda.*

Alison unplugged a lamp on a small table in the hallway right outside the bathroom, the only weapon she could find, and crept down the dark hall, feeling ahead with each leading foot to ensure the soundlessness of her steps. Panting, perspiration dampened her forehead. Her nose wrinkled against an offensive odor. *Jeez, did something die in here?*

Alison froze, trying to peer in the dark, swearing she saw the form of a man? A shadow? It seemed like it was moving, but it was way too tall to be a person. Did her eyes deceive her? She read something about a brain phenomenon where people see patterns in abstract shapes in the darkness even when one isn't there. Each passing moment seemed like an hour.

"Alison?"

Alison gasped. "Oh, God, it's you!"

The hall light switched on. Miranda stared at her with a questioning look. "If you like the lamp that much, all you had to do was ask. I would have given it to you."

"No, I thought I heard something. Did you just get up? Here, you shouldn't walk around by yourself." Alison took Miranda's arm with her free hand.

"I got up to go to the bathroom." Miranda hobbled toward her intended destination. "You're probably not used to the noises around here."

"I thought so too, but this one noise, I could swear I heard it in the kitchen, footsteps. I got ready just in case. I didn't want to see anything else happen to you."

"You and I survived probably the worst of the worst, and I'm still here. Looks like you're stuck with me."

Alison squinted her eyes and stuck out her lips into a pout. "Promise?"

"Yeah, promise. Okay, why don't you put down that lamp first? You're making me nervous, dangerous with that thing."

Alison giggled and put the lamp back down on the end table.

"Geeze, have you been working out?" Miranda squeezed her sister's arm with her free hand. "I hope I don't make you mad. Now I'm even more nervous."

Alison giggled again. *I hope this means things will continue to look up.*

4
THANKSGIVING

Miranda's favorite season, autumn, settled upon Davenport, blanketing colors upon the trees populating the soft, round mountainsides, making the quaint town appear as if it posed for a portrait. The historical buildings dressed in demure grays and pastels. Stark white church steeples challenged the orange, yellow, and red treetops for attention. Proper, immovable brick buildings, standing since the 1800s, lorded over the town, the figurative headmistresses in charge of discipline.

Autumn showered kindness that year, providing the residents with plenty of time to become reacquainted with the cold as the temperatures dropped in small increments. Long coats replaced sweaters and light jackets by Thanksgiving, and chatter of snow arose before Christmas. Miranda oft heard people parroting their thankfulness that the usual October blizzard bypassed them for a pleasant change.

Miranda and Alison usually spent Thanksgiving with Mr. and Mrs. Berkshire, family friends and the local fruit-and-vegetablestand owners. The girls knew the Berkshires their whole lives. They were as influential as the brick buildings on the town and infamous for their banter, mostly on Mrs. Berkshire's end. No one really knew for certain if the couple even liked each other.

During the holidays, the Berkshires stepped in to fill as many voids as they could after Alison and Miranda's parents died and Aunt Cheri left. However, Dan Foreman invited the sisters to a gathering at his house, so they quieted Mrs. Berkshire's protests and promised Christmas Day to her. Of course, they could bring their dates, as usual, Mrs. Berkshire winked.

"What do you think about this one? Too dressy? More for a night of dancing. Oh, there's this one. Ugh, that's right, this one says, oh, hi, these are my boobs, and by the way, I'm Alison." She held outfits up one by one as she appraised herself in the mirror.

Miranda sat on the edge of Alison's bed, trying her best to avoid flying clothing. "Why didn't you move into Mom's and Dad's room? I'm sure they would have wanted you to."

Alison stopped for a moment and turned to her. She shrugged. "I guess it's a lot of things. It's hard to explain." Her forehead furrowed. "You were sleeping in there for a while, so I didn't want to intrude on that. I also didn't want you to think that I was trying to replace them. I suppose, too, I didn't want to move their things out, you know? Sort of like they're..."

"Still here," Miranda whispered.

"Yeah."

The sisters held a gaze of mutual understanding. Miranda walked over to Alison's closet and picked out a burgundy dress. "This one is perfect. Not too slutty, not too dressy, not too business. It's the perfect fall color, it compliments your complexion and hair, and you look beautiful in it."

Alison beamed as she took the dress, held it up to her shoulders, and looked in the full-length mirror. "Thanks, Mira. Let me do my hair and makeup, and we'll go. Oh, I love what you're wearing, by the way." Alison stripped down to her bra and underwear and slipped the dress over her head.

Miranda hoped she would look like her in several years. Alison's face had changed since she was a teenager, but it was more like she grew into her looks. "Thanks." Miranda looked down at her royal blue dress with a simple leaf pattern, just above the knees and shrugged. "I'm in no rush. He's your boyfriend. You know how I feel about the holidays."

"Yeah, I guess things haven't been the same since Aunt Cheri moved away." Alison applied her mascara.

Since Mom and Dad died. When Miranda thought of the word home, it meant Christmas at home with her parents. Aunt Cheri would always have Thanksgiving at her house, but all that disappeared when she took the principal's position at a boarding school for girls in California after obtaining her doctorate in school administration. It was the change she needed, she expressed, to get over what Uncle Dave did to her, and a once-in-a-lifetime job opportunity.

While Miranda celebrated with her, of course, she couldn't help but feel the rest of what she considered "home" flew out to California. The holidays held nothing for her but the unsettling feeling of being a visitor at someone else's Hallmark family holiday and the twinge of emptiness at the loss of her own. This time of year served as a constant reminder of loss, a lackluster time of year devoid of all magic and full of empty promises. The only thing she had left of home was her parents' house and her sister, but fussing over dresses with Ali in the nearly empty house didn't do much to console her.

The ride to Dan Foreman's house in Elmswood took thirty minutes across town. Before long, the rows of buildings gave way to the tree-lined rural route roads of the suburbs nestled in the sides of the mountains surrounding Davenport. These suburban towns and villages comprised the richer communities of Davenport, evidence of robust economic times.

Though not a gated community, Elmswood had the reputation of one, especially with their private, well-paid police force, which was not at all shy about pulling over unfamiliar cars driving through late at night. The homes all smacked of upper middle class. Miranda had considered buying in Elmswood but didn't like the similarity of all the houses except for one or two features to produce the illusion of differentiation. Because of the lure of a short commute to her office, she had decided to buy on the outskirts of the downtown area within city limits and on a house that had a little more personality.

Dan's home contained tasteful, decorative items and furniture with muted colors and simple patterns, as if the items were trying to hide how much they really cost. Plus, Miranda imagined the housecleaner spent more time there than Dan did.

By the time everyone had finished the appetizers and congregated around the dining room table to admire the turkey Dan had spent the day basting, Miranda distinguished a perceptible slighting of the sisters from Dan's parents, Alastair and Ester of the Davenport Foremans. Even worse, Dan's brother turned out to be Steven, the troll who tortured her all throughout high school, but Mr. and Mrs. Foreman's behavior sent the entire evening over the top.

"So, Alison, Dan told us, although I find it difficult to imagine," Mrs. Foreman laughed with a grimace, "you jump out of planes, for a living?" She asked as if she heard a crazy rumor. Mrs. Foreman toyed with a necklace that Miranda would not have bought from a yard sale for five cents but saw in a Michéle Ferràr catalog for two-hundred dollars.

Alison smiled politely. "Yes, it's true. I am a certified skydiving instructor. I teach people how to skydive. I am also part of a skydiving show. We do the Fourth of July celebration every year at Manahassee State Park. Or at least, I used to. I am retired now."

Miranda's mouth hung open. "What? And when were you going to tell me this?" *Unbelievable. There she goes again, shutting me out.*

"I quit right after your accident to focus on you."

"Is George going to let you come back?"

"No. I want to go back to college, so it's not important."

"Oh." *Of course Alison deserved to go to college.* Miranda could never be mad at Alison for more than five seconds, her most admired but stymieing quality.

"Oh?" Mrs. Foreman seemed unaffected by the sisters' exchange. "What do you plan on doing now?"

"I studied nursing when I was younger. I never did get a chance to finish."

"That's because she was too busy taking care of me," Miranda smiled. "Alison put everything she had into giving me a normal childhood after my parents passed."

"It broke my heart when my Daniel split up with Sarah," Mrs. Foreman stated, bypassing all of Miranda's input. "She had such a wonderful wedding planned. She was a brain surgeon too."

Out of the corner of her eye, Miranda caught Alison cringing. *Mrs. Foreman must do this all the time.* Mr. Foreman and Steven didn't even lift their eyes at the way she spoke, as if she weren't speaking at all. Alison would never have the chance to show that she was a worthy match for Dan because in Mrs. Foreman's mind, there was no comparison. To her, her son had become a doctor, the most respected profession, and he gave up his perfect match, a woman in the profession she admired most.

Miranda had several wealthy clients, but they acted more like real people. They spoke as if they didn't have a care how much money anyone made. Mr. Foreman didn't speak much to anyone, as if any conversation were an inconvenience, and Mrs. Foreman spoke with an air, as if she were doing that person a favor by speaking with them at all.

"Mother, I'm sure no one here wants to hear about ancient history." Dan caught Alison's eyes and mouthed *I'm sorry.* She furnished a brave smile for him. He cleared his throat to shift the conversation to more productive pursuits. "So, Miranda, Alison told me you have an assistant now. How's that working out?" asked Dan.

"Oh, better than I expected. Tanya has been a dream. Alison has been my rock through all this, so clever of her to set this up for me even before I woke up. But, that's the type of person she is, so warm and caring." While Miranda's efforts to boost her sister's image were going to be fruitless, she couldn't help but try. She glanced often at Alison, who downed a full glass of wine when Mrs. Foreman pointed out all the wonderful strengths of Dan's ex-fiancé. Alison's smile conveyed her gratitude through her flushed face and glassy eyes.

"What happened?" Mr. Foreman asked, not looking up from his plate.

Finally, he speaks. "I had a car accident." Miranda preferred the rest of the night's conversation to focus on something else other than her health challenges, but it was better than Mrs. Foreman's inappropriate nattering.

"Oh, that's right," Steven said. "I remember reading a clip about it in the local newspaper. You're in there quite often. I read about you every year, just last week, as a matter of fact. You had a great turkey drive for Thanksgiving despite your accident this past summer. And by the way, how are you doing?"

Miranda's cheeks reddened. Why couldn't she take after Mom's side of the family like Alison? She bore her curse all of her life, her red hair and pale skin, always showing how she felt and broadcasting it to everyone else against her will. "Better. I have full use of my left hand now, and I'm not limping. I can't remember the accident and some time before that, and I get migraines."

"Sorry to hear it." Steven shoved a forkful of mashed potatoes in his mouth and smiled.

"Thanks." Miranda took a sip of wine. *Why is he being so friendly now? He was such a jerk in high school. He's part troll despite his good looks. Okay, he's hot. Not everyone has naturally black hair.* With dark brown eyes, tall, and a great build, she would have dated him in high school if Steven were mute. She couldn't believe her eyes when she entered Dan's house and saw him sitting on the couch in the oversized living room, and it shocked her to learn he and Dan were brothers. Well, by marriage. Dan's mother, Ester, married Steven's father, Alistair, she learned during the appetizers. But still, Dan's warmth exuded from him, and Steven was just so, Steven. She felt out of place at this gathering. She even missed the verbal wars Mrs. Berkshire waged against her husband during Thanksgiving dinner.

Dan stood up and clanged his fork against his glass. He paused for a thoughtful moment. "Thanksgiving. What a wonderful time of year to dwell upon our blessings. For me, I have the gifts of my family and new friends. I am thankful that this delightful young woman is still here with us." He raised his glass toward Miranda. Miranda cracked a compulsory smile, placing her fingers on either side of her face as her cheeks flushed. "I am also grateful that out of Miranda's accident and survival, this wonderful woman sitting next to me here has reentered my life." Dan placed his glass on the table, moved his chair back a bit, turned to Alison, and took her hands in his, gazing into her eyes. Dan took out a black velvet box from his jacket pocket, put it in the palm of his left hand, and opened it up to reveal the diamond ring in its interior. He got down on one knee.

All Alison could do was let the tears roll down her cheeks and nod. Dan stood up, placed the ring on her finger, and leaned over to kiss his new fiancé.

All these years, Miranda didn't think she ever saw Alison so happy, and she couldn't think of anyone else more deserving. She glanced at Steven. For the first time since she met him in middle school, they smiled at each other. The only people not smiling, Mr. and Mrs. Foreman, made Miranda grateful for the little happiness bubble enveloping Dan and Alison.

Miranda stood up. "Congrats, the both of you." She walked around the table and took her sister's hands. "I am so happy for you." Miranda and Alison hugged, Miranda resting her head on her sister's shoulder and Alison grasping Miranda around the back of her neck and rocking her from side to side. Miranda spied Steven and Dan speaking in low voices and glancing their way. They were talking about her. Steven wouldn't look her in the eye. Heat rose to her chest. He did the same thing in high school when plotting against her.

Mr. and Mrs. Foreman stood up. "Congratulations," Mr. Foreman took his son's hand, never breaking his stern expression. He nodded as if to say *I support your decision.*

"Are you sure this is what you want?" Mrs. Foreman asked Dan through a tight smile.

"Yes, Mother, this is what I want."

"Well, then, come here." Mrs. Foreman leaned forward to kiss Dan on his right cheek, then his left, and examined his face for remnants of her burgundy lipstick.

Uncouth. The word popped into Miranda's mind just like a mole in the Whack-a-Mole game at the fair. Didn't Mrs. Foreman realize that when she spoke out loud, everyone could hear her disapproval? The possibility that she didn't care bothered her even more than ignorance. And her horrible attitude toward Alison, the sweetest person anyone could imagine, made her blood boil with ire. If only she could, for one moment, say what she really felt.

Alison looked at Mrs. Foreman through narrowed eyes. An impish smile overcame her. "Mother!" She ran around Dan and wrapped her arms around the back of Mrs. Foreman's head, pulled her face close to her, and planted a big kiss on the never-ruffled Mrs. Foreman, who was unappreciative of this brand of affection; the grimace and flailing arms were a dead giveaway.

Dan and Steven turned toward the embracing women, mouths open as if it were the first time they ever saw another human muss their mother's perfectly coiffed hair. They looked at each other and smiled at her extreme discomfort. Miranda tried her best not to smirk, but it didn't work.

"Yes, dear, okay, okay, good, yes." Mrs. Foreman struggled to break Alison's embrace. She took Alison's arms by the elbows, slid her arms so she could take Alison's hands in hers, and attempted to smile, her pain showing through her grimace. "Congratulations."

She turned away from Alison. Steven moved in behind her to take his turn to offer a congratulatory hug to Alison.

Mrs. Foreman brushed off her jacket. "I hope she doesn't do that *every time*," she hissed.

Dan laughed. "I do. Come here, momma!" Dan wrapped his arms around his mother, who stiffened up like a board with rolling, impatient eyes.

Dan and Alison looked at each other over the shoulders of their congratulator, both with happy but slightly evil grins.

Mr. Foreman stepped over to Alison after she embraced Steven. "Welcome to the family." He shook Alison's hand. At long last, Mr. Foreman smiled.

"Excuse me. I have to go fix my hair." Mrs. Foreman went to the bathroom.

Dan shook his head. Alison grinned and shrugged. "My mother always said: when someone is not treating you well, kill them with kindness."

"Oh, I think you killed her alright," said Steve.

Miranda smiled. *That's my girl.* She found Mrs. Foreman's Achilles heel—human contact. Alison always complimented Miranda for her ability with numbers, but Alison possessed a subtle wisdom, which impressed Miranda more than her own skills for facts and calculations. Alison knew how to manage people. She never got into a conflict, always commanding a presence, always able to neutralize people with her kindness and steady temperament. Mrs. Foreman was certainly not the ideal in-law, but Alison would be able to handle her.

Moistness gathered on Miranda's forehead and under her arms. She fanned her face. Her chest tightened. She rubbed her eyes. What were those shadows surrounding her sister? *I must be getting a migraine. Damn, and me without my medication. I wonder if Dan has something to give me.* "Would you all excuse me for a moment? I think I'll get a breath of fresh air. I'm a little overheated."

"Oh, why don't you go through the sliding doors?" Dan pointed toward the kitchen. "I didn't have the chance to put away my outdoor furniture in the backyard."

"Thank you." Miranda walked through the sliding doors before she burned up.

Alison noted Steven's gaze. Steven's eyes lingered on Miranda as she slid the door open and stepped out into the cold night, as if she left a magical trail behind her. "Go on." Alison tossed her head in Miranda's direction.

Steven grinned.

Miranda leaned against the wall next to the sliding doors, gazing at the star-laden sky. Steven drew in an involuntary breath as the stars' faint light played off of Miranda's pale skin, as if she possessed a part of a constellation. Steven cleared his throat to cover up his excitement and pretended to be colder than he really felt.

Miranda gave a slight nod.

Steven balled up his fists and blew on them. "Big night, huh?"

Miranda nodded.

Steven cleared his throat again. "Nice night. Look at all those stars."

"Yep."

"You look beautiful tonight."

Miranda looked at him as if he wounded her.

Maybe he should apologize again? "You know, I am really sorry for being such a jerk in high school. I was really glad to hear you were coming to dinner so I would have the chance to apologize to you."

Miranda nodded.

"We're going to be in-laws now."

"Yep."

"Listen, why don't we get a cup of coffee after dinner? I really would like for us to get along, at least for your sister and my brother's sake."

Miranda's face flushed. "You know, this is what really pissed me off about you all throughout high school. All you do is manipulate. I see that hasn't changed."

"What?" Steven put his hands up with his shrugging shoulders. "Isn't it true? Don't we need to get along?"

"No. We can be cordial and civil during family gatherings, but we don't need to get along, talk outside of these gatherings, or know each other."

"Listen..."

"No, you listen for a change. If you wanted to have coffee with me, you shouldn't have tried to pull a ruse. I might have said yes if you had flat out asked me, despite the fact that you were such a jerk in high school."

"But I already apologized for that when you got here."

"And then you reminded me why we always fought."

"Okay, you're right. I'm sorry again."

"Stop apologizing. You're just being yourself. That's the problem."

Steven took in a quick breath. The tempo in his heart quickened. *This must be why I picked fights with her in high school.* The more his anger rose, the more he wanted to grab and kiss her, and because she possessed the ability to have her words cut to the quick, he often imagined many other naughty things. "Oh, and do you know your problem?" he challenged. Miranda's eyes flashed. *Damn, so beautiful.*

"Yeah, what's that?"

"You push everyone away."

Miranda pushed off the wall and faced Steven. "Hah! How dare you! You think you know me, but you don't know the first thing about me." The volume of her voice rose.

"Shhh. You don't want to ruin your sister's big night, do you?"

"Me? Ruin my sister's night? Well, I... I..."

Just as she was about to hit the ground, Steven caught Miranda in his arms.

• • •

When she awoke, Miranda lay on the couch in the living room. The last she remembered, the stars had turned into brilliant streaks of white light. Dan had his fingers on her wrist. Alison, Dan, and Steven looked worried. Mr. Foreman seemed surprised, and Mrs. Foreman looked displeased.

What the hell happened? I don't pass out. I have never fainted in my life. Ugh, now Steven's going to think he makes me swoon, egotistical bastard. Miranda blinked several times. It looked like there were black vines protruding from everyone there. *These migraines really mess with my vision. Dan said at times, my vision would be refracted, but he didn't mention anything about black vines sticking out from people.* Should she say something? They all might think she's hallucinating, or worse, crazy. As soon as she thought she might tell them, the blackness disappeared from around them—even Mrs. Foreman.

"Miranda. Okay, she's awake," Dan said.

"She's not going to die, is she?" Mrs. Foreman inquired as if Miranda's death would be an unpleasant inconvenience.

"Mother!" Steven shot her a look and shook his head.

"No, I'm fine." Miranda sat up. She still felt like she was on a ship but was determined to stand.

"As a rule, I would say it is probably not a big issue, but you had a concussion several months ago, Miranda. Maybe we should bring you in for a few tests as a precaution," Dan suggested.

"No way. I'm fine, really. I guess I got a little light headed. Where are my shoes?"

"I took them off. Here." Alison gave Miranda her black pumps. Miranda slipped them on her feet. "You know, Miranda, you should listen to Dan. I'm worried about you."

"I know. I'm fine."

"Is this the first time this happened since the accident?" Dan sat down next to Miranda on the couch.

"Yes."

"Do you feel nauseous? Any numbness or tingling anywhere?" asked Dan.

"No, none of those. Still a bit lightheaded, but I'll be okay." Miranda stood. "Let me take a few minutes to walk it off."

"Here." Steven rushed to her side and held out his arm. Too tired to argue and after flashing a dirty look, Miranda wrapped her arm in his and took a few unsteady steps forward.

Mrs. Foreman placed her hand on her husband's arm. "Alistair, why don't we clear away the dishes? Will you help me bring dessert and coffee to the table?"

"I'll have to bring Maria next time," Mr. Foreman muttered as they walked to the kitchen.

"Thanks, Mother. Oh, would you please pack some food for Miranda to take with her?" Dan asked. "I think she'll be fine," Dan comforted Alison. "Maybe she got overheated. The oven did warm up the house."

"Okay. But maybe she needs someone to stay with her tonight to keep an eye on her."

"Oh, no I don't," Miranda called back over her shoulder. She and Steven had made it across the living room. Not on Alison's special night.

"I'll do it," Steven volunteered, calling over his shoulder.

"Oh, no you won't." Miranda stopped walking, took her arm from Steven, and turned around. No way. Maybe she should go to the hospital.

"That is a great idea." Dan looked at Alison and smiled.

"Yes, I think so too." Alison clapped. "Thanks, Steven. Now I will rest easy tonight."

"It's a terrible idea. I'll be fine," Miranda insisted. Crud. What would she do with a troll at her house? She desperately scanned all corners of her knowledge to find a way out of it, but uncovered nothing.

"Here, Steve," said Dan, "why don't I get you some of my clothes so you have something to change into tomorrow?"

I wonder if he'll be able to pack a new personality in that bag as well. Miranda summoned all of her strength to resist speaking her thought out loud.

"I'll help you." Alison grabbed Dan's hand and the two and went upstairs.

"Great idea. I'll take good care of her," Steven promised.

"I appreciate your concern, really, but I'm fine now," Miranda called up the stairs after them. Miranda faced Steven. "I'm fine now. I'm calling a cab." She hoped the taxi could get there before Alison and Dan made it back down the stairs. As she attempted to make some strong strides to get her cell phone in her purse, her knees buckled under her, enough to send her stumbling.

Steven caught her once again. "I think you need to sit down and let me drive you home." He guided Miranda to the couch. He kneeled in front of her. "You know, outside, I didn't mean to make it seem like I was trying to manipulate you. Can we start over?"

Even though her head still spun, she couldn't help smirking. "I guess everyone deserves a do-over once in a while."

Steven made his best effort to seem as sincere as he could, taking her hands in his and looking into her eyes. "Miranda, would you like to have coffee with me sometime?"

"No."

The two stared at each other for a moment and then chuckled.

"How about this, then. When we get to your house, I'll make us both some decaf?" Steven asked.

Miranda paused for a moment. "I think I could live with that. Besides, it looks like I'm stuck with you for the night. No one is listening to me."

Steven shrugged and smiled. "You have a point there."

Dan came down the stairs with Alison behind him. "Here's your bag, Steve. I'll meet you in the front so I can go to the kitchen and get your doggie bag."

"Alright, let's get you home, Miss Miranda." Steven stood up, held out his hand, helped Miranda up, and looped his arm around her waist to support her.

"I'm sorry I ruined your big night, Alison."

"Oh, honey, you haven't." Alison took a step forward and put her lips to Miranda's ear. "Not even Mrs. Foreman can ruin this night. Don't worry." The sisters smiled at each other. "Call me the moment you two reach home so I know you have arrived in one piece."

"Okay, here we go." Steve helped Miranda walk to the front door.

Miranda caught Alison's eye and mouthed the words, *I hate you.*

Alison mouthed back *I know,* the corners of her mouth turning upwards and nodding.

Miranda mouthed back, *you're so obnoxious.*

Alison nodded again, smiling and giving her a thumbs-up.

Dan helped Steven walk Miranda to his car, instructing him on what symptoms constituted a medical emergency. Alison handed the bag through the window to Miranda.

Alison looked at the rear window of Steve's Toyota Corolla as they drove off. "I hope she's okay."

"I think so. Don't worry. Steve will take good care of her tonight."

"Yes, I know. I always knew those two liked each other."

Dan laughed. "Yes, me too."

5
Transition

"There we go. One step at a time." Steven guided Miranda up the stairs.

Miranda rolled her eyes. "You know, I feel fine now. You don't have to stay."

"What, and miss out on coffee? Besides, your sister warned me you would do this."

Miranda fumbled through her purse to find her keys. "Do what?"

"Refuse to rely on someone else for a change."

Miranda's face bunched up as if she ate a lemon. "My sister has a big mouth."

"Your sister is a saint."

Miranda put the key into the lock, opened the side door, and sighed. "Yeah, she's a saint."

"See, we agreed on something. Maybe by the end of the night, we'll find one more thing to agree on," Steven teased.

Miranda gazed at Steven. "Yeah, we'll see." Steven smiled back. He was being sweet and attentive, asking her how she felt on the ride home, and even letting her select the music to play on his satellite radio. Plus, anyone who spoke highly of Alison earned points in her book.

I wonder what he wants from me. High School Steven always had an ulterior motive. High School Steven never did anything unless it benefited him. Although, after meeting Ester and Alistair, it helped fill in a lot of blanks. Maybe this was New Steven. She hoped so. Most people didn't change from high school. The same people who gossiped in high school still spread rumors around town. They never grew out of it; they simply discovered a bigger venue.

Steven put his overnight bag down beside the door when they walked through it and locked the door with his free hand. The kitchen had just enough room for him to slide past Miranda to set the food on the kitchen counter. Miranda jumped a little, unaccustomed to having someone in her galley kitchen so close to her.

"I know where the kitchen is now. Ah, there's the living room. Let's get you settled here on the couch, and we'll see what goodies we have." Steven guided Miranda over to the couch, put her feet up, took off her shoes, and covered her with the afghan draped over the back of the couch, making sure she had her cell phone so she could call Alison.

She watched as Steven discovered the location of the items in the kitchen. He put their dinner in the microwave, asked for instructions on how to work her coffeepot, and opened drawers and cabinets to look for the silverware, plates, and napkins.

"You really don't have to do all this." Miranda yawned. The entire ordeal stole her energy.

"Think of it as my repentance for stealing your underwear in the eleventh grade."

"You didn't steal them. I gave them to you."

"I tricked you into it. I set up those cards so you would lose."

"I knew it!" The rush of heat crept up Miranda's cheeks. One more reason not to trust High School Steven.

Steven shot her a sheepish gaze. “Sorry.”

“Unbelievable.” Miranda folded her arms. Maybe he was still a troll after all.

The microwave beeped. “Ah, dinner is served,” said Steve, grateful he had something to take the focus off of his pubescent transgression.

Steven brought the meal and drinks to the wooden coffee table, a special table Miranda found at a yard sale when she first moved into the neighborhood. When she bought the missing pane of glass that went over the wood, it acted like a huge picture frame. Steven held the dishes and stood over the table gazing at her collection. “These are really nice. Did you take them?”

“Yes.”

“Wow, you have a good eye. Look at this elephant. Where did you take that one?”

“Borneo.”

“You’ve got the travel bug, huh? How many places have you been?”

“Enough.”

“Like where?”

“France, Spain, Portugal, Thailand, China, Borneo, Belize, Russia. But I haven’t had time to travel since the accident.”

He sat while holding the plates. “Don’t worry. You will again soon.” Steven spied a picture of Miranda in front of her Corvette. “Wow, nice Corvette.”

“Yeah, that’s my baby, Cherry Red. I really miss that car.”

“Oh, how could I forget?” Steve jumped up and trotted to the kitchen. He retrieved a lit candle, dimmed the lights, walked over to the coffee table, and placed it in the middle.

Miranda smiled. “You are certainly full of surprises tonight.”

“I wanted to make a good impression, well, at least to make it up to you for that card game.”

“It’s in your best interests not to mention that again.”

“Mention what again?”

"Yep, you got the idea. So, why do you seem, well, so human?" Miranda joked. This occasion, after all, marked the first time Steven didn't seem so Steven.

"Here, eat." Steven gave Miranda her plate. Miranda accepted it on her lap. "When I graduated college, I met the girl of my dreams. I mean, head over heels, one hundred percent in love. In no time, I had asked her to marry me. Then, she died in a car accident."

"Oh, Steven, I'm sorry." Miranda meant it, too. Why did car accidents always pop up in her life? Was someone unknown force trying to kill everyone she knew, herself included?

Steven nodded. "Somewhere along the way, I realized life taught me a cruel lesson. Karma, I think they call it? Don't ever let anyone tell you it doesn't exist, because man, it will kick you right in the ass." Steven shook his head.

"What do you mean karma?" Miranda asked.

"In high school, I was callous to your situation. I often thought after two years, you should just get over it already, move on, and stop your brooding. I thought you were doing it just for attention, and I'm ashamed. When I lost Hannah, I realized you never 'get over it.' I struggled with the senselessness of it all, which made it hard for me to move on. Life taught me that lesson I was missing, and I have been living with regret ever since. I realized there wasn't anything wrong with you. There was something wrong with me for judging you like that. So when I said sorry, I meant it."

Miranda and Steven held a long gaze. "Steven, that is probably the best apology I have ever received. I forgive you." *This is strange. I do forgive him. Maybe he has changed.*

"Thank you. I'm grateful you're still here so I had the chance to tell you. I couldn't believe my luck when I heard Alison hooked up with Dan, and I would be able to see you tonight at dinner."

He looked down. "Hey, you haven't touched your food. Don't you like it?"

"Oh, no, I love it. I'm not very hungry." Miranda set the food down on the table.

"Alison told me you would do this. She said to tell you, eat ten bites, and she will be happy, and not to worry because you are going to be okay."

Miranda giggled. "She's unbelievable. Okay, okay, ten bites. It's like she has a camera on me inside her head, you know?" She picked her plate back up. Alison always harped on her to eat more. Miranda didn't care a whit about her weight. She just didn't have much of an appetite most of the time.

"She seems to know you well."

"Like a book. I'm so happy for her and Dan. I worried that she hadn't met anyone. She's a lot like my mom. She would make a great mother." *But I don't feel like I know her at all,* remembering the bomb Alison dropped on her during dinner. She missed how they used to talk before Alison became her replacement mom. She supposed it was because of the burden placed on her. Maybe she thought she needed to act a certain way so she could maintain authority. Everything changed with her parents' death, even Alison, and Miranda resented it for a long while. She appreciated Alison's position and all she did for her when she matured enough to understand her sister's actions and inactions another way.

Steven smiled. "So would you."

Instead of responding, Miranda shoved a forkful of mashed potatoes into her mouth, hoping it would cover up her discomfort. "There, six bites, and I swear I can't eat another." She finished her mouthful and placed the plate on the coffee table.

"Good. Now I have another surprise." Steven put his plate down and patted his lap. "Put your feet up here. I will reveal to you one of my talents."

"Which is?" Miranda placed her feet obediently on his lap.

"Foot massages."

Miranda wrinkled her nose. "Are you sure?"

Steven didn't wait for her permission. He already had the covers off and started rubbing her toes. *How can this be relaxing when I'm worried if my feet smell?*

• • •

Miranda awoke at dawn. Steven's foot massage was so effective, she didn't remember when she fell asleep and couldn't remember when she had slept sounder. She heard him in the kitchen.

"Hey, how do you feel?"

Even through her sleepy eyes, with his shirt slightly rumpled and his hair tousled, he looked as good in the mornings as he did in the evenings. "Wow, you were not kidding. You have magic in those fingers." Miranda rubbed her face to wake herself up.

"Here, I have coffee if you're up to it. Lots of cream, lots of sugar?"

"Yeah, how did you... oh, Alison, right?"

"You got it."

Miranda shook her head in amazement, accepting the cup of coffee from Steven. "Did you sleep?"

"Yes, some."

"Here on the couch with me?"

"I did for a bit, but then I moved over to the recliner. That's pretty comfy, by the way."

"That's why I bought it."

"You didn't have eggs, so I went to the market on the corner. How do you like yours?"

"I don't."

"You don't like eggs?"

"Why would I like eggs? They look like snot."

"You're supposed to cook them first."

"Why, so I can eat cooked snot?"

Steven laughed. "You are original. Okay, how about pancakes then?" He rummaged around her kitchen cabinets.

"I'll tell you what." Miranda stood up. "I'll take you out for breakfast to thank you for watching over me last night. You won't find anything in those cabinets. I don't have much time to cook."

"You don't cook? What do you eat, then?"
"Salads, mostly. And stuff I can put in the microwave."
"Why don't you cook?"
Miranda shrugged.
"It reminds you of family, doesn't it?"
Miranda looked up at him. *He really gets me. Hello, New Steven.*
Steven smiled. "Okay, but I'm treating."
"No, I'm treating."
Steven smiled. "We'll see."

• • •

"So, who paid for breakfast?" Alison munched on her salad, eyes fixated on Miranda as if Alison were engrossed in a movie.

"Jeez, would you stop looking at me like that? You look like some sort of matchmaker ghoul." Miranda looked around The Big Easy Cajun Restaurant to see if anyone had noticed.

Alison smacked Miranda's arm. "Come on, who paid?" she interrogated through her mouthful of food.

Miranda folded her arms. "He did, the idiot. He paid the waitress twenty bucks to give the check to him."

"And?"

"And what?"

"Are you going to see each other again?"

"No."

Alison put down her fork on her plate and swallowed. "What?"

"We said our goodbyes and went on our way."

"He didn't ask you out on another date?"

"Nope."

"Really?"

"Nope."

"What?"

"I'm messing with you." Miranda reached over, grinning like an imp, and poked Alison's arm. "He said he needs help with his finances. He's coming over to the office next Monday. Then we'll see from there."

Alison breathed out a sigh of relief. "You are such a brat."

"And you're really nosy."

"Yeah, it's my job."

"No, it's not your job, but you do it anyway. And that's what I love about you."

Alison shook her head. "You're like a cinnamon bun wrapped in barbed wire."

Miranda wrinkled her nose. "And you're like a jar of honey."

Alison smiled. "You know, hon, I wanted to talk to you about our house."

"Okay, what about it?"

"Now, I don't want you to get upset. And I want you to know that it's only an idea, and I won't do anything unless you agree. Since Dan and I are getting married, I will move in with him. I thought if we had kids, we could keep our house so they have a place to move into when they get older. On the other hand, the upkeep could get expensive. The house is in decent shape now, but if we leave the house vacant for a long time, there's no guarantee that it will remain in sellable condition. Plus, if we sell the house now while the market is high, you and I could do something with that money, like maybe invest it to expand your charitable works or grow your business, or keep the money for your children and invest it. Your thoughts?" An uncomfortable smile crept up the corners of her mouth and rested there with her expectant eyes.

"Jeez, children? Steven and I haven't even been on our first date yet."

Alison rolled her eyes. "Yes, ha ha, very funny. Get serious."

"Sheesh, okay. My thoughts. I guess the idea makes me uncomfortable, but I knew we would have this conversation when you and Dan got engaged. The upkeep and the property taxes are significant. Our county charges one of the highest property tax rates in the state. Add in the insurance, and we'll pay out at least a grand per month just to keep up on those costs. I considered renting out the house to have income on the property and cover the costs, but we both don't have any experience as landlords, and I have heard of some real nightmares of what happens when you rent to the wrong people. Real estate always has some value, but the market goes up and down according to the health of the economy, and the market is really high right now. The house still looks great, thanks to you, but if we wait, you never know if a hurricane might roll through and damage the entire house. I suppose now is the best time to sell."

"Wow, really? You mean it?"

"Yes. Let's clean it up and put it on the market. I'll help."

Alison's mouth hung open for a moment. "That was so much easier than I expected."

Miranda smiled, always happy to shock her sister. The negative ways were much more fun, but she did enjoy shocking her in positive ways every once in a while to keep her on her toes. "Listen, when you almost die, you gain another perspective. When we lost Mom and Dad, I couldn't stomach the thought of letting go of our wonderful past filled with so many good memories. Because of you, you didn't force me to let go of my entire childhood. You know me. I've had these numbers rolling around in my head for a while. It would make more sense to have that cash working for us now rather than keeping up the house."

Alison stared at Miranda. "You know, I'll bet Mom and Dad are so proud of you, up in Heaven smiling." She pointed upward and sipped her coffee. "I'm proud of you too."

Typical Alison rhetoric, referring to Heaven and faith. Alison stopped inviting Miranda to church after Miranda came up with the perfect reply to get out of it—*I won't go, but you can pray for me.*

Why should she go to church? God couldn't exist. Why would God take away her parents, the best people of all? If God possesses total power, he could have prevented their death. Since he didn't, he must not be there. If he were, he would have heard her praying for her mother in the hospital. She found the idea of God not existing more acceptable than God existing but ignoring her pleas.

Alison sipped her coffee. "Okay, then. Listen, Dan and I are going away tomorrow for our own private celebration of our engagement."

Miranda smiled. "Oh, that's nice. I'll stop by the house to start cleaning out my room. Where are you going?"

"Not too far, in case Dan has to go to the hospital. You know that bed and breakfast right outside of town, the Victorian house those two guys restored?"

"Oh, the one with the room that has the bookcase that opens up into a marble bathroom with a Jacuzzi? I saw pictures. That place is so beautiful, lucky girl. That sounds wonderful. Have fun."

The sisters smiled at each other. "Alison, congrats again. I am so happy for you. Look at you. You're glowing. You deserve this."

"And so do you, sweetie. I hope you're this happy one day soon. You work all the time. Maybe it's time to slow down a bit and enjoy yourself."

Miranda shrugged. "Who knows? We'll see."

• • •

On Sunday, Miranda dressed in an old pair of jeans and sweatshirt and threw on her ski jacket. *Life is tough sometimes, but I'll have to be tougher than life,* she repeated on the drive over. She steeled herself so she would not spend the entire day crying.

"Are you sure you're going to be okay? It's not easy for anyone to give up their childhood home," Steven observed when Miranda declined his offer for dinner.

"No, I'll be fine. I'm going to pack and see what needs repairing or repainting."

She almost regretted passing on Steven's offer as she let herself into the house, but it felt too soon for her to be all raw and exposed in front of him. When she opened the door and walked into the living room, some empty cardboard boxes waited for her on the couch. Miranda turned on the Jamaican rum bottle lamp sitting on the end table, took off her jacket, and draped it over the top of the couch. She picked up the lamp and held it for a few minutes, tracing her finger along the colorful Jamaican lady. She could still hear her mother's laughter from the day they made the lamp together. Smiling, she turned it off, took off the lampshade, unplugged it, and put it on the table after she wrapped the cord around the lady.

A knock on the door. She jumped.

"Steven! What the hell are you doing here?"

Steven seemed surprised. "Not exactly the reception I had hoped for."

"Are you following me?"

Steven folded his arms. "What if I am? What if I followed you to make sure you're okay?"

Miranda sighed. "I'm sorry. That's sweet, really, in a stalker-y sort of way, but I'm fine. Thanks for stopping by."

Stalker? He shook his head and walked in. "I've been through this. You want me to stay."

"Oh? And what makes you say that?" Heat rose from her chest and crept past her sweatshirt collar.

"One, my sparkling personality," Steven grinned, holding up his pointer finger, striving for obnoxiousness.

"Ugh, get out." *Yep, there's the old Steven.* Miranda pushed him toward the door.

"And, B, because I've been through this, so I understand," he said a little softer. Miranda stopped pushing. "When I lost Hannah, I isolated myself for months. I pushed everyone away. Why bother, when they can up and die on you tomorrow, right?"

"Yeah." Miranda stood and stared at Steven, stunned at his ability to describe the way she had been feeling for years in only a few sentences and the reason why she threw herself into her career. So, that's what he meant in the backyard at Dan's house. Maybe he saw something in her she couldn't see.

"You know, we lived together for several months before we got engaged, and I went through all her things by myself. Besides losing her, it was the hardest thing I had to do. I wished I had someone there. You tried to pull your tough gal act on me over the telephone, but I didn't buy it. It doesn't matter when your parents died. It's still hard, whether their death was last week or seventeen years ago. So, I'm here to support you."

Miranda didn't know what emotion prevailed at the moment: irritation due to the undisputable truth of his statements or endearment because of his insistence to help her. "Okay. Thanks."

"I'm here to help. Just tell me what to do."

"I know one thing. It won't involve my underwear."

Steven smiled. "Yeah? What if it does?"

Miranda looked down and put her hands to her face, as if she could prevent the telltale color from creeping up her forehead. She cleared her throat. "I guess I walked into that one, didn't I?" A nervous laugh escaped her throat.

Steven smiled. "It was too easy. Now, what would you like to accomplish today?" He walked into the living room, and Miranda closed the front door.

"I thought I might go through the house to see if there's anything I wanted to keep. Alison has dibs on everything in the kitchen, but if there's any furniture or knickknacks I want, I could have them. She only wants one or two things, and they are already in her room. She said something about auctioning off the rest so she could raise a little money for my charity stuff."

Steve smiled. “That’s a nice idea. Why did you get into charity work?”

“My parents, in honor of them. They helped people in their practice right up until their death. I didn’t get into psychology like they did, so I figured I could help in a different way.” Because Miranda had sharp observation skills, her parents always encouraged her to get into psychology, but Miranda couldn’t bring herself to pursue a career in it. Too much poking around in other people’s misery would not have helped her at the time. She appreciated the safety of numbers. They didn’t cry or dig up old memories that she would rather keep buried.

Steven’s smile continued. She glanced down like an awkward teenager. Steven cleared his throat. “So, what room would you like to start in?”

“Here, I guess. Let me find some tape and packing stuff. Do you think you could wrap that lamp up somehow? Here, put your jacket with mine.” Miranda draped Steven’s jacket with hers over the back of the couch.

Steven took the box. “Neat lamp.”

“Yes, my mother and I made it together one weekend. She always bought books that had ten thousand craft projects. Soon after that she and my father died.”

“Do you have any bubble wrap?”

“Alison said she had some in the dining room cabinets. And Steven?”

“Yes?”

“Thanks.” A secret part of her hoped Steven would show up after all, the distraction she needed to keep her from crying all day.

Steven nodded.

Miranda walked into the dining room to look for the packing materials. Her eyes settled on the “piece of art” she had drawn on the wall in permanent marker when she was too young to know better, but old enough to remember her parents’ reaction. Instead of getting mad, her mother painted a frame around it and kept it.

Her father was less thrilled, but happy about how supportive her mother had been of her artistic efforts. Whenever the deep dark hole inside of her overtook her, the mural always helped her feel as if one day, the hole would fill up.

• • •

In the living room, Steven had the bottle lamp in his hand. The lamps, situated around the living room, flashed even though he had not turned them on. Steven looked down. *It couldn't be.* The lady lamp's light bulb flashed with the electrical cord still wrapped around the lady's body. Steven put the lamp down, careful not to let it drop, and stepped away from the table. *It couldn't be.* It still lit up along with the other lamps in the room.

• • •

In the dining room, Miranda opened the cabinets of an odd piece of furniture with six box-like units that had doors on the front. She recalled how much her mother loved endless storage possibilities. She discovered packing materials in the bottom middle cabinet. When she pulled out the bubble wrap and tape, some papers fell onto the floor. *What are those strange diagrams?* She picked up the scattered papers. She examined a photocopied diagram of the human body with wheels drawn at different points along the spine and head, labeled *Diagram 3 - The chakras, colors, and points of origin.*

What in the world is Alison reading? She drew in a quick breath when she saw her parents' names under the title *Police Accident Report Form.* She peered into the living room. Steven fussed with the bottle lamp.

She picked up the papers, walked to the living room, and took her jacket. "Steven, I forgot to do something at home. I have to go."

Steven's eyes widened. "Um, okay. Do you need me drive you home?"

"No, I have my car here, thanks. I appreciate you coming by."

"Will I still see you tomorrow?"

Miranda paused. "Oh, yes, our appointment. Tomorrow evening after work, right?"

"Yes. Are you sure you're okay? This is a bit sudden."

"No, I mean, yes, I'm good. It's important. That's all."

"Okay then. Miranda?" How could he bring up the odd occurrence? When the lights stopped flashing, the lamp was like any other unplugged lamp. He turned the switch several times, but he couldn't get the unplugged lamp to light up like it had before. He couldn't explain it, not for the life of him. "I'll see you tomorrow." Steven grabbed his jacket.

"Yep, see you tomorrow."

Steven climbed into his car. *It was just an electrical malfunction. She probably has something work-related she forgot.* He hoped if he said it enough times, he would eventually believe it.

• • •

Twinges of guilt plagued Miranda. She made herself a cup of her favorite tea and sat down in front of the pile of papers, yellowed on the corners with age. She pulled out the police report and stared at the title for a few minutes. Daggers stabbed in her chest. Her eyes wandered down to her parents' names. She took a shaky breath and continued to read the details of her parents' death. *Clear night. Tire tracks. Tree. Mile marker 15 on Route 25. Dr. Alan Sheppard dead on arrival.* Miranda gulped her tea to hold back tears.

She leafed through the other papers. She pulled out a newspaper clipping from behind several of the top papers, an article from The Davenport: *Local Psychologists, Drs. Allen Sheppard and Joy Sheppard, in Fatal Auto Accident.* She ran her fingers over the photos of her parents with their hair in some crazy 1980s professional hair style. *Funny how different generations have their own sense of what looks good.* Her eyes wandered down the page. She gasped when she saw the heap of twisted metal resembling the car from her childhood. It looked as if it had fused into the tree at the bottom of the mountain. She could see why her sister never shared this with her and almost regretted seeing it.

Miranda saw her sister's handwriting on a yellow sheet of lined paper from a legal pad. *Clear night. Not drunk. Halenbecker–no cause for the crash, not willing to look into it further. THINGS HAPPEN FOR A REASON!!!! Photocopies and accident–connection?????*

Halenbecker served as the chief of police throughout her entire childhood. Edward "Hal" Halenbecker had dinner over the house several times. She thought she heard Aunt Cheri mention that if it weren't for the fact that her brother-in-law consulted for the police department, he and Joy would still be at the bottom of the mountainside.

Miranda took the accident report, the newspaper article, and her sister's notes and put them into separate piles. She examined the colorful diagram that had caught her eye at the house. Her eyebrows furrowed. How could such an odd diagram have a connection to her parents' accident?

There were other diagrams, each as puzzling as the first. *Shapes in the Aura and Their Connection - Figure 10,* an illustration accompanying a "case" from the book. The "psychic" who worked on a man remotely detected a square over the man's right eye before the man revealed he was blind in that eye. The psychic also saw a WWI helmet from Germany. After a past life regression, the psychic reported that the man had lived a life as a WWI soldier and had been blinded during the war, all shared before the psychic learned of his blindness.

For *Psychic Tears in the Aura - Figure 21,* Miranda saw the tears noted in the different spots of the aura and the different physical ailments one could experience, as well as emotional and mental imbalances. She looked at the bottom of the photocopies. The only words there were *Id Speak.*

Miranda jumped when her cell phone rang. "Hello?"

"Hey, just got back. I see you were here, but you didn't get much done. I'm checking on you to see if you're okay," said Alison.

"Yes, I'm okay. It was harder than I thought, but something came up." Miranda glanced down at the pages.

"You mean, Steven? Did he stop by? He said he would try."

"What is this, a conspiracy?"

Alison laughed. "Yes, and we're all going tie you up and drag you down the aisle. I saw Steven at Dan's house, and he asked for the house address, mentioning he might check in on you. It sounded like a good idea."

"I knew you were involved somehow," Miranda pouted.

"Miranda, someone is taking a great interest in you, and he is cute and nice. Why don't you just enjoy it a while and see where it goes?"

Miranda laughed. "In other words, stop being a pain in the ass?"

"Well, um," Alison tittered. "When you put it that way..."

"Yeah, don't worry. I've got it covered. It was a very nice gesture, along with all of your efforts. But you have to start butting out now. I'm a big girl, and I can handle things on my own."

"Are you sure?"

"Yes. I realize what you are saying. We had a long talk. We'll see what happens. Okay?"

"Okay, butting out, for now. My job here is done."

The pride in her sister's voice grated on Miranda's ears. "Sheesh, Ali, you need a hobby."

"Shut up. I have one. Do you know what it is?"

"What?"

"Getting married."

Miranda laughed. "I can help."

"Aww, really? Thanks, Mira."

After a pause, Miranda said, "Ali, I hope you don't get mad..."

"What happened? Are you okay?"

"I'm fine, I promise. I found the papers."

"What papers?"

"The accident report."

A long sigh. "Oh, those papers. I wish you hadn't."

"I do too, in a way. I have them here with me. Ali, what are those weird diagrams, and why would you think they were connected to Mom and Dad's death?"

"Hon, it's nothing. Ignore it. Mom and Dad were getting into some strange stuff right before they died. I thought maybe it had some sort of connection to their death, only because they were researching it right before their passing. It was easier than accepting that their death had no reason. You know what I mean?"

"Yeah." Miranda knew exactly what she meant. "Why did you give up on that idea?"

"Because I thought Mom and Dad would want me to focus on you rather than grasping at straws to find some remote connection for something I couldn't change, no matter what I found out. Everyone told me it was unhealthy to pursue it. As time went on, I couldn't deny it. I had my plate full anyway. Until I joined that show, skydivers really don't make very much, even as instructors, and even with the life insurance, so I focused everything I could to make our situation work. Make sense?"

Miranda sighed. "Yeah, I know I didn't make things easy on you either. I'm sorry."

"Hey, I always understood the pain you were going through. And listen. Don't concern yourself with those papers. I don't want you digging up painful things right now. It doesn't make any sense. Understand?"

"I understand."

"Mira, I'm serious..."

"I know, I know. I get it."

"Okay. Why don't we start cleaning the house together, maybe this coming weekend?"

"I'd love nothing more."

When Miranda hung up, she whispered to herself, *Sorry, Ali. For some reason, I can't let this go.* The photo of the accident drew her eyes again like a magnet to metal. Maybe it contained the answers she needed. Or, maybe she'd feel closer to her parents. She walked to the other side of her table and opened her planner. She pointed to the next day: only one appointment in the afternoon before Steven would arrive at 6 P.M. Time enough to go to the site.

• • •

For the first time since her accident, Miranda had a tumultuous night of sleep. She dreamed of her parents' car careening down the mountainside into the tree from the photo. The scene remained on auto-loop until it melted into her crash, the crimson box truck's side yielding to her Cherry Red as the nose crumpled inward. She floated above as her body lay unconscious behind the wheel, reliving every moment of her crash she had all but forgotten.

Am I dead? She heard an annoying but familiar buzz in the distance. Its sound grew closer and closer. As she floated, dark clouds descended from the sky and blanketed everything below. *What is that? It couldn't be Heaven.*

When her alarm woke her, she had slept for a full half hour through its impetuous complaining, and it felt as if she hadn't slept a minute. The dream faded into the background. As she attempted to sit up, she squeezed her eyes shut due from blinding pain. *Probably from the lack of sleep.* When she swung her legs over the side of the bed, she winced. The pain worsened, and she got tunnel vision.

Her migraines had earned her the nickname "Little Grasshopper" from Dan. She told him when she had gotten her first one that she felt like a grasshopper because of the refracted vision.

Miranda made her way to her bathroom, painted and tiled all in white. She usually enjoyed the nice, clean look of the bathroom, but on mornings like these, with the sunlight streaming through the window, it blinded her. Wincing and shading her eyes, she opened the cabinet and grabbed the little brown bottle of pills. Only pain like this could make her swallow those damn things.

As Miranda filled the glass of water, she felt a tickle at the back of her neck. When she looked up, a flash in the mirror, the figure of a man stood behind her. The glass slipped from her fingers, shattering in the sink into tiny pieces, distracting her enough to look down for a nanosecond. She looked up again. He had vanished.

I better call Tanya and tell her to rearrange my appointments today. I have to go lie down. She stumbled out of the bathroom. *This is a really bad one if I'm seeing things that aren't there.*

• • •

Miranda awoke on the couch. She heard the radio playing "Blinded by the Light." She shook her head. Her parents used to listen to that song all the time. Who turned on the radio? Boy, she must have been out of it.

The pain and the halos had vanished. The grandfather clock chimed twice. She sighed and stood up from the couch. *Ugh, I hate losing my days to these migraines.* She pushed her arms through her favorite fuzzy button-up shirt and yanked on her stockings and jeans. No sense in freezing while she examined the accident site.

She grabbed her jacket, keys, and purse. On the way out, she pushed the button on the radio to turn it off. Miranda turned around. The radio switched back on again. She turned back around. She shook her head, staring at the radio. She pushed the button three times and turned it off. She made a mental note to call an electrician.

She walked through her little kitchen to the side door. She heard a bang behind her and then heavy footsteps. She gulped hard to abate her racing heart.

She whipped around. A towering, hulking man stood at the entrance of her kitchen. A pungent smell hit her nostrils. Her mouth watered. She resisted the urge to vomit. Her skin crawled with pins and needles. The memory of where she saw him overwhelmed her: the hospital room after the accident, in the mirror earlier that morning. A strong shadow concealed his facial features. He walked toward her, his heavy boots thudding with each step.

Miranda's hands shook violently as she commanded them to unlock the dead bolt. Her breath grated along her throat as her mind screamed at her for not being fast enough.

Suddenly, all of the windows exploded in front of her. A foreign, guttural sound emanated from the center of her being. Little shards of glass stung as they wormed their way into her skin. Trickles of blood tickled her face and arms.

As she turned to face her attacker, she searched in desperation for a weapon, only to find nothing.

The stranger took an empty wine bottle off of the countertop and overtook her in three steps. She could not escape his towering stature. Before she had time to react, he raised the wine bottle in the air.

"Lights out," he growled. Miranda was certain the end had arrived as the bottle crashed on top of her crown, splitting her mind in two.

6
REALITY

Miranda bolted upright. She had to get away. Looking down, she was so startled to be out of her clothes, she grasped and pulled at the hospital gown. She looked around the room, frantic to escape before the stranger returned.

"Whoa, whoa, hey. You're okay, you're okay." Steven placed his hands on her upper arms. "Dan, Alison, she's awake," he called behind him toward the open door. He put his face close to hers. "You're at Morningside Hospital."

Alison and Dan rushed into the room with a nurse. "Miranda!" Alison shoved Steven out of the way to sit on the bed and hug Miranda. Steven nearly toppled over. "What happened? Thank God you're okay."

Miranda pushed Alison off. "Did you catch him?"

"Catch who?" asked Dan.

"The tall man. He knocked me out."

"Okay, hold on a moment, Miranda. Let us check you out, and then we'll sit down and have a long talk," Dan conveyed in a soothing tone.

Miranda detected the difference between his medical-doctor mien rather than his usual, personable approach. Whatever concern Dan tried to hide, it didn't matter. Alison's expression said it all.

"Miranda, do you have any pain anywhere?" Dan asked. "Liz, please get her point-two-five milligrams of Alprazolam." The nurse nodded and left the room.

"No." Most likely the benefits of the adrenaline, she reasoned.

"Why don't you start by telling me what happened?" Dan asked.

"As I was leaving my house to run an errand, a man attacked me in my home. I couldn't get away from him. The glass from the windows on my door and the windows shattered all over me, and he hit me over the head. Next thing I know, I'm here." Her speech spurted out like gunfire. A wave of adrenalin-nausea overtook her.

"Are you sure that's what happened?" Dan asked in a calm, quiet tone.

"Yes, why?"

"Oh, God," Alison moaned. She put her hand up to her mouth, as if it could act as a blockade for her tears. Alison stood up in an attempt to hide her worry.

"What? Alison, what?" The lump in her throat grew. She swallowed but couldn't get it to go down. Alison never freaked out like this.

Dan took a deep breath. "Steven, why don't you tell Miranda how she got here?"

Steven sat on the chair beside the bed and took her hand. "Miranda, I found you on the floor of your house. I went to your office for our appointment. Tammy said you had canceled all your appointments for the day because of your migraine, so I stopped and bought some soup and rice from the Chinese restaurant you like, and I brought it over to check in on you. I rang the front doorbell, but you didn't answer. I grew worried because your car sat in the driveway, so I went to the side door. That's when I saw you on the floor of the kitchen. I didn't want to break the glass on the kitchen door because you would have gotten covered in it, so I walked around the house and broke a living room window, crawled in, and stayed by your side after I called 911. I called Dan to meet us here, and I rode in the ambulance with you."

"What? What do you mean? There was glass all over me!" Miranda gulped and looked down at her hands. "No!" They were cut-free. She leaped up, strode to the bathroom, and gazed in the mirror. Her image, unmarred, unbloodied, gazed back at her. She returned to the bed and sat down, dazed.

"Miranda, I swear to you, the only broken glass I saw was in the sink of your bathroom and the living room. Also, as I sat and waited for the ambulance to arrive, the operator asked me if I could see any injuries on your body. I didn't see any." He closed his eyes and shook his head as if it pained him. He gazed into her eyes. "Because I had to break in to get to you, the operator didn't see a need to send the police, so she sent the ambulance."

"No, I know what I saw. My head..." Miranda's hand flew up to her head, feeling her skull all around.

"Honey," Alison said. "When they brought you in, Dan sent you right away to do an x-ray and CAT scan. With my permission, they even tested you for drugs. Everything came out normal."

Miranda looked at Dan. "Is this true?"

Dan nodded. "Miranda, I could not find any conclusive cause for your blackout."

"No, you're making it up. I know what I saw. The glass was everywhere. I could feel the blood trickling down my face. This man, when I had my accident, he stood over me here in the hospital."

"Can you describe him?" asked Dan.

"He was really tall, and his face had a shadow cast over it. He also wore a brown leather jacket."

"I'll let the staff know to keep their eye out, just in case," said Dan.

"Just in case what?" Miranda looked at Dan. "Don't you guys believe me?" She looked at Alison and Steven. "Steven, you believe me, right?" Why should they? Miranda was quickly losing faith in herself. The nausea spread like a disease. *Is this what people go through when they lose their sanity?*

"Hon, if you want, I'll go to your house and have the police investigate," Alison offered. "I am a bit worried that you saw this guy while you were in the hospital." If she expressed her concerns that a man could be stalking Miranda, she might be able to get the police to come by to check out the house.

"Thanks, Ali. I would appreciate that." At least Ali was willing to believe in her, even when Miranda didn't know what to believe.

Miranda looked at Dan. "Could the migraine medication cause hallucinations?" *Please say yes.*

"Only if you've had a lot of it," Dan responded. "How many pills did you take?"

"Only one, and then I went to sleep."

"And you're not on any antidepressants?"

"No."

"And did you have any nausea, dizziness, palpitations, vomiting?"

"No."

"Well, what you say confirms the blood test. Everything was normal."

The nurse walked in with the medication. "Miranda, this will help you relax after the ordeal you had tonight." Dan gave Miranda the pills.

Miranda shook her head. "No way." What if the stranger hunted her down? She needed to stay alert.

Alison looked at her sister, doing her best to barricade her endless worry over her before her accident, during her accident, her fainting at Dan's house. Now this? "Hon, please, for tonight, to help you sleep. You went through a scary ordeal. Besides, Steven told me he'll stay to guard you. Right, Steve?"

"Yep, I'll be here the whole night."

"I feel okay now. I don't think I have to stay here. Can't I go home?"

"Miss Miranda," said Dan, "given your history with head trauma and because this is the second time you've lost consciousness since your accident, I would like you to stay for observation overnight. I have a buddy, a neuropsychiatrist, who will come and see you tomorrow."

"But..." Miranda started to object. Dan raised his hand.

"I know. Since I could not find any injuries or lesions on your brain, we need to explore other options. Hallucinations often have a physiological cause to them, which are treatable. Susceptibility to hallucinations increases after a traumatic brain injury. However, if it was a hallucination, what you saw was more complex than seeing a bunch of bunnies hopping around the room." Alison, Steven, and Miranda laughed. "I had a patient who saw that, really, a nine-year-old girl." Dan smiled, seeming satisfied his statement broke up some of the tension. "Or maybe the migraine medication caused an intense dream. Either way, I am keeping an open mind for you, Miranda. I need you to be open-minded too. Okay?"

Miranda sighed. "Yeah, thank you. I guess what you are saying makes sense. It's nice to know I'm in such good hands. Thanks, all of you. Sorry to worry you." Maybe the accident did cause hallucinations, but she doubted she dreamed the entire incident. She looked down again at her hands, the proof that it didn't happen right there in front of her. But to hallucinate the same man more than once? Maybe some help would do her some good.

Alison took Miranda's hands in hers. "We'll figure this out together. Let me get going. You know, Mira, I hope it was a dream."

"Yeah. I don't like it either way. I want to know what is going on."

"We all do," said Steven. "Hey, I'm sorry you're going through this. I'm here. Okay?"

"Okay, Miranda, I'm going to talk with the nurses, and I'll see you in the morning. You're in good hands here." Dan winked at his brother.

"I'm going to go call the police and meet them at your house. Thanks, Steve." Alison picked up her purse and coat.

"No need to thank me. I would stay even if no one had asked me." Steven winked at Miranda. Miranda's blasted cheeks burned.

"I'll see you at home." Alison kissed Dan.

"I'll walk you to the elevator, and you can give me another one of those." Dan put his arm around Alison. Dan and Alison closed the door.

Miranda smiled at Steve. "Thanks for staying and for finding me." She tried to say something else, but closed her mouth and leaned back on the bed.

Steven looked at her. "What's the matter, besides the obvious?"

Miranda sighed. "I don't want you thinking I'm a poor little victim you're always going to have to save. I can take care of myself. This isn't a good start to a relationship, or whatever this is between us. Besides, I could be losing my mind. Are you sure you want to get involved with me?" Miranda yawned, sleepy from the medication.

"Miranda, we've known each other for years, yes?"

"Yes."

Steven took Miranda's hands again and looked into her eyes. "I have thought a lot of things over the years about you, but those thoughts never included helpless victim, and you are the sanest person I have ever met. Understand? I am here because I've always had feelings for you. In high school, I was too immature to understand them and too scared to pursue them. Now, I'm not."

Miranda felt the telltale heat creep up her neck to her cheeks. "Oh."

"I am here because I want to be with you, at home, in a hospital room, on top of Mount Everest..."

"But, I'm going through such a hard time now..."

"Yes, I can see that, and I'm sorry. But if this is as bad as it gets, I think I'll stick around for easier times. This way, we'll have plenty of time to figure out whatever this is between us."

Wow. I really like this New Steven. She smiled and took Steven's hand, and wrapped her other arm around his forearm. Within seconds, she fell into a deep, drug-induced sleep.

• • •

Dan arrived at Miranda's room the next morning in time to witness shouting, a group of his colleagues exiting the room, nurses rushing to assist, and flying tongue depressors.

"Get out! All of you! What do you think I am, some sort of circus sideshow freak?"

Dan shook his head. *Oh boy. Alison warned me. Here it is: The Temper.*

He saw Steven walking as fast as he could manage with two cups of coffee in his hands. Dan shot him a look. Steven shrugged, his eyes wide and confused. "She wanted coffee. I was only gone for ten minutes."

Dan rolled his eyes. He looked at his colleagues. "Stay. I'll handle this."

He grabbed Steven by the elbow and led him into the war zone. "Miranda, it's me. Don't hit me with tongue depressors. Tell me what's going on."

Miranda, her face crimson, pointed at the door. "I'll tell you what's going on. I fell asleep when Steven went to get us some coffee. I couldn't keep my eyes open because of that damn pill, and when I woke up, these jokers were in the room, looking at me like an experiment and whispering to each other. I'm not a bug in a jar, and I'm not crazy. They need to treat me with more respect and dignity."

"Okay, okay, I'm sorry. This is a teaching hospital, but they should have waited until you woke up to get your consent. It won't happen again."

"You're right. I'm going home." Miranda grabbed her clothing from the closet and threw them on the bed.

"Miranda, please stay for a little longer and speak with Dr. Fine. Besides," Dan leaned over to speak in her ear, "if I don't do everything I can to help you, Alison will kill me. You know how she gets."

Miranda couldn't hold a straight face. *Alison never yelled, but when you've had your ears boxed by Alison Sheppard, you know you've been scolded.*

"So, help me out here, please, for me?" Dan smiled at her.

"Okay, sure," she said, taking a deep breath. "I'm sorry. Maybe I overreacted. I don't like being surprised."

"After what you have been through, I can see why," Dan agreed.

"Can I please put on my clothes, though? I'm tired of wearing hospital gowns."

Dan smiled. "Of course you can. We ran all of the physical tests we need. And we'll release you today after Dr. Fine and Dr. Gallagher have had the chance to speak with you."

"Okay, great." Miranda took a deep breath and picked up her clothes. She looked at Steven. "Mmm, coffee, thanks." She grabbed the cup with her free hand, stood on her tiptoes, kissed Steven on the cheek, and walked to the bathroom.

"Hmm, I wonder what she'd do for two cups." Steven raised his eyebrows like Groucho Marx.

"I heard that," Miranda yelled through the door.

Dan and Steven laughed. "So, Alison called this morning?" Dan asked.

"Yes, Miranda knows." Steven sat with his coffee and took a sip. "Want some?" He offered his cup to Dan.

"No thanks. You take too much sugar in yours."

Steven smiled. "More for me." He took a loud slurp from his cup.

"How did she take it?"

"She's confused. She insists the experience was so real."

"I also spoke with the hospital staff. I didn't expect much since so much time had passed, but none of them remember a man fitting that description."

Miranda stepped out of the bathroom. "Thanks for checking up on that. Yes, Alison called to let me know that the police didn't find anything."

A knock on the partially open door interrupted the conversation. "Hello?" A thin man with silver hair, silver-framed glasses, and a blue suit took a tentative step over the threshold of the room.

"Dr. Fine. Thanks for coming." Dan walked over and shook his hand. "Dr. Fine, this is my brother, Steven, and this is Miranda Sheppard."

"Dr. Foreman told me a bit about your history and your recent experience. Why don't we sit down, and you can tell me in your own words what happened?"

"Do you want us to leave?" asked Dan.

"I'll leave it up to Miranda." Dr. Fine glanced at Miranda.

"It's alright. They can stay."

"Okay. Why don't we sit?" Dr. Fine sat down on the chair and gestured over to the bed. Miranda walked over and sat and told Dr. Fine everything from the beginning.

"Dan tells me you have your own business. How is that going?" asked Dr. Fine.

"I'm lucky. That has been going pretty strong."

"I'm curious. How did your memory loss affect your business?"

"I am grateful that I cultivated good business practices. I take detailed notes, so that enabled me to read up on what I didn't remember."

Dr. Fine nodded. "Have you had any trouble remembering, such as what day it is, since the accident?"

"When I first woke up, yes, but I had been out for a while. Since then no."

"And you had a migraine yesterday morning, correct?"

"Yes."

Dr. Fine wrote some notes as Miranda told her about her medications. "You mentioned you were going to run errands when this happened?"

"Yes."

"Where were you going?"

Good question. "You know, I don't remember now."

Dr. Fine asked some more questions about her family history, and Miranda shared with him her childhood situation and how Alison stepped in to take care of her after her parents' death. After Dr. Fine finished making some notes in his book, he acknowledged, "Miranda, it sounds like you have had a lot going on. Your memory loss concerns me. If you agree, you can come see Dr. Gallagher at our office. He couldn't make it today. Would you like to do that?"

"Why do you want me to see Dr. Gallagher?"

"I do the medication and physiological side of our practice. He does the therapy."

Miranda tried to control the shakiness in her voice. "Why do you think I need therapy?" She looked down at her fidgeting hands in her lap. *I must really be going crazy.*

"I think you have a lot of unanswered questions. We could help you sort them out and recover some of the memory you lost, Dr. Gallagher's expertise. Sometimes, Ms. Sheppard, the type of event you experienced has physiological reasons, and sometimes, disorders can be responsible."

"It sounds like you think I imagined the whole thing." Defensiveness reared its ugly face, attempting to hide how fragile she felt. She just might have imagined the entire thing. How can a hallucination seem so real? She dammed the river of tears crouching at the corners of her eyes.

"Miss Sheppard," Dr. Fine peered at her over his silver glasses, "in the long run, isn't it most important for *you* to decide what happened? I have no judgment. In all honesty, I hope someone didn't enter your house to assault you. To me, the alternative explanation is much less frightening and treatable."

"What could cause something like this?"

"It could be a real event. TBI, Traumatic Brain Injury, could bring on hallucinations. You see, as a neuropsychiatrist, I look at both the physiological components as well as the psychological components. Since you had a head injury this past year, I would guess that your injury is still affecting you. If we can discover how this culminates in your daily life, we can find some answers for you. I can have my office call you for an appointment."

Miranda sighed. "Okay."

"Good, Ms. Sheppard. Here is my card. Heather, my office manager, will call you." Dr. Fine stuck out his hand. "We'll see you soon, and it was a pleasure meeting you."

Dan opened the door. "Let me walk you to the elevator. Miranda, I'll get the paperwork going for your release. Listen, no running a marathon today, doing power lifts, okay?

Miranda chuckled. "Okay."

"Would you like some company?" asked Steven. "I can make coffee again and give you one of my famous foot rubs."

Miranda sighed and smiled. "You know, that sounds nice."

Dan and Dr. Fine walked down the hall to the elevators. "Jerry, what do you think?"

Dr. Fine paused. "No brain lesions? The bloodwork was normal?"

Dan shook his head. "None. Her brain scan was clear. Bloodwork normal. No drugs or alcohol in her system."

"It could be any number of things. Migraines can cause hallucinations, but I've never heard of anything like this, with the vividness, the detail. I'm leaning toward TBI. It's not typical of head injury-related psychosis either, but we all know no absolutes exist in the world. She could have passed out and envisioned the entire scenario while unconscious or even semi-conscious. Dr. Gallagher will help pinpoint it. Could you please forward those CAT scans to my office?"

"Sure, no problem. Thanks for coming by on such short notice."

"You've done the same for me," Jerry smiled. The two arrived at the elevator. "Oh, by the way, congratulations on your engagement." Jerry patted Dan on the arm.

"Thanks," Dan smiled.

"This one finally roped you into domestic life?"

Dan laughed. "Yeah, I guess so." Dan pushed the elevator button.

"So, your fiancée is Miranda's sister?"

"Yes."

"And these are the same girls whose parents died in that crash some years ago?"

"Yes. Funny how life works out, isn't it? But Alison is an extraordinary woman. I've never been happier."

"Hmm," Jerry said, frowning.

"What?"

"Well, I find it interesting that Miranda's episodes both occurred during a time of transition. She's not the dramatic type, is she?"

Dan laughed. "Well, that's a loaded question, especially if you saw her this morning. But dramatic, as in attention-seeking? I don't think so. She's pretty independent, from what Alison told me, but she has a bit of a temper."

Jerry nodded. He would run it by Jack when he gave him the paperwork. The elevator doors opened.

"Here's your ride," said Dan. "Are you still up for our squash match this Thursday?"

"You bet. 1 P.M.?"

"You better be on your toes. You got the best of me last week, but I have a new strategy for beating you this week."

"Yeah, what's that?" Dr. Fine stepped onto the elevator.

"Get you drunk first."

Both men laughed. "Okay, Dan, see you Thursday." He waved as the elevator door closed. Dan nodded.

"Hey, handsome."

Dan turned around to the voice of his lovely new fiancée. Alison wore a silky little dress. His eyes followed it down to her mostly bare legs.

"Are you ready to spring our girl?" Alison asked.

"Yep, I was just going to start the paperwork."

"Okay. I'll go to her room to see if she needs anything. Steven's here too, right?"

"Yes, he stayed overnight."

"Wow. He's really smitten, huh?"

"Yes, and it seems Miranda's coming around too."

"Hmm, maybe there'll be a double wedding."

Dan half-smiled and raised an eyebrow. "Maybe." *Women and their romantic notions.* He found it one of Alison's endearing qualities. She had such a difficult time, but she still had the capacity to possess idyllic notions. She came across as all sweetness, but strength resided inside that soft exterior.

"So, what did the specialist say?"

"You'll have to talk to Miranda about that. Do you think you'd like to go out for an early lunch? I want to check on some other patients, and then I'm done for the day."

"I'll let you know. I want to see if Miranda needs anything first."

"Oh, Steven said he would take her home."

"Good. I'll say hello, find out what happened, and then I'll meet you in your office?"

"Great." Dan planted a kiss on Alison's cheek.

Alison walked down the corridor to Miranda's room. She tapped on the door. "Heeelloooo." She opened the door a crack.

Miranda and Steven sat on the bed kissing. Steven reached under Miranda's sweatshirt, rubbed her stomach, and moved his way up to her breasts. Miranda moaned as Steven rubbed her nipples lightly over her bra. Their kissing became hungrier.

Alison shut the door. She closed her eyes for a moment as that familiar warm wave washed over her, heightening her craving. She sighed and rapped on the door. She heard rustling behind the door before her sister said, "Come in."

Alison opened the door. Miranda's eyes were glazed over. Steven had moved over to the chair and crossed his legs. "Hey, you two. Came by to see how you're doing. I see everything is fine." Alison smiled. "Heh heh, sorry to interrupt."

"No, you're not," said Miranda

"Yeah, you're right. I'm not," Alison agreed. Steven laughed. Miranda scowled and crossed her arms. "So, how did it go?"

"I'm going to see a neuropsychologist and his partner, a therapist," said Miranda.

"Any ideas on what happened?"

"He said the injuries from the accident could have played a part."

"Okay. I'm sorry this happened, love, but it could be a good thing. Maybe you can recover some of your memory, right?"

"Yeah, I guess." Alison finally got her way. Maybe Alison could see that she was nuts all along. She dared not think or ask it.

"Dan's getting the paperwork ready to spring you. Do you need me to do anything?"

"No, I'm good. In fact, I'm glad nothing is wrong with my head, at least on the outside because I'm feeling pretty good at the moment, and Steven's going to give me a ride home."

"Yeah, and maybe he'll give you one when you get there too."

Steven smirked. He seemed to like that idea.

Miranda rolled her eyes. "Grow up."

Steven and Alison chuckled.

A nurse knocked on the door. "Hello, Miss Sheppard. I have your paperwork ready."

"Yes, I know the drill."

"Okay, hon, I'll go wait for Dan. He's taking me out to lunch."

"You go ahead. We've got this." Miranda grinned shyly at Steven.

"Okay, Miss Sheppard, let me go over the doctor's instructions."

Alison meandered to the elevator and took it up to the eighth floor. She walked to the office at the end of the hall, her fingers tracing Dan's name on the door, glued on with gold and black letters. She turned the handle. Images of Steven and Miranda still played out in her musings. She plunked down on the couch, let out a loud sigh, and looked around the office. Several neat piles of papers sat on Dan's spacious L-shaped desk. Hmm, if she took all the paperwork off and placed herself on top of the desk, they wouldn't knock into the computer sitting safely off to the left, but she decided against it, worried that it might annoy him if she moved everything.

She heard Dan in the hallway. "Yes, why don't you write it up? I'll take a look at it on Monday." He turned the handle and opened the door. Alison sat on the black leather couch.

"Hi there." She smiled.

Dan gazed down. Alison tantalized him in a way his ex-fiancé never could. The way her nipples poked through her silky little dress, that perfume she always wore that made his head forget everything else, the pride he felt when every man checked her out everywhere they went. *She's capable of driving any man crazy.* That dress rode all the way up, barely covering her. He angled his head down to peer up her skirt. Naked underneath. With a devilish grin, he locked the door.

Eventually, all the paperwork wound up on the floor.

7
DISCOVERY

Miranda had a list of excuses she was dying to give so she did not have to go to her appointment with Dr. Gallagher. If it weren't for her compulsive need to keep all the appointments she made and the unsettling feeling she should go, she probably would have used one of them.

"Ms. Sheppard?"

"Yep." Miranda put up her hand like roll call in school.

"Hi, I'm Dr. Gallagher." Dr. Gallagher's large, strong hand seemed to swallow up Miranda's tiny, pale one as they shook. It felt rough, as if he were a carpenter instead of a psychologist. "Come on back."

Miranda followed his stocky frame to his office. He was not the tallest man Miranda had ever met, about six foot, but his wide shoulders made him appear even taller. "Have a seat." He pointed to the chair in front of his desk.

"Thanks." Miranda sat in the cushioned chair. Dr. Gallagher had piercing blue eyes. If he weren't wearing a suit, she would have guessed he was in a motorcycle gang. White hair was scattered throughout his short black hair on his head and mustache, but his beard, which hung to the bottom of his neck, was almost all white, contrasting almost in defiance with his blue-collared shirt and his dark blue suit jacket. Because of his size and appearance, she might have found him intimidating, but his gaze was so warm and unassuming, it put her at ease.

"You know, most people don't want to be here," Dr. Gallagher said.

Miranda's heart jumped. "What makes you think I don't want to be here?"

Dr. Gallagher pressed his lips together and drew back the corners of his mouth. "After doing this for so many years, you learn a few things. Most people would rather run into a burning building to save someone's pet iguana than talk about their emotions."

Miranda laughed. "Yes, I know the feeling."

"Also, some are worried about the stigma."

"Yes," Miranda agreed.

"Some people feel annoyed because they would rather handle things themselves. They feel they have somehow failed or are not strong enough. Especially people who pride themselves on their independence."

Miranda looked down at her hands folded in her lap. Those were her very thoughts on the ride over. When Alison wanted to send her to see someone in Miranda's teenage years, she didn't go for that very reason, to make her parents proud of her for her capability of figuring things out on her own. "Yeah."

"And then some are not ready to deal with the pain. But I have a feeling you are not in that boat."

Miranda nodded.

"Don't worry. What you're feeling is common. Why confront issues that are upsetting or painful? It's our nature to protect ourselves from that pain."

"How are you doing this?" Miranda asked.

"Doing what?"

"It's like you were with me in my head during my car ride over."

Dr. Gallagher laughed. "I get that a lot."

"You're right. I don't really want to be here. I guess whatever's bothering me made me drive here to see you."

Dr. Gallagher nodded. "I like your honesty. Why don't you tell me what is going on?"

"Did you speak with your partner? Do I have to explain it all over again? Or maybe you can just read my mind." Miranda grinned. Why not take an opportunity to needle him a bit?

Gallagher laughed. *This one is going to be a trip.* "I understand it can be annoying, but hearing your take on what's going on will allow me to help you. It would be sort of like having a narrator step in and give me a summation of your experiences the other way."

"Okay, I get it. Sorry. I guess I'm frustrated. I haven't had an easy time."

Dr. Gallagher nodded, maintaining eye contact with Miranda, an invitation for her to continue.

Miranda told him everything from the beginning, how she saw this oversized gargantuan at the hospital, the aliens grabbing her wrists with tentacles, the dark vines at Thanksgiving, and the most recent incident.

"Oh, goodness," Dr. Gallagher said.

"I know, scary, right? Between that night and now, it's been driving me crazy. Um, maybe not crazy..."

"Don't worry," Dr. Gallagher held up a hand. "I know what you mean."

"Okay, good." The tension in Miranda's shoulders released. "I don't know what in the world happened. I haven't felt like this in a long time. It's unnerving."

"Feel like what?"

"Lost. Upset. Frustrated. Helpless. Like I don't have any control." The tears stung as they rolled down her face. She pulled at the tissue box in front of her on the doctor's desk. "See, I didn't want to do this." Crying always gave her an awful headache.

Dr. Gallagher nodded. He waited for Miranda to compose herself. "When is the last time you felt like this?"

"When my parents died."

"Oh, I'm sorry." His brow puckered. "When?"

"When I was eleven."

"That must have been very difficult."

"Yeah."

"I can see why you felt the way you did, at a loss, confused, frustrated. Understandable, given the circumstances."

"I'm lucky too. My sister Alison agreed to take care of me."

"And how old was she at the time?"

"Eighteen."

"That was nice of her, to say the least."

"Yes." Miranda wiped away the rest of her tears.

"Do you mind if I ask you a few questions?"

"What sort of questions?" Miranda eyed him suspiciously.

"About your family history and your background. I have some questions about your medical history as well."

"Why do you need to know that?"

"Because it helps me learn about you. You didn't hatch from an egg and grow up by yourself, right?"

Miranda laughed. "No."

"Okay, then. May I ask a few questions?"

"Sure."

"Here, I have a form. Is that okay?" Dr. Gallagher rifled through the papers on his desk.

"That's fine."

"Okay, thanks. Here it is." He held up a paper at arm's length to examine it. "I think." He fumbled for his reading glasses from the inner pocket of his suit jacket with his free hand, opened them, and perched them on his nose. Miranda smirked. "Ah, yes, here we go. So, are you from this area?"

"Yes, born and raised."

Dr. Gallagher scribbled on the paper, and then looked up at her. "What do you do?"

"I'm a certified public accountant."

"And Alison, what does she do?"

"She used to be a skydiver."

Dr. Gallagher raised his eyebrows. "Wow! What does she do now?"

"She quit after my car accident. She's thinking of going back to school. Right now, she's concentrating on moving and getting married. I kind of wished she had quit sooner."

"It sounds like it was a source of trouble in your relationship," Dr. Gallagher observed.

Miranda nodded. "I was going through so much. I wasn't easy to get along with at the time."

She explained her most recent revelation of how Alison had changed, seeming distant after her parents' death. Instead of being able to express it, she gave Alison a hard time over skydiving, but the fact that picturing her sister plummeting to her death every time she went to work didn't help at the time, and she didn't understand her sister's career choice. Miranda wouldn't even go see her shows at the park. That ate at her as she matured, realizing the missed opportunities to see Ali do something she really loved. They spent some time discussing Miranda's car accident as well, and she reported the details she remembered from her dream the morning of the latest incident.

"All your other memories are intact?" Dr. Gallagher asked.

"Yes. I remember my childhood, going to college, getting my CPA, and everything else."

"Was there any type of brain injury?"

"Just the concussion. All the x-rays were clean. No brain injury. I have a small scar right here." Miranda pointed to a fine line right above her eyebrow.

Dr. Gallagher leaned forward. "Huh. You can barely see it."

"I know. Alison said all the bruising and swelling scared the heck out of her. I had to go to physical therapy because my right leg was a bit crushed, and I had some trouble in my left arm. I was sore as hell."

Dr. Gallagher nodded. "I'm sure Dr. Foreman is sending over your records to this office. You signed all the forms, right?"

"Yes, your secretary took care of that with me today."

"Good." He put the pad of paper aside. He settled back into his chair, gazing at Miranda. "How would you describe your childhood?"

"Perfect, until my parents died. Then my childhood ended."

"What did your parents do?"

"They had a psychological practice together."

"Oh," Dr. Gallagher said, as if he remembered something he needed at the grocery store.

"What?"

"Joy and Allen, right?"

"Yes."

"I worked with them a couple of times. We did one or two joint research projects. I didn't realize you were their daughter."

Miranda smiled. "You met them, so you know how incredible they were."

"Oh, yes," Dr. Gallagher agreed. "They were at the top of their field, skilled clinicians."

"Yes. They had a very good reputation."

"They still do." Dr. Gallagher and Miranda smiled at each other. "So, it seems as if this most recent event has brought up some old feelings connected with your parents' death," Dr. Gallagher observed.

"Huh. I guess it has."

"You know, sometimes recent trauma can bring up painful past experiences. Even happy news can sometimes trigger painful past memories. There is an ancient part of us necessary for our survival, but doesn't have the power of higher reasoning. It makes associations like this all the time, even when it doesn't make sense to our higher reasoning. The car accident brought back painful feelings, yes?"

"Yes," Miranda agreed.

"And the event in your house has left you feeling lost, confused, frustrated. Yes?"

"Yes."

"So, that part of you in your subconscious associated the most recent painful event with the past painful event. This is why you are feeling emotions you consider 'old.'" Dr. Gallagher stuck up his pointer and middle fingers to make air-quotes. "Rather, they are the set of emotions that arise when painful situations come up in life, no matter what the painful situation is. Of course, every person has different reactions, and these sets of emotions might be different for each person. For you, it's a feeling of loss, frustration, anger, and confusion. You follow what I'm saying?"

"Yes. I'm starting to see it. So, there are things going on inside of my head that I am not aware of? Then, how do you know they're there?" Miranda narrowed her eyes.

"You do know on some level because I extracted the information based on what you shared with me. I have the experience and training to connect the dots. The language of the subconscious speaks through associations. When you were little, you were dealt a blow no eleven-year-old should have lived through. Another couple of painful and traumatic events came up within the past year, so that part of you, since it doesn't have higher reasoning, associated pain with pain. The first experience set up a default system: when in pain, refer to age eleven."

"Wow. I can't believe I understand this. You're talking about the id, right? I remember my parents teaching Alison and me." Her parents used to teach them psychological theories, so when she took it out of interest in college, it was like they imprinted them in her brain since birth. She had at least heard or recognized all of the concepts before.

Dr. Gallagher smiled and nodded. "It's a very simple process. The complicated part is learning to identify these inner mechanisms."

"What does this mean in terms of what I experienced?"

"Not sure at the moment, but I'm keeping an open mind." Dr. Gallagher furrowed his eyebrows as if many great thoughts resided in the creases of his forehead. "I'm curious. When you arrived home from the hospital, where was that wine bottle?"

Miranda closed her eyes. She pictured herself walking through the kitchen door with Steven. She focused on the kitchen counter. She opened her eyes and looked at Dr. Gallagher. "On the counter where I had left it, like it hadn't even moved."

Dr. Gallagher nodded. "Has anyone else heard or seen anything strange in your house?"

Miranda stared past Dr. Gallagher as she mulled over his question. Then, she gasped. "Yes, my sister! Right after my accident, she came to my house to take care of me. She said she thought she heard something in my hallway! Oh my God! I'm not crazy!" Her nervous energy released itself as a laugh.

Dr. Gallagher smiled. "Why don't you tell me about the incident?"

"Well," Miranda's voice shook, "she was in my bathroom and was so sure about hearing something in the hallway, she unplugged a lamp from its socket to use as a weapon. Oh, I'm so relieved." She wiped the corners of her eyes but then gasped again. "Oh, God." *There's no relief for me, is there?* "That means someone might've been in my house."

"May I call your sister to get her account of the incident?"

"Sure. I'll give you her cell phone. Dr. Gallagher, what happened to me? God, now I wish I dreamed the whole thing. You know what I mean?"

"Yes." Dr. Gallagher maintained a neutral expression. "Can you think of anything else about the most recent incident that struck you as odd?"

"Yes. Something smelled awful. I'm surprised it didn't burn off my nose hairs."

"What sort of smell? Like a skunk?"

"No. It was more like rotten eggs. Oh, crap. I smelled that in the hospital too." Anxiety crawled over her body, prickling her skin.

Dr. Gallagher nodded. "Miranda, has anything unusual happened since your most recent visit to the hospital?"

"No, but I feel creeped out now. I can't go home."

"Do you have anywhere you could stay?"

"Yes, I have a place or two. Oh, this will upset Alison. I'm upset."

"You're going to make arrangements, then. And we can still work on memory recovery together. Would you like my continued involvement, Miranda?"

"Yes, for certain. I still don't know what happened. And you're completely amazing, by the way. I thought I'd have to see you for months trying to figure out what happened."

Dr. Gallagher smiled. "Thanks. Let's meet in a couple of days, after you've settled in. Sound good?"

"Yes, that sounds great. Thanks."

"All right, then, let me walk you out to help Heather make room in my schedule for you."

8
PARANORMAL

At her next appointment, when Miranda had sat, Dr. Gallagher dropped a stack of printed papers on her lap.

"What's this?" Miranda asked.

"Before we go into that, have you found a place to stay?"

"Yes. I'm staying with Steven."

"Good. Do you feel a little safer now?"

"Yes." Miranda shuffled through the papers, glancing at the titles on the pages. "So, what is this stuff?"

"Remember when I told you I was going to be open-minded?" Dr. Gallagher sat on his burgundy, cushioned office chair behind his desk.

"Yes."

"I said it because I am open-minded."

"I commend you. You seem more open-minded than I am. Ghosts, possession, poltergeists. You took a chance showing me this stuff. How do you know I'm not going to call you a quack and run out of this office?"

Dr. Gallagher smiled. “The same way I knew you didn’t want to be here.”

“That could have been a lucky guess.”

“It could have been.” Dr. Gallagher paused for a moment. The night before, he didn’t get much sleep, struggling with bringing this content to Miranda. He was taking a big risk, introducing the supernatural without the client taking the lead. Didn’t his client deserve to explore everything, without closed-mindedness? Unlike so many other psychologists, he felt perfectly comfortable exploring existential questions. He resolved to share the reason for his unshakable faith, the reason why his instincts won out, and he packed the results of his overnight Internet search. “When I was 11 years old, I saw my first ghost—a solid, full-bodied apparition standing in my kitchen. It scared the crap out of me. I thought a stranger broke into our house. He and I locked eyes. I looked away to grab a weapon. When I looked back, he had vanished, all within the span of a few seconds. A few years later, my mother showed me some family photos, and I saw him in an old photograph: my father’s grandfather.”

Miranda sat wide-eyed. She experienced the same exact pattern of events in her bathroom with the whatever-it-was. Maybe she should be more open-minded.

“My parents raised me without a faith,” Dr. Gallagher continued. “I’ll tell you, the entire experience made me a believer. People who don’t believe in the paranormal haven’t experienced it for themselves. When you do, you have no choice but to believe. I think you know what I mean.”

“What makes you say that?”

“Since our last meeting, I’ve been going over your experience. It was very real to you, yet there isn’t any physical evidence that it happened. Your sister saw some movement and heard something in your house. I think now you know there is something real going on, and we don’t have any physical or physiological explanations for it.

I got my smack on the back of the head at eleven years old. You are in the same boat."

Miranda wrinkled her nose. "Do other people find this irritating?"

"What?"

"The way you're always right?"

Dr. Gallagher chuckled. "Yes, my wife."

"Yep, know how she feels." Miranda crossed her arms. *How the hell is he doing that?*

"So, you on board with this?"

"I'm not so sure. I don't think God exists."

"Why?"

"Because if he did, and he's supposed to be all about love, he wouldn't have taken my parents away from me." Her voice pitch rose slightly as she scowled.

"You don't have to acknowledge God's existence yet. All we have to do is explore every possibility. You know atoms exist, right?"

"Yes."

"How?"

"I learned it in science class."

"You know, people for thousands of years had an inkling that atoms existed, but until they actually saw these particles in the early and mid-1900s, no one knew for certain. Perhaps the spirit world is made of undetectable energy particles. So, do you think for the moment you could entertain the other possibilities?"

Miranda sighed. "I guess so." Maybe some natural phenomenon could explain things that only a few people claim to see. It could occur in the natural world anyway, but without a grand overseer. It was better than having to accept that she suffered from hallucinations or that God ignored her.

"Good. Now, as you can probably see from the research, I've looked into several types of possibilities."

"Demon possession?" Miranda held up the paper and frowned.

"I wanted to show that one to you because I think we can rule it out. What happened to you over the past several months does not follow the typical pattern of known cases of demon possession, such as levitation, psychic abilities, speaking in languages the person doesn't know. I think we're safe on this one, unless you floated all the way to your living room from your bedroom speaking Italian."

Miranda giggled. "No, I haven't."

"Okay, demon possession, cross out. There is a case of demon obsession, though, where a priest pissed off a demon, and the demon followed him around and pulled pranks, like messing with his toothpaste."

Miranda had to laugh despite the seriousness of her circumstances. "Toothpaste? What did he do to piss off a demon?"

"I don't know. I guess his holiness offended him. It seems demons go after spiritual warriors like priests because of what they represent. Again, doesn't fit your experiences either, but it's the only similar experience that I could see."

"Great. Demon obsession."

"Hey, maybe you're a spiritual warrior."

Miranda snorted. "Yeah, right. Me, a spiritual warrior." Not in her wildest dreams.

"The rotten egg smell concerns me, though, the only thing typically demon, or at least, according to a religious site I found on the Internet. A sulfuric odor could mean a demon attack."

Miranda shuddered.

"Don't think for a moment that I believe it. We're just going through some of the possibilities now. They're just stories, and they are unsubstantiated, but it's all we have to go on."

Miranda's face relaxed. "Yes, I know." She rifled through the papers and read. "What about hauntings and poltergeists?"

"As far as I can see, spirits have typical patterns of communication. The ghost I saw during my childhood occurs a lot less than other types of communications, such as tapping or banging, objects, doors, or furniture moving by themselves, hearing voices in your house, the lights flickering on and off, seeing orbs or energy balls, mists, things missing then reappearing again..." Dr. Gallagher paused. "Do any of these seem familiar to you?"

"Well, yes, actually. My sister heard and saw something, some footsteps, and she thought she saw someone in my house. I saw this man also in at least two different settings."

"It seems to follow you around, rather than having an attachment to a place or an object, and I did find one or two stories like that. No proof, just stories. Your last experience was violent, which points toward a poltergeist."

"You mean, like the movie?"

"In a way. There are people who experience poltergeist activity, I've heard. It's usually not extreme like in the movies, but I know some people where a ghost or spirit knocked everything out of the kitchen cabinets and dumped it on the floor and made books fly off a bookshelf. Has anything like that happened?"

"Nope, only what I told you. Um, do you think it's possible that this thing can hurt me?" Miranda looked down at her hands in her lap and rubbed them together. This was not the way she envisioned her own demise.

"It's not very likely."

"But, it could happen." Miranda tried to gulp back her tears.

"Listen, the chances of you getting hurt are slim. But I'll tell you what. If there is something in your house, I know a team that will investigate." Noticing her increasing uneasiness, he offered, "Let me know if you're overwhelmed."

"I'm overwhelmed."

"Okay, let's take a break and talk about your week."

Miranda took a deep breath. "It's good. Since I didn't know what was going on, I didn't want this whatever-it-is to follow me and hurt Alison, so I decided to stay with Steven because his building has a lot of security. There is someone at the desk around the clock, and there are security cameras in the lobby, the elevators, and the hallway."

"That's great. So, it's going well with Steven?"

"It's strange, staying with Steven, but he's been very supportive and healthy about the whole thing. He told me he's not taking this as me moving in. It's not putting a strain on us at all, and he's been very accommodating and understanding, like a fun sleepover with a good male friend. He even started looking into security systems for me."

"That's a great idea."

"Yes, I think so too. I'm looking into an entire system I can arm and disarm, has motion detectors, and a camera system. This way if that bastard shows up at my house again, or if he's still there, I can record him, and my whole house will be hard-wired into the security company. If the slightest thing goes wrong, the police will arrive in no time."

"You should see if the police would do a run-through of your house before you go back in case someone made a strange home somewhere, like in a crawl space. There have been cases of homeless people living in attics for weeks before the homeowners discovered them."

"Yes, that's a super creepy thought. Good idea."

"These sound like great precautions and will eliminate any possibility of a person living inside of your home besides you."

"I hope so. Having them check it one more time would make me feel more comfortable."

"There is a possibility that nothing will happen again."

"Yes, I've considered that. I have mixed feelings about that. You know, because part of me wants it to reveal itself again so I can figure out what it is, and part of me wants it to go away and leave me alone for the rest of my life."

"Yes, understandable." Dr. Gallagher was satisfied when all the stress left Miranda's face. "Now, I would like to revisit our conversation about the paranormal investigators, Mike and Joe Cavanaugh, brothers. They have all the equipment necessary to uncover any supernatural causes for the disturbances you experienced. They use a scientific approach. There have been great advances in the technology. If they don't get any evidence, they'll tell you. If they do get proof, you'll also know. They are well-respected in their field because they do not automatically assign paranormal reasons to occurrences."

"They don't have one of those television shows, do they?" Miranda asked uneasily.

"No." Dr. Gallagher smiled. "They're happy helping people explain the unexplainable."

"I'm not sure. It's one thing for my closest family members and some doctors to know. Now the circle is growing."

"Yes, I understand."

"Do you?" Miranda slanted her eyes.

"Sure. Even though people are more open-minded, a stigma surrounds the idea of the paranormal. Also, I noticed you like your privacy."

"Yeah. That really is irritating."

"What?"

"The fact you're right again."

Dr. Gallagher laughed.

Miranda crossed her arms. "How do you do that? It's almost word for word what I'm thinking in my head. It freaks me out."

"I'm sorry. I don't mean to freak you out. I'm not aware that I'm doing it half the time."

"I think I've entered the Twilight Zone."

"I'd like to welcome you to the Zone." Dr. Gallagher stuck out his hand.

Miranda giggled, a release of nervous energy, and shook Dr. Gallagher's hand.

"Don't worry. We'll figure this out."

"Maybe we will." Miranda, for a change, felt safe in Dr. Gallagher's hands.

9
Ghosthunting

"Are you sure the police checked the *whole* house?" Alison had begun packing the living room. As she piled her memories and items into boxes, she spoke to Miranda on the speaker phone.

"Yes, for the fortieth time, they checked the whole house." Miranda shook her head, looked at Steven, rolled her eyes, and pointed to the phone receiver. Steven put his hands up, shrugged his shoulders, and smirked.

"Maybe I should come over and check it myself." The statement served as a forewarning rather than a suggestion.

"No, no. Steven is here with me. The police did a walk-through with us. We checked every single nook and cranny of this house. I promise. They're almost done putting in the security system. You do not have to come over."

"Okay, only if you're sure. I trust you. I trust Steven too. This has been nerve-wracking."

"Yeah, I know. Sorry I'm such trouble."

"Oh, honey. You're no trouble at all. You never have been. Everything else in life is troublesome."

Miranda smiled and shook her head. "I can only aspire to be as good as you."

"You're already there."

"Okay, enough sweetness, before I need an insulin shot."

"Haha, yeah. So, when are the ghosthunters coming over?"

"Ugh, don't call them that. They're paranormal researchers."

"Yeah, those. When do they arrive?"

"Tonight. The brothers who run the organization know my doctor. They rearranged their schedule when Dr. Gallagher told them about my case."

"What time? I'll come over."

"You don't have to. It's okay."

"Yeah, you really think that's going to work? I'm coming over. What time are they going to be there?"

Miranda rolled her eyes and sighed. She knew better than to argue. "About eight."

"Fine, I'll see you at seven. And quit rolling your eyes at me."

Miranda laughed.

"Yep, can see you right through the phone. See you at seven."

"So, Alison's coming over to check your house, isn't she?" Steven smiled.

Miranda laughed. "Yeah. You're starting to get her, aren't you?"

"Was she always like this?"

"For the first couple of years after my parents died, we both walked around in a fog. It didn't feel real, you know. Then, at thirteen, I acted out. You saw what I went through, dying my hair, going Goth. I was tired of going on with life, pretending that everything was okay. I wanted my old life back. That's when she figured out how to step up. She wouldn't give up."

"I guess leaving you alone was something you never had to worry about. It almost seems like she set out to prove it to you."

Miranda laughed. "Yeah, ain't it the truth?"

"Ms. Sheppard." A man stepped into the kitchen. He wore a dark blue collared shirt with *Secure Home and Business* on the shirt pocket resting over his heart and tan pants. He reseated his dark blue cap on top of his head, revealing a shock of white hair. "Let me go over the checklist with you. I finished installing your new system."

"Okay." Miranda followed the man into her living room.

Harry, the security specialist, explained all of the ins and outs of working her new system with a camera in every room. He led them to Miranda's workspace in her living room. Her computer equipment, her filing cabinets, and a laptop sat in the middle of the desk. Harry explained that she should put her laptop away in case anyone breached her system and to have one laptop dedicated just for the security system. "All the video from the cameras can be accessed through your laptop, and the program I installed on it records for twenty-four straight hours. Once the recording is completed, it automatically saves it in a folder." After they completed the payment and paperwork, Miranda showed Harry out.

"There goes taking a trip or buying another Corvette for a while," Miranda laughed, shaking her head.

"Yes, but the fact you're going to be safe now is priceless." Steven circled his arms around her waist.

"Yeah, yeah, I guess so." Miranda smiled and kissed Steven on the lips.

Steven smiled back. "Oooo." He kissed her again.

"Helloooo." Alison rapped on the kitchen door. She turned the knob and let herself in.

Miranda and Steven laughed. "She has a knack for interrupting at the wrong moments, doesn't she?" Steven held his embrace around Miranda's waist and gazed down at her.

Miranda looked up at him and smiled. "You really are starting to get her."

"Hi guys." Alison set down a couple of big paper bags on the counter. Steven and Miranda walked to the kitchen. "I thought it would be nice to have some dinner together. I stopped at your favorite Chinese restaurant."

Miranda kissed Alison on the cheek. "Thank you. Very thoughtful. It smells delicious. How did you get over here so fast with all that food?"

"I called ahead, of course. I brought all your favorites."

"I'm pretty hungry." Steven peered over Miranda's shoulder into the bags.

"Good. There's plenty. So, why don't you give me the tour and show me this security system on steroids you got?"

"I'll get the food ready." Steven took out the plates and silverware from Miranda's kitchen cabinets and drawers.

"Alison, if you want to check out the house, why don't you say so?"

"Miranda, I want to check out the house."

"Didn't you check it when the cops were over?"

"Yes, but I want to check it *again.*"

Miranda rolled her eyes and shook her head. "Fine, go nuts."

Alison clapped her hands and smiled. "Yay." She took off her jacket and gloves and scurried down the hallway.

"Don't touch my stuff," Miranda yelled after her, her voice trailing off.

"I see this family has strong-headed women in it." Steven took the plates, napkins, and silverware over to the dining room table.

"More like bullheaded," Miranda laughed. "Yes, me included. I guess you have your hands full." She helped Steven set the table.

Steven set a plate down in front of each of the chairs. "It's funny. When you meet Alison, she doesn't really seem like that."

"Yeah, I know. When you get to know her, though, you start to realize she always gets her way. She won't nag, and she won't argue. She'll keep at you, always with a smile. Unless you know her, you don't even realize what's happening."

"What do you want to drink?"

"Water."

"Alison brought soda."

"Yuck. That's okay. I don't like the bubbles or all that sugar. It gives me a headache."

"More for me." Steven smiled.

Miranda sighed. Signs of Old Steven popped up like this every once in a while.

The front doorbell rang. "Dr. Gallagher, hello."

Dr. Gallagher's frame seemed to take up the entire doorway. He certainly wasn't Miranda's idea of typical attractiveness, but there was definitely something about him. Maybe his blue eyes made people want to pour out their souls to him. "Sorry, I guess I'm early. I went to a store nearby, and it didn't make sense for me to go all the way back across town."

"Not at all. It seems to be the trend for today." Miranda stepped aside for Dr. Gallagher to enter. "Here, let me take your coat." Dr. Gallagher handed Miranda his coat and baseball cap with *NESP* sewn onto the front of the hat. She took his coat and hat, hung them on a hanger, and put them into the closet opposite the front door. Miranda offered food and drink, all of which he declined.

Dr. Gallagher carefully noted as many details as he could about Miranda's house. The path leading to the front door started at the middle of the house and then veered off to the left corner where the front door stood underneath a small overhang. A closet sat in the small vestibule. Just beyond, a large living room, and through the living room, a small dining room just large enough for the table and chairs. The tiny kitchen lay directly beside the dining room, and beside the kitchen, a hallway, where he imagined were stairs to access the second story. The décor exuded simplicity. White walls, framed photos covering the walls, shelves with knickknacks, a few plants, the couch, a couple of lounge chairs, and a television on a small stand in the living room right off the kitchen, track lighting in the living room, and her workspace in the corner by the windows.

To an untrained eye, Miranda's house might have seemed immaculate, both in cleaning and organization. To Dr. Gallagher, it was Miranda's way to cope with loss; cleaning helps people feel like they have control. In the dining room, he saw a man placing some white cardboard containers from Lee's Chinese Restaurant in the middle of the table with serving utensils.

"Dr. Gallagher, this is my boyfriend, Steven."

"Pleased to meet you." Dr. Gallagher shook Steven's hand.

"Likewise. Are you sure you don't want anything to eat? I'll set another place for you."

"Thanks, no. It smells great, but I'm full."

"Okay, more for..."

Before Steven could finish his sentence, Miranda took one of the cloth napkins and threw it in his face. There. That should handle Old Steven.

Steven, laughing, caught the napkin.

Dr. Gallagher smiled.

Miranda narrowed her eyes at Steven. *He can be such a stinker sometimes.* Miranda just met her psychologist, and she didn't want things to go wrong, especially since he went out if his way for her.

Alison walked into the dining room. "Dr. Gallagher, this is my nosy sister Alison."

Alison and Steven laughed. "Nice to meet you." She shook Dr. Gallagher's hand. Dr. Gallagher smirked.

"Are you satisfied now?" Miranda crossed her arms.

"Yes, quite. I didn't find any hobos living in your attic, no secret passageways. Nice security system."

"Good. I'm glad you feel better."

"Yes, thanks."

"Dr. Gallagher, why don't you have a seat?" Miranda pointed to the dining room chair next to him.

"Thanks. So, the police didn't find anything?"

"Nope, and neither did Alison." Miranda pushed out her lips and scrunched her nose at Alison as they all sat down. Alison and Steven laughed again.

"I wanted to see for myself," Alison explained.

Dr. Gallagher acknowledged her with a nod and slight smile. "So, are you nervous about tonight?"

"Yes, a bit. I have no idea what to expect."

"I think we're all a little nervous," Alison accepted containers of food as Steven passed them around the table. "Here, Miranda." She passed a container to Miranda.

"Thanks. So, Dr. Gallagher, you seem like you work with your hands a lot. Do you have a hobby outside of listening to other people's woes?"

Dr. Gallagher noted the intentional shift in conversation. "Yes. I like to rebuild old cars and work on my motorcycle." Dr. Gallagher glanced at the small cuts and the telltale traces of black grease ground into the creases of his knuckles backyard mechanics are never able to scrub clean.

Steven swallowed his food. "Oh, you mean like muscle cars?"

"Yes, those, and all sorts of classic cars. I'm rebuilding a Camaro now."

"What year?" asked Steven.

"1980."

"Nice. What did you pay for it?"

"It wasn't running. It needed new wheel bearings, so I got it for fifty bucks."

"Wow. Next time I need to buy a car, I'm going shopping with you," Alison said.

Dr. Gallagher laughed.

"So, you restore the cars, then, for show?" Steven asked.

"No, I race them at the track."

Steven raised his eyebrows. "Oh, around an oval track?"

"In a straight line. Drag racing."

"Nice." Steven smiled approvingly.

"Dr. Gallagher, you are full of surprises," Miranda observed. "I have another question."

"Yes?"

"What do those initials stand for on your baseball cap?"

"NESP? The New England State Prison."

"Oh? Did someone you know work there?"

"When I turned twenty-one, I worked there for four years. They officially hired me as a correction officer, but because of my background in mental health, I took over the night shift counseling. I worked third shift, and the hired counselors turned their beepers off at night, so they came to rely on me to respond to emergencies. After a while, they called me at home because many of the inmates didn't want to talk to the hired counselors. I decided to go back to school and get my Ph. D. in Clinical Psychology."

Alison raised her eyebrows. "Wow. Dr. Gallagher, is prison really as bad as it's portrayed in the movies?"

"It's worse."

"Worse?" asked Steven.

"Yes. Worse. Imagine what it's like being in hell. It's worse than hell."

"Is that why you worked there for four years?" Miranda asked.

Dr. Gallagher paused, gazing at Miranda. "Correction officers have a shelf life of four years, the average rate of burnout. Four years in prison is like forty for any other profession. That's why the turnover is so high."

"Sorry. I didn't mean..." Miranda started. *Terrific. I haven't even known him for more than a couple of weeks, and I have already offended him.*

"No, nothing to be sorry about. People can't understand unless they go through the experience. And that experience, my dear," Dr. Gallagher said warmly, "is something I pray you never have to live through."

Her cheeks turned their usual crimson. Of course he understood she didn't mean anything by it. He seemed to understand everything.

The doorbell rang. "Is that them already?" Miranda jumped up and answered the door.

"Ms. Sheppard? Hi, I'm Mike Cavanaugh, and this is my brother Joe. Sorry we're a little early." They wore baseball caps and jackets embroidered with *Davenport Paranormal Research Society*. Both seemed just a bit older than her, but younger than Dr. Gallagher.

"Hi. Come in, please."

They nodded and stepped into the foyer.

"We moved some things around in our schedules to come right away." Joe, the taller, thinner one, picked up his bag after relinquishing his jacket. Mike, the stouter of the two, picked up a large backpack. "We thought we'd get an early start and set up our equipment."

"Thanks. I appreciate that. Everyone has been showing up early all day. I think we're all excited to find some answers." Miranda led them into the living room.

After the introductions and Alison offering some dinner and drinks, all politely declined, they sat in the living room, with the exception of Alison, who busied herself with cleaning up.

"Miss Sheppard," started Joe.

"Miranda, please."

"Okay, Miranda. We have a procedure. First, we'll interview all of you for first-hand accounts of the activity within the home. Then, we will have you take us on a tour of your home, and we'll set up equipment in hotspots, areas of concentrated activity. We'll conduct our investigation into the early hours of the morning. Does all that sound okay?"

"Yes, that's fine."

Joe reached into his pocket, pulled out a mini-recorder, turned it on, and placed it on the coffee table. "Okay, if you don't mind, would you please share with us what happened?"

Miranda recounted her experiences with the entity in her house, but then, when she awoke, there were no signs of a physical entry or altercation.

"What?" Joe and Mike exchanged shocked looks. "Get out," said Mike.

"With Dr. Gallagher's help, I realized that I wasn't the only one who experienced something in the house, which prompted his call to you."

"Who else experienced something here?" Mike looked around at everyone.

"Alison did, my sister. Ali," Miranda called.

"Coming." Alison wiped her hands with a dishtowel and sat on the chair opposite the easy chairs. "Yes. Miranda had gotten into a car accident. I thought I might..." Alison's voice broke. "Sorry, it's still hard for me to talk about." She cleared her throat.

"That's alright," Mike consoled. "That must have been difficult."

Alison nodded as she gained her composure and explained what she experienced in the apartment while watching over Miranda. Maybe that figure was real after all, she had been thinking prior to this meeting.

"So, you don't think you saw Miranda?" asked Joe.

"No, it couldn't have been."

"Why is that?" asked Mike.

"The build of the figure I saw would tower over all of us, even you, Dr. Gallagher. Her hair is long, but the person had short hair. I could see the bulk from his jacket, and I smelled this stinky smell too. I thought something died in the house."

"Oh, so you could actually see the form of the person?" Joe inquired.

"Yes, but when Miranda turned on the light, I thought I imagined it, and I put it out of my mind until Dr. Gallagher brought it up. When you stare into the dark, you can see all sorts of shapes, so I thought I was just experiencing that."

"Plus, her description of the man fits with what I saw, and we hadn't even discussed it," Miranda recounted. "Also, you should know I saw the same man in my bathroom behind me in the mirror a couple of hours before he hit me. I thought I had imagined it because I had a migraine earlier that day. I also saw him when I first woke up in the hospital after my car accident several months ago."

"Really?" Mike raised his eyebrows.

"Yes. While I floated in and out of consciousness, I saw him standing over me. I thought he might have been part of the hospital staff or something, but he had that same leather jacket on. I couldn't see the jacket at the time, but I could smell the leather. And I also smelled something like rotten eggs when he was around."

Miranda was certain that the story would make the two run screaming from the house, but they remained, seemingly unaffected. She believed if they had to, they would stare down the devil himself, like Dr. Gallagher.

"I never heard of a case like this," Joe admitted, "but we'll see if we can get some answers."

"Why don't you show us where the incidents occurred, and we'll get our cameras and equipment set up." Mike stood up and grabbed the mini-recorder.

Miranda arose from her seat. "Okay." Everyone followed her to the kitchen. "It happened there," she pointed, "right in front of the back door."

"Was it still light out?" asked Mike.

"Yes, and his face had a shadow over it, even though the light coming in from the windows should have lit up his face. I couldn't see any distinctive features."

"Huh. Maybe a shadow figure." Joe crossed his arms and gazed at the windows. "We should try and recreate that, Mike."

Mike nodded, strode over to the door, and looked around. "So, he appeared out of nowhere?"

"Yes. As I readied to leave, he stood right here." She pointed down to her feet. "He grabbed an empty wine bottle on the counter, right here."

"It's really narrow, so you couldn't get past him," Joe observed.

A nod. "He hit me over the head right in front of the door. Also, right before he attacked me, I thought all of the glass shattered on me, but that didn't turn out to be true."

Joe and Mike's shocked expressions morphed into puzzled looks. They looked over the back door and the windows. Joe tapped on the glass. Mike's eyes scoured the floor.

"It was so vivid. The glass shattered all over me. I saw my blood all over my hands, my arms. Steven found me and rescued me. I regained consciousness later that evening. When I woke up in the hospital, I had no injuries at all."

Joe shook his head. "God. That had to be scary."

Miranda nodded.

"Hey, look." Out of the corner of Mike's eye, he caught a glint of something shiny on the floor in the corner. He stooped down, put what seemed like nothing his hand, and he and Joe examined it.

Mike looked up. "I think it's a shard of glass."

Miranda, Alison, and Steven all looked at each other with wide eyes. Dr. Gallagher remained unflappable.

Miranda stepped over to him. Sure enough, a tiny sharp sliver one-half a centimeter long winked back at her. "I don't know whether to feel elated or terrified." A glass shard on the floor, but the glass in the windows and the door remained unmarred?

Joe put up his hands. "Let's not jump to conclusions yet. There could be an absolutely ordinary reason."

"Maybe someone dragged it in with their shoe," Steven suggested.

Miranda shot Steven a look. Was he suggesting she made everything up?

Alison touched Steve's arm. "No, Steve, you don't understand. Miranda would have noticed."

Miranda, hands on hips, looked at Dr. Gallagher. "What do you think?"

Dr. Gallagher folded his arms. "Now it's getting interesting."

Miranda stared for a moment, and then cracked up laughing. *Boy, he has a way with words, doesn't he?*

The laughter caught on like a contagion.

Mike, after doubled over with laughter, wiped his eyes. His friend Jack Gallagher sure knew how to break up tension in the room. "Well, we still have more ground to cover. Steven, can you please tell us what happened?"

Steven repeated what he explained to Miranda in the hospital.

"Did you see or hear anything unusual in the house? Smell anything?" Mike questioned.

"No, nothing. No signs of forced entry, no smells, nothing."

"Just to let you know, the police have been through the house twice now, and they haven't found anything," Alison interjected.

"Huh." Mike shook his head. "Why don't you show us where you had your experience, Alison."

Alison turned on the light and walked down the hallway on the other side of the kitchen wall. The group stepped over to watch. "I was in the bathroom when I heard a noise in the living room. As I said before, I thought I was hearing things, so I ignored it. Then I heard the footsteps, like someone had on a pair of boots. I know Miranda didn't have boots on. When I came out of the bathroom and looked down the hallway, it alarmed me because I saw what looked like a guy, right here." She pointed down to the floor. "When the hall light switched on, it was only Miranda."

"Did you hear Miranda get up or anything?" asked Joe.

"I'm not sure."

"But, you heard the footfall of boots, though?" Mike asked.

"Yes."

Mike took a beat. "Is it possible you heard the footsteps in the kitchen, and it sounded like they were in the living room?"

Alison shrugged and held up her hands.

"Part of what we do is to seek natural explanations for these types of occurrences. Sometimes, we find good explanations that have nothing to do with the supernatural," Joe explained.

"We'll be testing out this situation to see if we can recreate the phenomenon, as well as different ways something from the outside could possibly wind up on the floor. If we can, then we have a natural reason for the phenomenon to occur," Mike added.

"And if you can't?" Miranda hoped they would be able to explain everything away with simple, natural occurrences.

Joe shrugged. "Listen, if we can't, it doesn't mean it has to have a supernatural cause. It just means that we could not come up with a natural explanation, and we have a phenomenon we can't explain."

Miranda nodded. She took pleasure in the logic in Joe's explanations. The pressure in her chest released. Just because they couldn't explain it, it didn't mean Miranda was crazy, and it didn't mean that the weird crap had come from the supernatural.

"Is this the bathroom where you had your experience, Miranda?" Mike pointed down the hallway.

"Yes."

"I think all the activity is centered right around here on the first floor," Mike said to Joe.

"We should set up the cameras here, here, and here." Joe pointed to the three spots Miranda and Alison showed.

"I see you have a major security system here. I suggest keeping your eye on the footage and look through it every day to see if anything shows up on the video system," advised Joe. "We have come across some very good evidence of the paranormal with security cameras."

"Alright. That sounds like a good suggestion," Miranda agreed.

"Would you like to show us the rest of the house, and we can get started?" asked Joe.

"Sure." Miranda led everyone to the other parts of her house. To her, it was akin to exposing herself in front of strangers. Like everything else, she bit her lip and trudged through it. She was a survivor, just like her parents told her. After all, there had to be an explanation, and she steeled her resolve to make it through to the end.

• • •

Miranda sat on the couch with Alison and Steven and watched Mike and Joe set up their cameras. Miranda noticed that the brothers didn't seem to resemble each other. Mike had light skin, a stocky build, hazel eyes, and had no hair. Joe was thinner, had darker skin, and brown hair and eyes. When Miranda stated her observation, Mike laughed. "We get that a lot. Joe is the spitting image of my mother, and I look like my father. Irish side," he pointed to himself, "Italian side," he pointed to Joe.

Miranda smiled. "Ah, I see."

"Wow, look at all this equipment. How does one afford all of this?" Alison asked.

Mike glanced down at their collection of equipment with a faint smile. "We do this out of our own pockets. Our wives aren't happy about it."

Joe chuckled. "Yeah. Mine keeps at me to build model airplanes instead."

Everyone snickered except for Dr. Gallagher.

"You've been quiet," Miranda observed.

"Just paying attention. I've only been on one other outing with these gentlemen. I'm always interested to see the equipment they're using."

"Do you have an interest in gadgets?"

"More like photography. I think it's fascinating there has been such an influx in capturing images of unexplainable figures, orbs, mists, and things like that."

Miranda nodded. "Me too." She would totally be geeking out at that moment if it weren't for the bizarre, tall thing following her around.

"We share a hobby. What's your favorite subject to photograph?"

"I take trips around the world every year and go nuts with the camera, but with the security system, now," her hand swept toward the security cameras, "it'll be a while until I can get back to my hobby. I guess my hobby is expensive too," she shrugged.

Dr. Gallagher smiled. It was always nice to meet a fellow shutter bug, someone who understands the need to document one's life in images, transcending words. "Oh, believe me, I know all about expensive hobbies."

Miranda laughed. "Yeah, racing isn't exactly cheap."

"Okay." Mike stood up from the floor when he finished running the wires and positioning the camera. "All the computer equipment is set up as well as the cameras at all the hot spots. Since this is a smaller place, we suggest you all go somewhere for coffee for an hour or two so we can do an initial sweep to get baseline readings."

Joe looked up from fiddling with a camera. "When you return, we'll do another run-through with you in the house. We'll review all the evidence and get back to you in a few days."

"It usually takes us a week, but we are going to step it up so we can get it to you sooner," offered Mike.

"Thanks for that, really. I appreciate it. You guys up for coffee?" Miranda turned to Steven, Alison, and Dr. Gallagher.

"Yeah, a cup of joe, that sounds good," Alison said. Joe looked up and smiled at her. "Oh, um." Alison blushed.

"Yes, a cup of *coffee* sounds great," Steven reiterated with a wicked smile. Alison scrunched up her face and smacked him on the arm.

"Do you mind if I stay behind?" asked Dr. Gallagher. "I think it will be useful for me to see first-hand if they experience anything."

Miranda nodded. "I think that's a good idea."

"Enjoy your coffee." Dr. Gallagher waved.

"Okay. We'll be back." Miranda sauntered toward the closet. "Let's all go out through the front." Alison and Steven followed.

"You are such a flirt," Miranda teased, pinching Alison's arm. She opened the closet to retrieve the coats.

"I am not." Alison frowned, moved her arm away, and brushed off her sleeve.

"And you're spoken for too."

"Shut up."

"They are kind of cute."

Alison rolled her eyes and blew out a sigh. "You're such a child."

"Hello, brother of the fiancé, standing right here." Steven helped Miranda and Alison with their coats. "I can hear you, you know."

Miranda's eyes glowed with glee. Now she had something to tease her sister about. Best of all, she wouldn't have to think about what Mike and Joe would find in her house.

"Oh, I'd love a cup of jooooeee," Miranda exaggerated in a high tone, batting her eyelashes at Alison. Miranda cackled. Alison sighed and stomped out the front door.

"Sisters," Steven murmured, shaking his head and following Miranda to her car.

• • •

When Miranda, Steven, and Alison returned from the diner, Miranda had long given up on teasing her sister, and they had settled into a quiet contemplation of what information they would encounter upon their return.

"It's been quiet," Mike reported when they entered the front doorway. "That doesn't mean we won't find evidence on the audio and video. We haven't experienced anything while we did our run-through of your place, and we did some debunking. We couldn't quite recreate the footfall of the boots. We had to literally walk the ground with boots on. It was the only way we achieved the same effect. And, tried as we might, we could not recreate the appearance of that small piece of glass. We tried to get it caught in the boots and walk over to that corner. We even tried putting it on our sleeves and brushing it off, but it didn't really fall far enough to wind up in the corner. We also did not encounter any smells."

"Oh." Miranda, Alison, and Steven took off their coats. Anxiety pinched Miranda's face. Alison put her arm around her sister's shoulders.

"We would like to do the walk-through with you now, if you're up to it," Joe suggested as they walked into the living room.

"I'll be fine." Miranda relaxed the tension in her neck and shoulders. "I was hoping for an answer."

"I know," Mike consoled. "We still have many more steps to go, so don't despair. Our walk-through gave us a good baseline of what to expect in your home. From what you told us, the entity seems focused on you. It's possible it won't show itself unless you're here."

"Oh, God, I can't believe I forgot this." Steven smacked his head. "Miranda, when I came over to your parents' house that Sunday to help you pack, all the lamps in the living room switched on by themselves, including your Jamaican rum bottle lamp." How could he possibly forget? He couldn't believe Dr. Gallagher was going in this vein in the first place with all this baloney about ghosts, but considering what he experienced with the lamps, he started to think it would be a good idea.

"You mean the one I had unplugged?"

"Yes. It lit up right in my hands, with the cord still wrapped around the lamp."

"Why didn't you tell me?"

Steven felt like he had just carried out Operation Shock and Awe. He never had a group of people stare at him all at once with their mouths agape. "Gosh, I'm sorry. I was more concerned about you. First, you left the house that day in such a rush, and then all this craziness happened. I meant to tell you, but with everything going on, it slipped my mind. I thought it was a fluke of some sort. I was just going to suggest getting an electrician to check out the wiring, or ask you if the lamp had a hidden battery. It didn't even strike me that it could be related to all of this."

Miranda nodded. “Okay, I understand. You were more concerned about me.”

“So, now we have three separate locations.” Mike ran his hand over his head and blew out a breath.

Joe rubbed his hands together. “Let’s get going, then. We’ll walk through with you with the video and audio. Dr. Gallagher, Steven, Alison, would you all like to monitor some of the equipment, and we can all do this together?”

“Here, Dr. Gallagher, why don’t you hold the K-2 meter? Alison, would you like the thermal camera? And Steven, how about the EVP recorder?” Mike handed out the equipment in turn.

“EVP?” Alison asked.

“Electronic voice phenomenon.” Steven and Joe parroted each other. Steven shrugged. “I like watching those paranormal shows.”

“Yeah? Now you get to live it,” Miranda said wryly. Steven touched Miranda’s cheek and put his free arm around her shoulder. “What do we do now?”

Mike pointed toward the front door. “We can start in your foyer, if you like, and then work our way back.”

Joe switched on his video camera. “We will walk through the house and see if we can speak with the entity and encourage it to communicate with us.”

“This thermal camera is trippy.” Alison pointed the camera around the room.

Joe laughed. “Yeah, it’s strange at first. It registers everyone’s heat signatures. Every person and animal will show up as a red-to-orange color. I can’t tell you how many times we’ve investigated a house for unexplained noises and found rodents in the walls. One time, we found a family of squirrels in the attic. Also, if there is something paranormal occurring in the room, it will show up as red or orange without an explanation for why it’s there. For instance, once we investigated an attic, and there was an orange heat signature on a chair. We couldn’t explain why it was there, since no one touched or sat in the chair.”

Alison grinned as she focused the thermal camera on Joe while he was speaking. The red and orange colors moved as his mouth moved. She walked backwards a couple of steps and captured the group's heat signature.

"Hey, Mike, is this running now? What do I do with it?" asked Steven.

"Yeah, it's running now. We're recording. Dr. Gallagher, are you okay with yours?"

"I'm good. I've done this before."

"Oh, yeah, that's right." Mike smiled.

Alison frowned. "Um, Joe, you said everyone should come up as red or orange, right?"

"Yes, with bits of blue and green."

Dr. Gallagher took a couple of steps toward Miranda. "Are you ready for this?"

Miranda took a deep breath. "Yeah, as ready as I'll ever be."

"We're all right here to help you," Dr. Gallagher encouraged her.

"Yes, I know, and I do appreciate that. I don't think I could do it without you all. Thank you for setting this up. You've really gone out of your way."

Just then, the K-2 meter lit up and beeped in Dr. Gallagher's hand. Miranda and Dr. Gallagher looked down at the meter.

"Um, Joe, I think you need to come see this." A sense of urgency pressed upon Alison's words.

Everyone fell silent as they looked at Miranda. The K-2 meter, pointed straight at Miranda, flashed and beeped. Joe and Mike stepped over to Alison to look at the thermal camera.

"What? What is it?" Miranda gulped. That lump in her throat returned. She looked back down at the meter, and then at Alison, Mike, and Joe, who stared at the screen of the thermal camera, eyes wide and mouths open. Steven rushed over to the thermal camera and looked down. All eyes looked up to watch Miranda.

It seemed as if everyone collectively held their breath and waited. A palpable force hung in the air, pressing down, descending upon them. Mike and Joe moved their equipment around to catch what they could only sense. Time distorted and stretched as second by second, the grandfather clock's ticking slowed, almost coming to a complete stop. The group stood, frozen, wide-eyed. They waited for what seemed like an eternity.

The lights flickered. They all jumped. Miranda's radio turned on by itself, playing "Blinded by the Light." All eyes turned to look at the radio.

It started in the kitchen. An explosion, a shattering of glass. Then the dining room, each light bulb exploding in its socket. Joe and Mike continued to record through their cursing. Steven ran to Miranda and hugged her to cover her from shards of glass. Alison grabbed the afghan from the couch and pulled it over her head. Dr. Gallagher reached for a couch cushion and held it over him. The explosions of glass continued in succession from the dining room to the living room, the bulbs exploding over them, showering them with shards of glass.

Total darkness. A pause. All the equipment in everyone's hands exploded with loud pops and sparks, flashes of orange and yellow in the darkness. Everyone let out cries of shock and dropped their equipment. The cameras at the entrance of the kitchen and the hallway exploded and fell over, shattering into tiny pieces.

The last to go was the laptop. Sparks flew out of the keyboard, and flames licked up the screen.

10
FALLOUT

The acrid smell of burning plastic hung in the air. Dr. Gallagher, the first to react, threw the cushion to the couch, took his penlight out of the inner pocket of his suit jacket, and made his way to the kitchen. He took the afghan from Alison's shoulders and threw it onto the laptop and yanked on the laptop's cord to pull it out of the socket. Alison winced. Their mom crocheted the afghan, though she recognized the necessity for its sacrifice.

Mike and Joe took flashlights out of their pockets. "Is everyone alright?" asked Joe.

Every part of Miranda's body trembled, her breath rapid and erratic. Steven's arms encircled her, holding her up.

"What the fuck was that?" Alison shouted. "God, oh God, Miranda."

"I've got her." Steven held Miranda's trembling body.

"Here, have a flashlight." Joe brought one over to Steven. "Don't worry. I carry at least three with me at all times." He gave one to Alison.

"Here, come on," Steven spoke softly in Miranda's ear. He reached over with his free hand to flip over a couch cushion and then backed her up to sit down. Miranda clung to him, shaking.

Mike and Joe looked at each other. "The security system," they said together.

Mike knelt down in front of Miranda. "Joe has the same security system in his home. Do you mind if he takes a look at the footage?"

Miranda nodded, still shaking.

"Did you set up your password?" asked Joe.

Miranda shook her head.

"Here, honey." Alison ran to get a blanket from the closet and draped it over her. It didn't seem the blanket would help Miranda's shaking subside. Alison caught Dr. Gallagher's eye.

Dr. Gallagher motioned with his head. Alison stood up and followed.

"Does Miranda have a history of epilepsy, or does anyone have epilepsy in your family?" Dr. Gallagher inquired.

"No. Why?"

"I need you to call an ambulance."

Alison drew in her breath. "Are you sure that's necessary? She's been in the hospital so much in the past year."

Dr. Gallagher held her gaze. "The violent shaking is an extreme reaction to stress. Her system is shutting down. I need you to call an ambulance and get them over here right away, and please find an extra blanket to cover her." He witnessed a reaction just like that in the prison. An inmate shook, dropped to the ground, and died right before his eyes, even before they could get the medical team over. The stress caused a fatal heart attack.

Alison gulped and nodded, her eyes wide with worry. She went down the hallway to use the landline and retrieve another blanket, doing her best to avoid the crunching shards of glass.

Dr. Gallagher walked back to the living room. "Steven, let's see if we can get her to lie down."

"Okay. Miranda, here hon, come lie down." Steven guided Miranda's head onto his lap.

"Stroke her hair. That relaxes her," Alison called from the hallway.

"Let's get her feet elevated above her heart." Dr. Gallagher found some throw pillows, checked them for shards of glass, and placed them under Miranda's feet.

Steven ran his fingers through Miranda's hair. Miranda, still shivering, shut her eyes. "It's going to be okay, baby."

"It is?" The uncontrollable shaking in Miranda's body shook her voice.

"Of course it is. We'll get through this. We'll all be here, from beginning to end."

"Promise?" Miranda asked in a tiny shaking voice.

"Promise."

"And you won't die on me?"

"No, I won't die on you."

"Promise?"

Steven stroked her hair and looked into her eyes. "I promise."

"Here's an extra blanket." Alison draped a quilt their mother had made over Miranda. At least that one remained intact. "It's your favorite."

"Thank you," Miranda mouthed. "Alison. I'm sorry I told you not to come over. I'm so glad you're here." She didn't want to die, and she felt like she would at that very moment.

Alison took Miranda's hand and held it. "I'm always here." She kissed her forehead.

"Yeah, don't I know it." Despite the tension in the room, Alison marveled at Miranda's ability to make everyone chuckle despite the danger.

Alison retrieved the lamp she was going to use as a weapon earlier that year. She found an electrical outlet with her flashlight. Standing aside, she plugged it in, and switched it on, careful to keep an arm's distance in case this light exploded as well. Fortunately, whatever phenomenon responsible for the explosion of glass did not claim the bulb in the lamp. It provided enough light in the living room. Everyone switched off the flashlights.

Dr. Gallagher glanced at Alison. “Thanks. That’s helpful. Okay, Steven, I would like for you to take some deep breaths with Miranda. How does that sound?”

Steven nodded. “Okay, let’s breathe in.” Miranda nodded and took a shaky breath. “Good, now let it out. Good. Now again...”

Dr. Gallagher tapped Alison on the arm. “May I see you again in the kitchen for a moment?” he whispered in her ear.

Alison nodded and followed Dr. Gallagher.

They passed Mike, in the process of examining his equipment, picking up parts and pieces off the floor, and shaking his head. Dr. Gallagher tapped Mike on the arm and pointed at him, himself, and Alison, and pointed toward the kitchen. Mike nodded and followed.

“Okay, what did you see in the thermal camera?” Dr. Gallagher asked.

“I don’t know.” Mike shook his head. “In twenty years, I have never experienced anything like this. I feel bad. Maybe if we hadn’t confronted it that way...”

“Listen, we don’t know what happened,” Dr. Gallagher interrupted. “You said it yourself. If a reasonable explanation exists, we can’t rule it out, right?”

“Right,” Mike concurred. “When I looked at the thermal, I saw this black mass within Miranda’s heat signature. It looked like a gnarled, twisted tree root. It seemed to have these strange, almost like...” he paused as he struggled to explain the phenomenon.

“Fingers,” Alison continued. “They looked like black, long fingers, plugged into her up and down her spine coming out of a black twisted mass. Right?”

Mike nodded. “Yes, exactly.”

“And this was when the K-2 meter went crazy?” Dr. Gallagher prodded.

“Yup,” Alison confirmed.

"Then all the light bulbs blew, and the equipment exploded," Mike recounted.

"Hey." Joe walked over from the living room. Alison and Mike turned toward him.

"What did you find?" asked Mike.

"Nothing. The entire system white-screened, nothing but snow for the last several hours. Even our arrival had been wiped clean."

"Alright. I don't think we should tell Miranda about the black mass for the moment," Dr. Gallagher instructed. "Except for that anomaly, we can explain the rest as some sort of electrical malfunction or power surge."

Mike and Joe looked at each other. "I think we can do that," said Joe. "After all, we can't rule out the possibility of an electrical or equipment malfunction, no matter how strange it might seem. Although, most of our equipment runs on battery power."

Alison nodded. "We shouldn't discuss this evening at length for now. I've never seen her seem so fragile."

The siren of the ambulance sounded outside. Dr. Gallagher walked to the back door to greet a man and woman in blue shirts with patches reading *Davenport Morningside Hospital EMT*. The man bearing most of the equipment had brown hair and was tall and thin. The woman, shorter with dark brown hair, had a round face. Each had their names on their uniforms, Bill and Rita.

"Do you have oxygen with you?"

"Yes," replied Rita.

"Miranda Sheppard has had a traumatic incident, and her body has been shaking. She should be monitored, possibly overnight." Dr. Gallagher led them through the kitchen and into the living room.

Rita's feet crunched on some of the glass shards. She looked down at the floor, and then looked around. Dr. Gallagher led them through the dim light to the living room. "What in the world happened here?" she whispered loudly to Bill.

"It looks like a bomb went off," he replied.

Miranda still trembled. “Miranda.” Dr. Gallagher looked into her eyes. “I had your sister call an ambulance as a precaution.”

“Hello Miranda,” Rita said. “We’re going to check your blood pressure, and I’m going to put this over your mouth and nose so we can give you oxygen.”

Miranda nodded and reached for Steven’s hand. Steven grabbed her hand and squeezed.

Rita applied the mask over Miranda’s face. Miranda closed her eyes and breathed in.

Bill wrapped the blood pressure meter around Miranda’s arm and pumped. He took her wrist to measure her heart rate, and then took out a stethoscope and listened to Miranda’s heart.

“Are there any injuries?” Rita asked Steven.

“No,” he replied.

“Did she black out, lose consciousness?”

“No. She’s been shaking.”

“Did she fall and hit her head?”

“No.”

“Does she suffer from epilepsy or have a family history of epilepsy?”

Steven looked at Alison. “No,” Alison replied from behind Rita and Bill. She felt so lucky at that moment that Dr. Gallagher had such good training for emergency situations, the EMTs parroting his question from before.

“Is she on any medications?”

“She has medication for migraines,” Alison reported.

“Any allergies you know of?”

“No.”

“How about any allergies to medications?”

“No.”

Rita looked back at Bill when he took off the blood pressure meter. “Blood pressure, 70 over 40, pulse rate, 120 bpm’s, arrhythmia,” Bill reported.

Rita placed her hand on Miranda's arm. "Miranda?" Miranda opened her eyes. "Do you normally have low blood pressure?"

Miranda shook her head.

"Did you have something to eat and drink today?"

Miranda nodded.

"Have you lost consciousness?"

Miranda shook her head.

"Have you fainted or lost consciousness before, say within the past month or so?"

"She had a car accident several months ago and was unconscious for about a week, and has since had two episodes where she has lost consciousness." In the past, Miranda had a tendency of under-reporting her discomforts, the reason why Alison didn't leave it to Miranda.

Rita looked at Bill. "Take her in?"

Bill nodded.

"Okay," said Rita. "Her blood pressure is very low, and Bill detected an irregular heartbeat. I think we should take her in for overnight observation. Miranda." Rita placed her hand on her arm. "You understood what I told your sister and your husband, right?"

"He's her boyfriend," Alison corrected.

"Sorry, boyfriend. I don't think we can fit the stretcher through that kitchen."

"Is there another entrance?" Bill inquired.

"Don't worry. I'll carry her to the ambulance," Steven intimated.

Miranda took the mask off. "You're staying with me, so he won't come for me?"

Steven smiled at her, smoothing her hair. "There's no place I'd rather be."

Rita checked the oxygen tank and retook Miranda's pulse. Her expression had changed from professionalism to indignation. She stood up and pulled Dr. Gallagher aside.

"You introduced yourself as 'doctor,' right?" she hissed.

"Yes."

"Why aren't the police here, *doctor*?" She saturated the word doctor in sarcasm.

Dr. Gallagher drew in a breath to calm himself. "Rita, we had an electrical malfunction, and all the light bulbs exploded."

"Oh. She said a man is after her." Rita's eyes clouded with doubt.

"Miranda experienced an incident last week, but the electrical malfunction was the only incident tonight. She has fears associated with the incident from last week and had a bad reaction to the electrical malfunction. The police checked the house this afternoon."

Rita's expression changed. Her righteousness sail deflated. "Okay. Let's get her to the ambulance." She exited the door to get the stretcher ready.

Dr. Gallagher shook his head. No apology, of course. He let it go because Miranda's well-being was far more important.

Bill turned to Steven and Miranda. "Miss Sheppard. Are we ready?" Steven nodded, stood up, lifted Miranda, blankets and all, and carried Miranda to the side door through the kitchen with Bill holding the equipment.

"I'll get your coats." Alison ran to the hall closet and followed Steven and Miranda.

"She's off?" Dr. Gallagher asked Alison when she came back in.

"Yes. Off to Morningside again. Thanks for taking care of her, Dr. Gallagher. I would have never known to call an ambulance. I hope her heart is okay."

Mike and Joe were busy in the living room collecting the pieces they could salvage of their equipment. "I am so sorry about your equipment," said Alison. "Is there anything I can do?"

Mike waved his hand. "Don't worry about it. We have insurance."

"Oh, good," Alison put her hand to her chest and breathed a sigh of relief.

"Yeah, forget the equipment," Joe chimed in. "More importantly, is Miranda okay?"

"Yeah, she's in good hands. I'm going to the hospital to check in."

Dr. Gallagher gathered his things and walked over to Alison. "I'll swing by tonight to make sure she's calm and comfortable, and then I'll be back tomorrow morning."

"Okay, good. Thanks again."

Mike touched Alison's elbow. "Alison, I want to let you know that even though the equipment is a little worse for wear..."

"Understatement of the year." Joe rolled his eyes and laughed.

"...that we will still have our equipment expert salvage any recordings they could have captured," Mike continued, casting Joe a dirty look. "I hope some of the cards and drives on the devices aren't completely fried, and we can extract some sort of voice or image, or at least capture what occurred tonight."

"Okay, thanks. But please pass the information through me first rather than Miranda. I think we need to have Dr. Gallagher assess Miranda's condition first before we share anything."

"Yes, that's a good idea," Dr. Gallagher consented.

Despite their protests, Alison helped the gentlemen out. Dr. Gallagher seemed to meet excellent people. They were so professional, even offering to help clean up the glass. It didn't quell her apprehension when they said it was the most bizarre experience they've had to date.

"Miranda's had two traumatic incidences here. It might not be in her best interests for her to stay here." Dr. Gallagher stated upon Alison's return.

"If I know my sister, she's too stubborn to be kept out of her own home. She'll be back."

Dr. Gallagher's slight smile conveyed that Alison spoke the facts. "You're both survivors. And, if you feel the need to discuss anything with me, give me a call."

"Me? Oh, I'm okay now. I guess we really don't know for sure what happened tonight. I'm willing to say it was a huge electrical malfunction of some sort. I'll get an electrician in here to check the whole house." She didn't let on that the occurrence rattled her just as much on the inside as it had Miranda on the outside.

"That's a good idea."

Alison paused and frowned. "Doc?"

"Hmm?"

"What are the chances that what happened to Miranda, the dream of the guy hitting her on the head, was some sort of premonition?"

Dr. Gallagher shrugged. "I don't know. I wouldn't discount anything at this point." The pause grew between them as they fell into the deep well of their thoughts. Dr. Gallagher snapped awake. "Do you need a ride to the hospital?"

"No, that's okay. I think I should take my own car. I'll be staying at Dan's tonight." She didn't relish the idea of riding in the car with the doctor, as nice as he was. She needed time to collect herself, which to her, remained a private endeavor.

"Okay. I'm going now, then. You coming?"

"Yes. I'll meet you there. I'm going to lock up."

"Okay, see you there."

Alison shook her head and looked around the darkened house in wonderment. Not even a top-of-the-line security system could protect Miranda. Why all this trouble for her little sister? She gulped down the tears before they could spring out of her eyes.

11
Equilibrium

"Aortic Valve Regurgitation," Miranda stated when Alison walked into the hospital room. Steven had spent the night, looking messy and crumpled from sleeping on the flimsy convertible chair that turned into a cot, an item brought in from one of the birthing rooms. Dan granted him permission, agreeing she had to have a sentinel, a sensible precaution after he learned the sequence of events.

"Aortic Valve Regurgitation? What in the world is that?" Alison hung her purse and coat on the hook on the back of the room door.

"From what the heart specialist told me, it's when the aortic valve doesn't close all the way and some of the blood backs up into the heart chamber. He said it was due to the accident. Remember all those bruises I had on my chest from the accident when my baby's steering wheel compressed my chest?"

"Yeah, I do."

"He thinks the trauma was significant enough to damage the valve. It explains the blackouts too. They happened every time I got excited. They feel the injury was minor at first, which was why it didn't show when they brought me to the hospital, but the stress from the last several weeks made the condition more apparent."

"So, what does this mean? Do you need an operation?"

"No, not at this point, at any rate. Eventually, maybe. He said the results from the echocardiogram showed the damage isn't severe, so he's adopted a watch-and-wait stance. He gave me some meds too." Miranda made a face.

"And you're going to take those meds religiously, right?" Alison asserted.

"Don't worry, I'll make sure she does," affirmed Steven.

"Great, another conspiracy." Miranda rolled her eyes. She grabbed Steven's hand. "Hey, hon, would you mind getting us some coffee?"

"No! No, no, no. The doctor told you no caffeine, remember?"

Miranda grimaced. How could she get by without her daily coffee? "Decaf, then?"

"Nope. It still has a bit of caffeine in it. You'll have to have herbal tea."

Miranda wrinkled her nose. "Forget it. Just because I can't enjoy my morning java, it doesn't mean you two can't. I'll watch and live vicariously through you."

"No, that's alright. I'll give up caffeine too." Steven took Miranda's hand and kissed it.

Miranda smiled. "That's so sweet of you. I really appreciate that. I guess what I was trying to say is, I'm trying to get rid of you. I need to talk with Alison alone for a few minutes. Is that okay?"

"Oh, of course. Why didn't you say so? I'll see if they have any muffins. Sound good?"

"Delicious. Thanks, hon."

Steven stood up and checked for his wallet in his pocket. "Back in a few." Steven gave Miranda a peck on the lips and left.

"What's up? Is there something else?" Alison asked.

"You know, this morning, I had to laugh at myself because I realized I experienced an extreme situation last night, and if it weren't for that extreme situation, they might not have checked my heart, and I could have had this problem for a long time and not realized it, and it could have been a lot worse than this. Does this sound familiar to you?"

Alison's brow furrowed. "Yes."

"I'm sorry I gave you such a hard time over Aunt Cheri."

"It's okay."

"No, really, I'm so sorry. I didn't understand. But I sure do now, don't I?" Waiting for Alison to arrive that morning had been torture. Alison was just trying to do her best. Years ago, after Uncle Dave cheated on Aunt Cheri, Alison thought bringing Aunt Cheri for a skydiving lesson would help give her a new perspective on life. When they got to the ground, Aunt Cheri was having a heart attack. The attack was minor, and the entire incident saved Aunt Cheri's life, the minor attack uncovering a heart condition. If she had gone on without symptoms for years, her doctor explained, that heart attack could have been the one that killed her. Miranda always thought Alison careless for almost killing their mother's sister, but her own heart trouble gave her a whole new perspective. Miranda awoke with the feeling that she needed to make amends for giving her crap about it for years before she didn't have the chance any longer.

"You know, I'm not worried about all that now, Mira. Do you know what I really want?"

"What?"

"For you to be healthy and happy."

"I'll tell you what. I'll work on it. Maybe someday soon, I'll wake up, and I'll be the poster child for bliss and health. Okay?"

"Now you're making fun of me." Alison frowned.

"No, I'm not. I'm making a commitment, to myself and to you. You know me. No one can knock me down for long. I'll get right back up and fight again."

Alison smiled. "You know, that's what I told Dr. Gallagher."

"What, that I'm a pain in the ass?"

Alison and Miranda laughed. "No, I told him you are a very strong person. I'll let him figure out the rest for himself."

A knock sounded on the door. "Come in," Miranda invited. Dr. Gallagher stepped into the room.

"Hi, Dr. Gallagher." Miranda smiled at him. Alison waved hello.

"Hi, Miss Sheppard. And how are you doing today?"

"Better, thank you."

"Yes, you seem better," Dr. Gallagher agreed.

"I do feel much better. I'm not afraid anymore. A big weight has been lifted."

Dr. Gallagher had a quizzical look. "Why?"

"My heart valve in my aorta had gotten damaged in my car accident."

"I see. You seem to be almost excited about this piece of news," Dr. Gallagher observed.

"Yes, because the whole problem all along has been my health, my head and my heart injuries. I asked the doctor about the man I saw when I first woke up in the hospital and in my house, and he said anything is possible. Who knows how multiple health problems affect the brain? I could have had a strange dream or vision before I passed out."

"What about what I saw?" asked Alison.

"A coincidence. And last night could have been some sort of weird, electrical malfunction, and at the house too, when Steven saw all the lamps turn on. I had been having issues for a little while. The radio turned on by itself too. There could have been an electrical storm. They have been known to do crazy things."

"Yes, that's true," Dr. Gallagher agreed.

"So, yes, I'm happy. Now I can focus on getting better, and I'll be in the clear."

"Honey, what about the memory loss?" Alison asked.

"I can still work on that with Dr. Gallagher, right?"

"Of course," confirmed Dr. Gallagher.

"Hey," Steven opened the door, "Muffin Man has arrived." He shook the bag and placed it on Miranda's lap.

"Yum, thanks." Miranda kissed Steven on the cheek.

Just as Steven and Dr. Gallagher greeted each other, Dr. Fine poked his head in the door.

"Come in," invited Miranda.

"Thanks. I heard you were back in the hospital. I came to see how you are doing."

"Oh, they found a problem with my heart valve, which probably happened when I had my car accident."

"Oh, I'm sorry to hear that."

"No, it's okay. They caught it early. I could have died from a blood clot or something. Now we watch it. Who knows, maybe it'll even get better." Miranda's optimistic smile matched her tone.

"It's great to see you taking this in stride," remarked Dr. Fine, and he did not challenge Miranda's optimism. Aortic valve regurgitation did not heal on its own.

"Oh, I am." Miranda would much rather have a health problem than having a maniacal stalker ghost follow her around for the rest of her life. Even the idea of taking medication for the rest of her life seemed more attractive than the alternative.

"Great. Dr. Gallagher, I have some office matters to discuss with you." He pointed to the door.

"Sure. Miranda, I'm glad you're feeling better. I'll tell my receptionist to keep an eye out for your call so we can have our next appointment together."

"Okay. Thanks for everything, Dr. Gallagher, and thank you for stopping by."

Dr. Gallagher smiled. "Until next time, then." He and Dr. Fine exited the room.

Dr. Fine's demeanor changed the instant the door shut. "Really, Jack, ghosthunters?" he spat.

"How did you hear?"

"Through Dan Foreman. He's engaged to Miranda's sister. When were you going to tell me about this?"

"Today. I was on my way to the office."

"Can you explain to me how you could possibly coordinate such crap?" Dr. Gallagher never saw Fine so riled up. His face turned crimson and his eyes bulged as he pointed with such ferocity, his silver hair flopped over to the other side. "Did you suggest this?"

"Only to get an explanation for what happened to her." Dr. Gallagher pointed his finger toward Miranda's room.

"And then on top of that, she practically has a heart attack as a result of this, this, cockamamie, unbelievably stupid... Do you know the lawsuit you could have opened us up to? It's one thing if she called them herself..."

"Dr. Gallagher did the right thing." They both had not heard Alison open the door to Miranda's room and step into the hallway. Dr. Fine took a deep breath. Dr. Gallagher nodded his approval for Alison to join the conversation. "I came out here to speak with you both. I know she seems okay, but I'm worried."

"Why, Alison?" Dr. Fine asked.

"Because you weren't there, Dr. Fine. You didn't see the image that showed up in my sister's heat signature on the thermal camera. Because you weren't there when Miranda's house exploded. There is something going on, and we all witnessed it last night. Just because Miranda seems to have come up with her own explanation, it doesn't mean I'm convinced that she is going to be safe. She's a fighter, but she doesn't recognize her own vulnerabilities."

"What do you think happened last night?" Dr. Fine took another deep breath and swept his hair back in place.

"I'll tell you one thing. You can't explain it away through power surges and equipment malfunction. I saw the image in the thermal image. It didn't look like anyone else's heat signature. If the equipment had a malfunction, it would have shown up on everyone's heat signature. The moment we all looked at it together, something hung in the air, almost stifling. That's when it turned into a war zone."

Dr. Fine didn't respond. Doubt washed over his blue eyes.

"You don't believe. I can tell," Alison perceived.

"Believe in what?" Dr. Fine crossed his arms.

"In something larger. In spirits, ghosts, the afterlife. Am I correct?"

Dr. Fine rolled his eyes and looked off to the side.

"There's my answer. You know, my parents taught me quite a bit before their passing. I think they always hoped either Miranda or I would get into psychology like they did. One of the things they shared with me was that your own beliefs cannot affect or overshadow the way you view your clients. Everyone has their own perspective, and we have to maintain respectfulness of their understanding of reality. They taught you that in med school, didn't they, Dr. Fine?" Alison's eyes twinkled.

Dr. Fine narrowed his eyes.

Dr. Gallagher smirked, recognizing the dig on medicine versus psychology. She must have gotten that from Allen, Alison's father, who once complained about the medical community's lack of appreciation for those trained in therapy while they worked on their project together. Dr. Gallagher didn't disagree with him once.

"So, Dr. Fine, you can't possibly say we all shared a psychotic episode, and you can't write off or dismiss what has been going on with Miranda, and you can't explain why an unplugged lamp lit up in the hands of Miranda's boyfriend." Alison watched Dr. Fine for the reaction and saw it. *Shock is good for skeptics.* "As a matter of fact, I'm more concerned now than ever. I know you feel the same way, don't you, Dr. Gallagher. I saw it in your face. Please share your concerns with me."

Dr. Gallagher looked at Dr. Fine. Dr. Fine sighed, shrugged his shoulders, and put out his hand to motion for Dr. Gallagher to continue.

"You're right, Alison. I am concerned for Miranda. I can't tell you how many times some medical doctor, with no training in the human psyche..." (Dr. Gallagher aimed a sharp look at Dr. Fine. Dr. Fine gave him a sour look.) "...offered some off-the-wall explanation for my clients' experiences when they have no understanding of what occurs in a person's subconscious. Yes, I have concerns about Miranda also. She's in a state of denial due to the traumatic event last night. Her mind has come up with an explanation she can live with at the moment so she can continue functioning. She shut down her emotions so she can focus on her physical recovery. It is too much stress on her to think otherwise."

"I know. I saw her do it when she was a teenager. That's why I'm so worried. What do we do now?"

"We wait," recommended Dr. Gallagher.

"And that's it?"

"Yes, that's it. Confronting Miranda with issues she isn't ready to deal with is a dangerous thing to do, especially with trauma in her history. She has to dictate the pace. Then, we shall do our best to be there for her when she needs us. She has arrived at a state of equilibrium, where she can live for the moment and not fall apart on us. Let her focus on her heart problem and get better and stronger. I can guarantee all of this will resurface at some point. All we can do is wait and be there for her when it happens."

"So, we're going to do the same thing as we are with her heart. Watch and wait. Right?"

"Yes, exactly. Watch and wait."

As the conversation developed, the anger and skepticism left Dr. Fine's face.

"Okay. Thanks, Dr. Gallagher. I feel better now. I'll get Steven up to speed. I'm going back into the room and hang with my sister for a while, so I'll see you. Dr. Fine." Alison nodded his way.

"Alright. Don't hesitate to contact me if you need anything," Dr. Gallagher responded.

Alison nodded and walked into the room.

When the door shut, Dr. Gallagher turned to Dr. Fine. Dr. Gallagher knew if he waited a few more seconds, he would have gotten his apology. Instead, right before Dr. Fine offered it, Dr. Gallagher said, “Wow, she really nailed you, didn’t she?”

Dr. Fine’s expression went from apologetic to sour lemons. “Fuck you, Jack.”

Dr. Gallagher laughed. “See you at the office, Jerry.”

Dr. Fine stuck his middle finger up and stomped down the hallway. Dr. Gallagher chuckled, pleased that he could always bring out the best in his friend, Dr. Jerald Fine.

12
EVIDENCE

Joe Cavanaugh was the one to make the call to Alison. "Usually, we have a sit-down with the client to discuss our findings in person."

"I know." Alison cradled the phone on her shoulder while she pursued her ongoing quest to pack boxes from her parents' house. "This isn't the usual case, though."

"Yeah, I remember. In our experience, when we provide the evidence, the clients appreciate it. It enables them to either live with the entity or to take other steps."

"Steps?"

"You have to understand, poltergeist activity is rare. A majority of what we capture are EVPs. It's rarer to catch human forms on camera. In a majority of our cases, people are relieved that they aren't losing their minds, and if the entity doesn't pose any harm, they learn to coexist with it. Many are even happy to do so. For dangerous entities, and again, this is very rare, specialists help to remove them."

"Dr. Gallagher said he thought Miranda should not see any evidence at the moment. Were you guys able to catch anything?"

"Well..." Joe paused. "I think you all need to see this in person."

Alison heard the echo of Dr. Gallagher's advice. "If Miranda asks about seeing the evidence, then we should set the appointment so we can let her dictate the pace. Okay?"

"Sure, no problem. Sounds like a good idea. Mike will think so too. We'll wait to hear from you, then?"

Alison's thoughts warred against one another, but she soon found her resolve. "Listen. I think I need to see that evidence. When my parents passed, I never stopped looking out for Miranda. I'm not going to stop now. I will come over to your office and view the evidence there. I have to know what we're dealing with, and I have to learn of any immediate danger. I need to be prepared."

Joe paused. "I don't know. We pride ourselves on our ethics. We have to in this field. I can appreciate what you're saying, but what if she finds out you saw this information without her? Would she have trouble trusting you after that? What would that do to your relationship?"

"Hmm." Alison's thoughts skipped back to a mistake or two she made when Miranda was a teenager. *Miranda is slow to forgive.*

"I know it's difficult to let go sometimes. If you want to support and protect your sister, you need to keep everything on the table and trust that she is strong enough to handle it. I know as a parent, sometimes it's hard to do. Once you break that trust, it's difficult to get it back."

Alison sighed. "Yeah, I know you're right. I don't like it."

Joe laughed. "Who does?"

Tears spilled into Alison's voice. "She's had such a hard road. I wish I could take on this one battle for her so she doesn't have to."

"You know, someday, you are going to make a great parent."

Alison laughed, sniffing and wiping her tears.

"No really, you are."

"It's a fine line you parents walk, isn't it?"

"It certainly is. You let us know when she's ready, then."

"Okay. I'll call the moment she's ready. And thanks, Joe, for everything. You guys have been wonderful."

Alison hung up the phone, feeling like she was back in the hospital waiting for Miranda to wake up. The dread of what Joe and Mike's equipment captured sat on her chest. They found something. Otherwise, Joe would have told her they found nothing. She shuddered, and her energy drained. She took a blanket off the couch, wrapped it around her shoulders, and sat down at the dining room table.

She looked at the piles of papers on the table, musing over which cup of tea to make. The peculiar photocopies mixed in with her parent's accident report and news clippings drew her eyes. While the police conducted their first check through Miranda's house, she took the pile of papers off the table, hoping her sister would somehow forget the traumatic image of her parent's crumpled car. She suspected that the photo somehow triggered the most recent series of events.

She picked up the pile of papers and looked at the diagram of the chakras, a strange concept to her. Yet, as much as she believed in her Christian values, she couldn't help accepting the validity of this belief system, even though people cannot see an energy system. This is the reason she always felt that spirits and ghosts existed. Something she read a long time ago, about how the human eye is only capable of seeing certain spectrums of light, and shrimp can see 41 different colors that the human eye is not capable of seeing. How silly people can be. There could be plenty of things people cannot see that are actually there, but she knew many people who don't believe just because they can't see it, just like Dr. Fine. Humans are not physically capable of seeing everything, so how can people claim it doesn't exist just because they can't see it? It's like that tree in the woods. It still falls even if no one hears it.

The diagram had discs of energy in different colors mapped on the body in a straight line. *The illustrator did a great job.* Another diagram mapped the chakras in the front of the body and one for the back. She stared at the diagrams for several minutes. *No, it couldn't be!* She picked up a business card and dialed the number.

"Joe?"

"Yes?"

"It's Alison Sheppard again. I need to see the evidence right away."

"Alison..."

"Joe, it's important. Miranda could be in danger."

Joe paused. "I'll call Mike on his cell phone. Hold on." After a few moments, he said, "I've got him on the line. He said okay. How about tomorrow evening?"

"How about now? I'll drive to you. Say, in thirty minutes?"

"Hold on." Alison could hear bits and pieces of the muffled conversation. "Okay. Mike's driving over. We'll see you in a half an hour. Do you know our location?"

"Yeah. Thanks, Joe. I'll see you in a few."

• • •

Alison drove to the industrial part of town and arrived at Joe and Mike's office, a simple rectangular white metal building Alison often saw on construction sites to give construction workers a temporary office. She pulled her car alongside three other cars parked out in front.

Joe opened the door and greeted her. "So, what's the matter?"

Alison stepped into the building. Joe and Mike's collection of exploded equipment sat on a long banquet table in the middle of the room. They had computers and equipment along the walls on two other long banquet tables. A man sat at one of the computers who looked more like Mike's brother than Joe. He stood up when he saw Alison.

Mike pointed to the man. “This is Tim. He’s our equipment expert and all-around guru. We’re lucky enough that he’s related to us and doesn’t charge us much for his services.”

Tim smiled and reached his hand across the table. “Nothing, actually. Nice to meet you.”

“Likewise.” Alison glanced at Mike. “Another brother?”

“No, cousins.”

“Here, have a seat.” Joe motioned to a metal chair, and Alison sat. Mike, Joe, and Tim sat down.

Mike folded his arms and leaned back. “So, Alison, it sounded important. What’s going on?”

“First, show me what you have,” Alison replied.

“We’ve been working with Tim the moment we returned from your sister’s house to see if we could retrieve any evidence from the hard drives on our equipment.”

“You got what we saw?” Alison asked.

“Yes, from the thermal camera, enough to record the anomaly and get a snapshot of it.” Mike took a sheet of paper and handed it over the table to Alison.

I knew it. She took the paper from Mike. The glossy sheet contained the image. She squeezed her eyes shut.

“Do me a favor, Tim, would you?” Alison opened her eyes and handed the diagram of the chakra system to him. “Could you scan this and then print it up on that see-through stuff, you know, the plastic stuff you use for slide shows with an overhead projector? Do you have those? And, could you isolate Miranda’s heat signature to match this?”

“Yeah, sure.” Tim took the picture, lifted the lid of his scanner, slid the image onto the glass, and closed the lid. Mike and Joe exchanged questioning looks.

“Um, yes.” Joe cleared his throat and looked at Alison. “While Tim does that, we can play the recording.” He got up and sat down at the computer behind him. He turned his chair so he could use the computer and keep eye contact with Alison. "This was right before all the lights shattered."

Alison readied herself. "I'm okay. Play it."

Joe nodded and clicked on the file. A metallic, clicking, tinny, low-pitched growl emanated from the small computer speakers before the first explosion of glass.

"What the hell?" Alison's voice squeaked. "It doesn't even sound human."

"We don't know what it is," Mike admitted. "It could have something to do with the explosion or equipment malfunction. Have you ever heard that sound in Miranda's house?"

"No, never, but Miranda did say that the man's voice sounded like a growl."

"Here's the printout." Tim handed the vellum to Alison.

"You gentlemen wonder why I am so worried about Miranda? Look at this." She placed the transparency over the printout from the thermal camera. The diagram of the body's energy fields matched with the black areas within Miranda's image. She turned the overlapped images to the three men. They studied the images in silence for a few moments.

Joe seemed as if he was going to say something until confusion washed over his face. He took another breath and said, "So, what are we looking at?"

Alison removed the transparency from the image. "This is a diagram of the body's energy fields."

"Oh, yeah, that's the new age theory thingy." Tim took the vellum from Alison and held it up in the air and squinted at the diagram.

"Thingy?" asked Mike in a sarcastic tone.

Tim seemed oblivious to Mike in his excitement. "Yeah." He waved his hand in a circle next to his head as if it would help him find the right words. "You know, they're ..."

"Chakras," Alison interjected.

"Yes." Tim pointed at Alison with a satisfied look. "Yes. Chakras."

"What are those?" Mike asked.

"Some think they are the body's unseen energy fields. Edgar Cayce, a famous healer born over a hundred years ago, could see people's auras and energy fields."

Allison nodded. "They are more like energy centers for the body. When my parents passed, they had a whole stack of papers on the subject, like they were researching it." Alison gave a half-hearted laugh and shook her head. "I used to have this crazy idea that this stuff was somehow linked to their death."

"Yeah," Tim agreed, "and these energy centers all correspond to the functioning of the body. For instance, the green cone here governs the functioning of the heart. The chakras are located up and down the spine: red, orange, yellow, green, blue, indigo, and violet." Tim pointed to the chart as he spoke. "These are the major chakras, but there are minor ones as well mapped throughout the entire body."

Mike's forehead and nose wrinkled in skepticism. "If you can't see it, how do you know it's there?"

"Okay, think of astronomers. They are some of the few who are able to see planets and stars through their super duper high-powered telescopes. Only a handful of people around the world get to actually view other universes."

"I don't see how..."

Tim put up his hand. "It's related, so shut up a second."

Joe rolled his eyes. "See why we don't let him out much?" Joe joked.

Despite Alison's worry, she snickered.

Tim shot Joe a dirty look, but even his cousin's need to explain his behavior didn't sidetrack him. "There are people like Edgar Cayce who can see and read these energy fields. It's equivalent to a few people who have access to high-powered telescopes. Some people can see what others can't, sort of like they have their own telescopes."

Mike frowned and crossed his arms as he shook his head in disbelief.

"You are—such—a pain—in the ass!" Tim pointed his hand in between pauses for emphasis. "Mike, you hunt *ghosts*, and you have trouble believing what entire sects of Hinduism and Buddhism have believed for thousands of years?"

"Well, the only, and I mean, the *only* reason I believe in ghosts is because I have recorded them on tape and seen them with my own eyes. I have never seen energy fields. Not a one. You know I don't believe in all this stuff." He waved his hand around.

"But, Mike, don't you think we should give this a second look? I mean, isn't it strange that the image matches up perfectly to these chakras?" Joe opened his eyes wide, his glance leading Mike's gaze over to Alison.

Alison sat, quiet and bewildered, her hands folded in front of her.

"Sorry," said Joe. "They've been doing this for forever."

"Yeah, sorry." Mike rubbed his head. "Tim always gets me riled up. I guess he knows how to punch my buttons."

"Yeah, same here," Tim apologized. "I guess we're both a bit bullheaded."

Alison provided a forgiving smile. "Dealing with the bullheaded is my specialty."

"You know, though, I don't believe in all this. That's why we never bring a psychic with us. I know some groups use them. I never believed in them," Mike explained.

"I know how you feel," Alison replied. "I thought all this stuff was pretty weird too. The new age movement is really what brought all this stuff to the West, but I think Tim has a good point. Maybe it has some sort of wisdom to help Miranda."

"Any ideas?" Joe looked around.

"The question is why Miranda has this black mass in her aura where her chakras are," Tim mused.

"Yes, exactly what we saw that night, and what I have been wondering since." Alison's face conveyed her worry. "The thing that frightens me most is that it seems to have plugged into the center of her chakras."

"While we shouldn't rule it out, the image seems to be too specific for a camera malfunction," Mike noted.

"Could her car accident and your parents' deaths have caused a strange shift in her aura?" Joe suggested.

"That's a good theory. We should write these down, sort of like the brainstorming sessions we have at work." Tim grabbed a marker and then walked a few steps to grab a white board. "Okay, number one." He wrote the number and circled it. "Strange shift in aura."

"I know what really scares me. I don't even want to say it." Alison looked down at her clasped hands.

"That somehow we captured an entity that has a hold of your sister?" asked Mike.

Alison nodded at her interwoven fingers. "Yes, that's it. It's too horrible. I wouldn't even know where to start. And what would happen to her? If we rip it out of her, would there be anything of her left? If it is an entity, it is already powerful enough to render Miranda unconscious for an entire afternoon and to cause her light bulbs to shatter, sort of like it's gaining strength. What will it be capable of doing next time... when..."

"Theory two." Tim wrote the number and circled it. "Entity occupying Miranda." Alison's shoulders bent under the weight of the statement. Mike shot Tim a shut-up-look, waving his hand underneath his chin. "Yeah, well, I'll ..." He sat down and put the cap on the marker. "Shut up."

Finally. Mike reached his hand across the table and placed it on top of Alison's folded hands. "It doesn't mean it's true. They're just ideas, theories, so we can try and describe something that we've never come across before."

"Yeah, I mean, you could see an expert in this sort of thing. Someone who knows more about energy fields and such," Joe proposed.

"I wish we had more answers for you. We don't know a whole lot about this subject," Mike admitted.

"As a matter of fact, I wouldn't even know who to contact," Joe apologized. "The only thing I would recommend is to bring the evidence to Dr. Gallagher. Maybe he would have some ideas on how to approach this or who you could go see."

"How are you going to handle this with Miranda?" asked Mike. "Is she doing better?"

"I don't really know what to do. Through the event at her house, the doctors discovered she has a heart condition. Plus, she's already written off the entire experience as an electrical malfunction. It might make her feel better to believe that so she can focus on her health, but because of what we've seen here tonight, I'm not going to rest until I find out what this is."

"Really?" Joe's eyes widened. "God, am I glad Dr. Gallagher was there."

"Yeah, me too. He had the training to know something was wrong. We were able to get her to the hospital right away before anything major happened, and now the doctors are monitoring her health, so..." Alison's voice traipsed off as she looked down at the evidence.

"Listen, if you want Miranda to see the evidence, don't hesitate to call us. We'll help you in any way we can," Mike put forward.

"I appreciate that," Alison replied. "You guys have been wonderful. Thanks for everything. I'm going to call Dr. Gallagher right now. Do you think you can email me the EVP?"

Tim put up his finger. "Sure, but you'll have to get the program we have in order to listen to it. I can come by and install it for you if you like."

"That's so sweet." Alison smiled. "Yes, as soon as you can."

"Why don't I follow you home?"

"That's perfect. This way, I can get together with Dr. Gallagher tomorrow night. I'll have you put it on my laptop. I'll get my car warmed up and wait for you. Joe, Mike, thanks again. I don't know what I would have done without you guys."

"It's our pleasure." Joe stood up and put out his hand across the table. Alison shook it.

"And please, keep us updated and let us know what's going on." Mike shook Alison's hand.

"I will. I'll wait in my car." Alison took her purse and the printouts and went to her car.

Tim peered out the window and watched her go down the stairs. Mike and Joe sat down and exchanged knowing looks.

"So, Tim, that's nice of you." Mike folded his arms.

"I do what I can," said Tim absentmindedly. He took out a laptop from underneath one of the tables.

"Yeah, very charitable, almost noble." Joe put out his hand and pointed it toward Tim to emphasize his words.

"What can I say? I'm a humanitarian." Tim took a container of breath mints out of his pocket and popped one into his mouth. "See you guys later." He grabbed his jacket.

Mike tapped Joe on the arm, smiling and motioning him to look. "You know, she's engaged." Tim's hand froze on the doorknob.

"Yeah, to a famous brain surgeon, I heard." Joe smirked.

Tim gritted his teeth "Shit," he muttered. He turned the knob and opened the front door.

"Have fuuuuun," Joe and Mike called after him.

Tim spun around and slanted his eyes at them. "You're just jealous." Mike and Joe laughed hard, Joe almost falling off of his chair. Tim whirled back around, slammed the door behind him, and marched down the stairs.

Joe and Mike laughed as Alison and Tim's cars pulled away. Mike wiped a tear from the corner of his eye. "At least he's not boring."

"Yeah." Joe gasped, trying his best to regain his composure.

13
NOTHING

Dr. Gallagher had a plastic container on his desk and finished chewing his mouthful. “Mmm, sorry. Have a seat.” He motioned to the chair in front of his desk.

“It’s okay. I’m infringing upon your lunch hour. Thanks for seeing me so soon. It smells good. What is it?” Alison put her purse down on the floor and slung her coat over the back of the chair. She sat down, holding a folder and her laptop. Miranda nailed it. Dr. Gallagher looked like a biker stuffed into a suit. Yet, there was something about his eyes: not the fact that they were blue, although, Alison did like blue eyes. It was like he had lived three lifetimes. Was that a smirk she saw when she thought about Miranda’s comment? She warned Alison about Dr. Gallagher’s extrasensory abilities too.

“Garbanzo beans and tomatoes.” He closed the lid of the container and put it aside.

“Really?”

"I know. I don't come across as a bean type of guy. My wife makes it for me. She thinks feeding me vegetarian dishes will keep me alive longer. She's probably right. I'm lucky enough she's able to cook things that taste good."

Alison chuckled. "It sounds like you're very lucky."

Dr. Gallagher smiled. "Do you want some?"

"Oh, no, thanks."

Dr. Gallagher smiled. "So, whatchya got there?" Dr. Gallagher motioned his head toward the file and laptop in Alison's hands.

Alison first opened her laptop. The audio program appeared on the screen. "Okay, listen to this." She played the recording that shook every one of her vertebrae.

Dr. Gallagher frowned. "That's creepy. But it sounds metallic, almost mechanical. Could it be a sound the equipment made before it exploded?"

"I'm not sure. Then there's this." Alison opened the folder and placed the images in front of Dr. Gallagher.

Dr. Gallagher looked down and took in a deep breath. "Okay, I see what you mean. No one else has this in the image except for your sister, and there are black, um, they look like spikes or vines protruding into your sister's energy centers. This is also not the type of equipment that would detect tumors."

"So, I don't have to explain any of this to you?" She hadn't realized that Dr. Gallagher was well-read, further dispelling the biker image.

"Not at all. I'm very familiar with the belief and theory behind chakras."

Alison put her hands up and shrugged. "What in the world is this thing, and why does it seem to have a hold of my sister?"

"The first thing I would do is call the brothers and see what type of camera they use. Then, I would call the manufacturer of that camera and show them the image to see if this could be an equipment malfunction."

"That's true. It could still be an equipment malfunction, even though we initially thought it would not be likely. But if it's not, then what?"

"I have some people I can consult. Say, do you want to call Mike and Joe and see if they can tell us the name of the manufacturer now?"

"Yes! The sooner, the better."

Dr. Gallagher took his reading glasses out of his jacket pocket and looked under several papers on his desk. "Ah, here it is." He held the card at various arm lengths to read it. "I think."

Alison smirked.

After some polite chitchat and note-taking, Dr. Gallagher hung up the telephone. "Okay, Joe gave me all of the information, and he's sending over the FLIR image. Let's see if I got that email." He turned to the computer at the corner of his desk. "Got it right here. Ready to call?"

Alison nodded.

"Here we go." He dialed the number. "I'm going to put this on speakerphone so we can both hear."

"Yes, that's great."

After three rings, someone picked up the line. "Hello, this is Tara, tech support. How can I help you?"

"My name is Dr. Gallagher, and I'm here with Alison Sheppard. Joe Cavanaugh gave us your name and number. I have a piece of evidence I would like for you to examine. We have an anomaly on an image captured on one of the cameras you manufacture, and we need to know if it's something you could help us explain."

"Are you having a problem with the camera itself?"

"I don't know if the Cavanaughs had the chance to tell you, but the camera exploded."

A pause. "Excuse me?"

"Hello, Tara, this is Alison. Let me explain. Joe and Mike Cavanaugh conducted an investigation at my sister's house. Something strange occurred. All of the equipment exploded."

"Did they have the camera on battery power or plugged into the wall at the time?"

"I used the FLIR camera, and at the time, it was running on battery."

Another pause. "I've never heard anything like this before. If you're calling about the warranty, you'll have to have the Cavanaughs call back during business hours."

"No, Miss, you misunderstand," stated Dr. Gallagher. "We need to see if you could help us with an image we recovered from the camera. We saw this image live on the FLIR right before the explosion."

"Oh. You were able to recover it from the hard drive after the explosion. Correct?"

"Yes," Dr. Gallagher confirmed.

"Okay. What did you want to know?"

"May I email you the picture?"

"Sure. Go to the website and click on *Contact Us*. You can send attachments. We get inquiries like this a lot. I should see it in a moment."

After typing for a few moments, Dr. Gallagher announced, "Okay, it's sent."

"I see it now. That was fast today. I see the FLIR image. So, what do you want to know?"

"Do you see the black mass in the image?"

"Yes, I see the people with unremarkable heat signatures except for the one who has a black mass within the heat signature, and it even seems to be affecting the colors that normally show up within a FLIR image, such as orange and red. That's very strange."

"What could cause something like this to show up in someone's heat signature?" asked Alison.

"These cameras have sensors detecting the temperature of the object or person. If the sensor failed, you would have seen flashes on the screen of the camera, and you would see either no image or something consistent across the image. You can really tell camera malfunctions. I would have to say this is not a camera malfunction."

Alison gulped. "Then what do you think this is?"

"Hmm. Something the person wore could have deflected the sensor."

"She wore a normal cotton shirt. I know because I bought it for her for Christmas."

"Cotton wouldn't do that. It's only a theory, but..."

"A theory would be much better than nothing, so please share your thoughts." Alison clasped her hands and waited for the reply. No camera malfunction meant dealing with the unknown. How could they identify what this was out of a universe of possibilities?

"It doesn't really exist in nature except for black holes and dark matter, but there's the theory of a perfect black body. And, no, it's not a porno film." Tara chortled to silence on the other end. "Sorry, my friends always comment on my racy sense of humor. A perfect black body absorbs all wavelengths of light and does not allow any light reflection to escape. Since it does not reflect any light rays, it is considered a perfect black body."

"I don't understand," said Alison. "It gets dark every night and you really can't see anything on a cloudy night with no moon."

"That's a lack of available light. I am talking about an object or phenomenon absorbing any and all light entering it. Think about how we see. Objects and even people absorb light rays, but not all. Some get reflected, and we see color from the reflected ray of light. With grass, for instance, all bands of light are absorbed except for the green ray of light. Perfect black bodies absorb all light rays and reflect none."

"But, this image was taken with a thermal camera," observed Alison.

"Yes. Theoretically, a thermal camera would be able to pick up a perfect black body because black bodies have a constant temperature. It takes very high temperatures of one thousand Kelvin and above to even start seeing the radiation from a black body, and you see radiation when the black body converts thermal energy into electromagnetic energy, therefore electromagnetic radiation."

"How do you know all of this, Tara?" Dr. Gallagher asked.

"It's better to be a thermal camera technician than an out-of-work astrophysicist. Now, see here, the person in this photo, she has the black mass in the center, and the rest of her body temperature is cool. Oh, and around the black mass, there's almost what one would consider an event horizon. You see, thermal cameras can detect small differences in temperature as well, and there is a slight temperature difference all around the black mass, which means it could have an event horizon, what is theorized to be the surface of the point of no return around a black hole. Huh. So, there seems to be an energy that is acting like a mini black hole in the person, sucking up all other bands of light from the person's body of energy without freeze-drying her physical body cells." The excitement in Tara's voice was apparent to her listeners.

"So, you're saying, if this does exist, it shouldn't exist in a person?" asked Alison.

"Yes, essentially. Also, because I'm not seeing any red or orange in the person with the black mass as the people around her have, it's almost like, well ..."

"Whatever it is, it's feeding off of her energy," Alison deduced.

"Well, yeah," Tara agreed. "It's acting like a black hole that's absorbing all of the electromagnetic radiation from the person in the image."

Alison gulped. "Do you have any ideas on how one would get rid of a perfect black body?"

"It depends on the composition of the black body. In nature, a perfect black body is actually the cosmic microwaves left over from the big bang. They have a temperature of 2.7 Kelvin, which is, like, really, really, really cold. To cancel that out, you would have to send out a microwave from the same point of origin and have the same exact amplitude to cancel out another microwave. Or another theory is to have something that will exert as much force on it so it cancels out the microwave. Or, to send microwaves that have the same amplitude, but are perfectly out of sync so they cancel each other out. But according to quantum physics, you can't have, say, an electron sending out more than one wave. It would require another electron located in the same exact position, or co-located, emitting a wave with the same amplitude and frequency.

"As it is, these microwaves are everywhere. You can listen to them if you have a low-noise antenna, which is how the microwave radiation left over from the big bang was discovered. The entire universe is filled with this radiation, which includes Earth. The good candidate for the composition for this black mass could be microwaves left over from the big bang."

"Let me see if I've got this," said Dr. Gallagher. "If a perfect black body was partially or wholly made of the microwave radiation, there wouldn't be a way to cancel out the microwaves."

"I'm really confused," Alison admitted. "Do black bodies exist or not?"

"Okay. In nature, the examples I gave you are *nearly* perfect black bodies. They have a constant temperature and absorb all wavelengths of light, as long as the wavelength does not surpass the mass of the black body. All living things give off electromagnetic waves ranging from short waves to long waves. Humans give off infrared electromagnetic waves, which are on the longer end of the spectrum. Black bodies, on the other hand, regardless of what they are made of, have a constant temperature below absolute zero. Since they absorb *all* wavelengths of light, which include gamma rays, the shortest and most harmful to humans, to the longest, which are radio waves, it does not radiate anything at all. So, at room temperature, the body would appear black, just like the picture you captured on your FLIR. And, it just so happens that substances like water or black, dull surfaces are great absorbers of electromagnetic radiation, so your entity might just have enough low-level energy to suck out the body's electromagnetic energy without freezing the entire body with extreme freezing temperatures. Plus, in order to release all of the wavelengths of light and turn it into radiation, it takes extremely high temperatures of five hundred degrees Celsius. These conditions could be replicated so that it acts similarly to a black body, but nothing we know of in nature is a *perfect* black body."

"I think I'm getting it." Alison squinted as she concentrated. She liked biology so much more. It deals with the tangible. "So, if this really were a black body, it actually would absorb all the light and radiation from the energy sources around it."

"Yes, you got it," said Tara.

"And since black bodies really don't exist in nature, there really isn't any known way to get rid of a black body?"

"I wouldn't say that. You would just have to find out what the substance is made of. If you can figure that out, there is an antithesis for it."

Alison rubbed the center of her forehead. Pretty soon, Miranda wouldn't be the only one who got migraines. "Thank you very much for your time, Tara."

When they said their goodbyes, Alison closed her eyes. "This has not made me feel any better."

"Alison, don't jump to any conclusions here. These theories might seem to fit, but as she said, black bodies really don't exist in nature."

"That we know of," Alison pointed out.

"Yes, that we know of, but it's improbable. I hoped for a more ordinary explanation."

"So did I. Typical. Nothing about Miranda is ordinary."

Dr. Gallagher grinned slightly and shook his head. "Yes, I gathered that much."

"So, what now, Dr. Gallagher?"

"I think we need to disprove this theory."

"How are we going to do that?"

"I have a friend who is in charge of the world's most powerful MRI."

Alison's eyebrows lifted. "Really?"

"Yes. If there really is anything within Miranda's energy field that has an electromagnetic presence, we should be able to capture it again. Then, we will know for certain."

Alison paused. "And what if there is something inside of her? How in the world do we deal with that?"

Dr. Gallagher looked steadily at Alison. "I don't know. But we'll figure it out."

"How can you be so certain?"

"Because I have faith."

Dr. Gallagher's reference to the conversation she had in the hallway of the hospital with Dr. Fine did not go unnoticed. "Okay, then. How do we tell Miranda without scaring the crap out of her or pissing her off?"

• • •

"Alison, when my brother said you are full of surprises, I never expected this." Steven's dark eyes shot daggers, first at her, then at Dr. Gallagher.

"Listen. I'm concerned. Okay, more like worried sick." Alison never thought that when she brought Steven to Dr. Gallagher's office, he would put up roadblocks.

"Alison, we all are. That's why I don't want you to breathe a word of this nonsense to her. Not now. And Dr. Gallagher, I'm surprised, no, shocked, that you would go along with this. And Alison, I'm shocked that you went behind her back pursuing this, this garbage. I entertained your little ghost hunt, and look what happened. It nearly killed her."

"Aren't you the least bit worried about this? I mean, look at this thing." Alison pointed to the picture on Dr. Gallagher's desk.

"Do you know what that is, Alison?" Steven picked up the papers. "To me, absolute crap." He threw them onto the desk. "You heard the doctor. Everything that has happened to her at this point was related to her heart condition."

"And what about what we all saw that night? What about what you saw? You know it wasn't nothing. I can feel it, Steven. Something is wrong, very wrong. I saw this man, this thing, in her hallway."

"Which you wrote off as your imagination. Do you know what this could do to her? I'm not sure she can survive through this *again*. And I'm not going to allow anyone, not even you, to make it worse, because I'm not going to live through this *again*." The volume of Steven's voice rose as his words blasted like a spray of bullets.

"Live through what?" asked Dr. Gallagher.

Steven pressed his lips together and breathed deeply through his nose. He pointed to the both of them. "You drop this. And I don't ever want to hear it again. She's going to be fine, the way she is, right now. And that's the way it's going to stay."

Steven's eyes darted back and forth to Dr. Gallagher and Alison. He swiped his jacket off of the chair and slammed the door behind him.

"He lost his fiancé when he was in college," Alison explained to Dr. Gallagher.

Dr. Gallagher nodded.

"Do you think we're making something out of nothing?" asked Alison.

"I wouldn't pursue it if I thought it was nothing."

"What do we do now?"

"There is nothing else to do. The last thing we want to do is to create more havoc in Miranda's life. I know you want to find this out, but it's not going to happen. Sometimes, we have to let people progress at their own pace."

"And hopefully by then, it's not too late," Alison said.

"Yes. Miranda is on her own schedule. We can't rush that along."

14
DREAM

Miranda took off her coat and sat down in the chair in front of Dr. Gallagher's desk. "Did my call surprise you?"

"Do you think I should be?"

"Um, I don't know. That's why I asked."

"No, not really."

"Why?"

He shrugged. "I figured something would come up."

"How did you know?"

"The degree's on the wall." He pointed behind him.

Miranda giggled. "Thank you for seeing me so soon."

"No problem. How have you been this past month?"

"I dreamed about my mother. It was so vivid. It felt like she had visited me."

Dr. Gallagher raised his eyebrows. "Oh?"

"I thought it might upset Alison if I told her about it."

"And Steven?"

"I don't know. He's been so protective lately. I didn't want to worry him. I needed someone neutral to talk to."

"Most people do."

"I guess I can see why."

"So, tell me about this dream."

"In the dream, I sat at a picnic table in the back of the cabin my family used to rent every summer in my childhood. We used to spend weeks there. It was such a beautiful scene, you know, where you look at a photo and it looks too beautiful to be real. I could even smell the pine trees and see the lady slippers."

"Sounds beautiful."

"Yes. And I was so relaxed. Then I saw her. She wore one of those long, flowing dresses she used to wear. She looked radiant, beautiful, and young. She sat down beside me, and we hugged." Teardrops snaked their way down Miranda's face. "I was so happy to see my mom. I cried for what seemed like forever." She grabbed a bunch of tissues from the tissue box in front of her on Dr. Gallagher's desk. "She kissed me on the cheek and told me I had to start paying attention."

"To what?"

"She said, 'You have to start paying attention to you.'"

Dr. Gallagher nodded.

"But then if it was really her... is she okay?" Her eyes brimmed with tears. The end of the dream left a bottomless pit in her stomach.

"Okay, Miranda, I want you to take a deep breath for me. Come on, I'll do it with you." Dr. Gallagher took a deep breath. Miranda followed. "Better?"

Miranda nodded. "Yeah. Sorry. Why does it feel like I lost my mother yesterday when I think about her?"

Dr. Gallagher gave her a soft look. "Because love is not bound by space or time."

Miranda gasped, almost jumping out of her chair. "How did you know?"

Dr. Gallagher's eyes widened with surprise. "Know what?"

"How did you know what she said in my dream? I asked her the same question, and she said what you said, word for word. How the fuck did you know that?"

Dr. Gallagher paused. "It's something that happens to me a lot. But there's another possibility here."

"Yes?"

"Some people are sure they are visited by a relative, friend, or someone they know who has passed while they are sleeping. This could be a true spirit communication."

"No! Oh, shit, I hope not!"

Dr. Gallagher put out his hand. "Miranda. Tell me the rest of your dream. I promise you, we'll make sense of it together. It's my specialty."

"Did you know this is the first dream I've had since I remembered my car accident?"

Dr. Gallagher nodded, waiting.

"If the dream had ended there, I would have been so happy. I would have felt like I received a true visitation from my mother. But, when we finally finished hugging, I looked at her, and her head looked as it did, right after, right after the accident." Miranda's voice got stuck in her throat as more tears welled up. She took one of the tissues in her hand, wiped below her eyes, and then pinched her nose. "That's when it got scary."

Dr. Gallagher nodded and raised his eyebrows a little in expectation for her to continue.

"Her eyes turned black, then her face, and then everything around me. The darkness pierced my body everywhere." Miranda's voice trailed off, as if the memory of the dream made her ache. "I screamed, and then I woke up."

"Where did the darkness pierce you?"

"Through my forehead, my neck, my chest, my stomach. Everywhere."

Dr. Gallagher stared at her for a few moments. Was that shock she saw on his face for a millisecond? Dr. Gallagher's years of training enabled him to hide his feelings under a cloak of professionalism. Because of her parents, she understood that. To break it for a moment must have meant he knew something.

"I think it's time you, Alison, and Steven come in here together. You need to tell them your dream."

"Why?"

"You have something important to tell them, and they will want to be there for you. Why don't you give them the chance to do that?"

"Be there for me?"

"Yes. If Steven and Alison are available, I'll make some time for you all tonight after the rest of my appointments."

"You think we should all meet with you?"

"Yes. If it were easy for you to share your dream with Alison and Steven, you would have done it already. I'll be here to support you."

• • •

The month of March was always deceptive in Davenport. A general sentiment circulated among the residents that every year: Punxsutawney Phil forgot them and left them to brave the bitter cold winds and the snow storms that blanketed the product of older snow storms, lumps of hard ice mixed with grit, dust, and dirt, with fresh, newer snow. The snow in March fell to the ground in beleaguered clumps of ice rather than merrily drifting in the air as beautiful little fluffs of sparkly snow as they do in December, like the snowflakes themselves had tired of winter. Most years, winter did not release its hold until the middle of April, when the timid sun finally peaked from behind the clouds to relinquish the stronghold of the final bits of dirty snow clinging to the earth.

Miranda was still trying to work off the chill when she, Steven, and Alison arrived at the office. Dr. Gallagher sat at the receptionist's desk poking at the keyboard.

"Hi everyone." Dr. Gallagher stood up. "Come on back." He opened the door to the hallway. Dr. Gallagher had placed four chairs in the middle of his room in a circle. He sat in the chair closest to his desk. "Here, have a seat."

"Thanks." Miranda sat in one of the chairs with her jacket still on, folding her arms in front of her.

"Cold?" Steven dragged his seat next to hers and put his arm around her shoulders.

Miranda offered a smile. "You're so good to me." Steven smiled back.

Alison settled into her chair. "So, Mira, hon, what's going on?"

Miranda looked at Dr. Gallagher. "Miranda has something to share with the both of you."

"Guys, I dreamed about Mom."

Alison nodded. Steven wrapped his other arm around her and hugged her.

"I can see why that would be upsetting, but that's also good, isn't it?" Alison inquired.

"Yeah, in a sense, but not for the reason you think."

"Okay." Expectation saturated Alison's voice.

Miranda conveyed to Alison what she conveyed to Dr. Gallagher earlier in the afternoon.

Alison gasped.

"What?"

"I can see why you wanted us here tonight, Dr. Gallagher."

"Why?" Miranda asked.

"Because, hon, the paranormal researchers, Joe and Mike, they called with some evidence. I convinced them to let me see it without you so you could focus on the health of your heart. I hope you're not angry, but I wanted to see if I could help while you recovered."

Steve glared at Dr. Gallagher and Alison.

"What? Why didn't you tell me?"

"Because, hon, your heart specialist convinced you that everything you experienced had to do with your heart condition and electrical malfunctions. Remember? It seemed to be what you needed to believe."

"You know, and it could still be nothing. It was just a dream, after all." Steven glowered at Alison. Alison looked at him, pressing her lips together and opened her eyes wide, conveying *shut up and get on board with this.*

Miranda turned toward Steven. "Steven." Miranda searched his eyes, "I don't think it was just a dream. When I told Dr. Gallagher about it, I asked him why it feels like I lost my mother just yesterday, and he said, 'because love is not bound by space or time.' My mom said those same words to me in my dream."

"Miranda, it could be a coincidence. Didn't I read that in a greeting card once?" Steven gave Dr. Gallagher a dirty look.

Dr. Gallagher, instead of taking the bait, said, "You seem angry, Steven."

Steven stood up. "Miranda, we should go. I've had enough of this. I entertained this little ghost hunt until I almost lost you that night."

"Well, you didn't. A problem got detected early. I'm lucky."

"If we continue on this hocus pocus *crap*, with this *quack,* how long is it going to take for your heart to give out? Tomorrow? No, I'm not doing this. I think we should go, now."

Miranda's face puckered up in shock. "Steven. It's not a coincidence, and it's not crap. It's me. I can't believe I'm hearing this from you."

"So, you're telling me you no longer believe this happened because of your heart condition? That there is some spook flying around doing all of this?"

"No, I'm not saying that at all. I don't know what it is. Steven, have you met anyone on the planet or even heard of anyone experiencing what I have this past year alone?"

"No, but it could be a string of unfortunate incidences, and that's it."

"And what about all the lights exploding in my house? And seeing that man in my house and in the hospital, and Alison seeing him in my house? And the light bulb lighting up in an unplugged lamp? And my radio turning on by itself? Can you explain all that away?" Steven folded his arms, the maddest Miranda had ever seen him.

Electrical malfunction. Drugs they gave her in the hospital. Alison's imagination. An electrical storm. Electrical malfunction. While Steven didn't "explain it all away" out loud, he took satisfaction from listing them mentally.

"Hey, you promised me that night in the hospital that you would be here for me no matter what. You look like you're ready to go back on your promise."

Steven unfolded his arms and placed his hand over her hand resting on the arm of the chair. Miranda was satisfied when her statement dissipated all signs of Old Steven.

"No, I'll never go back on my promise to you. I'll be here, no matter what, but I just can't live through it again."

"Live through what?"

"I don't want to lose you."

Miranda looked into Steven's eyes. "You won't. I promise. I'll fight for every breath of life I have. Okay?"

Steven nodded. "Everything seems so fragile."

"Sometimes life seems like that when we are feeling fragile," Dr. Gallagher noted.

"Yeah," Steven said, putting his head down. He raised his head and met Dr. Gallagher's gaze. "Sorry, for, you know, the quack thing."

Dr. Gallagher held his stare and nodded. He wasn't Steve's hugest fan, but he knew better. At times like these, he was grateful for his professional training. Otherwise, he would have told Steve to shut the fuck up or punched him in the jaw like he used to when he was young and living in the Bronx, asking him if he enjoyed sipping all of his meals through a straw. He turned his gaze to Alison. “Why don’t you share what you found?”

“Yes. I found it in the pile of paperwork you took from the house, Mira. You had it on the table when I went through the house with the police. I grabbed the paperwork because I thought it might have had something to do with your incident, and I didn’t want it upsetting you further. When I came across that diagram, I ran straight over to Mike and Joe and had them show me the evidence. Sure enough, they were able to retrieve the image we saw on the thermal camera that night. Dr. Gallagher said we needed to share this information with you when you were ready, and here we are. Are you mad that I didn’t wait for you?”

Miranda took a deep breath. “No. I guess I needed to adjust to my new life without coffee and taking better care of my heart, and all in the midst of tax season. I wasn’t in any place to confront this. I guess Mom came to me when she knew I was ready.”

“So, Miranda, it sounds like you’re convinced she visited you,” observed Dr. Gallagher.

“I’m not sure yet. For the first time in years, a part of me is hoping it was my mom. I still don’t know the reason for all the creepiness at the end of the dream. At any rate, it brought me here.”

“I think I can help with that.” Alison showed Miranda the image she received from Mike and Joe. “This is what the brothers gave me.”

Miranda looked at the image, her eyes wide with shock. “This is what I saw in my dream. Why did you bring it?”

“A hunch. Okay, now look at this.” Alison took the transparency of the diagram of the chakras and placed it over Miranda’s heat signature. The chakras showed through the blackness within Miranda’s heat signature.

Miranda rubbed her forehead. “What does this all mean?”

“We don’t know,” Dr. Gallagher admitted. “Alison and I called the FLIR camera manufacturer to see if it had to do with the explosion somehow, or a malfunction of some sort. The manufacturer could not explain the picture or the presence of the blackness."

"The technician we spoke with said the picture reminded her of a theoretical situation, a perfect black body, like a black hole," Alison reported. "She was an out-of-work astrophysicist before she became a camera technician."

"How lucky," Miranda said dryly. "So, what does this mean for me? I have some sort of black hole sucking all the life out of me?"

"Honestly, I'm not buying into it at the moment," Dr. Gallagher admitted, "but I think I have a way to find out what's going on. A friend of mine runs the most powerful magnetic resonance imaging ever made. It is one hundred teslas. It's in its experimental phases now. Only one or two individuals in the world have ever been scanned by this MRI."

"Are there any harmful side effects?" asked Alison.

"My friend, Dr. Tetenbaum, said they did the first test subject two years ago. The person had some dizziness, but nothing since then."

"MRIs have been used safely for years, but with the tesla so high, it makes me a bit nervous, especially with her heart," said Steven.

"Do you think it could prove for certain if I have anything in my body living there without my permission?" asked Miranda.

"I think this is our best shot," said Dr. Gallagher. "I'll call my friend tonight and get an appointment for you and verify the possible effects on your heart. When would you like to go?"

"How about tomorrow?" asked Miranda.

Steven took Miranda's hand. "Miranda, shouldn't we think about this a little more?"

"What is there to think about? There's nothing else on the planet that could help. This is the closest thing to certain I have right now. I might as well confront this now and get it over with. Then we can deal with the outcome." She looked into his eyes. "I can't live like this anymore. I'm afraid to stay in my own house. I want to move on. I have been dealing with this for almost a year now. I need to know as soon as possible. Don't you want that for me?"

"Of course I do, but I don't want you to die in the process."

"Steven, if this is really some unknown entity, it might kill me anyway. I think this will save my life. For me, it's worth the risk."

Steven sighed. "Okay, yes. If this is what you want, I support you no matter what."

Miranda kissed him on the cheek. "Thanks, darling."

Alison breathed a sigh of relief. "Finally." Miranda cast an inquisitive look. "Oh, I've wanted this to happen for a month now."

"I know." Miranda walked over and hugged her.

Alison stepped back and held Miranda's face in her hands. "I'll be there too. We'll see what this thing is, if it's anything at all. It could be what Steven said, a string of unfortunate, but very strange incidences."

"Yes, and I want to emphasize that Steven is more likely correct about this than this theory we are investigating." Dr. Gallagher caught Steven's look of approval. The best way to win over dissidents, he found, is to compliment them. "We're just being thorough. If nothing shows on the MRI, then we know for certain. You know, this MRI is the only one of its kind. You will be the third person in the world to undergo this procedure. We will be able to see what is going on inside of you, including your heart. You will probably have the best picture of your entire heart your doctor has ever seen."

Miranda raised her eyebrows. "Wow, well, that's good."

"That I like." Steven squeezed Miranda's hand.

"So. How about that? We might be close," Alison reflected out loud.

Miranda did not want to put her faith in something that might not pan out, but she couldn't help but feel hopeful that an end was near. "Yes. We'll see tomorrow, won't we?"

15
MRI

Dr. Gallagher called Dr. Tetenbaum the moment the trio left. It was nice to see Miranda leave on a high note for a change. He arranged for everyone to meet him at Dr. Abraham Tetenbaum's office at seven in the evening the next day. Because he got Miranda to sign the agreement to allow Dr. Gallagher to speak with Dr. Tetenbaum about her case, he hooked his interest by sharing details and the photo from the thermal image. By the time he finished, Abe eagerly accepted the opportunity to run Miranda through the MRI. While he and Abe were still skeptical of the unknown, they were both confident that Miranda's body contained a secret that could possibly teach the world something new. Yet, unlike many doctors, he and Dr. Tetenbaum were willing to explore supernatural possibilities, whereas many in the medical field, the psychological field, and the scientific communities shunned such thoughts. This, he felt, would work to Miranda's advantage.

On the drive over to Abe's office, Dr. Gallagher reflected on how much he enjoyed his friend. Dr. Gallagher didn't find many people very interesting. Abe remained the exception because he was exceptional. The fact that Dr. Tetenbaum was the scientist who headed the team that created the MRI with funding from Davenport University titillated Dr. Gallagher.

When he arrived, Miranda, Steven, and Alison were already in the waiting room. "I see you found your way," Dr. Gallagher observed.

Miranda stood up to greet him. "Yes, your directions were very good. Dr. Tetenbaum asked if we wanted to get an early start, but I thought we should wait for you."

"Thanks for that. I hope you didn't wait long."

"No, we've only been here for a few minutes. I'm excited to get some answers. I hope he can read them today and tell me what he thinks."

"I'm not sure. I believe he'll be able to at least tell us a little something, but I think he'll want to write up a full report for us."

"Any idea how much this will cost?" Miranda asked nervously.

"Not a dime. Your case piqued his interest, which is why he agreed to use grant money and see you so soon." Dr. Tetenbaum had explained that the grant money allowed for "interesting cases."

"Yes, this is very exciting." Dr. Tetenbaum entered the room and extended his hand to Dr. Gallagher. "Hey, Jack. Good seeing you again." Abe and Dr. Gallagher shook hands.

Dr. Gallagher noticed his friend had stray strands of white hair all around his head of dark hair, some new additions from the last time they saw each other several months ago. He was still the same, tall, lanky Abe, although his skin was puffy and a bit wrinkled under his eyes. *He must be overworking himself with this project.*

"Yes, very exciting indeed," continued Dr. Tetenbaum. "This case is unlike any I have ever heard. We will be exploring your body in as close to an atomic level as humanly possible. In examining the physical, we will see, without question, the substance of the dark anomaly that appeared during your ghost hunt if it is in your body. It could be a strange tumor, or it could be absolutely nothing at all.

I'm gunning for the latter. However, if what you have is extraordinary with an explanation extending outside the realm of what we know scientifically, it could be the discovery of the century.

"With our first two subjects, there were some images that showed within the outline of the body. We thought it might be the effect of the tesla. But now, we have you, Miss Sheppard, who might have something within your field of energy that is only detectable with thermal image cameras because nothing unusual has shown on your x-rays for you this past year, correct?"

"Yes, that's correct."

"Now, if something is hanging onto your electromagnetic field of energy, and it's not quite physical, and it's more ethereal in nature, theoretically, we might be able to pick that up in the MRI image. Also, it will help us delineate the body's natural energy system as well. For instance, a lot of what scientists learned about the human brain came from cases where something had gone wrong. It helped us pinpoint normal brain functioning. For the first time, this could prove whether or not physical bodies have an unseen, energetic component. This could turn the scientific world on its head and upset everything we think we know, proof beyond reproach." His eyes gleamed. "So, Miss Sheppard, how does it feel to be the center of a possible earth-shattering discovery?"

Dr. Gallagher, unlike Abe, noticed Miranda's pallor blanch. "I think for the moment, figuring out what is going on with her would be a big relief."

"Oh, yes, of course. That's the best part, helping you figure out what's going on," Dr. Tetenbaum said. "Sorry, I don't get out much."

"I can tell," Steven muttered under his breath. Miranda jabbed her elbow into his rib. He let out a soft *umph*. Alison looked at the both of them and frowned. Dr. Tetenbaum didn't seem to notice.

"Yes, well, why don't we get started, then?" Dr. Tetenbaum gestured his head toward the door and led them to the back.

All the walls donned bright white, creating a sterile feeling. The control room for the MRI contained a large and complex control panel and a windowpane built into the wall above it.

"There are more buttons here than for an airplane," remarked Steven.

"Ah, yes, this is my cockpit. And that's not even the prettiest part. Watch this." He opened an electrical fuse box and threw the switches up.

The lights illuminated a large room through the window pane. One would not guess the immense size of the building from the front. Alison and Miranda couldn't help but let out utterances of admiration when the machine appeared into view. The unit sat in the middle of the room, white and tall, with a perfectly round, gigantic tube on the top of it, almost as tall as the ceiling. Miranda estimated it to be at least fifteen feet high.

"Are you going to give me a map to get into that thing? I might get lost in there," Miranda commented.

Dr. Tetenbaum laughed. "Yeah, I know. A bit big, huh? The coil for the magnet alone weighs almost fifty tons. You can't even imagine the hole we had to dig and how much concrete we had to use so the floor wouldn't cave in. And there are thousands of miles of wires made of copper and silver, making it also the world's most expensive MRI, to the tune of one hundred and fifty million. Between that and having to create a second energy field around the unit to cancel out the first so it's safe to use, it is a mammoth. This wing of this facility had been constructed to accommodate the MRI. First, we set the concrete, and two additional walls were built. Then, we installed the MRI and finished the building extension's third wall, doorway, and roof. As a result, we have an MRI that generates 100 teslas."

Dr. Gallagher's jaw dropped open. "When I had my MRI done for my back, the unit was three teslas, and it was one of the most powerful units at the time."

Dr. Tetenbaum nodded. "Yes, most MRIs still are between one and three teslas. Only a few have eleven-point-seventy-five teslas, even today. This MRI trumps all of them."

Dr. Gallagher's admiration for his friend multiplied. He couldn't even imagine what it took to design the MRI. His brain didn't work like that. It was more inclined toward seeing what others cannot see from their own words, thoughts, and behaviors.

"How in the world did you get a magnet like this? I would imagine it's not the sort of thing people have lying around," Alison pointed out.

Dr. Tetenbaum laughed. "The University of Florida worked for years perfecting the world's most powerful magnet. When they first began testing the magnet, they had to begin at lower teslas. They slowly bumped up the tesla a little at a time until they were able to run the magnet without it collapsing in on itself because of the sheer force the magnet creates. Once they made it through the testing, we were the first to obtain the coils and install it in the most advanced design for an MRI to date. With this magnet, man is on the brink of discovering the mysteries of the universe as well as the mysteries of man. Our solar system and beyond are within our grasp. This one hundred-tesla magnet will also be used in space shuttles instead of rocket fuel."

Dr. Tetenbaum paused while everyone expressed amazement.

"Okay, Miranda, I have this gown for you. There's a restroom right here." He opened a door revealing a small bathroom with a toilet, sink, and an end table next to the sink. "You can leave your stuff in there if you want, and you can leave on your undergarments."

"May I wear my shoes?"

"Oh, here," he said, providing her with some paper slippers and cap. "The room is sealed so it remains clean and dust free. When you get a unit like this worth hundreds of millions of dollars, spending a fraction of that to secure it in a clean environment seems like a bargain."

"Okay, this is it," Miranda looked at Dr. Gallagher, Alison, and Steven.

Alison held both of Miranda's hands. Steven kissed her on the head.

Miranda felt like she was going to the moon in a shower cap as she changed into the gown. When she came out, Dr. Tetenbaum had the same paper slippers and cap over his feet and head with the addition of a yellow jumper. "Ready?"

"As ready as I'll ever be."

"Okay, this way." He pointed to a door. "You'll feel like you're in a wind tunnel for about five seconds due to the vacuum. It will pick up stray particles from our hair and skin."

They entered the doorway. Miranda felt the pressure from the vacuum tingle her skin. She jumped a little at the sound and the feeling.

"Yeah, it's weird at first," Dr. Tetenbaum shouted over the suction sound. "You'd be surprised at the particles that house themselves on our body and hair alone."

Miranda nodded. The door opened, and Dr. Tetenbaum led Miranda across the floor.

It looked even larger when she stood next to it. "I don't think I've ever felt so tiny," remarked Miranda.

Dr. Tetenbaum laughed. "Yeah, it'll do that to you. The stairs are in the back here. I'll walk up with you. The table will slide into the place where we will obtain the most vivid pictures of you." Miranda ascended the stairs, Dr. Tetenbaum following behind her. "We will be in constant communication. At any time during the process, you can call out. The scan won't take long at all, only a five-minute process from start to finish. When we constructed this thing, we considered the comfort of human subjects, so we soundproofed it. The first person I ever had in the MRI fell asleep. There is a bit of a 'chugging' sound, similar to being on a train." They arrived at the top of the stairs. "Here it is." He pointed to the back of the MRI. The table was designed to slide into a smaller tube. He pointed. "You will slide in feet first."

"It's kind of small in there, isn't it?"

"Oh, yes, sorry. Because the magnetic field is so high, it has to be a closed unit instead of an open one. There are ways to cancel out the magnetic field when the tesla is a lot smaller. But with a bigger unit like this, we had to enclose the unit as well as establishing a self-canceling field. It's safer for you."

Miranda breathed in and let out a big sigh. "Okay." Miranda slid onto the cushioned table.

"Great. Now, I will let you know when the unit is ready to start. I can play some music in there for you if you like. When I tell you, you'll have to lie as still as you can and hold your breath for several seconds at a time. After the machine has powered down, I'll come back and get you. Sound okay?"

Miranda hoped her smile covered her nervousness. "Yes."

"And don't worry. We've taken every precaution into account."

Miranda nodded. When Dr. Tetenbaum descended the stairs, she closed her eyes and waited. As promised, the table moved forward into the smaller tube. *It's a good thing I'm not claustrophobic.* On the inside, it was a typical MRI: white tube, close quarters. The only one she recalled seeing was when the hospital assessed her mother's brain for signs of life after her parents' accident; Miranda was not conscious during her own MRIs.

"Hello, Miranda. You can hear me, and I can hear you, correct?" Dr. Tetenbaum verified over the intercom.

"Yes, I can hear you fine."

"Great. You'll start hearing that chugging noise. Let me know if you need anything."

"Okay."

"Would you like to listen to some music?"

"No, thanks. I'm fine."

"Alright, then. I'll let you know when it's ready."

Miranda heard the chugging noise of the machine as it powered up. She could see why the first person fell asleep. The white noise and the gentle vibration lulled her. Her eyelids drooped.

"Okay, Miranda, in a moment, it'll be time for you to lie as still as you can. There will be a point I will ask you to hold your breath, but I'll let you know when."

"Okay."

"Um, Miranda, hold on a second, okay?"

"Okay."

Suddenly, she heard a high whirring sound. "Dr. Tetenbaum?" She looked around with trepidation. The pitch drove higher and louder. "Dr. Tetenbaum." Miranda's heart pounded. "Dr. Tetenbaum!" She brought her hands up to her ears. She craned her neck to look behind her. The round door remained sealed. The area in front of her was open, but the only way she could get out was to slide out of the hole where she would have a twelve-foot drop to the floor. "Help," she screeched. She banged on the sides of the machine. "Let me out, you multimillion-dollar piece of shit!"

Miranda screamed and blacked out once again.

16
FORGOTTEN

"You know, I told Harlan, I said, Harlan, you have to keep better receipts. I've been telling him for years. Of course, he doesn't listen." Mrs. Berkshire waved her hand like she normally did when it came to discussing the exchanges between her and her husband.

Miranda Sheppard blinked several times.

"What's the matter, dear? Do you have something in your eye?" asked Mrs. Berkshire.

"Oh, no. I'm fine. Would you excuse me for a moment?" Miranda stood up from her desk.

"Sure dear. Take your time. Harlan's running the shop at the moment, and I sure do enjoy seeing you girls."

"Thanks. I'll be right back."

Miranda shut and locked the door behind her, sat on the toilet lid, and put her head in her hands. She didn't remember how she had gotten to her office that day or her entire morning.

She got up and splashed some water on her face. Before she could really mull over the memory lapse, she heard a knock on the door. "Miranda, dear, are you okay in there? You know, I have something in my purse for bellyaches."

Miranda smiled and shook her head. Mrs. Berkshire was like everyone's grandmother. "No, thanks, Mrs. Berkshire. I'm fine. I'll be out in a moment."

"Okay, dear."

Miranda took one last look in the mirror. She examined the slight scar she had on her forehead from the car accident last May. Steven joked it made her look like a sexy pirate. She guessed he wanted her to smile and think about him when she looked at her scar instead of it making her sad and depressed. It worked. Smiling, she took a breath and opened the door.

"Okay, let's take a look at the rest of those receipts."

• • •

Dr. Gallagher jumped up from the seat at his desk. He had the distinct feeling he had been somewhere or was supposed to be somewhere, but forgot... he couldn't put his finger on it.

"Dr. Gallagher. Your two o'clock appointment is here." Heather's voice emanated from the intercom.

He looked down as if she spoke an alien language.

"Dr. Gallagher. Dr. Gallagher?"

He cleared his throat and put his finger on the intercom button. "Heather, give me a few."

"Okay, Dr. Gallagher."

He never recalled feeling so disoriented. He tried to remember what he did that morning. He couldn't even remember the date. He leaned over to his computer and opened his organizing program. March 21st. What did he do yesterday?

He poked the keyboard and opened up March 20th on his calendar. *7 PM M. S. at A. T.'s. Who in the world is M. S.? Was I drugged? How can I not remember what happened in the last twenty-four hours?*

The only person he could think about with the initials A. T. was his friend, Dr. Abraham Tetenbaum. *Did I see him last night?* No way could he sit with a client without knowing if he was right in the head himself. He had to see Abe and figure out what happened.

"Heather, an emergency has come up. I'll leave through the back. Would you please tell my two o'clock, and would you please call the rest of my appointments and reschedule them for me?"

"Is everything alright, Dr. Gallagher?"

"It will be. I might need a few days to work it out. Do you think you could call my appointments for the week?"

"What do I tell Mr. Sneed? He's here now. You know how he gets." She lowered her voice.

He shook his head. He could almost hear Mr. Sneed reciting the mileage over to his office to the third decimal place, how much gas it cost him down to the half penny to drive over there, and an itinerary of the activities he could have accomplished if he hadn't wasted all his time coming to the office. "Tell him I apologize for the inconvenience, and his next appointment won't be billed toward his maximum for the year."

"Okay. Thanks, that'll work. Good luck, Dr. Gallagher."

"Thanks, Heather."

Dr. Gallagher printed up the page from March 20th out of his planner and grabbed his car keys, jacket, and baseball cap.

• • •

The drive to Dr. Tetenbaum's office seemed like an eternity due to his growing worry, even though their offices were but a short distance from each other.

"Jack." Dr. Tetenbaum walked over to Dr. Gallagher and shook his hand. "This is a pleasant surprise. How's the wife?"

"Good. So, you don't remember me coming by last night?"

"Last night? We haven't seen each other in quite a while. But I'll tell you what. Let's remedy that now and have a bite to eat, and we can talk about it. I'm starved."

"Wait a second," Dr. Gallagher started to protest.

"No, it's my treat. I won't take no for an answer." He took his jacket out of the closet.

"Abe, listen..."

"Look." Abe pointed out the window. "We can see it from here. They have the best codfish you've ever tasted. It looks like a little hole in the wall, doesn't it?"

Dr. Gallagher sighed. Getting Abe to listen, a lot of times, was like trying to herd cats. He trudged the one-hundred feet to the restaurant with Abe and sat down at a small table. The tables and chairs reminded him of the ones from the break room where he did his internship decades ago, with Formica tops and orange seats that looked like a scoop with four legs. There were a couple of older men behind the counter that seemed to do everything from taking the money to cooking and delivering the food. They both wore white t-shirts that could have easily been undershirts, and white, stained aprons.

Abe ordered for the both of them and sipped on his drink. "Now that the food is on the way," he picked up a dry, hard breadstick from the plastic red basket in the middle of the table, "what is this about seeing me last night?" He munched on the breadstick.

"Here, look at this." Dr. Gallagher took the folded paper out of his pocket and showed him, pointing to Dr. Tetenbaum's initials.

"Yes, those are my initials alright."

"I had a strange experience. Today, at two o'clock, I found myself in my office. I don't remember how I got there. As a matter of fact, I don't remember much about the last twenty-four hours. When I checked my planner, your initials showed up at seven o'clock last night, along with the initials M. S. Do you know who that is, or do you know what happened last night?"

"Hmm." Dr. Tetenbaum tapped his chin with his breadstick. "You know, come to think of it, I don't remember much about the last day or so either. I've been working so hard on this project, I thought I lapsed because of the lack of sleep. But since you are much more lucid than I have ever been, and you say you don't remember, now I'm concerned. What could have caused something like this to happen?" he mused. As he took an absentminded, loud, crunchy bite on his breadstick, bits of crumbs collected on the front of his shirt.

His friend could be a bit on the eccentric side, but on occasion, Dr. Gallagher couldn't help but make a face when something about his behavior struck him the wrong way. He made one of those faces just then and shook his head. As usual, Abe was oblivious. "I don't know. I hoped we could easily explain it."

The two sat in silence for a couple of minutes, lost in their own thoughts, processing possible causes for a shared memory lapse.

"Maybe someone drugged and mugged us," suggested Abe.

"That scenario would work if I didn't have you in my planner. But that occurred to me too."

"Why not? They could have drugged us when we met here. Maybe the mysterious M. S. drugged and mugged us."

Dr. Gallagher nodded. He couldn't deny the possibility of that scenario, but he didn't feel like he had gotten drugged, and he still had his wallet, plus not a scratch on him. Someone drugged him and his wife while they were on vacation in Florida. He remembers what it felt like the day after, and he didn't feel like that at the moment. Plus, even in his drugged state, he remembered what happened, including breaking the arm of the person trying to steal his wallet and take his wife away from him.

One of the cooks from behind the counter brought the food out. "Here you go, Abe." The man's voice sounded like gravel. He placed the plates down on the table, and he nodded to Dr. Gallagher. The skin on his face was wrinkly, but not sagging. Dr. Gallagher put him at about sixty years old. He had a bulbous nose that fit oddly well with his paunchy body.

"Thanks, Frank." Abe sniffed deeply over his plate. "Get ready for the best fish you've ever tasted. See, you don't need a flashy restaurant in the chic part of town."

"Aren't you a bit worried you don't remember anything about the last twenty-four hours?"

"Nah, not really. I'm more concerned you're concerned. I guess I would have ignored it if you hadn't thought it was important."

Dr. Gallagher frowned. His friend's indifference wore on his nerves. Or, maybe his nerves made it difficult to tolerate uncertainty. "How can you ignore a twenty-four-hour lapse of memory?"

"Because memory isn't as consistent as people would like to think it is. It changes and morphs over time. It doesn't get set in concrete. One day, it's there in the front of your brain," he pointed to his temple with his finger, "and the next day it's gone." He fanned out his hand for emphasis. "Sure, I pay attention, I remember, but I guess I don't really care that I have a block of time I don't remember." He shrugged, cut a piece of fish, and stuck it in his mouth.

"I do know all of that. I help people all day long with memory issues. I never had it happen to me," Dr. Gallagher said through his teeth.

"Now, come on, Jack. Calm down. We'll figure it out. We'll use the scientific method. You can't eat your fish clenching your jaw like that anyway. Try it. It tastes best when it's hot. Besides, Frank gets a bit sensitive when people don't eat the food."

Dr. Gallagher rolled his eyes. "Scientific method." Abe's way of chiding him. Dr. Gallagher didn't even like fish. He stuck a piece in his mouth and looked over to the counter. Sure enough, Frank was leaning over the counter and peering at him. Dr. Gallagher nodded and forced a smile at Frank, chewing his bite. Frank nodded and went back to the stove.

"So, what does logic dictate?" Abe asked. "If you were scheduled to see me last night, and you made it over, possibly with a third party we don't remember at the moment, we all had some sort of experience together right around seven o'clock that wiped our slates clean. Say, maybe that's the reason why the MRI doesn't work today."

"Your MRI, the one that costs like, hundreds of millions of dollars, is broken?" Dr. Gallagher asked in disbelief. "And you failed to tell me this, why?"

"It didn't seem important until now. Yes, and an expensive part of it too. The coils that generate the one hundred teslas for the unit melted, and we have no explanation for it. We tried to look on the surveillance recording because as you know, a multimillion-dollar system requires a security system. However, all the security footage had for us was snow. We've been working on it all day, or at least, as far as I can remember, until now. These coils cost millions of dollars. We'll be down for quite a while."

"And you're not upset?"

"Of course I'm upset. But I can't control it, so I'm not going to continue to agonize over it. I guess it's one of those healthy coping mechanisms you're always talking about." Dr. Tetenbaum winked. When he saw the expression on Dr. Gallagher's face, Abe's smile disappeared, and he sighed. "You should have seen me earlier," he admitted. "I was fit to be tied. We have no explanation for what happened to our machine until you showed up this afternoon."

"What do you mean by that?"

"We have two odd occurrences. You show up here, memory free, and all the coils are melted on the unit, and my cockpit is out of commission. Plus, we can't account for a third party. We thought it could have been some sort of electrical malfunction..."

Dr. Gallagher sat up straight. "What did you say?"

"An electrical malfunction." Dr. Tetenbaum paused, tilting his head. "What?"

"I don't know. That sounds familiar for some reason. It's the worst case of déjà vu."

"Maybe you're starting to remember."

"I hope so. So, what works on your MRI?"

"The MRI's built-in video surveillance system—we got that back right before you showed. Unfortunately, the MRI itself is still out of order, but it would seem if anything occurred here last night, that video might prove valuable. We might even have an image in the machine. If an image was taken, I'd probably be able to get to it now."

"Abe, that would be great."

"I finished my lunch and you barely touched yours, so let's get a container for it, and we can go back to the office. Hey, Frank. Do you think we could get a doggie bag here?" Frank shuffled over with a container. "Thanks. See you tomorrow."

Frank nodded.

"You know, Frank is a very funny guy when you get him going," said Dr. Tetenbaum when they stepped outside the restaurant.

Dr. Gallagher looked over his shoulder. Frank stood in the front window of the restaurant, wearing the same expression he did for the entirety of their lunch. "I'm sure," Dr. Gallagher agreed despite the fact that he was unsure if Frank even knew what a sense of humor was.

Dr. Tetenbaum led Dr. Gallagher back to his facility, this time taking him through a locked side entrance leading them straight into the control room. Through the window, he saw a couple of men in lab coats, paper slippers, and paper caps working on the massive unit. Dr. Gallagher couldn't help but feel a welling of admiration when he saw the machine.

Dr. Tetenbaum leaned over the intercom's microphone. "How's it going in there, Cecil?"

"It's going. The coil manufacturer said they can have a new set of coils for us in a few months. They want the old set back to see if they can help us figure out the malfunction and to recycle the materials. We're going over the circuit board now. Everything still seems to be in order."

"That's good. At least those components haven't been fried. So we can access the videos and computer files, right?"

"Yes, you should be all clear, but why do you want to look at those?" asked Cecil.

"Call it a hunch."

"Oh, no, not that. The last time you had one of those we wound up lost in a cornfield."

"Quit your complaining. It allowed us the time to relax and commune with nature," Abe stated with a flourish of his arm.

"Until that farmer thought we were stealing his corn and brought out his shotgun."

Dr. Tetenbaum seemed indifferent as he booted up the screen and pushed a bunch of buttons. "We were driving home from a conference," he explained without turning around. "As you can probably imagine, there have been great advances in the last ten years for MRIs. Believe it or not, those digital cameras you're always raving about have made a great contribution to the advancement of the way MRIs are transmitted from analog to digital, resulting in clearer pictures in a shorter amount of time, and the system runs more efficiently overall. What a wonderful time we live in. I mean, when we were kids, computers filled entire rooms, and you had to be a programmer in order to even use a desktop computer because there wasn't even such a thing as software. Amazing, isn't it?"

"Yes, I'll have to agree with you on that one."

"Yep, fun stuff." Dr. Tetenbaum clicked on some file folders on the screen of his computer. "I'm in the software program now, and I'm looking for something with yesterday's date. And look, here it is."

Dr. Gallagher peered over him at the screen. There was a file folder labeled Miranda Sheppard-Jack Gallagher. The date under the folder, 3-20.

"I've never had the pleasure of introducing a memory before," Dr. Tetenbaum gloated.

Dr. Gallagher rolled his eyes. "Abe, open..."

"Yes, yes. Opening. You get to do that sort of thing all day long, so I was thinking how cool it is to be able to do it for the first time..."

"Abe!"

"Yes, here we go." He double-clicked on the folder. The folder had two files in it, one for the video footage and the next for the image the MRI took. He opened the video footage. A software program opened up, and a black and white image of a young woman in her twenties appeared on the screen. As the video continued, she banged on the wall of the tube and shouted. Then the image turned to snow.

"Do you recognize that woman?" asked Dr. Gallagher.

"No. Do you?"

Dr. Gallagher shook his head. "We were both here for this? How could we not remember this woman or the circumstances that brought her here?"

"You know, Jack. For the first time in a long time, I don't have any answers. As a matter of fact, I'm dumbfounded." Dr. Tetenbaum opened up the second file containing the images the MRI took. "Okay, we did manage to get a full body scan."

"Magnificent!" The clarity of the picture was beyond anything Dr. Gallagher could have imagined. In the three-tesla MRI he had a decade and a half ago, they could see what the one-tesla MRI could not pick up—the bone fragment spiking through his nerves. In the three-tesla MRI, the bones and cartilage appeared as mere shadows. He had felt fortunate that the three-tesla MRI picked up anything at all because until then, the doctors told him that all his pain was in his head, when in fact, all the pain was in his spine all along, just like he told them. After all, with his training, education, and experience, he knew the difference.

At one hundred teslas, it was like seeing a high-tech, sci-fi, three-dimensional body scanner. Even though they managed to capture a full-body scan without focusing in on a particular part of the body, he could see each nerve ending of the entire nervous system, every fold in the brain, and every capillary of the cardiovascular system.

"Yes, I know, it is breathtaking, isn't it?" Dr. Tetenbaum grinned as if it gave him peace of mind.

"It is beautiful. But, what is this around here?" Dr. Gallagher pointed to areas of darkness throughout Miranda's body. It didn't seem like something that could ever be a part of a human. It looked like a massive root system entwined within areas of her body, but it seemed to superimpose itself all throughout. "It seems to be there, all up and down her spine, with finger-like protrusions, but look at all these things here." He pointed to the dark vine-like cords throughout her system. "Is it a malfunction of the equipment of some sort, you know, before it melted?"

Dr. Tetenbaum frowned, absorbed in the image. "That's not normal. That's not what I've seen from our first two subjects. One had a brain tumor. The other had cancer. I don't know why we took an image of this person, but it wasn't for the thrill of it. There is something going on here, but it's not cancer."

"What do you mean?"

"Here." He opened up another folder and brought an image up on the screen. "Look here. You can actually see the tumor in the brain, its shape, and its substance. Now see this one, the cancer patient, we can see the cancerous cells, clearly identifiable from the healthy cells."

"Wow, look at that. I feel like I just got close and personal with cancer. I can't believe I'm actually looking at real cancer cells inside the body without a biopsy."

Dr. Tetenbaum nodded. "Now, take a look at Miranda's image. It almost looks like black plasma or tar-like tendrils. And see how it's intertwined throughout her spine, here, here, here, here," he pointed to the base of her spine, around her belly button, the solar plexus, and in the middle of the chest at the heart, "and here at the throat, and here at her forehead. There's no way this is an equipment malfunction. There is too much detail. And look here."

He pointed to a dark area around her head. "This almost looks like the shape of an eye, and here, a face. This is the strangest thing I've ever seen. As a matter of fact, this collection of tendrils looks like an entire body, superimposed over this woman's body."

Dr. Gallagher examined the face shape. It wasn't as clearly defined as Miranda's body, but he could see something that looked like it had some definition. It drew him in. Could it actually be looking back at him? He stared for a full minute. *I must be seeing things.* The eyes appeared to open and stare back at him. A chill traveled straight down his spine. "This is helping. I think I'm starting to remember. Abe, would you please print me up a copy of this?"

"Sure. What do you suppose this could be?"

"I still don't know. But I know where to go next. Would you also email me that video?"

"Okay." Dr. Tetenbaum sent the email. It took several minutes for the image to print in high resolution, but the system had a top printer because, as Abe said, a multimillion dollar MRI needed to have a top printing system. "Done, and done."

"Abe, thanks for everything." He patted his friend on the shoulder.

"No problem. You'll keep me updated, then?"

"I thought you didn't care about not remembering."

"What can I say? You know scientists. The curiosity always gets the better of me. Good thing I'm not a cat, right?"

Dr. Gallagher smiled. "I'll keep you posted."

"Thanks. Say hello to your wife for me."

"I will. You better think when you have some free time if I do, though, because her next question will be, 'When are you coming over for dinner?'"

Dr. Tetenbaum laughed. "I do love her lemon chicken. I'll check my schedule and let you know."

• • •

Outside the office, Dr. Gallagher called his wife to let her know he would be home late, and as he predicted, she asked when Abe was coming over. He drove to his office. He wished he had some dinner. The thought of his wife's lemon chicken heightened his appetite, but he wasn't willing to eat his doggie bag of smelly fish or stop to satiate his hunger, too eager to get to the office to find more answers. If Miranda was a client, he should have a file and notes on her.

He sat at the receptionist's computer in the darkened, quiet office and typed in *Sheppard, M.* to find the file number. Nothing came up in the system. Frowning, he walked to his office. If she were a client, why wouldn't her name show up?

He went to his desk and looked for her file. He rummaged around the surface, lifting piles of papers. He opened up his top drawer and found a file sitting inside without a name or case number on it. When he opened it up, he saw her name.

Miranda Sheppard. 29 years of age. CPA. Parents died when she was eleven. Raised by sister Alison. Car accident, loss of memory. Paranormal research? He looked at the images from the paranormal research session he didn't remember attending. He wasn't sure Mike and Joe would remember either. The same black areas on the MRI matched the black areas in her thermal image. He took out the image and placed it next to the thermal image printout. He stared wide-eyed at both images, side by side, as he thought of that young woman, trapped in the MRI, scared out of her mind. His heart pulsed in his ears. He had to contact her.

17
DÉJÀ VU

At nine o'clock at night, Dr. Gallagher arrived at Miranda's house, relieved to see a light on in her home at the far corner.

"Who is it?" Miranda peered through the peephole.

"Ms. Sheppard. My name is Dr. Gallagher. May I speak with you? I have an important matter to discuss with you."

"May I see some identification?"

Dr. Gallagher opened up his wallet and held up his license. "Here's my card, also." He slid them underneath the door.

"What is this regarding?" Miranda asked through the door.

"Ms. Sheppard. You and I know each other. You are an accountant. You have a sister named Alison and a boyfriend named Steven. You got into a car accident last May, you still get migraines, and you have a heart condition. As of two o'clock this afternoon, you found yourself in your office, and you had no idea how you got there because the last twenty-four hours are a blank."

What the hell? Who in the world was stalking her? How could he know this? "Go away, or I'll call the police." Her voice pitched with fear. "I have a very, very big dog in here. He's a man-eater. Go away, or he'll have you as a snack." She thought those fake recordings of vicious dogs were stupid, but she sure wished she had it at that moment.

"Ms. Sheppard, I know this is disconcerting. I felt the same way this afternoon. I know because the same exact thing happened to me at the same exact time." He paused and listened. No movement from the other side. "Ms. Sheppard. I normally wouldn't do this, but this has been a very bizarre afternoon, and I am concerned for your safety. I'm concerned for *my* safety. Would you please open the door so we can figure this out?"

Miranda unlocked the door and opened it. She stepped aside and motioned for him to enter.

Talk about déjà vu. The woman had a deep-red hair color and pale skin. He knew a girl growing up who would turn crimson at the slightest embarrassment, same hair and skin. He imagined it happened with Ms. Sheppard as well. He followed her to the living room.

"Let me take your coat."

Dr. Gallagher handed Miranda his coat and baseball cap with the embroidered letters, NESP. She paused as she looked at the cap. "I have the worst case of déjà vu looking at you, like I'm in a fog." She shook her head. "I normally wouldn't have even let you in, but I feel like I know you, except I can't place from where. I should know where I was yesterday and today, but it's like putting something down and misplacing it for a few minutes until you find it again."

"I know. That's been happening to me today, too."

"Here, have a seat." She motioned to the couch.

Dr. Gallagher sat down as she sat on the recliner. He had been here before. How? When? Is this what it felt like for his clients to struggle with remembering?

"So, how did you know what I went through this afternoon? Were you inside my head somehow? I can hardly believe you're real."

Dr. Gallagher couldn't help but chuckle. "Oh, I'm real. Ask my wife. She'll tell you."

Miranda smiled. "You do seem familiar. I don't know where we've met. Did you know my parents?"

Dr. Gallagher nodded. "I read in my notes that I did work with them on a couple of research projects. I think we made this connection during one of our therapy sessions."

"Therapy? With you?"

Dr. Gallagher took a deep breath. This was going to be a hard sell. "Ms. Sheppard, apparently, you are my client." He handed her a copy of the file he read in his office. "You came to me several months ago because you had a car accident and then a bizarre incident that led you to my office."

"Really?" Her tone was skeptical. "Why don't we remember each other? And why don't I remember this bizarre incident?"

"Honestly, I don't know. All I know right now is that we don't remember the last twenty-four hours, and neither did the man who took an MRI of your body last night at 7 PM."

Miranda's expression was incredulous. "I had an MRI? Last night?"

"Yes, and not just any MRI. You had it taken with the most powerful MRI available on the planet."

Miranda shook her head. "You have to be speaking about someone else. I couldn't have possibly..." her voice trailed off, as if the thought caused her pain. "Why in the world would I agree to have this MRI?"

Dr. Gallagher pulled out the thermal image. "Because of this."

"This is me? This isn't me. Who are all these people in the image? This is baloney. That's what this is." Maybe this was some sort of scam. She thought about getting her cell phone ready in case he asked for money or threatened her.

"I can see why you would say that." Dr. Gallagher pulled out a copy of the MRI printout. "You see, I had your initials in my planner for last night. I met with you and my friend, the head scientist in charge of constructing the MRI at the University of Davenport. From what I read in my notes, my friend agreed to run you through the MRI because of this thermal image. Then, something went wrong. Before the MRI blew up, we managed to get this one image from it. The black areas within your body match up with the thermal image."

Miranda glanced down at the images, stood up, and paced. "What the fuck is this?" Logic dictated that the images were some sort of scam, but somehow, she knew he spoke the truth.

"I don't know. Dr. Tetenbaum, the MRI guy, was also able to capture this." Dr. Gallagher took out his laptop and turned it on. He opened the file Abe sent him and turned it around to Miranda.

Miranda watched intently. She handed Dr. Gallagher his laptop. "What the fuck did you two do to me? Did you sickos drug me?"

Dr. Gallagher worked to maintain his cool. "Miranda, please, take some time to read the file before you jump to any conclusions. You can read an account of everything that has transpired between us for the last several months. When I saw the video, I didn't wait one second more. I came right over because I was concerned. If we do have a therapist-client relationship, I want to continue that relationship. If you are in any danger, I want to help you."

"Why do you think this is dangerous for me?"

"The video, for one. Whatever happened, it contained enough power to melt the ten-million-dollar coils on the MRI."

Miranda inhaled in a deep breath as her eyes opened wide. Her head reeled. How could she not remember? It just wasn't possible. Pursuing therapy, an MRI, a ghost hunt? She certainly would have remembered. Right?

Right?

She couldn't remember what she did for the last 24 hours. And Dr. What's-his-face looked so familiar, the only reason she didn't kick him out for knowing so much about her, which was so super creepy, she felt pinpricks all around her skin.

Dr. Gallagher continued. "And the fact we can't explain how the same anomaly showed up on two different images with two different instruments, exactly the same way. We could say it was an equipment malfunction if it only showed up on one. But we can't really say that because here it is, an exact duplicate on the other. I believe that is why we went to have the MRI done. We wanted to see if the anomaly would show up again. The MRI contains the world's strongest magnet, which would prove you have something dwelling inside of you, and we need to address it as soon as possible."

"What in the world do we do with all this? What can we do now?" Miranda closed her eyes as if she was hoping Dr. Gallagher would disappear.

"I do have someone we can see. We can see her tomorrow morning. Can you do the same?"

"Tomorrow's Friday. I think I can." Even though it was tax season, she tried to keep her Fridays light and not make any appointments.

"Okay. Let me call her now, right here, and we can confirm it." Dr. Gallagher took out his cell phone. "Hi, Grace. It's Jack. Yes, she's doing well, thank you. Yes, her lemon chicken is still really good. Of course I will, but you know she'll just want you to come over again for dinner. Grace, the reason I'm calling is because I have a situation, and I could use your expertise. It's very difficult to explain over the telephone. Can I bring a client and see you tomorrow morning? Yes, it's that important. Tonight? Now?" He looked at Miranda. Miranda shrugged as she considered it, and then nodded her head. "Yes, we can come now. How did you... never mind. You know the way you always know, right? Okay, we'll see you in twenty minutes."

Miranda had already gotten up and put on her boots. "Ready."

"Are you okay with this?"

"I have to be. I might be scared, and I might not like it, but I have to face it. If this thing has been able to wipe our memories clean it could be dangerous." In the past, she preferred to avoid her pain, but... it was difficult to put into words. She just met, well, remet this doctor, but she already felt like she knew him. Something seemed so familiar about him, and his blue eyes carried so much concern for her. Plus, he seemed just as upset. Regardless of her personal feelings for him, they both experienced an event at the same exact time, and he had information that he could only know if they did spend some time together. The sooner she worked with him, the sooner they would both find their answers.

Dr. Gallagher nodded. "I admire your courage, Ms. Sheppard."

"Who are we going to see?" Miranda gathered her purse and coat.

"Grace. She has been my mentor for years. If anyone knows what to make of all of this, she will."

• • •

Miranda liked Grace's apartment. Not the biggest apartment she had seen, but the rooms were spacious enough to sport darker, warm-colored walls without a closed-in feeling that paired well with the big, soft furniture and décor, a concerted, effective effort to create an atmosphere of comfort, easing Miranda's edginess, the thing she needed. Entering the apartment felt like a safe haven.

Miranda hoped she aged well, like Grace. Her hair was still blond and pretty, her smile unfettered with lines around her hazel eyes and mouth that characteristically come with age, and she didn't have that pulled, stretched look common with facelifts.

"Miranda, this is Dr. Grace Kelly," Dr. Gallagher said.

"Really?" Miranda shook Grace's hand.

"Yes, really. My mother loved the princess. No relation, though. As a child, I didn't enjoy having the name, but right before my mother passed, she told me that I had always been her little princess. Now, I love my name." Grace took Miranda and Dr. Gallagher's jackets. "Come have a seat." She extended her hand toward the sofa.

Dr. Gallager sat. "Thank you. Grace, we've experienced something you may not have come across before. We were hoping you could point us in a direction."

Dr. Gallagher ran through a synopsis of the content in the file and what they experienced in the last twenty-four hours. Grace examined the images and the diagram of the chakras.

"And that is all we know," Dr. Gallagher concluded.

"Do you still have no memory of your last several months with each other?" Dr. Kelly asked.

"It seems familiar, but I don't remember it as if I lived through it," Miranda said.

"Same here," said Dr. Gallagher.

Dr. Kelly thought for a moment. If she ever trusted anyone, it was Jack Gallagher. Grace was the last person to discount anything as impossible, and if she were anyone else, she would most likely suspect shared hysteria. *Good thing I'm not everyone else.* "I could do some relaxation techniques. Maybe it will allow you access to the memories."

"You mean, like hypnosis?" asked Miranda.

"It's more like meditation. I'm not sure if it's a good idea to confront this head on yet, so meditation will be a good way to work around it. It's quiet around here this time of night, but I'll play some music for white noise. Why don't you make yourselves comfortable any way you like, and I'll get the music ready."

Dr. Gallagher spied the reclining chair. He pointed and asked Miranda, "Do you mind?"

"No, that's okay. You have it. I'll take the couch," Miranda took off her boots and slid her legs onto the couch. Dr. Gallagher sat on the recliner and pushed the handle to put his legs out.

"Do you want anything to eat or drink before we begin?" Dr. Kelly called.

"Nope, I'm good here," said Miranda.

"Same." Starved as he was, a full stomach would make him fall asleep. Meditation and a full stomach paired with his daily back and neck pain didn't mix.

"Okay, then. I think we're ready to begin." Dr. Kelly started the music, a collection of soft wind instruments with ocean waves set in the background, walked over to her chair, and sat down.

"I see you both have gotten comfortable. Good. Now, I want you to listen to the music and close your eyes. Listen to the ocean waves in the background. Take in a deep breath, visualizing golden, white light. Hold it and feel the light spreading to all parts of your body. Listen to the music. Feel the waves wash over you, relaxing all your muscles.

"There is a part of your mind that is like a recorder of everything you ever said, done, and experienced. You have full access to those files now. Open the file from yesterday. Allow yourself to become part of the scene." Dr. Kelly paused for a few moments.

Miranda's muscles complied with the soothing tone of Dr. Kelly's voice. She saw a giant brick wall. She gulped, and her stomach tightened.

"Miranda, what do you see?"

"A brick wall."

"So do I," Dr. Gallagher confirmed.

Dr. Kelly frowned. *If they both see a wall, chances are, something else created it.*

"When most people see a brick wall, they perceive it as a block. They think it has physical substance to it. They think they have to walk around it, break through it, or climb over it. Your walls do not have to have any substance to them. Your walls have no permanence to them. You see your walls melt away to reveal the truth."

Miranda felt like she should be upset, but the meditation put her at a distance from it, like an outside observer. *I can't believe this is working.* Dr. Kelly's voice was so calm and soothing. She saw a white light surround her and the wall dissipate into a wispy vapor.

"Now your walls should have disappeared. It's time to go back to yesterday. Everything has been recorded and stored in your memory. All you have to do is access it, and you will remember what happened. In your mind, you might see the connection to that memory as a road or tunnel. Go through that tunnel or walk down that road now. When you arrive, you will see what has been blocked."

Miranda relaxed almost to the point of falling asleep. She found herself on a dirt road surrounded by trees, the road to the lake where her family vacationed during her childhood. She looked around and sniffed the fresh air. Fresh-cut grass tingled her nose, intermingling with the smell of water from the lake. She walked to the cabin they rented every summer. It felt like home again.

Her hand shook as she reached for the door handle. *Is Mom here?* She peeked inside and looked around. All the wonderful memories rushed in when she took a deep breath, making her eyes sting with wistfulness and longing for a time when life was nearly perfect and she was almost always happy.

"Hello, Mom?" she called in a tiny, hopeful voice.

Her mother appeared from the kitchen. She had on a t-shirt and jean shorts, same blond ponytail, her cheeks sun-kissed and her skin smoothed by lake water and country air.

Unable to do anything else, Miranda stood and stared. Her mother smiled and extended her arms. Miranda rushed into them.

18
Journey

Dr. Gallagher had been through these sessions with Grace before. *She is the master of meditation.* She taught him all of her techniques while under her guidance as he worked to obtain his license in clinical psychology. He melted into the easy chair. *I'll have to ask her where she bought this recliner.* The nagging pain in his back and neck and his empty, growling stomach kept sleeping at bay.

He saw his brick wall evaporate. He scanned his surroundings. He could hear the sound of a rushing river, and in front of him stood a footbridge set in concrete on either side. He smelled the fresh water. He looked over the side and saw the rushing water beneath him. Never had his meditation seemed so real-to-life.

He came to the end of the bridge and looked around, transporting him back to the Bronx, right in front of his old high school. Three kids walked toward him. *Why do they look familiar?*

"Gimme your jacket," one of the kids threatened. These kids tried to mug him when he was a freshman in high school. He looked around. This time, Dr. Gallagher's friends were not there to back him up.

"I don't think so."

The kid took out a knife. "Give me your jacket and your fucking shoes. And if you don't, I'll take all your clothes, and you'll be naked *and* bleeding."

As he had so many years ago, Dr. Gallagher kicked the knife out of the kid's hand, punched him in the nose, and knocked him to the ground, and his friends ran off and left him. The kid squirmed around on the ground, struggling to get up and holding his hand to the front of his face. The blood protruded from his fingers and sopped the front of his shirt. "You broke my fucking nose!"

"And I'll break the rest of your goddamn bones if you even dare get up!" Staying down after a blow meant submission of his opponent, a feat he had to accomplish over and over again as a teenager. "Next are both your knees. Or how about that hand of yours that pointed that goddamned, mother-fucking knife at my throat?"

The kid cowered on the ground and held his bleeding nose.

Dr. Gallagher gave him a menacing stare and turned. His large hands made perfect weapons. They carried him successfully through countless fights when he balled them into a fist, and the strength in his frame ensured that once hit, his opponents avoided getting back up again to fight him even when they were capable.

He took ten steps. Suddenly, his back stung, almost knocking him to the ground. He winced and flung himself around. He looked up. The "L," what they called the subway tracks in the Bronx, hung high above him in the air. The gang competing with the Grim Reapers for turf near the park surrounded him, a reenactment of the gang fight he endured thirty years ago. He faced the teenager with the chain. His opponent's black leather jacket reflected the dim light of the 7-Eleven, and his three friends, one with a baseball bat, and one with a knife. The guy swung the chain to hit him again. Dr. Gallagher planted his feet, a trick he learned in karate class. All four rushed at him.

The boys attacking him vanished and turned into inmates. Dr. Gallagher looked around. The scene had morphed into the rotunda at the New England State Prison and placed him in the middle of the riot that had broken out while he worked there. He and his friend Jeff, another correction officer, stood back-to-back, several inmates rushing them at a time. Having no time to appreciate seeing his friend again, even if it were in a meditative vision, Dr. Gallagher blocked two blows but was hit several more times in various areas of his body. Behind them, fifty more inmates readied themselves for their shot to become king of the cellblock, the status inmates obtained for killing a correction officer.

"Jeff!" More inmates rushed toward him.

"Yeah."

"Listen. We have to make it out of here. We are not going down, no matter what. We stay back-to-back. I got your back and you got mine. And you go for the kill. Got it?"

"I got your back, Jack."

An inmate swung at Jack. Jack took the inmate's arm in his large hands and produced a cracking sound. The inmate screamed, his arm hanging at this side, and he hit the floor. Upon witnessing the ease Jack broke their fellow inmate's arm, the shock value made some inmates take a step back, but three others charged at Jack. Jack took the arm of one guy, pulled him in, and smacked him in the face with Jack's large, hard elbow. The guy in the middle—his crotch had a meeting with Jack's foot. He screamed and hit the floor in agony.

Jack's fighting prowess didn't faze the last guy. He towered over everyone else, a full head taller than the other men, even Jack. Since he didn't have anything else to do for the last six years other than work out, he built up his six-foot-six frame into a wall of muscle, which is why the other inmates called him Brick. He glowered, looking as if he wanted to taste Jack's blood.

Jack took one look at him and kicked him right on the kneecap. Brick bent over, howling and holding his knee. Jack kicked him square in the face. Brick went down hard. Blood spurted between his fingers. Brick removed his hand and spat out his front teeth.

A lull came over the other seventy inmates. A dark, tall figure appeared from the back of the crowd. The inmates, as if this man were the alpha male, kowtowed to him as he walked toward Jack, taking him aback. *This didn't happen during the riot.* He readied himself as the figure drew closer. The towering figure stepped in front of him, his face darkened over. *What the fuck is going on?*

"Miranda is mine." The towering figure brought a steel bar down on him. Suddenly, Dr. Gallagher remembered everything.

• • •

Miranda and her mother stood at the front door hugging. She wanted to stay in her mother's arms forever.

Her mother whispered in her ear. "Come out to the lake with me. We have to be quiet because he might hear." She pointed up.

"Who?"

"Him."

"You mean, God?" Miranda asked incredulously.

Her mother shook her head. "The opposite of God," she whispered. She motioned her daughter to follow her.

Miranda followed her mother through the small house and out the back. They went down a path and sat at the picnic table overlooking the lake.

Joy took her daughter's hands when they sat down. "Honey, listen to me now. I'll always love you, and I'm always here to protect you no matter what."

"Mom, you're scaring me."

"I'm scared too."

"You mean, dead people get scared? Why?"

Her mother held her gaze. "When your father and I passed, Alison had wondered if our passing was more than a car accident. She has really great instincts without even knowing it."

Something gnawed in the pit of Miranda's stomach.

"She was right, in a sense. Your father and I had stumbled onto something, ancient wisdom combined with modern knowledge. We experienced this reality one day with a shared client. The person was very sick. He felt listless, and he said he felt like half a person. We didn't know what to do with him. It led us to a book, and it described what our patient was experiencing to a tee. We followed the directives in the book, and we cured the patient. It's when we actually saw our first id. Because of our experiences, we set out to prove it exists."

Miranda's mind flashed to the set of papers she found at the house. "You mean, those weird pictures from *Id Speak?*"

"Yes. That's good. You're starting to remember." Joy took her daughter's hands and held them. "Almost twenty years ago, the technology wasn't even there. That MRI you had yesterday was beyond our wildest dreams."

Miranda recalled the video of her trapped inside of the tube of the MRI, pounding on the walls to get out. "Mom, what happened to me yesterday? And why was Alison right?"

"Our accident. We veered off the road because there was someone standing in the middle of it, or so we thought."

A tear trickled down Miranda's cheek. "Who was it?"

"We didn't know for a long time. But then, we started to understand when you got into your car accident."

"Was the same person involved in my car accident?"

"In a way. He's trying to gain full possession of you."

“What in the world do you mean by that Mom?” *Oh God, what in the world was happening? How could any of this be real at all?*

Joy helped her daughter wipe her tears and took her hands again. “I don’t have much time, my love. We guided you toward finding Dr. Gallagher. Remember, you’re not alone. We will do as much as we can to help you fight. Keep us here.” She pointed to Miranda’s heart. “It is your connection to the light. Remember, love is not bound by space or time.”

Everything went dark. Her mother disappeared. Two dark eyes peered at her. “Lights out,” they growled.

19
REVELATION

Dr. Kelly sat and observed the two. Dr. Gallagher thrashed around a bit, and Miranda had tears on her cheek. Dr. Gallagher and Miranda sat up at the same time, both breathing like they had just run a marathon. Dr. Gallagher jumped up. He looked around the room, dazed, almost like he expected someone to be there.

"I remember everything," Miranda exclaimed.

"So do I."

They seemed troubled to Dr. Kelly. "So, tell me what happened. Who wants to go first?"

"I had a vision about my mother. She helped me remember everything. And I saw him. I don't know what to think."

"I saw him too," Dr. Gallagher chimed.

"Oh, Dr. Gallagher. I am happy to hear you say that. I'm sorry for the way I acted tonight."

"It's alright, Miranda."

"Who did you both see?" asked Dr. Kelly.

"It was the man standing over me in the hospital. He was in my house, and Alison, my sister, saw him, and he hit me over the head. Oh, my God, Alison, Steven. Do you think they remember anything at all?" The entity blocked their memories. *This must mean we uncovered its existence during the MRI.* For the first time since her journey began over a year ago, she fully realized the precariousness of her situation. It took over her entire body, her hands trembling.

"Probably not because Dr. Tetenbaum didn't remember either," Dr. Gallagher reported.

"It should stay that way. Alison took care of me. She should be happy and marry, no matter..." she paused when her throat became thick with oncoming tears, "...no matter what happens to me. God, what is this thing? What do I do?" Miranda stood up and paced. "I can't believe this, but I wish I was crazy. I wish I had cancer like I first thought. At least I would know what I am fighting. Is it a spirit? How in the world could he wipe out our memories? What the fuck does he want with me? And he's inside of me, somewhere?" She sobbed, clutching her chest. "How could this happen? How can I not feel that he's there? How gross is that?" There was no denying it; an entity housed itself in her body. The ghosthunter's image capture, the MRI, and now both she and Dr. Gallagher saw this monstrosity of a man... or whatever it was.

Dr. Kelly offered Miranda a box of tissues. Miranda shook her head and plunked down on the couch. Dr. Kelly sat next to her and put her arm around Miranda's shoulder, and then looked up at Dr. Gallagher.

After decades of practice, Dr. Gallagher had built a wall around his heart so he didn't get dragged down into other people's pain. Otherwise, he would become a useless pile of mush. He had helped all sorts of people identify ghosts and demons from their past, figuratively speaking. Distance is healthy for therapists. With this young woman, nothing was identifiable. For the first time in a long time, Miranda's pain tugged at his heart. How to explain the unexplainable? Yet, most everything in the universe contained patterns. There had to be something they could analyze that would at least help them understand the entity, if not the nature of it, then its behavior. "Because it went through a lot of trouble to stay hidden. Let's think back, now that you've recovered everything. What was your first hint that something was wrong?"

Miranda wiped her eyes and nose. Her expression changed from moment to moment as various thoughts and feelings flashed before her, indicating a revelation grew near.

"I remember," she said, almost in awe. "I remember the trouble I had sleeping for months. Is it connected somehow?"

"Yes, if that is the first thing that came to mind. What do you think it could be?" asked Dr. Gallagher. This was good. It was ground they had not had the chance to cover.

"Everything was going fine. I mean, I had a tough childhood with my parents' death, but these days, who doesn't? In honor of my parents, I straightened up. I moved on. Everything was fine until I had trouble sleeping."

"Why do you think you had trouble sleeping?" asked Dr. Gallagher.

"I don't know." Miranda jumped up. "It's what started all those trips to the doctors. I was tested for everything from cancer to a yeast infection. No one could peg a cause. Dr. Singer, the oncologist, referred me to you. I should have listened."

"Okay, Miranda. Take a few breaths and try and clear your mind a little," said Dr. Kelly.

Miranda took a few deep breaths. *Okay, calm down. I'm not alone.* Another image blazoned in front of her eyes. "I know. I haven't remembered this in months. Oh, God, they were horrible images. They haunted me. I thought I was losing my mind. I couldn't sleep for more than ten minutes at a time."

"Can you describe the images?" asked Dr. Gallagher.

Miranda closed her eyes. "The world was in disarray, destroyed beyond our comprehension. Everyone just lost it, and the images I saw, they were worse than war, worse than death. It was like hell.

And these creatures, black, ugly. Blackness covered the entire planet. I couldn't do anything to stop it. And what felt like an all-night nightmare would only be five minutes of restless sleep. Then the entire thing would reset, and I would see it over and over again. And I couldn't sleep, night after night after night. I felt like they were chasing me. If this is our destiny, everything we know and love will be gone forever!" What a nightmare her existence had been. She was so tired, she would fall asleep sitting up, all of the time. She had fallen asleep right in front of a client. She was more annoyed and embarrassed than the client, who was so sweet, all she did was express concern for her. She remained in a state of exhaustion, the images haunting her every time she closed her eyes. It was hell, not being able to sleep even though exhaustion permeated her entire existence.

Oh God, Dr. Gallagher thought. This wasn't a hallucination. Miranda housed a visitor who was not only black of substance but had the darkest intentions. *Could he be teaching her to envision the worst that could possibly happen to humanity, what could be the most sadistic and painful, what we could do to each other? What did I get myself into?*

He looked over at Dr. Kelly. *Grace, so intuitive. She knows what this all means.* While Dr. Kelly was the one who trained him to use his facial expressions as part of his therapy, he knew her "tells," the shifting of her legs, pressing her lips together. She got it too. This could be bigger than any one of them.

Dr. Gallagher frowned. "We don't really have any precedents to go by, so we need to make sense of it ourselves. We'll take this piece-by-piece to observe patterns. So, before that, it sounded like life was the way you wanted it. Anything lacking at that point?"

"I did wish I had a boyfriend or something, but I figured that would come with time when the right one came along, so I didn't worry about it. When I felt lonely, I visited Alison."

"Okay, so life was moving along, and it sounds like you were satisfied for the most part. And the death of your parents?"

"Of course, I miss them every day, still, but I'm an adult now. As angry as I was, I think I outgrew a lot of those old feelings."

Dr. Gallagher made a mental note to come back to that later, knowing full well that after a tragic event, people don't *outgrow* the feelings related to that loss: they transition, they learn to cope, and they grow from the experience if they deal with those feelings constructively. "Then the images and lack of sleep, right?"

"Yes."

"And how about after your accident?"

"I had no memory of the accident or the disturbing dreams."

"You didn't remember the months before your accident, the lack of sleep?"

"No. But I did keep a journal." Miranda's eyes lit up for just a moment. Where was that thing? "But I don't know where it is now."

Dr. Gallagher frowned and rubbed his beard. "That's okay. You're remembering a lot without it for the moment. The insomnia could be the point of entry, when he first tried to settle in, working to weaken you until he could take hold. Grace, it sounds like we need to make a chart."

"It sure does. I'll get a marker and a board." As Grace looked for a piece of poster board, she reflected upon how far Dr. Gallagher had come. When he interned under her, she spotted his talent. There are so many out there who aren't talented in what they do, and unfortunately, this holds true in the field of psychology and medicine. She was happy to have Dr. Gallagher as a student because at least she could say that she helped one person find his true calling. She found a poster board and marker and brought it out to the living room.

Dr. Gallagher laid the poster board flat on the coffee table. "So," he uncapped the marker and wrote as he spoke, "the first time you noticed something was wrong, when would you say, February, January?"

"End of January."

"Okay. Then you had trouble sleeping, for how long?"

"Several months, right up to my accident, and it probably caused my accident."

"Right. Okay." Dr. Gallagher marked the poster board. "So, the accident occurred, and you were unconscious for a while, right?"

"About a week or so."

"That's when you first saw him?"

"Yes, in the hospital, but I thought I had a hallucination while I was under. Do you agree this is when he really, um, moved into me?" *How disgusting!*

"He could have taken advantage of the accident to take hold. Then after the accident, you regained consciousness, no memory of not being able to sleep. You attributed that to the accident, correct?"

"Yes."

"He could have blocked your memories. We know now that he's capable of it. Then what is the next occurrence?"

"Hmm." Miranda put her hand on her chin as she thought. She described the vine-like apparitions she thought she saw around everyone when she came to during Thanksgiving dinner. Dr. Gallagher diligently made notes.

"Okay, so, you got dizzy at Thanksgiving dinner. What's next?"

"Um, then Alison told me about her intentions to sell the house, and I went to go clear out some of my stuff. Jeez, I have to get going on that. That's when I found those papers, the research my parents were doing right before their passing. My Mom said in my, um, what do you call it? My vision, I guess. She said that she and my father were trying to find a way to prove the existence of the id. Then they had their accident. She didn't go into details about it, but she said they saw a man standing in the middle of the road, and they veered to avoid hitting him, and that's when the car veered off the road and down the side of the mountain."

"Hmm." Dr. Gallagher flipped over the poster board and wrote the parents' research and their accident on the back. "Okay. What's next?"

Miranda thought for a moment. "When I discovered that paperwork and read through it, my sister had made some notes. She suspected all along that there was more to my parents' accident. I wanted to go investigate the site where my parents crashed. I had a migraine that morning, and I had planned to meet Steven in the evening at my office, so I wanted to go in the afternoon to check it out."

"Migraine, then you went to go investigate the site?"

"No. I didn't remember this when I first saw you, but I never made it there. That's when I guess I knew I saw him for certain, in the mirror in my bathroom, and then in my kitchen." She shuddered. *What does he want from me? Why can't I feel him all of the time?*

"Alright, got it."

"Then, we discovered that Alison saw the man right after my accident in my house when she took care of me."

"So we have several appearances total by that time, not including what your parents saw before their accident, correct?"

"Yes."

"Okay." He backtracked to Miranda's accident and wrote in Alison's sighting.

"After that, I put in my security system, and we got the paranormal researchers over to the house."

"So, when we tried to capture its image, it seemed to defend itself again, and it blew up all the light bulbs on your bottom floor," observed Dr. Gallagher.

"Yes. And I found out I have a heart condition related to the accident."

"Then what?"

"Alison, I guess, received the thermal image. We decided to do the MRI after I dreamed about my mother."

"Okay, so MRI, then it wiped out, let's see, one, two, three... at least five people's memories, and it melted the coils on the MRI."

"And that takes us to now. I saw him again in my vision. My mother warned me about him. She told me to hold my love for her in my heart, that it would give me hope and help save me somehow."

"Did she tell you anything else?"

"She said something about fighting the darkness."

Dr. Gallagher wrote those revelations inside quotation marks.

"And, she told me she and my father guided me to you."

Dr. Gallagher smiled and nodded. "In the vision, what triggered the return of your memory?"

"What my mom said to me in my first dream; love is not bound by space or time. And right after that, he came in and said 'lights out' again, and it snapped me awake."

"Yes, I saw him too, at the end of mine, and that's when I came out of it too."

"What did he say to you?" asked Dr. Kelly.

"To leave Miranda alone." He worded this carefully so the poor woman would not fall into a blind panic. As it was, he saw nearly every emotion pass over her face as she struggled to remember the involvement the entity had in many points of her life. This woman had a lot of skill and resources, but he didn't want to send her over the edge.

Miranda shuddered. "Oh!" she exclaimed. "And I had that creepy dream the morning before my crash, and I think I remember something while I was in the hospital. Do you think that's important?"

"I think everything is important," said Dr. Gallagher. "Tell me about it."

"In the dream, I had this feeling the stars were all examining me, like I was an experiment. Then I saw these black eyes, the same ones in my meditative vision. I also saw the same black vines I saw around my sister and the Foremans during Thanksgiving dinner as I woke up on the couch."

Dr. Gallagher took notes. "Tell me more about the incident in the hospital."

"While I was half in and out of it and on the respirator, I dreamed these dark aliens had tied my wrists. They were black and kind of slimy and were made completely of tentacles, but they seemed to be in the shape of a body like ours. They told me at the hospital that this is a common false memory that happens when they stick that tube down your throat, but I don't think it's a false memory in my case. Oh, and the last and the worst, right after my crash, I think I visited hell." Miranda shared every vision that had been forced on her as they made her watch, almost like they were trying to train her to accept total dehumanization, erasing her humanity altogether. Miranda took a deep breath. "Before the accident, it felt like something external was trying to break in. After the accident, I saw the same images, but instead of being able to avoid them, like I was in my waking hours, I was..." Anger and pain flared, stealing the breath away from her lungs as she remembered the violation. "They forced me to watch everything they wish to rain down upon mankind, while I was unconscious and unable to defend myself. It was worse than even the sickest of imaginations could imagine. Then, after that, everything felt to me as if it was, well, internalized."

Dr. Gallagher thought it best to withhold how much the information bothered him, so he continued, business as usual. Working in the prison, he heard what he surmised was the worst of the worst: a serial killer's childhood, the abject abuse and neglect, and how the serial killer lived out his life afterwards. Miranda's experiences were quickly becoming the most awful set of circumstances he had ever heard. It bothered him more than a little bit, and containing his discomfort became more and more of a challenge as Miranda spoke. "Okay, let's see if the pattern emerges. Can you see anything?"

Miranda studied the poster board. "I can see in the first several months with the insomnia, that's probably when he first arrived. But, why at that point?"

"Like you said, it sounded like you were at the calmest point of your life. You had a tough childhood because of the loss of your parents, but you are well-established as an adult. You refocused your energy when you were a teenager so your conscious mind wouldn't focus on it. Unfortunately, your fight for survival made it easier for him to normalize himself to your energy because your parent's death and its profound effects weren't really resolved but went into hiding. Also, it seems like you were sensing his presence in the semi-conscious state. Look, you have the images right before you fall asleep and that dream right before your accident. It's almost like he had to create the accident so he could move in and then remain hidden and undetected."

Miranda stared at the poster board. "It seems like when I was just about to discover something about him, he would wipe out my memory. Look, after the accident, memory loss. Then I read the paperwork and wanted to visit the site where my parents died. Memory loss. Then he blew everything up when Mike and Joe visited, I think, so he could hide himself."

"Yes, good point, almost like he is trying to buy time." Dr. Gallagher made notes on the board, hoping that "buying time" did not matriculate into the worst of his fears. "But, he couldn't destroy everything because we got our first image, the thermal image."

"Yes, and the MRI."

"The electromagnetic energy from the MRI coils and magnetic field gave him a boost of power so he could wipe out all our memories." Again, in an attempt to not allow his fears to overtake Miranda, he didn't speak about how this was most likely another stalling tactic. The entity could not wipe out their memories completely. He and Miranda's entire relationship was based upon finding out what exactly was going on with her, so it was more difficult for the entity to erase itself from their memories. However, he did take note of the fact that it would be a lot less likely for Alison and Steven to remember Miranda's trouble as nothing else but her heart condition. At the very least, it slowed Miranda and Dr. Gallagher down for 24 hours, and it shrank the circle of people who knew about the entity. "At least we know what it did and some reasons as to why it did it. Now we have to figure out what it is."

"Why has it latched onto me? Dr. Gallagher, why do I remember everything now, and why did we both see him in our vision? It's almost like it allowed us to remember all of this. This couldn't be good for him."

"I don't think he has a choice. These memories have become part of your conscious process, almost like..." Dr. Gallagher paused.

"Almost like it doesn't have control of all the processes," Dr. Kelly suggested. "Notice, even when it had enough energy blow up the MRI, it was only able to put up a figurative wall between the subconscious and the conscious. Plus, although Miranda didn't know it at the time, she could actually sense him when she was in a semi-conscious state, upon falling asleep and waking."

"So, it can't control all of me." It was the first time Dr. Gallagher saw Miranda get excited. "It can't control all of my thoughts, and it can't control my will, and it can't control my physical body."

"So acting now to get rid of it is essential," Dr. Kelly observed.

"But we do know for certain it's here," Dr. Gallagher added. "So, where do you think we should start?"

Grace thought for a moment. "One thing I noticed. When Miranda's parents started their research, the entity made sure he played a factor in their early demise. I think we should obtain a copy of that book, *Id Speak*, somehow, but it's not easy to get. I think I know where I can send you. He has an extensive library of unique books. Here." She wrote down the name and address. "You tell him Grace Kelly sent you, although you won't need to."

Dr. Gallagher cocked his head to one side. *I wonder what she meant by that?*

"So, Jack. What did you see in your vision?" Grace looked into his eyes.

From Dr. Gallagher's grimace, she gathered it was not pleasant to remember.

"It's not important. It's all water under the bridge."

20
FAITH

Grace never spoke of any other human being in derogatory terms. The adjectives she used to describe Dr. Widener were *colorful* and *reclusive*. She warned Dr. Gallagher that Dr. Widener didn't have a telephone and had cut himself off from the modern world for his sabbatical. Instead of traveling to Europe, Dr. Kelly shared, he decided to "take his sabbatical on an inward journey."

Dr. Widener lived a couple of hours outside Davenport, beyond the more affluent neighborhoods and into the countryside that supplied much of the local area with its fruits, vegetables, and livestock. Dr. Gallagher offered to drive, observing the all-nighter had taken its toll on Miranda. Besides, he told her, he had pulled so many all-nighters throughout his young adult life, it did not require much effort to pull another one. What he didn't divulge—at this point, his back and neck pain was so profound, it radiated from the core of his bones, making sleep impossible. He had become so accustomed to hiding his condition that Miranda did not notice his slight winces and limping to the car. Corporate America is usually not very kind to people with disabilities, and before he went into the partnership with Jerry, he had to pretend that nothing bothered him, doing his best not to stand out in any way, and certainly not asking his jobs for accommodations that he should have been able to access according to the Disability Act. Miranda reclined the passenger's seat, and the moment they reached the city's outer limits, the white landscape lulled her to sleep.

They traveled up and down the roads hugging the contour of the mountains. Despite his pain, Dr. Gallagher also found himself becoming sleepy from the monotony of the desolate landscape. He enjoyed springtime rather than winter. The landscape transformed from boring, monotonous, and scrubby to rich, green, and lush. The air smelled fresher, and he loved to open the windows and breathe in the smells of earth as signs of life sprouted from the trees through the sunshine, which almost never made an appearance through the gray clouds of winter.

Two hours after they embarked upon their journey, Dr. Gallagher found Dr. Widener's house set back from the road, almost like it had been erected in secrecy. Grace warned him: all he would see were trees and a large wall of shrubbery. When he drove down the driveway, which was more like a small road, he saw the evergreen trees planted together in a row, forming almost a fortress, and a row of evergreen shrubs providing a wall directly behind the tree trunks. They did a very good job of concealing the house behind them.

Dr. Gallagher tapped Miranda's arm. "We're here." She was well into dreamland. Miranda's breath made a raspy, soft, airy noise. "Miranda." He picked her hand up and dropped it in her lap. He shook his head. He decided to give her a few more minutes of sleep.

If he didn't find the car to be such a painful place to sleep, he would have considered getting some rest himself. If he were still in his twenties and convinced he would live forever, he would have had no problem getting a little shut-eye wherever he pleased, but with the deep ache in his bones, he couldn't even consider it. If he had known how he was going to feel in twenty years, he would not have gotten into so many fistfights in his youth. He rubbed his neck, sore and swollen after the long drive and the constant supply of snow. *We really have to move,* he thought, down south where winters wouldn't be as difficult on him.

"Miranda, we're here." Dr. Gallagher shook Miranda's shoulder until he saw some movement.

Miranda took in a deep breath and stretched. Her eyes fluttered open for a moment and then shut again. Going on empty made her stomach feel like it had gut rot. "God, life sucks without caffeine. How long have I been out for?"

"Almost two hours. You ready for this?"

She opened her eyes, but all she could do was squint against the bright light reflecting off the snow. Her face scrunched up as she smacked her lips. She dug through her purse to find a mint and popped one in her mouth. She offered one to Dr. Gallagher. He nodded and took one from the little tin box. "No, but I'm going anyway. Is there even a house here?"

"Yes. Grace said it's behind the bushes."

Miranda put her seat back up, groaned and stretched again, and rubbed her face with both her hands, allowing her hands to stop and rest on her cheeks, and squished them together. "I miss caffeinated coffee," she said through her puckered lips.

Dr. Gallagher laughed. His wife and he had decided long ago to not have children, but if he had any, he wouldn't have minded it if they turned out like Miranda and Alison. "Come on."

They got out of the car and ventured down the pathway in front of the bushes, their feet crunching on old snow that had formed a hollow top layer, as if the flakes unionized to protect the softer, bottom layers from the elements.

Dr. Gallagher rang the doorbell. "Dr. Kelly said sometimes it takes a while for him to answer the door."

Miranda nodded, imagining a fragile, little old man.

After a few moments passed, Dr. Gallagher depressed the doorbell's button again, this time resting on it then letting it go a bit slower to extend its sound.

"Yes, yes, coming," said a male voice, and after some shuffling from behind the door, the door opened. From Grace's description, Dr. Gallagher expected someone more like his friend Abe, eccentric and outlandish, but Dr. Widener didn't seem like that at all. Average height, thin. Hs hair, not very short or long, black with streaks of white. Dr. Gallagher estimated that Dr. Kelly and Dr. Widener were probably around the same age. He donned a knitted black shirt and dark gray pants. "Just finishing the preparations," Dr. Widener stated instead of greeting them with the normal hello.

"Preparations?" asked Dr. Gallagher. "I'm sorry, you must..."

"Jack, right? And this, this is Miranda." Dr. Widener took her hands and smiled.

"Oh, Dr. Kelly said you don't have a phone," said Miranda.

"I don't. Come, come in."

"Email? A cell phone?" Miranda followed him inside.

"No, none of those things. All the modern trappings, the Internet, the social networks, chatting, texting, television, they distract us, and you can't be a good listener when you're distracted. I happen to be a great listener, my dear. In the middle of my meditations this morning, they told me you were on your way, so I made the preparations."

"They?" echoed Dr. Gallagher.

Dr. Widener stopped and turned to the both of them in the foyer. "Spirits who help me."

"You mean, spirit guides?" Dr. Gallagher's tone conveyed his skepticism.

"Yes. They find titles or names distasteful, so I call them those who help me."

"So, you hear voices in your head?" asked Miranda.

"Yes, dear, but don't worry. They aren't crazy voices suggesting that I knock off the gas station on the corner, or dogs telling me to kill couples making out in cars. They tell me things I need to know, such as your arrival, for instance, and how important your case is for mankind."

Mankind? "Why," was all Miranda could muster.

"Because, my dear, you are the first person to have parts of your ethereal emotional body captured in an image, something that has been unattainable until now, and I'm not talking about those silly aura pictures meant to bilk people out of their money at psychic fairs. Now, come, come." He motioned with his hand, leading them into his living room.

Books lined all of the walls from floor to ceiling. Miranda loved to read, but Dr. Widener took book ownership to a different height—literally. "Wow. How many books do you have?"

"Approximately eight thousand books and counting. This room isn't the only place I have books. They've taken over other rooms in my house. I think I need more shelves," he contemplated, as if it were the first time this thought occurred to him.

"Why do you keep them all? Aren't they available in a library?" asked Miranda.

"Not unless you want to make a trip to Lilydale."

"Lilydale?" asked Dr. Gallagher.

"Lilydale, New York, the headquarters for the spiritualist movement. Come, please sit." He motioned for Miranda to sit on the futon. Miranda complied. Dr. Gallagher sat on a recliner next to the futon. The room décor exuded simplicity: unassuming furniture, including all of the shelves that housed his library, and a quiet, burgundy carpet.

Dr. Widener sat on a rustic, cushioned brown chair. "You must be hungry and tired after the long drive. Do you want to rest here a while, catch up on some sleep?"

"Oh, I don't know." Miranda looked at Dr. Gallagher to see his reaction.

"I would, but my wife is expecting me home," said Dr. Gallagher.

"Yes, your pain sometimes is overwhelming, isn't it?" asked Dr. Widener.

"I didn't say anything about my pain." *How did he know?*

"Aside from the shifting in your seat and the expression in your eyes, I can feel the pain in your neck and back. Right there, there, and there." Dr. Widener pointed to three areas on the neck and back.

"Oh, I'm sorry, Dr. Gallagher," said Miranda. *How selfish of me. I'm so caught up in my own pain that I couldn't see his.*

Dr. Gallagher looked at him in amazement. "I have had neck and back operations in those exact locations."

"The operations only did so much."

"Yes again."

"As you know, Dr. Gallagher, the subconscious is the last frontier that no one wants to explore. Don't give up in your fight against this pain. Your subconscious has many reasons why it is in pain, and the physical pain is only part of it. Ah, you have done all the conscious work. You are very strong in yourself and you came to peace with your past. My, and so many challenges you have overcome. You haven't been taught yet about the roots. And therein lies the way we are going to help our Miranda." He turned his head to smile and look at her.

"I feel see-through right now. How did you get to be the way you are?" Even though Dr. Widener didn't just analyze Miranda in thirty seconds, she had no doubt he could do the same with her.

Dr. Widener laughed. "Oh, my dear, I told you. It's nothing special. I'm a good listener, like our friend here, Jack. Instead of talking myself out of the information I receive, I listen and take note. You do the same, don't you Jack, except you don't know what it is and where it comes from. All you know is that you've been able to do it since you can remember."

"You know, Miranda is the reason why we're here."

"Okay, I'll stop poking around, Jack. But we are going to have to go through these things piece by piece if you want to help Miss

Miranda. Here, let me get the food and drink, and we can all sit and chat a while."

When Dr. Widener left the room and they could hear him clanking dishes and glasses in the kitchen, Miranda turned to Dr. Gallagher and opened her mouth wide to show her astonishment. "He's amazing," she whispered. Despite her worry, she couldn't help but giggle. "How does it feel, being on the receiving end for a change?"

Dr. Gallagher shook his head. He couldn't deny that Dr. Widener had amazed him, and he did feel transparent to him, like Miranda had stated, but it was disconcerting. He didn't want things in his past resurrected just because someone was capable of poking around in his head without permission. Maybe this was how his clients felt about him. Luckily, none of them punched him in the mouth for it.

Dr. Widener came back out with a tray containing a teapot, several envelopes of teas, and some baked goods. "When I went on sabbatical, I decided that I had to become self-sufficient, so I learned how to bake my favorite coffeehouse muffins without all the junk. Try them. And I see you have a heart condition, dear, so I have several types of herbal teas for you. Besides, I think you and Dr. Gallagher should rest a while before you go anywhere." Dr. Widener set the drinks and food on the coffee table, and then sat back down on the brown chair. "Please, help yourselves."

"Maybe later, thank you." Dr. Gallagher waved his hand in refusal.

Miranda politely complied, taking a cup of herbal tea and a muffin. She bit into it. "Mmm, this is good." She was hungry and did enjoy lemon poppy seed muffins.

"Thank you, dear. To answer your question from before, I decided to ignore all of those things we are taught while growing up. How many times were you told to ignore your feelings, it's your imagination? Countless, I bet, by parents, teachers, friends. It's counterintuitive and counterproductive. I mean, through my practice, I always knew I had something. I was right too many times about things I couldn't have possibly known, like you, Jack." He glanced at Dr. Gallagher. Dr. Gallagher held his gaze. "But, when I focused on myself, you know, releasing all the past I carried around, that's when everything kicked in. It's the pain. The pain, no matter what type it is or the cause of it, blocks everything you want in your life, from our full potential."

"So, you learned about all this from meditating?" asked Miranda.

"No. As you can see, I also read a lot."

Miranda giggled.

"And this is what brought you here. A book containing the information you need. Correct?"

Miranda nodded.

Dr. Widener stood up and walked over to his desk. He went to a pile of books and took the top book off, walked over to Dr. Gallagher, and handed it to him. "This book contains everything you need."

"This is the book we came for," Dr. Gallagher said. *Son of a gun! How in the world is he doing this?* He glanced around casually, looking for any signs of a telephone.

Miranda gasped. "You gave us *Id Speak*?"

"Yes. I have other copies of that book, so you can have this one. It's a gem." Dr. Widener sat next to Miranda on the futon. "And Miranda," he placed his hand on top of her hands. "I want you to know, you are capable of defeating this. It's inside of you."

"What? The strange thing?"

"The ability to take control and banish it forever."

"How do you know?"

"The same way I knew your name. And the faith your mother and father have in you."

Miranda's eyes watered. "You can see them?"

Dr. Widener nodded. "Your mother says love is not bound by space or time."

Miranda gasped and put her hand to her mouth, tears budding at the corner of her eyes.

"They have always been with you, right by your side. They have shown you signs they were here. If you stop telling yourself those signs were only your imagination, a coincidence, or faulty wiring, you can start noticing them for yourself."

Miranda nodded, crying and sniffing, Yes, she has told herself all those things over the years. Dr. Widener got up and strode over to the end table to grab a tissue and handed it to Miranda. Miranda took it and held it under her nose.

"They won't give up until you are free of his oppression."

Dr. Gallagher sat forward during this interaction, listening intently. "So then, you can tell us what this thing is, once and for all? I mean, you have all this information about us, right? So, they should give you the most important piece of information. What the hell is this thing? Why has it decided to move into her subconscious?"

"I don't know," Dr. Widener admitted.

Dr. Gallagher's mouth hung open. He sat forward in his seat. "You—don't—know. You don't know? How could you not know? We barely had to open our mouths since we've been here. You rattled off ten thousand things about us only we would know, unless you spoke to Grace during our ride over here."

"Which would mean Grace, our good friend, one of the best people you have ever met, is somehow part of a charade? I am shown what I am shown. You should know, Jack..."

"All right, you can hold it right there." Dr. Gallagher stood up, his anger overriding the pain in his back and neck. "You can stop comparing me to you right now. We are in no way similar. You have no idea who I am and what I've been through."

Dr. Widener paused, unfazed. "I see I've poked a sore spot, Jack. Where do you think your gift comes from?"

"It's not a gift. I've just been through so much shit in my life, I can tell."

"Tell what?" asked Dr. Widener.

"I can tell what people are thinking and feeling. There's nothing psychic about it," although he couldn't ever figure out how he did it, "and I resent being categorized with those phonies and frauds. It's just good observation skills, based on the profession I have been practicing for decades," he concluded after thinking about it time and again.

"So, it's the label you don't like. Do you think I'm a phony?"

Dr. Gallagher glared at him.

"Yes?"

"Dr. Gallagher." Confusion knitted Miranda's eyebrows together. "You said you saw a ghost when you were little and that you're open-minded. How could you not believe this is really happening?"

"There's God and there's spirits, but the one thing I will not believe is that they talk to some guy in the middle of the mountains." Dr. Gallagher's voice rose as he pointed to Dr. Widener.

"I think God has you on a crash course today because I'm seeing a scene you experienced. You are surrounded by a bunch of men in orange suits. You are fighting with them. There is a man behind you, fighting by your side. Much smaller than you. It feels like a fight to the death. They intend to kill you and your friend."

Dr. Gallagher's head reeled. He sat back down on the chair, hard. "Only my wife knows this story, the prison guards, and the men at the prison, and most of them are still there serving life sentences or are dead. While I was a correction officer, we were trapped, locked in the rotunda with over one hundred prisoners. How did... how did..." For the first time in years, Dr. Gallagher had no words to say. He didn't even tell Grace about this experience.

"Jeff. He was on a helicopter that crashed in Afghanistan two years later."

Dr. Gallagher was again speechless. That's what he had been told, but he didn't know if the prison lied about it or it was just a rumor. He had hoped it wasn't true, and the confirmation overwhelmed him. He surprised himself when he heard his voice crack and felt tears sting his eyes. He cleared his throat and pressed his fingers into his forehead above his eyes. He cleared his throat again and looked up. "Yeah, well, Jeff was, is the best. I don't know if I would have made it out without him."

"And same goes for him," Dr. Widener said.

Dr. Gallagher looked at him. His anger had left. Only exhaustion remained.

"I am only shown what I am meant to see. The only being who knows everything is God. All the rest of us, we are here to learn and grow and try and be as much like God as we can, in our thoughts, our deeds, and our hearts. I'm not talking angry, judgmental, control freak, wipe everyone out with a horrific flood God either. Loving, accepting God. At peace God. And the same goes for you. You are shown the information because you have spirits and angels watching out for you, and they've always been there, even as thick-headed as you are."

Dr. Gallagher laughed, shaking his head. That's what his wife tells him all the time.

"And you are shown things because you are a healer. You hear and see things, yes, in part, because of who you are and where you come from, but also, with the love and help of spirit. You are a warrior. And you can use this now to help Miranda."

Miranda sat in stunned silence.

They both faced her. "My dear, how do you feel now?" asked Dr. Widener.

"I am feeling this can't even be real. If I didn't witness it for myself, I wouldn't have believed it. My mother and father's death ruined any faith I might have had in a god. I was so mad. If God really loved me, I felt," her voice cracked, "why in the world would he allow this to happen? Why would he break my heart like this?" Talking about their death, recalling the intensity of the pain from the period in her life, made it feel as fresh as yesterday. "He couldn't possibly exist, I decided, and I moved on. I thought my sister foolish when she went to church and tried to get me to go. Now, with so much evidence, how can I deny it? My parent's love for me, it will always be here for me, won't it?"

Dr. Widener nodded.

"And they've been here, all this time, watching over me?"

He nodded again.

"Would you please tell them all I've ever wanted to do was make them proud?"

"Darling, you did, all by yourself. They see and hear everything. You don't need me to speak with them. And they'll try and answer you back, like hearing that song on the radio in your car every summer for the last thirteen years on your birthday. That isn't a coincidence. That's them."

Miranda gasped. "It was our last summer together as a family, and we were going up to the lake together. Ali was going to be a senior. And this song from the seventies was playing. My parents said they grew up listening to it and sang it on the top of their lungs. Ali and I were in the back seat, holding our ears, and they cracked up laughing like crazy. We yelled at them that the words didn't even make any sense." Miranda choked as she laughed and cried at the same time.

Dr. Gallagher asked a question he instinctively knew Dr. Widener could answer. "So, what was the name of the song, Dr. Widener?"

Dr. Widener paused for a moment. "I'm seeing a very bright light, almost blinding."

Miranda's tears returned. "The song's title, 'Blinded by the Light'."

"Manfred Mann's Earth Band," Dr. Gallagher and Dr. Widener echoed.

They sat as Miranda cried. At last, she had her parents back. Dr. Widener patted the back of Miranda's hand on her lap. After a few minutes, she collected herself. "Well, then, Dr. Widener. What do we do now?"

"First of all, my dear, my first name is Favian. When I was younger and very immature, I would tell the ladies they could call me by my nickname, their Favorite."

Miranda laughed and wiped her eyes.

"We rest, my dear," Favian continued. "Spirit gave you both a crash course in faith. It takes some people an entire lifetime to achieve what you both had in the last hour. I congratulate you. I have set up my guest rooms for the two of you. You will stay and be my guests for the weekend. I'll let you know when dinner is ready. Jack, you have some studying to do." He pointed to the book.

Jack nodded. "I'm looking forward to it."

Favian walked to the bookshelf and took out a book. "Like I said, I have more than one copy, so here you go, dear." He handed the book to Miranda. "Come this way." He motioned for them to follow. He led them through the kitchen, large enough to be defined as such, but small enough where a table could not fit, and led them up the stairs. "I know, an odd place for a staircase, through the kitchen, right? I happen to enjoy odd things, part of the reason why I enjoy this house. Try to read as much as you can of the book, and we'll discuss it. I love conversation around the dinner table."

• • •

When Miranda woke up, although her eyes were laden with exhaustion, she still felt better. She heard the sound and smells of cooking wafting up from the kitchen. She stretched and yawned. She was too alert to go back to sleep.

Favian had pointed out the towels he had placed on the bureau and the bathroom when he settled her into her room. She took the towel and padded down the hallway, but the old floor creaked in protest despite her efforts.

When she came out of the bathroom, she found Dr. Gallagher waiting at the door. The puffiness underneath his eyes made him seem haggard.

"Hi. How are you feeling?"

Dr. Gallagher waved his hand. "I'm feeling how I'm feeling. Not much I can do about it. How are you?"

She looked down at her feet. "As good as I can be, I guess. I've been waiting a long time for an answer to my problems. I hope this weekend will be the end."

"Me too."

The two paused. Miranda gazed into Dr. Gallagher's eyes. "How is it that I haven't noticed your physical discomfort before this? Have I really been so self-absorbed?"

"No, not at all. I do much better when I'm in my own environment, so you wouldn't have noticed unless I was having a really bad day or hurt myself. I have my bed set up at home so I can get the sleep I need. I have special chairs in my home and office to fully support my back. When I get into unfamiliar environments, that's when I get into trouble. It's hard for other people to understand why I limp when I get up from a hard wooden chair. Something that is a bit uncomfortable for you can be devastating to me and send me to bed for a week. Besides, you pay me to pay attention to you. It's my job to express myself in a way that is focused on you, and so you don't notice anything about me. So, don't feel bad. Okay?"

"Okay." After a bit of a pause, she asked, "What if we can't get an answer this weekend?"

"Then we'll move on, try something else."

Miranda frowned.

"Try to focus on the task at hand at the moment. Let's see if we can get through this book this afternoon, and we'll see what answers it gives us."

"Okay. I think I can do that. Try not to think about the worst-case scenario, right? I guess that's hard to do because when I was eleven, I had to live through my worst-case scenario."

Dr. Gallagher nodded. "But sometimes in life, we don't have to live through our worst-case scenario, the worst of our fears. Sometimes, we get to live out our dreams too."

"Promise?"

Dr. Gallagher smiled and nodded. "What are your dreams, Miranda?"

"For the longest time, it was traveling the world. I did do a bunch of traveling, but I'm not so sure that's my dream anymore. I think now my dream is to settle down with Steven, if he'll have me, and we can live life together. You know, have some kids, and my sister and I can meet at the park and watch our children play together. That's what I want."

"Did you call Steven or Alison to let them know you're here?"

"As luck would have it, Steven's at a conference this weekend."

"That's almost a little too convenient."

"I know. Almost like it was meant to be."

"And your sister?"

"Unfortunately, she's used to me disappearing for a few days at a time. She's learned over the years that sometimes I need a few days to myself to collect my thoughts. She won't think anything of it now that she doesn't remember." Besides, what would she tell her? She can always tell if something is going on with her, and the last thing Miranda needed at that moment was Alison's persistent, polite digging.

"It's your call, but it's probably best that we don't involve her and Steven for the moment." Dr. Gallagher didn't want to say it out loud. Usually, he would support packing up someone's family into a van, need be, and cart them to their family member in trouble, but Miranda's dangerous situation encouraged him to recommend keeping her family members at a distance and in the dark. Less people to worry about meant that Dr. Gallagher could focus on Miranda and get her free from the entity. Once that occurred, who knew what shape Miranda would be in, and who knew if the entity would go people-hopping after that? Then it would certainly be a mess indeed.

Miranda's thoughts walked along the same line. "Yes, Alison and Steven should stay away, far away. She should stay a safe distance from me at the moment. I would never be able to live if..." She couldn't even finish the sentence. Naturally, Dr. Gallagher seemed to understand, looking upon her with kindness. After a moment, Miranda asked, "What about your wife? Does she know you'll be absent?"

Dr. Gallagher followed along with the switch in subject, which would hopefully help keep her calm. "Oh, yes. I called her while you slept in the car. I had a feeling we would be here for a little while."

"And she doesn't mind you going off with a young woman to some place for the weekend?"

"No, not at all."

"Wow. I've never met anyone like that."

Dr. Gallagher smiled. "Yes, she's very understanding. We know each other well. We have built a great deal of trust over the years, and she's not jealous or an insecure person."

"I can't imagine she would be, with you around all the time."

Dr. Gallagher smiled. "Exactly."

Miranda smiled back. "I'm going to see what this book is all about."

"Yes, me too."

"See you in a bit." Miranda walked to her room.

Dr. Gallagher nodded. He entered the bathroom.

• • •

"The meal is delicious," Miranda complimented her host. "And I love the candles and everything." Engaging in normal social interaction helped distract Miranda from what could possibly be the most upsetting experience of anyone's life. Without Alison and Steven's support, she felt grateful to drink up the attention and conversation from the doctors. So many doctors in her life now. Her parents spoke a lot like they had, sharing the latest study's findings about schizophrenia, or debating on the latest medication used for mental disorders. For this reason, she found the educational chit-chat comforting and interesting where others would be bored. She also found while many of her classmates in elementary school struggled with the cruelty of others, she possessed the skill to identify why certain kids acted the way they did, helping her to separate herself from their unkindness, and also possessing more compassion for them than they most likely deserved. Oh, yes, her parents left an indelible, kind, and somewhat nerdy mark on her.

"Thank you, my dear," replied Favian.

"Yes, it's quite good," said Dr. Gallagher.

"I know; it's not like your wife's cooking. I try, though." Favian gave a small shrug.

Dr. Gallagher grinned. "It's almost like it's not fair for the rest of the cooking world. She really does have a gift."

"I like the way you talk about your wife. I hope Steven and I are that close. Would you say you found the right one?"

"Sure, it's that. It's a lot of things. Many people don't realize that even when you find the right one, it takes a conscious effort to work on your relationship. All people have issues from their past affecting their present relationship with their partner. But if you want a long-term, close relationship with someone, you don't run away. You make an agreement to stay and work it out, no matter what, and to be responsible for your end of the relationship."

"Okay. I think I can do that."

Dr. Gallagher smiled. "I know you can."

"So, did you both get a good rest?" asked Favian.

"Yes, thanks. I feel a bit better," said Miranda. At least, sleep stopped the feeling that what was happening to her wasn't the end of the world.

"And you, Jack?"

"I got a bit of sleep, thanks, and I read almost half the book. It is interesting."

"I thought it was interesting too," said Miranda. "Thank goodness my parents taught Ali and me some things over the years as we were growing up. I would ask them what they do and how they help people, and they taught us about the id, ego, and superego and stuff. It feels like I've known about Sigmund Freud all my life. When you and I spoke the first time, Dr. Gallagher, you had jogged my memory about things I hadn't thought about in years. But it's coming back to me now."

"That's good because it will make it easier for you to grasp these concepts." Favian cut into his game hen. "It's almost tragic that Freud's theories are often summarized in a few paragraphs in Psychology 101, and that's the end of it. We're taught that his ideas are outdated, even. So, what have you understood from what you've read so far, dear?"

Miranda finished her bite. "It was interesting because it combines Freud's knowledge and theories with these ideas about energy fields and chakras. Freud was the first to realize there is a metaphysical part to us attached to the body somehow, which he called the id. Although, he didn't say the word 'metaphysical,' but in essence, what are our body of thoughts and emotions? The author proposed the id is attached into the middle of all our chakras, sort of like the dark substance in the MRI." The thought prompted Miranda to put down her fork, leaving her meal half eaten. "Does this mean it has possession of my id?"

"It could have attached onto your roots," stated Dr. Gallagher.

"I guess I didn't get to that part. What do you mean by the roots?"

Dr. Gallagher finished chewing his bite. "Trauma has an unseen, metaphysical component to it. It creates these dark, metaphysical roots, and if you remove those roots, you can eradicate the source of people's pain. Reading this part helped me realize the reason people do not progress in therapy for years. They cannot get to the source, or root, of their problems, mostly because it's too painful to face, and the world's psychologists are not aware of their presence. When people do face them, they can be eradicated. Sometimes, they heal spontaneously. But mostly, from some of the case studies he included, people had to face the experiences that created these roots, and then there is a process to actually remove the roots."

"That's a great summary, Jack," Favian complimented. "So simple, isn't it? Needless to say, the book never did get the attention it deserves because unless you have the ability to see the root system created by trauma in individuals, you really can't make the connection for others. Dr. O'Connor has that ability, apparently, which is why his system cannot be replicated easily. However, with your MRI, the entity has latched onto those roots in your id, which serves as the manager for your subconscious. You are the first person, Miranda, where it has been possible to see what exists in your subconscious because of the entity. Losing your parents seemed to hit your body down to the core of all of your chakras."

"That makes sense," Miranda admitted. "That's how I felt at the time. Like there was nothing true or honest in the world, and my entire body was shaken to its core."

"Yes. That description matches your MRI. The possibilities of this are mind-blowing. This is what makes your case so exciting. You have given the human race the first map of what happens to the ethereal body, what changes happen within it when a painful event occurs. This could mean the end of many illnesses, especially ones caused by stress or anxiety. It's the missing link for the mind-body connection."

Miranda was not quite sure how to respond or feel about being the first roadmap of pain for the human race. Plus, she had a weird whatever-the-hell-it-was using her past trauma to latch onto her. Her anger simmered at the thought.

"As I read, it occurred to me people might have mistaken the id for the soul," stated Dr. Gallagher.

"Yes, I think so," said Favian. "There is a difference between the ethereal bodies and the soul. The ethereal bodies are directly attached to our physical bodies, and it's the blueprint for our physical bodies. The id is one of those ethereal bodies. The id looks like us in every way and can detach itself from our bodies. Ids were put there to give our species the drive to survive, no matter what the circumstances. The ones who used their higher reasoning to take an ethical pause during a life and death situation are the ones who perish. That is what the id is there for, to ensure our safety and to procreate.

"Plus, the id has its own rudimentary organizational process. It manages all of our 'root systems.' It understands our experiences on a three or four-year-old level, so it's not very complex. When something upsetting happens, it automatically goes into protection mode and quickly manages the information so we can return to a state of equilibrium as fast as possible. It throws up defenses, something Freud's daughter, Anna, had explained. Freud provided us all with an elementary map of the subconscious. Now we are able to use Dr. O'Connor's more detailed map to help Miss Miranda.

"So, do you see, Miranda? We have an energetic system inside of all of us, there to ensure our survival. It has limited capacity to reason, and the defense mechanisms kick in to help protect us. The ego and superego are where our higher reasoning capabilities are located. We have metaphysical inner structures, and there has not been a way to prove their existence, so most people deny it, or if they do acknowledge they exist, they can only allude to them in general, nonspecific terms.

"We are on the cusp of understanding the human experience. On the inside, we are all the same. We are all interconnected with each other and the cosmos, with spirit and the earth, but we are all under the illusion that we are all different."

Favian looked around the table at the empty plates. "Ah, yes, the sign of wonderful dinnertime conversation," he crowed to show his pleasure. "Plates lying fallow upon a dinner table, long left cold and empty, for fear they would miss one beautiful word of the tantalizing conversation around the dinner table."

"Here, let me help you with these." Miranda got up and grabbed her plate.

"Oh, my dear, you don't have to," said Favian.

"No, I insist." Miranda walked into the kitchen with an armful of plates and glasses. Favian looked at Dr. Gallagher. "Why don't you see if you can relax your back on that easy chair?" He had noticed the way Dr. Gallagher squirmed in his seat at the table.

"That sounds good. Thanks." He got up from the table, wincing, and hobbled over to the chair in the living room. It was more like a living area rather than a separate room. The couch and chairs, along with the dining room table, the books and all the shelving, and some drawers and other storage bins, all in one giant room together. He liked the homey feel it gave the place, and at that moment, he appreciated the fact he didn't have far to walk to the recliner. He sat down on the chair and put out the legs.

Miranda, after several trips back and forth from the table, had already started scraping the dishes and washing them in the sink. Realizing his protests wouldn't go anywhere, Favian pulled out a dishtowel.

Miranda looked at Favian. "I appreciate your help. I've learned so much."

Favian smiled. "You're welcome."

After a moment's silence, Miranda asked, "So, tell me about your sabbatical. From what I understand of sabbaticals, you are studying something of interest to you for a full year?"

"Yes, that's it."

"So, what are you studying?"

"Where psychology and religion interrelate."

"All religions? You're studying all the religions around the world and how all of them have psychological aspects?"

"Yes."

"That sounds like more of a lifetime of study."

Favian laughed. “Yes, it has been a lifetime of study. This year is more of gathering all the information I’ve read and making it into a book or two.”

“I think it’s going to be a great book... or two.”

Favian smiled, drying a plate.

After a moment’s pause, she asked, “So, when did you first realize you could do what you do?”

“I don’t know. It started as knowing I knew certain things. I didn’t understand the why or the process, much like our friend Jack. I would know when people intended to visit without them having to call first: you know, little things. When I read the information from the New Age movement, that’s when it started to click. It seemed like the more I read, the more I realized what is possible for us humans, the more I opened up to it.”

“How about the stuff you told us tonight? Did you read a lot of it, or did you get that information from other means?”

“I was able to read some, and I was able to receive some during my meditations. And I want to let you know, I usually don’t haul off and slam people with a whole bunch of stuff from their past like that. It would make most people run the opposite way screaming. It usually doesn’t work like that, and this was the first time I’ve been able to know so much all at one time. It’s sort of like they downloaded information about you both into my brain. It feels like I’ve known you for years. It’s been an extraordinary day for me too.”

“I didn’t know that. Thanks for letting me know. How does it usually work?”

“When I do that sort of work, the person in front of me has to acknowledge the information. It’s part of the process. They have to demonstrate a readiness to accept the information passed onto them. I don’t know if you have seen these psychic mediums working in groups. They don’t go up to a person and say, hi Joe, I have your mother Ethel here, and she knows you missed your dentist appointment yesterday. It would make most people shut down.

They have to stand up and accept the information. It's gentler than what happened here today."

"So, it was special for Dr. Gallagher and me, and it was special for you too."

"Yes."

"I think that's all the dishes. Let's see about those pots and pans."

"No, that's okay. Let them soak overnight. They were a bit sticky. Oh, and speaking of sticky, I have some baked apples, if you would like some dessert."

"Oh, no thanks. I'm full. Maybe for breakfast tomorrow, with some yogurt?"

"What a nice idea. For breakfast, then."

"I'm a bit tired, so I think I'll take my book and go to bed. I'll try to get through it all tonight."

"Good. If you need anything, don't feel shy. My house, your house. And if you feel like you need to talk to me tonight, knock on my door. I'll be in my bedroom doing my evening exercises and meditations, but don't worry. If you need to speak with someone, if something is the matter, come get me. Okay?"

"Okay. Promise. If I need anything, I'll let you know. And thanks again." Miranda walked up the stairs.

Favian smiled after her. Perhaps Jack was up for more lively debate. When he walked into the living room, he saw Dr. Gallagher asleep on the recliner. He wrote him a note, put a blanket over him, turned off the light, and climbed the stairs to his room.

21
INTROSPECTION

Miranda had no idea what to expect when she awoke the next morning. Favian was puttering around the kitchen when Miranda emerged from the staircase. The homey feel of Favian's presence and the demure atmosphere of the house relaxed her jangled nerves.

"How are you this morning? Did you sleep well?" asked Favian.

"Yes, thanks. How about you?"

"Good, as always. Why don't you have a seat? Breakfast is on the table."

As promised, Favian had the baked apples and yogurt with some rolls, tea, and coffee set out on the dining room table.

Dr. Gallagher was already seated at the table. After waking up, feeling disoriented, and being able to let his pain subside so he could stand up, he took the note and put it in his pocket. "How did you sleep?" Miranda asked Dr. Gallagher, taking a seat at the table.

"Much better in the chair, thank you. And you?"

"Soundly, thanks. I guess I was exhausted."

Favian strolled in carrying some butter and jam. "Good. Everyone has rested well. We have a lot to do today. My neighbor makes this jam. She grows her own berries in her garden. It's really delicious." He put the jar on the table.

"So, you do get out once in a while," Miranda observed.

"The only way I could avoid going out at all is to be self-sufficient, but let's face it; no one is totally self-sufficient these days. I would have no time to write my books." He sat down. "Please, have some breakfast."

"Thank you." Miranda took some herbal tea and scooped some apples and yogurt on her plate and spooned little bites into her mouth. Dr. Gallagher took a roll and butter.

"So, I know only a bit about what has been going on, Miranda. I need to know what has been happening, in your own words, and you too, Jack. I think it will help clarify the direction we need to pursue."

"Why don't you start?" Dr. Gallagher said to Miranda.

Miranda told Dr. Widener a synopsis of what she, Dr. Gallagher, and Dr. Kelly had discussed before their road trip to see Favian.

"Dr. Gallagher, do you have anything to add?" asked Favian.

"Upon hearing what happened with Miranda, my immediate opinion was that it wasn't a hallucination, based on my experience in working with patients with psychosis. I thought it could have been some sort of dream when she had passed out. Maybe she thought she was awake when she was really unconscious. Sometimes, people have dreams that are so realistic, they are not aware they are sleeping until they wake up. Miranda didn't have that opportunity, because she remained unconscious for a few hours after she saw the stranger in her house, but when we went the paranormal route, we found the pieces of evidence, the FLIR image and the MRI. The attack upon Miranda was violent, swift, and calculated. It doesn't follow the pattern of demon possession, nasty spirits, or poltergeist activity. Miranda's entity only reacts when we approach it."

"It seems like your visitor has been doing everything it can to remain hidden." Favian grabbed a roll from the plate in the middle of the table. He spread a generous amount of jam on it. "It's strange that Alison had spotted it, out and wandering around, while Miranda slept."

"We charted its appearances with Dr. Kelly," said Miranda. "We found that it seems to be in my subconscious, where it remains hidden most of the time, until we try and call it out or stumble upon it."

"Hmm," Favian hummed. "Have you had anything else unusual happen other than those occurrences?"

"No."

"Except for your blackouts, have you experienced any lapses in time?"

"Except for my accident and the two blackouts, none."

"So your memory was consistent except for the blackouts and the erasure of your memory, including the experience you shared with several others?"

"Yes."

"Why do you think it felt like it needed to attack you in your house?"

"Because I was about to visit the accident site where my parents perished."

"Mmm hmm," Favian nodded. "Perhaps he didn't want your subconscious to get stirred up. It might have helped your healing process to see the site. If it had, he might have lost his host, so he felt like he had no choice but to put you out and make you forget your mission—an effective tactic. Even though he risked revealing his identity, it wouldn't have mattered as much as the healing process, which could have ousted him. Sound about right, Jack?"

"Yes, now that you mention it. While I read the rest of that book this morning, I learned more about the roots and thought that's what the entity is holding onto."

"Yes, I was doing a little more reading too," said Miranda. "This doctor claimed to heal a lot of people as part of a study?"

"Yes, he did, and he continues to in his practice."

"How do we know it's all real?" asked Miranda.

"Because I have experienced some of the things he did in his book, except I didn't know what I was seeing," said Favian. "So has Jack here. Right, Jack?"

Dr. Gallagher found Favian's habit of drawing him into the conversation in this manner irritating, but he politely nodded his head in agreement. After all, this was about Miranda, not his issues with Favian.

"People really don't know what to believe until they live through it themselves. Right?" Favian continued.

Miranda nodded. "Yes, I think so."

"To me, it all makes sense," agreed Dr. Gallagher. "It fits with what I've seen in my practice. If ridding people of these roots is possible, what used to take years in therapy to work out can happen in a matter of months."

"I'm sorry, but I am still a bit confused about how all of this is going to help me," said Miranda.

"My dear," said Favian, "it has everything to do with you. How do you think this entity is living inside of you, how it's been able to camp out for almost a year?"

"The black roots inside of me? Ugh, that sounds so yucky." The words left a bad taste in her mouth and turned her stomach sour. She put down her fork and pushed the plate forward despite the fact that the baked apples were among the best she had ever tasted.

"Don't worry, dear, we all have them. Until now, it took years for people to resolve, if they could resolve them at all."

"Even you have them?" asked Miranda.

"Yes."

"What are your roots connected to, Favian?" Dr. Gallagher looked at him intently. "You seem to know ours pretty well."

Favian coughed and looked down. "As I said, I can only see what I am being shown. Honestly, I didn't know that this entire phenomenon was real until I experienced it myself." Miranda seemed disappointed. He needed to even the balance of power. He cleared his throat and looked intently at Miranda. "I lost my parents at a young age also. I was five. Two gunmen killed them. They entered our home, busted right through the front door. My mother ran and hid me in my closet behind all of my toys. I heard the shots. They took some jewelry and our television. That was it. They killed my wonderful parents over a lousy $800 in merchandise. I hid until the cops arrived. I had soiled myself when the shots rang out. There is nothing worse than not knowing. When the police came, they shielded me from the scene, hiding my eyes. They called the social worker. She was kind enough to clean me up. My grandmother came and got me, and I lived with her. I lost her to cancer when I was seventeen."

Miranda's eyes stung. She reached across the table and squeezed Favian's hand.

"I'm sorry," Dr. Gallagher said. "Truly." His early irritation melted away. That explained Favian's behavior, the way he was always referring to him as "our friend Jack." Maybe a sabbatical alone in his house was not the best thing for Favian. He seemed to need companionship.

"As you can imagine, I don't like talking about it, but not because it brings up bad memories. It does, but I've had forty years of dealing with this. I had spent half of my life recovering from this incident. Now, it's usually much more painful for people to hear than it is for me to tell them about it." With a kind look, he patted Miranda on the back of her hand. Miranda nodded and wiped her eyes. "I guess for the first twenty years, I focused on what I lacked. I even played super sleuth for a while, returning to my old neighborhood to ask the neighbors what they saw that day. They never caught the guys for the crime they committed against me, but I did find out their identities. They were both arrested for other crimes. One was arrested on a forgery charge two years later, raped and stabbed in prison, and died from his wounds. The other raped and murdered a nine-year-old girl and is in prison, awaiting his day of execution."

"Huh. Karma," said Dr. Gallagher.

"Yes, I think so. That's when I learned, even when people wrong you, you do not have to worry about revenge. What they do to themselves will catch up with them and do a much better job. It's made it a lot easier for me to forgive them."

"Yeah, forgiveness," Miranda said sardonically. She wished it always worked out like that. "My mother said in my vision this freak inside of me killed her and my father. I know how you feel."

Favian paused, squinting and cocking his head as if he saw something in the distance, then looked over to Miranda. "How sure are you that it was your mother in the vision?"

"Why?" Miranda asked. Anxiety fluttered from her stomach to her throat.

"How do you know some part of it wasn't the entity itself rather than your mother?"

"Why would the entity tell her something like that?" asked Dr. Gallagher.

"Think about it. We don't know for certain if it's true."

"You mean the dream and the vision are not real? Then what about all this connecting stuff I did yesterday?" Her cheeks reddened. "Was that not real too?"

Favian held up his hand. "No, no, I'm not saying that, dear. The vision seems a bit suspect to me. If your mom wants to help you confront this entity so you could banish it, why would she tell you something that would make it almost impossible for you to do it right now, here with us today? It's natural to go through an angry phase, ensuring that you will not heal right away. It takes time to process those feelings."

Miranda was still upset, but what Favian said made sense, although she wasn't ready to admit it out loud. "So I can know the truth and go into it with my eyes open."

"How do you know it's not the entity playing havoc on your emotional state, keeping you down by feeding you false information?"

"Yes, that does make sense," said Dr. Gallagher. "It's very difficult to go through all the steps at once to forgive someone, and he knew it. Forgiveness is a process, and it's something that takes time. He would be able to hold onto that black root if he caused a great deal of anger and revenge in you, Miranda, because look now, you're not in the emotional state to let go." While Dr. Gallagher wasn't sure about the verity of Favian's statements, he saw the cleverness in his use of doubt—cast doubt on the reason for Miranda's anger and release her from its hold. Whatever the truth, it would come out at some time down the road, during a time where they were better equipped to deal with the issue at hand and know what was true and what was a lie.

"So, the vision I had at Dr. Kelly's house was not real?"

"Ah, my dear, it was real," said Favian, "and I feel it was your mother for the most part, but for a moment, he was able to interfere and manipulate you into a specific emotional state. There is nothing in the world that could make you hang onto a bad experience better than hate and anger. The more you hate him, the more off balance you are, even if it's just for the moment it hits you, the better he can control and manipulate you because you are holding onto that dark root."

"So, he'll lie and deceive so he doesn't lose his parking space," Dr. Gallagher added.

Miranda looked at the pile of apples and yogurt still left on her plate, unable to look up. "I was so excited my mother came see me in my dreams and visions. It was so much like her, saying things like you can conquer the darkness with the light of my love for you. Why would the entity say something like that?"

"I think it was her, dear, until the entity had to step in and was forced to shut it down," reasoned Favian. "He held true to his pattern. He stepped in so you are kept in the dark. The longer you are kept in the dark, the longer he gets to keep, um, his parking space." He pointed his fork at Dr. Gallagher to give him credit for coining the term. "Ah, yes. Life is about patterns. Patterns are all around us. Patterns are within us. Patterns are in our past lives, in our DNA. And no matter where this entity is from, he has patterns too, which makes him more predictable."

"It does make sense when you break it down that way," agreed Miranda. "But, that even makes me mad. How *dare* he use the memory of my mother against me."

"My dear," said Favian, "it seems like he knows how to push your buttons. And it would make sense that he has access to all this information if he's been in your subconscious for a while."

"Are you trying to say he knows me better than I know myself?"

Favian and Dr. Gallagher glanced at each other. That is exactly what Dr. Gallagher feared.

"He's trying to make sure he doesn't lose his host, so he's lying and cheating and doing anything he can to manipulate you," said Favian. "You have to become impervious to him and not allow him to manipulate you like this."

"How am I not supposed to get mad?" Miranda stood up and pushed back her chair.

"Getting mad is understandable. So is the anger you felt when your parents passed," said Dr. Gallagher in a soothing voice.

"How can I not be angry? I am. I am fucking pissed off," she exclaimed, her face crimson. "First, I lose the best parents in the world. And I mean *the best*. They did everything with us. They played with us. They always said the right things. They were never mean, they didn't yell, and they loved each other to the end. And then one day, they were gone. Yes, I was pissed. I still am," she yelled. "How can I not be mad? Who is there to forgive? God? Why should I, when he took away my life because there is really no other explanation for what happened to them. Now you're saying that I finally have someone to hate. I have someone who is victimizing me and responsible for the death of my parents. I finally have some sort of sense of what happened to them, and you're saying I can't trust that? What the hell is true, then? So I'm back to my parents' accident having no cosmic purpose, and a stupid fucking whatever-it-is living inside of me for probably the same stupid reason why my parents aren't here, for no purpose whatsoever, and I'm still pissed! How can you possibly expect me to be anything else? I have a huge hole in my life, in my heart, and it'll never go away!" Tears gradually overtook her voice until she sat down, arms crossed, with a plunk.

"My dear, you hit upon your root," said Favian in an even tone. Dr. Gallagher nodded.

"You feel like you did when you were eleven and lost them, right?" asked Dr. Gallagher.

Miranda's eyes flashed angrily as she responded. "Yes, I do."

Favian sat back in his chair and gazed at her. "Now we have our focal point for our session today."

"I'm sorry." The heat in her cheeks dissipated. "I haven't lost it like that in years."

"That's the root, my dear," said Favian. "You could be going along, and everything is fine. Then all the sudden, something triggers it, pokes at that open wound, and you feel like you're five or eleven again, and all that progress you feel like you've made seems to evaporate."

"On top of that, anger is the second phase for the phases of grieving."

Miranda nodded. Even though it was still early, her bones ached with exhaustion. Yes, yes, the phases of grieving. The one thing mushroom-head, her school's counselor, parroted was the grieving process. Several times. The only thing she really said. It didn't help her to grieve any faster or better. Maybe she never got through the anger phase.

"Forgiveness isn't something you do for another person. It's a gift you give yourself," said Favian. "You can still forgive. You can forgive the entire host of angels and God, even the Holy Spirit if you like. You can forgive Buddha. You can forgive your parents for not being there. You can even forgive the entity inside of you. Only then will you be able to release him and let him go. He can't hold on..."

The lights flickered.

Dr. Gallagher looked around. "All the lights are off, Favian."

"Oh no." Miranda shrunk in her seat. "Not again."

Favian got up and ran to the kitchen. He opened up the box and switched off the main breaker. The activity ceased.

"Quick thinking," Dr. Gallagher complimented. Favian nodded and sat back down.

"I think you are close, darling. We've angered it. It feels threatened," observed Favian. "I think it's time to move onto the next step." He stood up. "My dear, you might have this resolved within the hour. Follow me. I'll clean up later."

The house hadn't appeared as big from the outside to Miranda. Favian brought them up to a third floor containing three more rooms, windows allowing enough available light. Two of the rooms had piles of books occupying most of the floor, some waist high.

When he opened the door to the third room, Miranda drew in a breath.

"I know, intense color, isn't it?" Favian acknowledged.

"I think I saw this color on a fish in a pet store once." Miranda looked around.

Dr. Gallagher blinked. "Whew, talk about royal blue."

"Yes. It's the royal-bluest paint I could find."

"What are we going to do in this room today?" asked Dr. Gallagher.

"I've been working on an introspective experiment with consciousness levels. I spend hours in this room sometimes. It is part of my sabbatical inward. I am trying to draw a more detailed map of the human consciousness and subconscious."

"How long have you been doing this?" asked Dr. Gallagher.

"Only for a month or so."

"And how is it going?" asked Miranda.

"As you can see, I had my first moment of perfect clarity before your arrival. I guess there had to be a catalyst before I obtained some results."

Miranda's eyes adjusted to the color. The room wasn't very big and didn't have a window. Three recliners faced a different wall in the room. White, cylindrical candles, an incense burner, and an old-fashioned CD player had been placed on top of a small coffee table off to the right along the wall. She could still smell the lingering odor of the incense permeating every nook and cranny in the room.

"Why do you have so many recliners in here?" asked Miranda.

"Once a week, I have a couple of neighbors come over and participate in my experiments with the subconscious and the spiritual world. I want to see if having people here with me will clarify the results of my meditations."

"Oh, you mean, the jelly lady?" Miranda inquired.

Favian nodded and smirked.

"Have you made any progress?" asked Dr. Gallagher.

"I only started this past week. I'll let you know when I have more information. Now," Favian clapped his hands and rubbed them together, "when this whole thing started, you became aware of this entity while you were in a semi-conscious state, right before you fell asleep, for the most part. The official term for it is called hypnagogia. When mapped on an EEG, this corresponds to theta brain waves. We are going to try and get you as close to the threshold consciousness as we can and keep you in it until you have the answers you need."

"You mean, like when one undergoes hypnosis?" asked Miranda.

"People are fully conscious when under hypnosis, but in a total, relaxed state and a state of increased suggestibility. Today, we are going to try and get you on the threshold of sleep and waking. In theory, if we pay attention to the patterns you and Dr. Gallagher discovered, you should be able to gain access to this entity's hiding place, draw it out, and see if we can confront it."

"Are you sure that's a good idea?" asked Dr. Gallagher. "It had a violent reaction every time we were upon discovering it, photographing it, filming it."

"I have thought about that. There's another pattern you both should have noticed. It had plenty of power from devices around it when it mustered a violent reaction. This time, we are going to limit its power sources. The radio is operating only on battery power, and the electrical power to the house remains off.

"When I devised this room, I took everything into account. I chose this color blue because it is the color of the communication chakra. I find it enhances my sessions with my guides as they help me understand more about the spirit world. The uniform color in the room creates sort of a Ganzfeld effect. And, I have angled the chairs in this room so we don't see each other in our peripheral vision."

"What's a Ganzfeld effect?" asked Miranda.

"It's a type of a sensory deprivation, like when monks go into a cave to gain spiritual insight or going into pitch-black isolation tanks. Because of the uniform visual field, it has been known to produce hallucinations," Dr. Gallagher explained.

"So, you want me to hallucinate?" asked Miranda with some trepidation. Her heart beat like a freight train gathering speed, but she told herself that she should trust him. Her parents trusted Dr. Gallagher when they partnered on their project, and Dr. Gallagher trusted Dr. Kelly, who trusted Favian. The unknown territory frayed her nerves, but she tried to remain open-minded. She had no choice. She couldn't think of anything within this world that would sufficiently explain her experiences.

"Not dysfunctional hallucinations. It's the eventual product of staring at a uniform blank wall for an extended period of time. It's a well-documented phenomenon. In reality, though, scientists have used the term hallucinations to describe phenomenon that has not been explained through science or even ghost sightings."

"Oh," said Miranda. The butterflies from her stomach rose to her chest.

"Now, this is my plan," Favian continued. "The walls will produce a Ganzfeld-type effect. I will burn frankincense and sage. It will stimulate your sense of smell, and it has been used for centuries to encourage contact with the spirit world. A CD will play to regulate the brainwaves by using sound pulses, and it will bring down the brain waves to the theta state as well as provide a background noise to help minimize auditory distractions. I am going to bring you through a series of exercises while meditating to help give you all the psychic protection you need in case we make contact, and it will help us all get into the brain wave pattern we need. I think we should go right after that big root and pull it out with the help of my spirit guides. And, Dr. Gallagher and I will be right here by your side this time." He looked into Miranda's eyes. "Does that make you feel better, dear?"

"Yes. I don't feel like I'm going into this alone." He sounded so experienced. Maybe this time, it would go better, and then she would be rid of this nuisance.

"At least we are trying to minimize all the known risks," said Favian. "Now, Miranda, since we suspect that the entity is attached to your metaphysical black roots, it's possible you will be confronted with some painful memories today. Are you ready to confront those memories and release them?"

Miranda nodded, taking a deep breath. "I'm ready."

"Okay. I'm going to light the incense and turn on the CD. Why don't you get comfortable?"

"The recliner, as usual, Dr. Gallagher?" asked Miranda.

"Thank you, yes," he said. He looked into Miranda's eyes. "Everything is going to be okay." Even if he wasn't sure, he had to try and convince her.

Miranda nodded, forcing a slight smile. Dr. Gallagher put his hand on her shoulder and patted it, smiling back. After they took their seats, Favian lit the incense, pressed play on the CD player, and sat down in his recliner. A pulsing sound came over the speakers.

Miranda made a face. "That's not relaxing at all."

"I know. Give it a chance. Here, I'll turn it down a little. Is that better?"

"Yes. I guess I can live with it now. So, we sit here and stare at the wall?"

"Yes," Favian replied.

"I was kidding."

Dr. Gallagher and Favian chuckled.

"If you feel like you want to close your eyes, then you can. Do what is comfortable for you. I'm closing the door now, and it's going to get dark in here."

Miranda shrugged. "Okay."

Favian sat down on his recliner. "Let's begin with a prayer. We ask God and Michael the Archangel to protect us on our journey today. Please give us the strength and guidance needed in our battle against this entity for the life of one of your most precious children, Miranda. Amen."

"Amen," echoed Dr. Gallagher and Miranda.

"Let us begin by breathing. Draw your breath in, visualizing a golden, white light. It is going to protect you and infuse you with God's love. Hold for a count of four, and breathe out again, blowing out any anxiety, stress, and fear, envisioning muddy colors." After twenty breaths, he spoke in a quiet, even monotone, matching the tone and speed of his voice with the slowing, pulsing sound of the CD. "Now, envision that the golden white light has engulfed your entire body. Feel the light infusing every atom and electron of your being. The light filters down to your feet and then burrows down into the core of the earth. You are now grounded to the earth. It will cleanse your body and aura with its energy. In partnership, we go forward today into the unknown, protected and loved. There isn't any room for fear inside of us."

The warmth spread throughout Miranda's body. She stared at the wall, listening to the sound of the pulsing tone. The absolute darkness of the room helped her body achieve total relaxation.

Favian continued to speak in the same, calming monotone. "Now imagine a dirt road. It leads us to a scene. We see the source of Miranda's root."

If Dr. Gallagher weren't so calm, he would have been very excited. He saw a dirt road. Miranda and Favian walked beside him. All three of them remained silent as they looked around. They could still hear the beating of the recording in the background, pulsing steadily. Dr. Gallagher and Favian stayed on either side of Miranda. They could see trees and wood farm fences lining the road, and the smell of fresh cut grass stung their noses. Horses lazed in the fields. They saw a large lake and a rustic cabin.

Favian put his hand on Miranda's arm. "Where are we Miranda?"

"At the cabin where my family spent our summers."

"Why are we here?" asked Dr. Gallagher.

She shrugged.

They walked up the stairs and went to the front door. Miranda took a deep breath and tried the handle to the front door. It opened and they went inside.

"Mom?" Miranda called.

They paused to listen for an answer. There wasn't any response, the pulsing forever present. Miranda walked inside with the two men behind her. She couldn't help but think of a saying she heard once—*expect the unexpected.*

"Oscar Wilde," Favian whispered in her ear.

"What?" The tension made her throat feel tight.

"'To expect the unexpected shows a thoroughly modern intellect.' Oscar Wilde."

"How did you do that?"

"We're all tuned into the same brainwaves. I hear you loud and clear."

"So do I," Dr. Gallagher confirmed.

"That's good. We'll be able to monitor what's happening," said Favian.

By that point, they had walked to the kitchen table. Instead of seeing her mother there, she saw him. Even though it was a sunny day with sunlight pouring through the kitchen window onto the table in front of him, his face remained shadowed over, the same as when she saw him in the hospital and her house.

Dr. Gallagher noticed he, the creature, was exactly as Miranda had described him. Apprehension rose from the pit of his stomach; it tasted like bile. The same instinct that kept him alive in the prison riot rose to alert him of trouble.

"Sit." The entity motioned to the chairs across from him.

Miranda first thought his voice sounded like a growl, but when she really listened, it sounded more like a tinny rasp, sort of like an artificial voice, much like the recording that was captured before this vile creature exploded her house. She looked at Dr. Gallagher and Favian. Dr. Gallagher shrugged and motioned to the chairs, taking a seat on Miranda's right. Miranda and Favian followed suit, taking their seats in front of them.

"I met you here, Miranda, so we could have a place where you felt comfortable," the entity said in his low rasp.

"I haven't felt comfortable since your arrival," Miranda retorted. Favian put his hand on her shoulder, feeling her hostility.

To Dr. Gallagher, the entity looked like a regular person, although much larger than an average male. He estimated his height at six-foot-ten. He tried to look into the entity's eyes, but no matter how he looked, he only peered into darkness. It was like no light could ever penetrate it to reveal the ugly truth on the inside. He could see the outline of some features, the eyes, the nose, his lips, but they were concealed under a shroud of darkness. He could even smell the leather from his jacket. Never had he heard or read of such a creature. Could he be a ghost, some sort of spirit, or a demon?

"No, not a ghost, spirit, or demon, Jack," the entity said. "Yes, I can read all of your thoughts too. Same brain waves, as our bright Favian has stated. But if you feel the need to talk, as humans often do, then blather away."

"Humans?" asked Dr. Gallagher. "If we are humans, then what are you?"

"I am. I exist."

"But you're not human," stated Favian.

The entity's dark eyes flashed under the shroud of the shadows. "Yes, you're right. I'm not human."

"What are you, then? And why the fuck have you been making my life absolute hell?" Miranda's voice rose.

"Ah, yes." The entity sniffed as if he smelled a sweet flower. "All that anger. It's what keeps me tied to you so well. It's why I have been able to remain with you. We will be tied for all eternity," he said in a menacing voice and leaned forward. "And if you think this is hell, you're in for a surprise."

Miranda narrowed her eyes, holding the entity's gaze. "I'm not scared of you. Not anymore. I'm sick of you. You have to leave."

"I won't. You'll never be able to do it. You humans. You think anything is possible, but you are all bound by your past. It ties your hands. And what do you do? Instead of confronting it, you hide it, stow it away. Right, Jack?" The entity turned his gaze over to Dr. Gallagher.

Dr. Gallagher stared. He could feel a hostile, terrifying power emanating from the entity that he never felt from any other source. He couldn't shake the feeling that something was very wrong.

"I know. I feel it too," Favian said, glancing over to Jack. Jack acknowledged the statement with his eyes.

"Ah, yes, our intuitive," the entity snorted. "So scarred by his past, he hides it by following a path of salvation, of enlightenment, when in fact, he's a scared little kid who wet his pants in the closet instead of saving his parents." The entity's tone relayed that he knew what he was saying to Favian, leveling the most hurtful statement he could, and he was enjoying it.

"You leave him alone!" Miranda shouted.

Favian put his hand on Miranda's shoulder. He tilted his head and narrowed his eyes, as if the statement made him curious. He expected the backlash. "Don't feed into it. He feels threatened."

The entity laughed in a low, raspy chuckle. "If that's what you want to believe, you clueless flea."

"Cursed, grinning villain."

Another low chuckle. "In time, I'll make you all forget all of this again, and forever this time. Like you humans, we too learn from our mistakes."

"Who exactly, again, is we?" asked Dr. Gallagher.

"My kind," he growled.

"What is your kind?" Miranda needed to vomit, but she wouldn't give him the satisfaction. She tried to swallow the feeling. It didn't help the churning in her stomach. "And why do you smell so bad?"

"My kind," the entity stated, ignoring Miranda's comment. "My kind is bent on the destruction of your kind."

"Why? What did we ever do to you?" asked Favian.

"He loved you best," the entity said.

Favian narrowed his eyes and tilted his head. "I thought you said you weren't a demon."

"We aren't. We are a separate species made by our father."

"And who is your father?" asked Favian.

"Lucifer." The last syllable of the evil name sounded like an extended, low growl. His sinister eyes gleamed at Miranda from the shadows.

"And this doesn't make you a demon, how?" asked Miranda impatiently.

"We are not demons from this world. Demons are limited in their power over the humans of this earth. They're bottom feeders. They can only enter people who are so weak and feeble-minded, they do not have any free will, and if they are not baptized. Or, they ask the demons to enter them willingly.

"On the other hand, our kind is not ruled by free will. We can come and take you over as we please. Humans have absolutely no natural defenses against our kind. My kind is able to occupy anyone who has some sort of blackness in their heart, caused by your pathetic existence, whether or not you succumb to our father Lucifer, whether or not you believe in the afterlife, in spirit, blah blah blah. There is no protection from my type. Your God and his pathetic little angels have no influence. We were created to have a presence here in this world."

"You mean, anyone who has been upset or has a trauma in their history can be occupied by you?" asked Dr. Gallagher. *Oh, crap. If what he was saying is true, they had to fight alien super-demons, version 2.0. New demon, new rules.*

"Yes, which means we will have control of all of God's little pets because after all, who hasn't experienced some sort of trauma?" His arrogant stare bore down on Miranda. Favian took Miranda's hand and squeezed it. She squeezed back, never taking her eyes off the demon. "And we shall carry on the wonderful work you humans started. You will all be our slaves, and our father will be your master."

"You're lying," said Miranda.

"Lying? Why would *we* lie? That's something humans do. No, we tell the truth. Even those bottom feeders, the demons, they don't lie. None of us do. After all, my father is an angel."

"Yeah, he's an angel," Miranda snorted.

The demon ignored her comment. "There's no need. You humans do it for us. You begin with lying to yourself, so you don't have to see how pathetic your existence really is. The most damage we can do to you is to tell the truth. That's when we cause the most chaos," he chuckled.

"He's lying. I can tell," said Dr. Gallagher.

"How?" asked Miranda.

"His lips are moving."

An ominous, metallic clicking emanated from the depths of his throat, a chuckle that chilled every cell of Miranda's body.

Favian sat back and crossed his arms. A series of facts crossed his vision. He had to say them out loud before he ran out of time. "You have more substance than an angel or spirit, giving you more power here in the physical world. You are in between the physical and the spiritual, so you can move in and take over the body's energy with your black energy. Your daddy, Lucifer, could not create you on this planet, so he sought out the universe for a suitable planet to create the army that would end all humans, since the black roots is the one thing that is consistent within every human being. Your planet couldn't accommodate and nurture physical beings like we have here on earth, so this is the best that you could do. Right?"

The entity glowered at him. "Right again, asshole."

Favian stood his ground, unaffected. "How did you get here?"

The entity chuckled in a low rumble, sounding more like thunder on the horizon. "Many perfect black energies exist in the universe. They serve as portals. They are well beyond you peons' comprehension. You have inherited limited vision. You're all so small, insignificant. There are many things your kind cannot even sense about the physical realities of the universe. It's all about magnetism, and there are many magnetic paths I was able to take that led me from star to star. Your star has these magnetic paths too, and it led me almost right to your front door, and then, into the depths of sweet Miranda's soul."

Miranda never experienced something as ominous and threatening as the alien-demon's smile creating a deep dark chasm where his face should have been. The evil surpassed anything she could ever imagine, anything she had seen or heard from earth. The realization and the abject loss of hope created what felt like an illness radiating throughout her entire being.

"Oh, yes, there's plenty of darkness for my kind to come and occupy and spread. And it's a matter of time until my entire planet comes with me. And we will exact our revenge, and our father will be avenged."

Dr. Gallagher glared at him. "How many are here now?"

Favian perceived the hostility and anger wafting off of the entity. "You're the test run, right? So if it blows up in your face, your planet doesn't lose all of your kind."

He glowered at Favian.

"Why me?" asked Miranda. Although she could barely speak, she held her determination to face him.

The demon chuckled again. "Because you are my match."

"Oh?" Indignation welled up, outstripping the fear. "This is your last day on earth. I will face all of my fears, even the stupid one about spiders, and I will eradicate you and your kind from the face of the earth."

The entity didn't waver in the face of Miranda's stand. "You are like little ants under a magnifying glass to us. Flies we can snatch out of the air and pull off the wings."

"Come on, fellas." She stood up. "We have work to do."

Dr. Gallagher and Favian rose. They turned to walk out of the kitchen.

The entity looked at Miranda's back with intent. Miranda gasped and held her chest. She collapsed to the floor.

Dr. Gallagher stooped down and put her upper body on his lap. "Stop! Don't, or I swear..."

The entity strode over and stood in front of them. "I can let you live, or I can take your life away in an instant."

"Fine. Go ahead and kill me," she shouted at him, choking. "At least your ugly, smelly ass won't be here."

"Or, I can kill all the people you've ever met from the day of your birth until this very moment, and that's including your pathetic little boyfriend and your sister. I can even have them all die by your hand." He looked at Favian.

Favian's eyes darted between the alien-demon and Miranda as she struggled to breathe. The entity's loathing washed over him from the shadows.

The entity released its hold on Miranda. Dr. Gallagher stood up to assist Miranda and with every intention to get everyone out of there as quickly as possible.

Miranda, panting, took Dr. Gallagher's hand and stood up, but bent over with her hand on her chest until she gained her composure. "Get out of my way. You're gone, and there's nothing you can do."

Again, the rumble rose from the entity's throat. He looked at Favian. Favian collapsed to the floor, clutching his chest and gasping for air.

"This is ridiculous. Come on, let's wake up," said Dr. Gallagher. "Wake up!" He shook Favian's shoulders. Favian clutched his chest, his eyes bulging as if he were being strangled.

"Wake up!"

22
GONE

They all found themselves in Favian's blue room, kneeling at Favian's side. Dr. Gallagher opened the door to let in the available light from the hallway.

Miranda's tears fell on Favian's cheeks.

"Oh, my dear, don't cry," he whispered in between erratic breaths. He put his hand up to her wet cheek.

"I'm calling 911. I'll go to your neighbor's house." Dr. Gallagher stood up.

"No. They won't get here in time. He gave me massive heart failure." He winced and clutched his chest. Spittles of blood protruded from his lips. "He wants me... (a gasp)... to die. I was just about to map the entire subconscious. Now I can't finish my work."

Miranda sobbed. "But, you can't die, Favian, because you're my favorite." She knew better than to pray. It never worked for her to bring the ones she loves from the brink of death.

His smile laced with pain. "I was too much of a threat to him. He was able to get at me because of the brainwaves, the similarity in our backgrounds. Oh, Jack," Favian said sadly, "I'm sorry we couldn't finish with you. What you have in store..."

Miranda's lower lip trembled at Favian's agonizing moan. She clutched Favian's hand. Favian looked into her eyes. "Miranda, we were so close," said Favian. He spat up spots of blood. "Don't give up." He clutched at his chest as he got another sharp pain and cried out. Then his body went limp.

Miranda looked into his eyes. Favian took his last, painful breath, the death rattle sounding in his chest. His body relaxed. She took his hand from the side of her face and grasped it tightly in her hands. He seemed at peace. Suddenly, he looked at her with purpose. "Don't give up, Miranda." Miranda gasped and looked up at Dr. Gallagher to see if he noticed it too. The look of shock told her he also heard Miranda's mother's voice from Favian's lips.

Favian stopped breathing. His eyes remained wide open, staring into the great void.

Miranda brought Favian's hand up to her forehead, clutching it with both hands. "No, no," she sobbed.

Dr. Gallagher's training from the prison kicked in. He rushed to his side and depressed underneath his chest cavity, but blood spewed from Favian's mouth. There was so much of it that he couldn't give him the breath of life.

Miranda held onto Favian's hand, begging, "Please, please," hoping that somehow this was some sort of sick joke, and Favian would wake up and carry on chatting.

After several more chest compressions, Dr. Gallagher stopped. The blood spread and seeped into the carpet. "He's gone."

Miranda sunk into a deluge of tears, clutching Favian's hand.

Dr. Gallagher ran his hand through his hair. He had seen his share of people pass during his time in the prison, but the sequence of events shocked even him. He got up and stood for a moment, trying to think of what to do next.

"Come on, Miranda. We have to go to the neighbor's house and call 911."

"No. I don't want to leave him." Miranda's voice shook.

Dr. Gallagher blew out his breath. "Miranda, I know you're upset. I am too. But there's only so much we can do at this point. The police need to come here and handle this. Then we should think of what we are going to do next."

Miranda stood up. "*We* are going to do nothing. That's what we're going to do." She sniffed and wiped her eyes.

"Miranda, you heard. You can't give up. We're close."

"That's exactly what I'm going to do. I'm going to give up. That's it. He won. Do you want to die?" she yelled. "I'm not going to have another death over my head. I'm not going to have him kill my boyfriend or my sister, or my aunt in California, or any of my clients, or *you*!" She jabbed her finger toward him. "It's done. I'm done."

"Listen. We can discuss our options later. Right now, let's make sure our friend is taken care of. Okay?"

Miranda sniffed. Her eyes filled with tears again when she looked down at Favian. "I'll stay here to watch over him. You go call." *My fault. This is my fault. All my fault. He's dead because of me.*

"You'll be here when I get back, right?" Dr. Gallagher asked.

"Yes."

"Promise?"

Miranda nodded, staring at Favian.

"Miranda..."

"I promise. Yes. I promise."

Dr. Gallagher had no choice. She wouldn't come with him, and he couldn't leave Favian there alone to rot, and there weren't any bars on his cell phone. He left to see if Favian's neighbor was home.

Favian's neighbor turned out to be jelly lady. She seemed really nice and allowed Dr. Gallagher to use the phone. He spoke with her briefly to inform her of Favian's passing, describing what he was going to tell the officers when they arrived. She cried a bit, but he had to excuse himself so he could return check on Miranda and be there when the police arrived.

He hurried back to his car, sped down the road to the driveway, and walked back to the house. The front door stood wide open. "Miranda." His stomach sunk to his feet, like he rode on a really fast elevator going down. "Miranda." He rushed through the living room, the kitchen, where a few drawers were opened and the contents emptied onto the floor, and up the stairs, the adrenaline numbing his pain. He got to the blue room, opened the door, and found Favian still on the floor, a blanket over him. The CD player was smashed to bits. A note lay on the chair beside Favian.

Dr. Gallagher shook his head. He squeezed his eyes shut and rubbed his face. He picked up the note.

Dr. Gallagher,

Thank you for everything you have done for me. I'm sorry I lied to you. I don't want you to die too, so I'm going away, and I'm never coming back. Please tell my sister and Steven I love them both with all of my heart and find a way to explain why I can't ever see them again. I hope you have a long and beautiful life filled with happiness.

Miranda Sheppard

Shit. This fresh trauma put them back to square one, maybe even further than that.

Dr. Gallagher folded the note and stuck it in his pocket. His gaze lingered on Favian for one final moment, and he turned to go downstairs and greet the officers when they arrived.

Instead, the officers greeted him with their weapons drawn. "Whoa." Dr. Gallagher put his hands up. "I called you, Dr. Gallagher. The body is upstairs."

The officers lowered their weapons. "Sorry. The front door was wide open. We thought someone might be in trouble," stated one of the officers.

To Dr. Gallagher, they both seemed young enough to be his sons. Kids with guns. "No, no trouble. My colleague passed. He's upstairs."

"This is Officer Wright, and I'm Officer Rong."

"Come on." *You have got to be kidding.*

They had already pulled out their identifications to verify their names. "Oh, I see," he said when he saw the spelling of their names. "Sorry."

"No matter. We're used to it. Our captain has a twisted sense of humor, so he couldn't resist putting us together as partners from day one," said Officer Rong.

"I'll go." Officer Wright pointed upstairs.

His partner nodded back at him. Officer Wright walked through the living room, looking around as he went as if he expected someone to jump out. He found the stairs and climbed.

"So, tell me what happened." Officer Rong pulled out his notepad and a pen.

"It's pretty simple. We were all upstairs on the third floor. Dr. Widener was helping me with a client. Then, he suddenly keeled over and died."

"Did you try reviving him?"

"Yes. For several minutes."

"Where is your client now?" The officer looked around.

"I'm glad you asked. I need your help. My client was distraught after Favian, Dr. Widener, passed. I asked her to stay here when I went to call you guys, but when I returned, she was gone. I'm afraid the trauma of witnessing someone passing has upset her so much she might be in danger. Could you help me track her down?"

"Yeah, sure."

Officer Wright came down the stairs. "Who put the blanket over the body?" he asked.

"It must have been my client."

"And where is she now?" asked Officer Wright.

"She's MIA," said Officer Rong.

Officer Wright paused, looking intently at Dr. Gallagher. "Why would she run off?"

"We were here as Dr. Widener's guests. We provided her with joint therapy as we helped her work through some issues. We were all inside that blue room, and he stood up and fell to the floor. I had no choice. After I tried to revive Dr. Widener for several minutes, I had to go to the neighbor's house and give you guys a call. I didn't think she would run off. I was wondering if you could help me find her. I just want to make sure she's okay."

The officers looked at each other. Their suspicious glances conveyed they remained unconvinced.

"Listen, when an autopsy is performed on poor Dr. Widener, I am one hundred percent confident the coroner will find that he had a massive heart attack. He clutched his chest, gasped for air, and fell over. My client was in a fragile state. I need to find her and make sure she's okay. She needs our help now."

"One more question," said Officer Rong. "Why did you have to go to a neighbor's house to call us?"

"Dr. Widener doesn't have a phone, and my cell phone doesn't get any bars up here."

"Okay." Rong made a note of it in his book. "What is the name of your client?"

"Miranda Sheppard."

Rong wrote the name in his book. "How do you think she left? Did she steal a car, walk?"

"I had my car. I drove to the neighbor's house and back. Favian could have a car."

Rong looked at Wright. "Let's take a look outside."

Wright nodded. "Be right back." He strode out the back door through the kitchen.

Rong looked at Dr. Gallagher. "This Miranda, she a tough case?"

Dr. Gallagher returned his gaze, perceiving something lay behind the innocent inquiry. "I can't divulge any of my client's information to you other than what I've told you to ensure her safety. She's not violent. She doesn't have any firearms or weapons. She's a woman who needs help."

"Right," Officer Rong said skeptically. "The only thing she's capable of so far is stealing a car and killing herself, right? You know, I haven't been an officer for that long, but I've seen a couple of situations where people get desperate..."

"Officer. Miranda is a pillar in her community, very well-respected, and she does not have a history of violence or mental illness. Witnessing the death of Dr. Widener triggered a traumatic memory from her childhood, so she ran." Rong stared at Dr. Gallagher. "Listen. I was a correction officer when I was your age. If there was anything you needed to know that would endanger you or your partner, I would tell you."

"Oh? Where did you serve?"

"NESP, twenty years ago."

"That would put you there during the riots."

"I'm surprised you know about that."

"My father has been working there for the last twenty years. He's retiring this year. I grew up hearing about these two officers trapped in the rotunda for twelve hours fighting off a hundred inmates."

"Who's your father?"

"Lieutenant Victor Abbott. Step-dad, actually."

Dr. Gallagher nodded. He hoped for the sake of this man that Vic had mellowed out over the years because he was one of those dicks who worked during the second shift. He didn't want to say anything to the boy. Perhaps he already knew how much of a dick his father could be.

"You were one of them, weren't you?"

Dr. Gallagher only stared, neither confirming nor denying it. People tried to take credit for surviving the twelve-hour riot, some of the losers on the first shift, bragging about it when they did not have any role in it at all. People who actually do live through something of that magnitude would rather not mention it at all. The emotions, the memories of finally making it out alive. He usually felt much better off not saying anything.

Officer Wright came back in through the front door. "It seems like a car was there, but it's missing now. Do you know what type of car Mr. Widener had?

"No, I don't."

"It's okay. We'll look it up in our system." Wright looked at Rong. "Let's call this in and get the coroner in here to handle the body. Do you know if he has any relatives?"

"I'll give you the name of a colleague of mine. She might have more information on his family situation. I'll give you my card and write her name on the back." The officers nodded.

Dr. Gallagher walked to an end table in the dining room to have a spot to write the information. He put his hand in his pocket and pulled out a pen and a business card. He bent over to write Grace's information on the back. He saw a picture of Dr. Widener on the table in front of him. He seemed so happy in the photo, holding up a good-sized fish, twice the size of his head, with a lake in the background.

Of course! He quickly wrote Grace and Miranda's information on the card and stood up, wincing from the pain in his back.

When he hobbled over to the kitchen, he heard Rong speaking with Wright: *Yes, that's him. He's one of the guys. Yes, a hundred of them. Yes, twelve hours. My stepdad told me all about it. They devastated all one hundred...* They stopped talking and looked up at him as he entered the room.

"Here's my card. Call me if you need anything else and if you find Miranda."

"Yeah, sure Dr. Gallagher," said Wright. His expression had changed. He looked at Dr. Gallagher with respect. "We'll call you the moment we find anything out."

"Gentlemen, unless there's anything else I can do for you, I will take my leave."

"Sure, Dr. Gallagher," said Rong. "We'll handle everything. I'm sorry for your loss."

"Me too. Dr. Widener was a rare individual. I didn't know him long, but there is less light on the earth today without him." Rong and Wright nodded. "Thanks, gentlemen. I'm going to gather my things. Take care."

Dr. Gallagher went to the bedroom and took his file, the book Dr. Widener had given him and Miranda, and his keys. Then he looked around Miranda's room and found her keys and book on the table next to the bed. He nodded to the officers on the way out and headed to his car.

On the way, he finally got some bars ten minutes out. He called Grace's number and heard her voice mail. "Grace," he started the message. He paused, trying to figure out what to say next. "I have some bad news. Dr. Widener, Favian, he passed today. I'll explain it all to you later. I have to find Miranda. She's missing. I'll check in with you when I can."

He sighed as he hung up. *Great message.* Hello, your friend is dead, talk to you later. He wasn't sure if he'd have the chance to talk with her later, and he wanted her to hear it from him before she heard it from anyone else. He wasn't sure if he was going to survive, but he couldn't leave Miranda out there all alone in the state she was in.

Dr. Gallagher dialed home. "Hi." He put the phone down in the cell phone cradle and put his wife on speaker.

"Hi, hon. How's your case going?"

"Not well. I need to take the weekend to work on it."

"Is everything okay?" she asked.

She knew better. She could always tell. "No, it's not. I hope it will be soon."

"Jack, you're making me nervous."

"Don't worry. I'll be fine. I love you, and I can't wait to be home soon."

"Okay. Thanks for letting me know. You'll call me the moment you're on your way?"

"Yes, of course."

"Okay, love you."

"Love you too, horny slut." Oh, how he loved that about her, and loved egging her on. She transcended any label anyone could tag on her. He could not care less what others thought of his open and free wife. They were just jealous. No one could surpass the passionate love affair they had for the last twenty years.

As predicted, his wife laughed. "Yeah, get home soon, and I'll prove it to you."

There it was—the motivation he needed. When he fought through those 100+ inmates, landing thousands of blows over twelve hours, he arrived to a point where succumbing seemed easier than continuing to fight. His arms and legs felt like lead weights, and sheer will was the only force driving his fists to protect himself. Those little pieces, visions he could grasp onto, his dog, his father, fueled his body to overcome his utter exhaustion and his will to stay alive.

"Sounds good. I'll hold you to it." Dr. Gallagher felt his resolve solidifying like it had during the riot at the prison. No entity, no matter what corner of the universe it came from, was going to prevent him from returning home to his best friend and true love. He used this feeling to beat back any fear. He has had to get into fight mode before. This was no different—just another fight for a battle-weary warrior.

As he contended with the long stretch of highway and winter snow, he worked out his next move. First, he had to track down Miranda and then devise a plan to rid her of this thing once and for all. Her life and the life of the world depended on her success.

He drove the two-hour drive in an hour and a half, straight to her house. He used her keys to open the door.

"Miranda? Miranda, it's Dr. Gallagher." He waited and looked around. When he didn't hear anything, he ventured into the house.

The overcast sky produced a gloom through the windows. He turned on the kitchen light and made his way through to the living room. Something would tell him which lake Miranda's family went to on their vacations every year.

First, he walked through the entire house to see if she was lying unconscious somewhere. Empty. He went back to the living room, turned on the lights, and stood in the room looking around. She had many photos, in frames on her tables, on the wall, and in photo albums on the bookshelves. He smiled at the picture of her and Alison making silly faces as children and then one of them in the same frame making the same silly faces as adults.

He spied a family picture with water in the background. *Yes,* he said under his breath when he took the photo out of the frame. *Good girl.* Miranda's organizational skills would save her life that day. He read the back of the photo. *Mom, Dad, Me, Sissy, at Lake Ocelot.* It was like the stars had aligned. He knew exactly where Lake Ocelot was. It would require another two-hour ride north.

As he drove up, he didn't know how he was going to find the cabin, but was grateful for the bit of sunlight left. The days were growing longer instead of shorter. The ride also gave him a bit of time to contemplate how they were going to accomplish what seemed like an impossible task.

In his twenty years of practice, he never witnessed the decimation of another person in a few seconds. The entity knew exactly what to do to make sure Miranda felt powerless, and it was very effective. Why wouldn't it be? By this time, the entity knew what made her tick and all of her weaknesses, which explained his arrogance. He was holding all the cards, and Miranda has none. He knew everything about her, more than she knew about herself, a terrifying fact. She doesn't know anything about him, his species or his weaknesses. *And neither do I.*

He started with what he did know. It had killed Favian, but his death had a dual purpose Now, Favian would not be able to finish mapping out the subconscious.

However, the entity hadn't killed him, at least not yet. Whether or not this had to do with some purpose, the alien's weakness, or just dumb luck, he didn't know.

Welcome to Lake Ocelot. The sun had disappeared over the horizon. He had approximately twenty more minutes until the houses became engulfed in darkness. The houses ranged from small and rustic to larger and elaborate. He had gotten lost at the lake once but never had the chance to drive around it.

He noticed a dirt road, slammed on his brakes, and got out of the car. To his amazement, he stood on the same dirt road he saw in the shared vision with Favian and Miranda, except it was blanketed in snow with only one set of fresh tire tracks. He got back into the driver's seat, backed up his car five feet, and drove down the road.

Everything was exactly as he had seen it earlier that morning, the trees and fences, the large field off to the left. He slammed on his brakes again. He drank in the cabin from the meditative journey. He saw a blue Suburban parked outside, most likely Favian's car.

With no time to lose, he ran up the porch stairs and knocked on the door.

"Miranda. It's Dr. Gallagher." He paused, listening. He banged on the door. "Miranda," he yelled. "Miranda Sheppard."

He looked in the window: no lights shined from inside. He made his way around the house. He was tall enough to see into the windows. She lay on the couch in the main room.

He ran to the back of the house. He tried to break open the door. When it didn't yield, he took a rock to break a window on the back porch, but it had already been smashed, letting him know that Miranda had actually broken into the cabin. He used the rock to create a larger opening and squeezed himself through.

He rushed to her side. Her cheeks were stained with tears. She clutched a photo of her family in her right hand. "Miranda." No response. He put his fingers to her neck. He detected a pulse. He looked over on the table. He saw five different bottles of prescription medication. "Shit." He didn't have his reading glasses.

He held out one of the bottles and squinted. Shit. Sleeping pills. He could only assume that the rest were sleeping pills as well. He shook every one of them. Empty, except for one, which had a single pill in it.

Shit.

He dialed 911.

23
BULLETPROOF

Dr. Gallagher followed the ambulance to the hospital in his car. The EMTs intubated Miranda and then pumped her stomach. They said her pulse was erratic. Dr. Gallagher told them about her heart condition. They knew what to do.

He waited in the hospital overnight while they worked on stabilizing Miranda. By the time Miranda made it out of the I.C.U., the morning sun had just peeked over the horizon.

Dr. Gallagher was determined to stay at the hospital so he could speak with Miranda right when she woke up. He needed to speak with her before she went to the psych unit if that's what it was going to take to keep her safe.

Normally, he would have notified the family immediately so they could be there to support their family member, but if the alien-demon killed Alison and Steven too, then there would be no hope for Miranda, who treaded on fragile ground. Calling them after Favian's death would be nothing short of irresponsible.

He made the call to Grace early in the morning. He didn't see the sense in putting it off; he needed her help again.

Grace answered her phone. He told her all the details of their weekend. When he had finished, there was a long pause.

"So, he's getting more powerful," she observed.

"It seems to be the case."

"When we execute our next move, we have to make sure it's going to be bulletproof."

"Yes."

"I have one more person I can call. He's probably our last resource." *And hopefully, we won't kill him too.*

"Hopefully, we won't kill him too," Dr. Gallagher repeated.

Grace laughed a dry laugh. Jack always seemed to amaze her every once in a while, parroting her thoughts word for word. "Well, Jack. It's not only about us anymore, is it? At the end of this, if we told everyone how we saved the planet, if we come out of this alive, we would get laughed right out of our profession and probably be accused of creating an elaborate hoax and planting false memories in your client's head. I think the entity knows how to use our weakness against us—our defense mechanisms. He is hiding under the very thing that keeps us stable and sane every day. Miranda has you and me in her corner, and we're not giving up on her. Can you imagine the number of people who will not be so lucky?"

"I think that thought scares me more than anything," Dr. Gallagher admitted. "If these psychic roots really do exist, and the entities need their energy to feed off of their victims and take over their bodies, and everyone on the planet has them as Favian stated, then we really are doomed."

He hung up with Grace. He called his wife, Officer Rong to let him know he found Miranda, and his office to rearrange his schedule again. He went to the restroom and rinsed off his face, throwing some water over his hair with his hand. Exhaustion settled in as an ache in his bones. He supported himself on the sink, resting upon one hand. He turned off the water and stayed bent over the sink, supporting himself with both hands so that he didn't keel over from exhaustion. He raised his head and looked at himself in the mirror.

He saw him. A flash in the mirror behind him, his black shining eyes piercing through the darkness of his face. A pungent smell made Dr. Gallagher cough and then turned into a sickening feeling in the pit of his stomach. The entity had his wife and a large blade. He held her by the hair, his hand pulling on a fistful of her blond locks, her beautiful green eyes wide with terror. He took the blade and sliced off her head. Her body hit the floor with a terrifying thunk. Her blood spattered all over the mirror. He could feel the warm ooze gushing onto his back. He cried out and whipped around. He kicked each of the doors open, surprising a slender, short man in his fifties, ripping the stall apart. Naturally, he shouted at Dr. Gallagher and ran out of the bathroom after he pulled up his pants, but for obvious reasons, Dr. Gallagher had no concern for social politeness. No sign of his wife or the entity. He looked in the mirror. No blood on his back.

He took some deep breaths. He knew what he saw and felt, much like Miranda had. The hallucination seemed so real-to-life. To him, it spoke to her strength, how she hadn't attempted suicide before this. His call to his wife verified that she was home and safe.

The relief allowed him to refocus. Now it was personal. He would make sure Miranda would find her strength again and vanquish the alien-demon from existence. That smelly-assed alien-demon picked a fight with the wrong person.

When he walked out of the bathroom, one of the nurses told him that Miranda was waking up. Before he went to her room, he spoke with the psychiatrist on duty. He assured him he would be in the room in several minutes.

Miranda lay on her side facing the door. She glared at him when he sat down.

"Why did you save me?" Her voice rasped from intubation.

"Because part of you wanted to be saved," he replied.

"What makes you think that? Don't you think five bottles of sleeping pills are enough?"

"If you really wanted to kill yourself, you wouldn't have made yourself so easy to find."

"You should have let me die. Then he would have been gone." Hot tears rolled down her cheeks. She gasped. "You didn't call Alison, did you? Oh, God, she can't come anywhere near me. How could you... Please tell me..."

Before her anxiety got out of control, he said, "No, of course not. Not without your consent."

She took a few deep breaths. Good, calmer, just what he needed to continue.

"I know you felt overwhelmed, that there was no hope in conquering the darkness inside of you. That's why most people attempt suicide."

Instead, tears cascaded down Miranda's cheeks. "Now it's really all my fault. I don't deserve being saved. I'm so ashamed."

Dr. Gallagher glanced at her. He suspected a lingering childhood issue. "What do you mean?"

Her words spilled out, intermittent with sobs. "When I was a teenager, I buried all my pain. Alison tried and tried to help me, but I was too scared to admit it to anyone. I should have, and it might not have been as bad as I imagined it would be. I should have just told her. Now, we all might have to pay because I didn't have the courage to admit it. I'm so sorry! It's all my fault, all my fault." Her shoulders shook as she buried her face in her hands.

"Admit what, Miranda?" he gently prodded.

Miranda took a deep, shaky breath and sniffed. "I wanted to die when my parents died so I could be with them. By 13 years old, I had a plan to do it. Alison thought I didn't believe they were around, that I didn't believe in God. Before meeting Favian, I still wasn't sure. But I knew one thing. Taking the risk to be with them again was better than having to live without them. Even the prospect of nothingness after dying was better than having to continue living in such pain and agony.

"If I had only said it out loud, then maybe I would have met you when I was younger, and you could have helped me even back then. But because I didn't, this stupid alien-demon asshole has moved in, and I have no idea on how I'm going to get him out. The best thing is to end me, and then the world will be free of it."

Miranda sobbed. Dr. Gallagher placed his fingers under her chin so he could look into her tear-stained eyes, which glowed bright green. His wife's eyes did that too when she cried. "He's getting smarter. I saw him. He's threatening my family too. And if he can do that, if you die, he could easily find another now, and he could go after your sister or Steven without you here to protect them. We need you, Miranda."

Miranda's eyes opened wide with horror. She took a shaky breath.

"We're in this together. We have to see this through to the end. I'm not giving up, and I won't let you give up."

She gulped and nodded.

"Do you know what thought scares me more, though?"

She looked at him and waited for his answer.

"The thought of dealing with your sister upon your passing."

Miranda's laugh turned into a choke. It was true; she could be scarier to face that an alien-demon bent on destroying humankind. She wiped her eyes. "Yeah, she wouldn't have taken that too well."

"I bet she would have killed me herself." Dr. Gallagher found over the years that the best way to snap a person out of despondency was to say something completely bizarre. It pleased him to see it worked once again.

"Yeah, I know she would have."

"Do you want me to inform Steven or Alison of your status?"

Miranda shook her head. "No, no. They need to stay away from me, where they will be safe. They don't remember. They wouldn't understand. They would be angry and upset, and I don't want to do that to them." Anything she told them would sound like crazy talk. Better not to say anything at all, to keep them completely out of it until she could sort it all out.

Dr. Gallagher nodded. "I have an idea in the meantime."

Miranda wiped her eyes and waited.

"In my experience, medication chemically alters the body, even shutting down the subconscious at times. I'll bet if we put you on an anti-depressant, it would put handcuffs on the entity for the moment."

She paused as she thought about his idea. "Do you think that will really work?"

"It's worth a try. A low dose, maybe."

"I'm willing to try."

"Alright. I'll get the psychiatrist on staff to prescribe it and get you started on it."

"Okay." She liked the idea of binding the hands of this horrible creature inside of her.

Within the hour, the psychiatrist came to visit Miranda.

"Hello, Ms. Sheppard?" The psychiatrist's hair was short and blond. He seemed like he was in his late thirties, and he carried a clipboard.

"Yes," she replied.

"I'm Dr. Svoboda. How are you feeling today?"

"Tired. Queasy."

"Yes, common complaints, considering what you've experienced over the last twenty-four hours. I'm here to do an assessment. Do you think you're up to it?"

"What's the assessment for?"

"It's hospital procedure. I need to learn what happened, the circumstances that brought you here, and I make recommendations based upon what we discuss here. Okay?"

Miranda looked at Dr. Gallagher. He gave her a slight nod. She nodded her consent.

Dr. Svoboda stepped into the room and stood next to the bed. "I'm going to ask some basic questions. Do you know what time it is?"

"Is this part of the assessment, or do you want to know what time it is?"

Dr. Svoboda smiled. "It's part of the exam."

"There's no clock in here and my watch is missing, but I think it's sometime in the morning."

"It's ten-thirty," said Dr. Svoboda. "Very good. Do you know where you are?"

"I'm in a hospital probably somewhere near Lake Ocelot."

"Good. And what is your name and age?"

"Miranda Sheppard. Twenty-nine years old."

"Good. Okay, Ms. Sheppard. Why don't you tell me what happened yesterday?"

Miranda sighed. "It was a rough day yesterday. My great friend, Favian Widener, died. I was there when it happened. It brought me back to my parent's death. I lost it."

"What do you mean, lost it?"

"I took off and drove straight up here. I broke into the cabin my parents rented every single summer. I wanted to feel close to them again."

Dr. Svoboda nodded, waiting for her to continue.

"Yes, I had come up here intending to killing myself. But I guess I was crying for help. I have been avoiding the way I feel about losing my parents for so long. When my friend died right in front of me yesterday, it all came out. I realize that I finally need to confront what brought me to this point in my life. I will work hard with Dr. Gallagher to make sure that happens, and I can get back to the life I worked so hard in building."

"Where are you from?"

"Davenport."

"That's a two-hour drive, right?"

"Yes."

"So, your friend died in front of you yesterday, and it brought you back to when you lost your parents. What age were you?"

"Eleven."

"Who raised you after that?"

"My sister."

"How is your relationship with her?"

"I love her to death."

"Dr. Gallagher found you?"

"Yes. I guess I made it easy for him to find me. I realize now there is a part of me that doesn't want to die, so I'm going to fight to get myself back to where I was."

Dr. Svoboda nodded, marking some items on his clipboard. "Dr. Gallagher thought you might benefit from an anti-depressant. Do you agree with that statement?"

"Yes. We discussed it. I think that would be good for me."

"He's going to drive you home today and see you on an outpatient basis if I release you?"

"Yes."

Dr. Svoboda looked at Dr. Gallagher. Dr. Gallagher nodded. Dr. Svoboda made some more notes on his clipboard. "Okay. I don't see any reason why you couldn't go home today, Miranda. You seem lucid, your speech is clear, there are no signs of cognitive deficits, and you seem like you have knowledge of how you got here and a clear image of where you want to be. And Miss Sheppard," said Dr. Svoboda.

"Yes?"

"I'm going to have you sign a contract for life. It's an agreement that you will not ever do this again. You will agree to get the help you need before it ever gets out of hand. If you sign the contract, I will release you today."

Miranda looked at Dr. Gallagher. He nodded.

"Okay, fine."

"Good." Dr. Svoboda made a note on his chart. "I'll get the paperwork started, and I'll see if they can fulfill your prescription at the pharmacy downstairs. Dr. Gallagher, Ms. Sheppard, nice to meet you. Good luck to you, Ms. Sheppard."

"Thank you, doctor," said Miranda.

Dr. Svoboda nodded and walked out of the room.

"Was that okay?" asked Miranda.

"Of course it was," said Dr. Gallagher. "Why wouldn't it be?"

"I feel like I lied to him to get him to release me."

"You didn't, though. Aren't you going to face your fears and work hard to get yourself back to your old life?"

"Yes."

"Then you didn't lie."

"But I didn't tell him the entire truth." Miranda never felt guilty before about telling little lies or omitting part of the truth, but the events over the last twenty-four hours made her examine her own actions. Not confronting the truth of how she felt all those years, all of those pent-up feelings about her parents' passing, the little white lies to Alison to keep her big nose out of her business, was how she got into this mess in the first place. Her first opportunity for perfect honesty, and she couldn't bring herself to do it. Was she really a bad person?

"If you did, he probably would have us both locked up. Listen, when you go to the grocery store, do you tell the cashier all the truths about your life at that very moment?"

Miranda laughed. "No, of course not."

"So, it's not appropriate then, to tell her what you had for breakfast that morning, or how your bowel movements went, their shape, size, color, odor?"

Miranda wrinkled her nose. "Okay, I get it."

"Because I heard someone do that once, and now, I can't unhear it. I can tell you all about it if you like."

Miranda laughed. "Okay, enough. I get it."

Dr. Gallagher laughed. "Good."

"What did you tell the cops when they arrived?" asked Miranda.

"I did what you did. I told them the truth, but not the circumstances of it. I didn't show them your note implicating yourself because the note held no truth. You're not responsible for what happened. I didn't tell them about the entity."

"Did you tell them I stole Favian's car?"

"I didn't know you stole his car. They figured that one out for themselves. You might receive a call from an Officer Rong. He said there probably won't be any charges against you, considering the owner of the car is not alive to press charges and cannot verify if he lent you the car or not."

"Oh," said Miranda. "I feel bad. I've never done anything like that in my life."

"I think Favian would understand."

Miranda nodded, looking down. "I guess I should get dressed."

"That's a good idea."

• • •

As they walked out the front door of the hospital, Miranda asked, "So, what's the plan?"

"It's back to Grace's house." He headed for the hospital parking lot.

"Have you slept at all?"

"It doesn't matter," he said.

"It sure does matter. We have a long drive. How about I drive to Grace's house and you rest a while?"

"No, that's okay. I'll drive." They reached Dr. Gallagher's car. He stood on the driver's side of his Challenger Hellcat, plum purple, fumbling for his keys through his jacket pocket. He found them, and as he tried to unlock his door, they fell to the ground. He sighed, exasperated, and winced as he bent down to retrieve them.

Miranda ran around the car, stooped down, and picked up the keys.

"Thanks," said Dr. Gallagher, holding out his hand.

Miranda shook her head. "I'm driving, and that's the end of it."

"No, I'm driving." He reached for his keys.

She snatched them away from him and shook her head. "You know, I might have been full of sleeping pills, but at least I was the one that got some sleep. You didn't get any. It's the only way I'll get into the car with you."

"Why would I give you my keys? You stole a car yesterday," he said crankily.

Miranda laughed. "Come on, doc. You know I love cars. I've always wanted to drive a Challenger. I'll treat yours like it's my baby."

"First of all," he said, holding up his pointer finger, "No one drives my car except for me. Second, no one drives my car except for me, and third, no one drives my car except for me." He held out his hand and waited.

Miranda hesitated.

"Listen. We can't risk it. We don't know what the entity will do. He might try to kill us while you're driving, and right now, it's more dangerous than me being tired."

"Oh. I didn't think of that."

"That's okay. I'll tell you what. I'm more comfortable driving anyway because it helps me keep my mind off the pain in my neck and back. Why don't we talk on the ride down? It'll help keep me awake."

Miranda sighed. "Okay, fine." She walked around and got into the passenger's seat.

When he started the car, he looked at Miranda. "It was a sweet gesture, really. I appreciate it."

Miranda smiled.

"I have a request."

Miranda nodded and waited.

"Would you open your purse and show me you don't have any more pills?"

"Oh," she said, looking downcast. "You don't trust me? I'm not a pill addict. I got all of those prescriptions filled when I had insomnia." *Great. Now he thinks I'm going to attempt suicide every five minutes. Have I lost all control? Am I really that bad off?*

"I know. I trust you. We don't know what the alien is capable of, so it's best to make sure."

"Okay, I guess I understand." She opened her purse and turned all her pockets inside out, revealing to Dr. Gallagher's satisfaction that her pockets were empty and her purse only had the anti-depressants.

"Great. Thanks, Miranda. Let's get going." Dr. Gallagher pulled out of the parking lot. As they made their way over to the highway, Dr. Gallagher deliberated how he was going to cram two years of therapy into two hours.

When they reached the highway, Miranda asked, "So, Dr. Gallagher, what type of cars do you like?"

Dr. Gallagher grinned. She chose the right topic to keep him awake. "I like the older muscle cars. Challengers, obviously, and Road Runners. I had a Chevy Nova I miss. I also like Corvettes. I had a 1969 Corvette once."

"Cool. I love Corvettes." She shared the story of her Cherry Red. "What happened to yours?"

"It got stolen."

"Aww, sorry."

"It's okay."

"You don't seem very upset about it."

"I had cars stolen before that."

"How many?"

"Um, let's see." Dr. Gallagher mentally counted. "About six."

"Six?"

"When I was growing up, we lived right on the border of the Bronx. My road got hit up a lot. My parents, my siblings, and I all had cars, five in total, and one building parking space, so we had to park them out on the road. I never wanted to drive around in a beater, so I always found nice cars. We would rebuild them and race them on the Hutch."

"The Hutch?"

"It's a parkway. We'd go out at three in the morning, block traffic for a few minutes, and have our race."

"Is that legal?"

Dr. Gallagher smiled. "We were kids. We had a racing club. There weren't any tracks to go to in the Bronx. Otherwise, we would have done that for fun. The next best thing was the Hutch at three in the morning. Eventually, the media caught wind of our races. The news crew had filmed me as the flag man."

"No way." Mouth agape, she tittered.

"Yeah. When that happened and I wound up on the six o'clock news, it put an end to our club. Because of the media attention, the cops caught up to us and parked themselves in the parking lot of our hangout and would hand out tickets for everything under the sun, even had a few of our friends' cars towed away for not being street-ready."

"Aww, too bad."

"Yeah, what can you do? You know the funny thing about it? My wife saw that newscast and remembers seeing me on television years before we got together as a couple."

"No way!" Miranda guffawed.

Dr. Gallagher nodded and smiled. *Even under the direst of circumstances, finding opportunities to laugh is crucial to keeping our sanity.* "Yup. When we remember it from time to time, my wife jokes that she was seeing her future husband, the derelict."

"Oh my gosh!" Miranda doubled over in laughter. "So, you two grew up in the same area?"

"Yes."

"Maybe that's why you get along so well."

"Maybe," Dr. Gallagher agreed.

After a moment of silence, Miranda said, "I guess I'm having trouble believing what happened this past weekend."

"What do you mean? We lived through it together."

"I don't know. It's kind of blowing my mind. An alien-demon came all the way from God-knows-where to camp out inside of me? Me? Why me? Now, in order for these weird demon things to leave us alone, I have to figure out a way to conquer them, otherwise, they are going to come and take over all of us? Not only that, I have to figure out my emotional shit," she shook her head and paused, "to save the planet? I mean, come on," she said, folding her arms. "It sounds like a bad sci-fi movie or something."

Dr. Gallagher's suspicions about the grand plan of the alien demons were far more expansive than the distance the alien must have traveled to occupy Miranda. Instead of expressing them, he asked, "You want to know my thoughts?"

Miranda nodded.

"I think he chose someone who is very intelligent and has had a healthy upbringing. Remember, I met your parents. They were two of the healthiest, most constructive people I ever met. I bet he hoped to remain hidden, learn and incorporate all of your body and mind's energies, and eventually possess your conscious mind. If he could do that, then they could take over anyone on the planet, and there wouldn't be a thing we could do about it.

"Fortunately for us, he has had trouble with his plan from the start. The light and love inside of you have been much harder for him to conquer than he originally thought. Also, humans are much more intuitive than they gave us credit. Your body and mind reacted when he initiated his takeover of you. It shows he can be fought."

A pause. Miranda: "You know, if I had only dealt with my parents' death then, when my sister told me to all those years ago instead of burying it, none of this would have happened."

"There's no guarantee of that. Even if the therapy helped, your black roots could have still been there. It caused you a great deal of pain. Humans don't want to live in pain all the time, so we do everything we can to bring ourselves back to no pain, even if we have to lie to ourselves."

"You mean, like I did, trying to tell myself nothing odd or extraterrestrial was occurring with me, and I blamed it all on my heart condition?"

"Yes, that's it. You did what you needed at the time to put some very painful things out of your mind and concentrate on your health. You see, sometimes it's a good thing. It helps us survive that situation for the moment. But it stays in the subconscious, and unknown to the consciousness, it constantly affects our thoughts, feelings, and actions. It comes up in dreams, and at the most inappropriate moments, flashing through our minds."

"Yes, that's exactly what happened to me, the dream with my mother."

"Right again. It's about pain management, except it's emotional pain. It never goes away, but we keep trying to bury it so we can ensure our day-to-day survival.

"That's when the problem starts. It's only meant to be a short-term solution; there comes a time when burying it no longer works. Something always triggers the memory and all its feelings, and it comes back up again.

"Unless we are taught a healthy way to manage emotional pain, we do the easiest thing for the moment, and avoid it or bury it. Unfortunately, the extraterrestrial demons are using this aspect of humanity as their way in."

Miranda nodded. Dr. Gallagher could see her mind working to process the information, a good sign.

"So, what do I have to do?"

"I'm not really sure. I've never worked with metaphysical black roots before. Even though I've never seen them, I think they exist. I'm not sure how it all fits together with this alien and how it has attached onto you, but if we can figure that out, we can defeat him."

"Oh, did you remember to grab our books?" asked Miranda.

"Yes. I have your copy too, and my files. They're in the back seat."

"Okay, good. I'd love to share it with Ali, and Steven too." That is, if she made it out alive. How she ached for Alison's calming presence. Miranda resisted the urge to call her. The least she could do was keep Ali safe after everything she sacrificed for her. Maybe her parents would be there to help her, watching over her, even though she couldn't see or hear them. After another long pause, Miranda asked, "So how do you let go? I mean, I think about my parents, and it still hurts. How could that pain possibly go away? I'll always miss them and feel sad they weren't there for my prom or they won't be there for my wedding or to see my children grow. My parents would have made the best grandparents. Now, I have none to offer my children. How can I not be sad every time I think about them? Every time anything good happens in my life, anytime the holidays come around, there is an event going on, marriage, kids, accomplishments, they are not here to enjoy it with me. How can I start looking at only the positives in my life with a constant hole?"

"It's understandable. I've worked with a lot of people who have trouble letting go of being sad. Even when a person comes to the acceptance phase, that sadness can still be there because it's the only part that people feel they have left, until they realize they don't have to hold onto the sadness to have a piece of their lost loved one: they can instead remember their feeling of love or a good memory to honor them. Or sometimes, they feel guilty letting go of that sadness, even at great cost to themselves. They feel if they stop mourning over their loss, they will somehow dishonor their loved one."

"I don't feel guilty. I want them back, even now. I'll never get back what I lost, and it makes me mad."

"There's a point in our lives when we have to ask if the anger is doing us any good. Anger is a normal, human reaction to certain situations, and you are justified in your anger."

"I didn't think I was still as angry as I was, as I am. I guess I did bury it. And you're right. It's really not working for me anymore. I have to find a way to move on without it. I didn't realize how much the anger permeated everything in my life. I thought I had moved on, but I always carried it around with me, so it never completely went away."

"What else do you think you can do besides letting go of the anger?"

Miranda thought for a moment. "I can stop focusing on what I lost. I should focus on what I still have, what I can have in the future. Maybe I can work to fill the holes in my life. I can't replace my parents, but maybe I can look forward to the good things that I have and can still happen to me. I have Alison, I now have Steven. Plus, I think knowing my parents are always around me makes me feel a little better."

"It's amazing, the gift Favian gave us."

"What, you mean the books?"

"No. Faith."

Dr. Gallagher stopped the car in front of an open parking spot. Miranda's look had changed from anxiety to peace, pleasing Dr. Gallagher. She seemed ready to fight. Plus, no major attack from the alien-demon while she processed the past, an excellent sign that the antidepressant had done its job. Something told him, as always, it wouldn't be as easy as lifting the entity away from Miranda, but for a change, he hoped with his wife's maddening optimism it would be.

"Here already?"

"Like Favian said, it's the magic of good conversation." Dr. Gallagher winced as he turned around to park the car.

"Would you like me to park the car for you?"

"No, that's okay." He looked her in the eyes. "How about you drive when we're ready to go home?"

Miranda smiled. It meant he expected her to make it through, but also as important, he trusted her. Car aficionados do not allow others to drive their cars unless they really trust a person. "That sounds fine."

• • •

When Grace opened the door, all it took was one look for Dr. Gallagher to know what the last twenty-four hours had been like for her. Dr. Gallagher opened up his arms, and they embraced.

Dr. Kelly patted Dr. Gallagher's arm, and she backed up a step, wiping her eyes. She looked at forlorn Miranda and took her hands. "It's not your fault. I have a feeling Favian knew what was coming."

Miranda nodded. The women embraced.

"Oh!" Dr. Gallagher's utterance made Miranda jump and face him. "Favian left me a note! I didn't have a chance to read it." He pulled out his glasses and the letter and read:

Hey Jack. Hope you had a good sleep. I didn't want to upset Miranda. Such a sweet soul. My spirit guides informed me, this could be my last day on earth. I'm hoping it's not. I have unfinished business. Please make sure Grace receives all my books. I know she doesn't have room for them all. I trust she will do what is best for them. Also, see if she will take over my research, if she has an interest in pursuing it. I uncovered some materials from the worlds' religions that might interest all of you. And, my friend Jack, please protect our dear Miranda. One day, our dearest Miranda will save the entire world.

Miranda put her face in her hands and cried. Whereas before her heart ached with guilt, she now ached with his absence. He spent his last days caring for her, feeding her, encouraging her. He put himself in the way of danger to save her. He entered the meditative state knowing full well he would never come out of it. How can they do this without him?

It took so much for Dr. Gallagher to cry. His pain and anguish had to boil over for a tear to rise. Favian kept bringing up what he perceived could be Dr. Gallagher's downfall in the face of the beast, bugging him to protect himself, and Dr. Gallagher thought upon him unkindly. His tear was a result of the realization that he judged another individual without merit. He wished he had him back so they could really pursue friendship. He only spent a couple of days with him, but he missed his presence as if he had known him all his life. The surprise of this feeling produced a couple more tears.

The letter didn't surprise Grace at all, even though it made her cry for the thousandth time that day. Grace met Favian when he used to give psychic medium readings. She was the recipient of a spiritual message from her mother. It made such a significant impact on her life that she took it upon herself to form a friendship with him.

What an easy man to befriend. He taught her how to meditate. They talked about everything. They even had sex occasionally. Why didn't she marry him? She supposed in time, they would have the opportunity to pursue it, but it never seemed to matriculate. Now, they would never have the time to discuss the origins of the universe, to bare their souls to each other, or to see if their long-time relationship could be taken further. She already missed their weekend-long discussions. He was the only person on earth who knew what happened to her and listened to her without judgment.

Grace took Miranda by the hands again. There was something in Grace's eyes Dr. Gallagher had never seen before—anger. "Come on in, and let's get the bastard."

Miranda nodded.

Grace led them into the living room. An older gentleman sat in a chair facing the doorway of the living room. Not one of his features stood out as particularly ugly or handsome. Miranda thought he was good looking, even at his age, even though he had no hair. It was something about the way he held himself, the way he gazed upon them as they entered the room, the fire and intensity in his blue eyes.

"Jack, Miranda, when I heard what happened to Favian, I decided to call in the big guns. This is Dr. John O'Connor," she announced with some flourish.

"Dr. O'Connor? The one who wrote *Id Speak*?" asked Miranda. *Another doctor? Fine. Another doctor. Safety in numbers, right?*

What would be in store for her now? Would she go full-out *Exorcist* and throw up green, smelly ooze on them? Would they have to take on the beast to kill it like the priest had in the movie, killing themselves in the process? Favian's death hung around her neck like an albatross necklace. Would someone else have to die too before this disgusting alien-demon could be driven out from her and the earth?

She had more difficulty trying to focus on the task rather than get caught in the well of hatred toward the entity. Her mom always said that when people act despicably, love them all the more. It means that they have had such a terrible life. No one had ever loved them fully for themselves. They never connected with anyone who was able to show them love without abuse. Their reality is literal hell. When people act abominably, they need love in their lives most of all. This was why Joy Sheppard remained the most excellent person Miranda had the privilege to know.

She was just along for the ride now, a passenger in her own fate, this cliché unsettling her to the point of unhinging. She had no idea how to banish an alien-demon.

Growing up, Miranda wanted to be the first at something. Now, she got to become a living example of the negative side of being the first. No precedent existed, so they had nothing to refer to, nothing to guide them toward success. She always envisioned herself discovering a treasure for the first time, or uncovering an unsolved mystery, not discovering how to vanquish a parasitic alien-demon species from the earth. How she wished with all her heart to discover buried treasure rather than what she was experiencing.

Thank goodness she was lucky. She had Dr. Gallagher, Dr. Kelly, and Dr. O'Connor helping her. If she had discovered all of this garbage on her own, she would have struggled to get one person to believe in her. Other psychologists might have locked her away in a ward or treated her for delusions and paranoia. She wouldn't know where to go, who to turn to, or what to do. She would probably just lie down and die. Now, she had three who actually brought her to this point, and she didn't even have to convince them otherwise. Even though she had no idea how to solve her own problems, and she felt like a passenger in her own fate, there was no better time for her to feel like that and have these three people on her side, people who might actually be able to help her where there was no hope. *Good. Bring on the world's doctors and have them all believe her.* The more people who believed her, the less likely the annihilation of the human race would come to pass.

"Yes, that's me." Dr. O'Connor stood and stuck out his hand. "You must be Miranda." He looked toward Dr. Gallagher. "And you must be Jack." O'Connor and Gallagher shook hands. "When Grace told me what happened, I flew out on the first plane. Miranda, at the moment, you are the most important person in the entire world. You hold the key to saving our entire planet from hostile takeover."

Miranda's stomach heaved, and she swallowed.

"Have you not realized this?" he asked.

"No, I have. It's just strange to hear it."

Dr. O'Connor nodded. "You can say that again, sister," he said.

Sister? Dr. Gallagher and Grace laughed a little in response to Miranda's look in spite of the seriousness of the matter, making Miranda grin.

"Good," Dr. O'Connor said, satisfied he was able to break up some of the tension. People don't think clearly with too much stress. "Glad to see you can still laugh a little. We are going to have to hang onto what makes us humans feel good."

"Would you like some food or drink?" asked Grace. "You are going to need to keep your energy up."

Miranda wrinkled her nose and shook her head. "No thanks. You'd be surprised how much you don't want to eat after having your stomach pumped." There was a sentence Miranda never thought she would say out loud to another human being, and here she was uttering it to a room full of people.

Grace nodded and looked to Dr. Gallagher.

"Nah, I'm good, thanks."

"Please, have a seat." Grace sat on the same chair as she did the last time they visited. Miranda and Dr. Gallagher walked over to the couch and sat down.

Dr. O'Connor sat again, his expression grave. "Miranda, I know you've probably explained your experiences about a dozen times, but I'll need you to explain what has transpired from the moment you first noticed something was the matter until now."

"That's okay. I'm used to it." Miranda told her story again from the beginning. She shared how Dr. O'Connor's book served as an inspiration for idea of the blue room. After she was done conveying their arrival at Favian's house, her rising emotions forced her to pause. "I'm sorry. It still upsets me to think about what happened at that house. This wonderful man who extended himself to help me died at the hands of this beast. He was probably one of the kindest persons I have ever met, and now he's gone."

"When I spoke with the police," Dr. Gallagher interjected, "they said the coroner had never seen a heart failure like this. It almost looked like his heart had been ripped in half."

Dr. O'Connor seemed to be in contemplation. "Did Favian have any past trauma?"

"Yes, actually. His parents were murdered."

"Interesting," Dr. O'Connor mused. "The demon could have accessed Favian because the meditation put you all on the same brainwaves. Then, the similarity in life experiences provided him the opportunity to attack and kill Favian, making the mental and emotional trauma physical."

Dr. Gallagher nodded. "His heart was broken."

"Do you think that's why I'm having problems with my heart now?" Miranda asked. "It's not some random thing that happened to me with my car accident?"

"The world is not as random as most people think," Dr. O'Connor observed. "In my studies, I found that emotional issues often manifest themselves into the physical. It sometimes takes twenty or even thirty years, but eventually, chronic emotional issues can seep into the physical body."

A tear betrayed Miranda and rolled down her cheek. "When Favian was killed, I lost it. I felt responsible. I still do. I brought this thing to his house, and it killed him."

Grace sighed and closed her eyes, evidence of the pain the mentioning of her friend brought up. "Because of him, we know more about the demon. He used his own death as a teaching tool. He's very brave."

"No braver than you all are." said Miranda. "You're probably the only people on the planet now who know about this and believe me. I'm very grateful."

"And so are we for you, Miranda," said Grace. "We appreciate your willingness to fight. This demon might have entered our dimension through you, but it will also leave through you. We'll all make sure of it. We have to. It's up to us." She gazed upon Dr. Gallagher, Miranda, and Dr. O'Connor. "We have to save ourselves and everyone else."

Miranda nodded. "As I have asked you so many times before, what now?"

"I think we should rest and have some dinner before our first session," said Grace. "You all had long journeys. We need to keep up our strength. If anyone wants to take a nap, I have an extra bed in my spare room, and I can put someone in my bed also while I work on things. Jack? You look more worn out than an old rug." He didn't even look like he had the energy to put on a fresh change of clothes.

Dr. Gallagher chuckled and stood up. “I am. I’ll give it a try.” He needed the rest. Miranda might not be able to put herself back together again if he died too.

Grace led him to her bedroom. “I’ll work on some dinner. Maybe I’ll order out.”

Dr. Gallagher nodded. “Grace...” he started.

“I’m not ready to talk about it right now, Jack.” She put up her hand. “Tomorrow will be another day, and we can talk about our inner turmoil to our hearts’ content. Okay?”

Jack nodded. He learned the grieving process well when he lost his father to cancer. *She’ll share in her own time.*

24
STAB

Grace walked back into the living room and sat down on the couch next to Miranda. "When was the last time you were able to do something fun and relaxing? You know, where you could zone out, do something mindless?"

Miranda paused for a moment. "I can't even remember."

"We are going to remedy that right now. What would you like to do?"

Miranda thought for a moment. "Watch a movie and eat popcorn. My family and I used to see a movie once a month together. I would enjoy that."

Grace smiled at Miranda and patted her knee. "You shall have it. Do you have a favorite you would like to watch, or would you like to watch something you've never seen before?"

Miranda thought for a moment. "Do you think we could rent *Caddyshack*? It was my mom's favorite movie."

"Even better, I have *Caddyshack* in my collection. I'll start it and make the popcorn. Anything to drink?"

"Just water. Thanks so much."

It was the first time Grace ever saw Miranda smile. She smiled back, went to the kitchen, and took out a bag of popcorn from the box.

Dr. O'Connor got up and walked to the kitchen. "That's a smart thing to do." He leaned on the countertop. Grace stuck the bag of popcorn in the microwave.

Dr. Kelly shrugged as she set the timer. "The girl is responsible for saving the entire planet from enslavement. This might be hers and our last night here on earth. She feels isolated from her family and boyfriend at the moment. It's smart of her to keep her family away from harm, but it's not doing her much good. She has been living with the crushing stress of an auto accident, a heart valve problem, and possession, in addition to the trauma that goes along with these events and witnessing the death of another human being. I think it's easy to say she deserves a little R and R." She started the power. After a moment, the cheerful smell and sound of popping corn filled the kitchen.

"I agree. It'll be good for her to reenergize before our session tonight. Like exorcisms, we could be in for a hard road."

Grace frowned. "You know, when I first read your book, I felt like someone finally got it. Everything I had been seeing in my practice but couldn't explain, you explained it. It's amazing to me that no one seems to get it. I stopped talking about the id and the ego years ago because I would get dirty looks."

Dr. O'Connor laughed. "Yeah, believe me, I know the feeling."

The popcorn had stopped popping. She took the bag out of the microwave and pulled apart the top. The steam rose from the bag. She looked down for a moment as if something pained her, and then looked at Dr. O'Connor. "Are you as terrified as I am?"

"I'm not sure."

"When Jack and Miranda came to me, I knew something odd was going on, but I didn't know the extent of it. I can't believe Favian died," she composed herself after she choked up a bit, "and I have no idea how we can ensure the survival of this girl, of our species. Do you know the amount of trouble we're all in?"

"I think I do. Why don't you tell me what you think?"

"I think we're in big trouble. I don't know if we can do this. This demon seems to know all of our vulnerabilities, our shortsightedness, our limitations, and can use each one of them to stay hidden and undetected. It knows us better than we know ourselves. Humans have no idea what exactly goes on inside of them. Yet, this thing knows exactly what makes us tick.

"I'm most terrified because it's not human, so we can't reason with it. It's not physical, so we can't overpower it. Yet, it's as real as the ghosts and demons that haunt us from our past.

"And, in order to rid ourselves from its grasp, it forces us to confront the deep, dark secrets that we spend a lifetime hiding from ourselves, the most terrifying of fears buried deep within ourselves. It's less terrifying to travel to the far reaches of our solar system or climb Mt. Everest. As a species, our notions of bravery are all external. Yet, no one is brave enough to go to the scariest place of all, the root of all our fears. It's not even evil that we have to conquer. They are forcing us to conquer the things inside ourselves that are more terrifying than any ghost, demon, or monster any human could dream up. There's nothing external to fight, yet it's more terrifying than anything that can darken our doorstep.

"Because we can't prove their existence, most people will not believe these demons are even there. Most people don't even believe in the existence of the subconscious or the id. After over a hundred years since Freud detected these metaphysical structures, if the human race isn't sold that they exist, how are we possibly going to convince people that we are under attack from an unseen enemy who takes over parts of them that they feel aren't there? Yes, I believe in the metaphysical black roots that collect as a result of upsetting experiences and trauma. We are most likely the only ones on earth who do.

"It's our own ignorance, our own closed-mindedness that will leave the entire planet vulnerable. Our skepticism is built into us as a survival mechanism, and society does more than encourage it; it demands it. To use our doubt against us will literally end humankind.

"How can we fight against that? And, if we actually pull off the impossible and save this poor woman, we are always going to have to worry about every single person in the human race, about ourselves. We could be at war with these beings for the rest of our lives, if we live at all. Who will be under attack next? Who do we tell? It knows we can't go to other people for help. I think we would have better luck getting help if we all stated we saw a UFO. There is no one to help us. What do we do? Call the police? A psychic? A priest? The president? What can they do? What in the world are we going to do?"

"I know someone who can help," said Dr. Gallagher. Grace and Dr. O'Connor turned around.

"Who?" asked Grace.

"Dr. Abraham Tetenbaum."

Grace poured Miranda's popcorn into a bowl for her. "Oh, you mean the head of the MRI you've been telling us about?"

"Yes. I have a feeling if anyone could help us put a plan together, he could. He'll give us the missing pieces we need."

"Shall we have him come here?" Grace asked.

"He mentioned he had some equipment at his house, so he wanted us to go there after dinner. I described the entire situation to him. He understands what we're up against."

Grace picked up the popcorn bowl. "You couldn't sleep?"

"No." The bed was like sleeping on a board, but he didn't want to hurt his host's feelings. Dr. Gallagher got out of bed before it crippled him for the night.

"Since you're up, then, let me get this popcorn out to Miranda and put the movie in for her, and we can decide what to do." Grace brought the popcorn and water to the living room.

"So, Dr. O'Connor. Do you have the same understanding of our situation that Grace has?"

Dr. O'Connor nodded. "Yeah, we're fucked unless we can do something."

Dr. Gallagher laughed. "You have a way with words. Reminds me of being in the Bronx. I hear you can see ids."

"To me, it's as plain as the nose on your face."

"These roots. You see them too?"

Dr. O'Connor nodded.

"We're all riddled with them, Favian said."

Dr. O'Connor nodded again.

Grace returned. "Okay, she's all settled. Why don't we sit in here?" Grace motioned to her kitchen table.

Dr. O'Connor and Dr. Gallagher looked at the chairs. Dr. O'Connor sat down, wincing.

"You know, you're vulnerable, Dr. Gallagher," Dr. O'Connor observed.

Dr. Gallagher laughed. "And why do you say that?"

Dr. O'Connor gave him a sharp look. "Your pain is what the demon will attack first."

"Then everyone is vulnerable, Dr. O'Connor. Do you know anyone who doesn't carry with them some sort of pain? So, you can see my roots, then?"

"You mean the one that happened when you were twenty-three? And one when you were eight. And another when you were eighteen. You haven't lived an easy life, have you, Dr. Gallagher?"

Dr. Gallagher returned his stare. "You can call me Jack."

"Then, you can call me Dr. O'Connor... or John."

"Okay, John. As the expert, what is the procedure for helping this girl?"

"It sounds like you helped her process on the car ride over, correct?"

"Yes."

"*Id Speak* is about the root system resulting from traumatic events and how Freud's theories are interconnected with the belief of the human body's energy system."

"Yes. I read through it," said Jack. "So, how does this translate into helping Miranda?"

"We remove the roots, and we capture the alien."

"And how do you propose we do that?" asked Jack.

"First, I'll do what I always do. I will locate the roots."

"How do you do that?"

"Miranda's roots are all up and down her spine, each having a plug that goes into her chakras, the red, orange, yellow, green, blue, indigo, and violet."

"Oh, you saw the MRI, then?" Jack asked.

"No, Jack," Grace interjected. "You took your copies with you when you went to Favian's house. Remember?"

"And I left my folder in the back seat of my car, so that means..." Jack paused and looked at John.

"I saw it, the patterns of trauma. It hits them on every level of their lives–on the physical, emotional, mental, and spiritual levels. That is why the root attached to all of her chakras. The fact that it is plugged into her chakras right in the center of them means that the tragedy she faced as a child completely affected her id."

"Right." Grace pointed. "Because Miranda's root is exactly where her id is located, right?"

John nodded. "The id is plugged into these energy centers. It makes her a perfect candidate for possession. The entity has been able to plug into the center of all her energy centers all at once because that's where her roots are located.

"There is a front and back part to the chakras, the energy wheels. The conscious is located in the front, and the subconscious is located in the back, and the id is plugged right in the middle of the chakras. The demon is intermingled with her entire id and that black root. Her id could be overtaken even as we speak, using her trauma as an in for possession."

Grace shook her head. "That poor girl. She was so devastated when her parents passed."

"So, what did I see on the MRI?" asked Jack. "Was it the alien, or was that actually her id?" He shuddered as he recalled the black eyes that almost seemed to be staring at him from the image.

"I think it's an intermingling of both you saw," said John.

"How do you see ids?"

"I don't know. I've always been able to see them. I didn't know what they were at first. Then, when I began my practice and studied other worldviews of the human body, I realized there were emotional connections to what I saw, and it began making sense. I mapped the accounts of my clients' experiences to the physical symptoms they experienced, and I observed that each and every single time, these traumatic experiences corresponded with the roots I was seeing. I connected their trauma with these energy centers on a whim one day, actually, to see what happened. According to what I had read until that point, each energy center contains the body's physical functioning. Red governs the body's energy, orange, the sexual organs and spleen, yellow, the nervous system and brain, green, the heart, blue, the throat and communication, indigo, eyesight and the third eye, and violet at the top of the head connects our energy field to spirit. There is some variation on this understanding depending on a person's cultural orientation. People have known for a long time there is a mind-body connection, but until I made that discovery, it was the missing link."

"Okay, now I understand about the root system, and we know where Miranda's main roots are. How do we get rid of them?" asked Jack.

"We pull them out."

"How do we do that?" Grace asked.

"I have spirit guides who help me do it. I ask them for help, and they help me and the client transform the energy of the dark roots into golden light. If she releases the issues keeping the black root there, the thing won't have anything to hold onto within her, and it will force him to leave... hopefully."

"It's our best bet." Grace looked at Jack, whose brow had knitted into wavy lines of concern. "What is it, Jack?"

"I saw him right after I spoke with you, in the hospital."

"You saw him in the visions, right?" asked John.

"No, well, yes, but I saw him another time, at the hospital. He appeared behind me in the mirror of the bathroom right after we spoke on the phone, Grace. He looked as real as you and me. He sliced off my wife's head. When I turned around there was no one there."

Grace's hand flew up to her mouth, her eyes filling with tears.

"Now this fight is personal for me, too. No one threatens the ones I love and gets away with it."

"After you and Miranda shared the vision, he's able to access you," John hypothesized. According to what was explained to him, the entity was bound because he was a match for Miranda. He hoped this didn't mean that it was finding a way to move between people.

"So now what?" asked Grace. "Does this change things?"

"No, not really. We have to take an extra precaution. The plan is still the same."

Grace jumped. "Oh, Miranda. Is something wrong?"

Miranda gazed down at the floor.

Grace put her hand to her nose as the pungent smell of sulfur hit her nose.

Dr. Gallagher's pulse raced. "Miranda?"

Miranda raised her head. Her eyes glowed black. Grace gasped. John and Jack looked at each other and nodded. Jack felt like he was back in the prison, readying himself to fight. Jack looked down to Miranda's side. She held a twelve-inch blade. *Where in the world did she get that?*

"Wait until I have this simpering little fool kill your wife, Jack, and everyone you know."

Jack's heart pounded in his ears.

Grace could hear another voice overlaying Miranda's, a lower, tinny, growling voice.

Before any of them could rise from their chairs, the lights flashed. Total darkness. Grace reached for Dr. Gallagher's hand. He could hear Grace panting. The lights flashed like a strobe light.

Miranda reappeared right behind Grace. She stabbed Grace through the back of her seat with the knife. Grace's body convulsed.

The shock and horror that registered on her face were unlike any other experience Jack had witnessed, the knowledge that something has happened and there wasn't any hope to reverse the events. The knife impaled her from back to front, the bloody blade poking through her chest, the front of her shirt saturated in her own blood. Grace coughed blood out of her mouth.

Miranda's eyes glowed black as she laughed at their horror. "You should see your faces," she laughed, pointing with a bloody finger. As the lights flashed, they could see quips of Miranda leaning over and licking the blood dripping out of Grace's mouth. Grace made a gurgling sound. Miranda took the blood from the front of Grace's neck and wiped her own face with it, smiling.

Jack cried out. He and John jumped out of their chairs to restrain Miranda, but she had disappeared. The lights came back on.

Jack knelt down next to Grace. She was still coughing.

"Grace, Grace, it's okay. There's nothing there. Look down."

Grace looked down at her hands and chest. Sure enough, there was no sign of blood. She drew in gasps of air, feeling her chest frantically where the hole had been and stood up.

"It's okay. You're okay." Jack took the shaking Grace into his arms.

It felt so real. If the scene had continued on, it could have killed her.

"Miranda!" With Grace still gasping and coughing, they ran to the living room.

Grace grasped at Jack's hand and drew in a quick breath. Miranda lay on the couch, fast asleep with the popcorn bowl in her lap, while Rodney Dangerfield stated he understood why tigers eat their young and rolled his eyes.

They silently walked back to the kitchen. “Jack,” said John.

“Yeah?”

“I think you better call your friend and have him come over now.”

“I think that’s a good idea.”

Grace nodded.

Jack took out his cell phone.

25
Preparation

"Abe, thanks for coming so soon." Jack shook Abe's hand.

"Oh, believe me, Jack, part of me can't help but be excited. Who else will be able to say that he played a part in eradicating the earth of a parasitic species of extraterrestrial demons bent on enslaving the human population and taking over the world?"

Jack shook his head. Typical Abe. He didn't have to jog his memory much after his visit. With the discussion between them, the memory of that night had returned on its own.

"Besides, I get to levy a little payback. That entity destroyed my one hundred and fifty million dollar MRI. So, where is Miranda?"

"Sleeping in the guest room," said Jack.

"Is she aware of what happened?"

"No."

Abe looked at Grace. "My dear hostess, is it okay if I leave my equipment here by the door?"

"Yes, it certainly is. Dinner's on its way. We can sit and tell you what happened and formulate a plan for tonight."

"That sounds good. Thanks, Grace." Abe smiled warmly.

Grace smiled back. There was something about Abe that reminded her of Favian. Usually, eccentric people are brilliant and very sweet on the inside, and the conversation is much more interesting. Her most successful romances had been with eccentric people. "Abe, this is Dr. John O'Connor. John, Abe. Make yourselves comfortable." Grace headed into the kitchen.

The men nodded to each other and settled down into the living room. "So Abe," John started, "Jack tells me you're the guy who took that beautiful image of Miranda."

"Yes, that's me," said Abe affably.

"It's the most powerful MRI ever made?"

"Yes, it is."

"So, how do you get a job like that?"

"You lead a team of scientists to design it." Abe provided the same explanation of the MRI to John as he had to Miranda and the crew the night he took the MRI of Miranda.

"Ah." John nodded. "Amazing."

Grace came out of the kitchen with a tray. "Here's the coffee and tea." Jack stood up to help her set the tray on the table.

"You didn't have to go through all this trouble." John reached forward to set the tray down with Jack.

"I was thinking the same thing," said Abe.

"Oh, no, it relaxes me, to sit with a cup of coffee or my favorite tea, and believe me, I need to relax right now." Grace sat with Jack on the couch.

"Oh, yes, I can imagine. I'm so sorry. That must have been awful. I ran right over when I heard," Abe consoled.

Wow, genuine concern. It's something Grace hadn't seen for quite a while outside her circle of friends. But then again, who else would Jack be friends with other than exceptional people? "Jack brought you up to speed?"

Abe nodded. "What's the plan? It seems to be getting stronger."

"The plan is still the same," Jack explained. "We are going to help her remove her roots so the entity no longer has anything to latch onto. We're hoping with the removal of the trauma, it won't have enough to hold onto with the id alone. It's going to be a fight. We let her rest for a little while so she can have the strength to make it through the session. We might have to have several sessions until it releases its hold on her. And, we have to make sure that this process doesn't put too much strain on her heart. We could lose her."

Abe rubbed his chin, lost in thought. "Let's see what we already know. Even though it claimed to be part of Lucifer's army, we simply don't know if there's any truth to it. But if it is true, the implications are almost biblical. We know it's ethereal enough to remain hidden from its host, but physical enough to produce hallucinations, materialize and walk around when its host is in the semi-conscious state, kill other people when it finds a connection through these roots and possibly brain waves, and destroy physical equipment if it's hopped up with enough electromagnetic energy. Even though the magnet coils on my MRI are made of silver and copper, it was able to melt the coils before it was drawn into them.

"It seems to feed off its host by consuming all rays of light of the chakra energies. In this regard, it acts like a perfect black body, and it could be made of cosmic elements left over from the big bang. Perhaps that's how it was able to travel here, using electromagnetic energy fields and the electromagnetic radiation from the big bang, or even black holes themselves, using them as a portal. Huh." It seemed like Abe had a light bulb light up.

"What is it, Abe?" asked Grace.

"Interesting. If Lucifer is using cosmic microwaves that have been around since the genesis of our universe to end us, he is perverting the 'alpha and omega,' a phrase from the Christian 'Book of Revelations.' And, the alien-demons have the ability to pervert and override the in-dwelling of Christ and the Holy Spirit."

Grace shifted her weight in her seat. "In-dwelling? What's that?"

"Christians believe if one accepts Christ as the Savior, it enables spirit to dwell inside of you, implying that people who accept God and Christ in their lives as absolute powers have a protection against evil spirits.

"Even those who have some sort of spiritual protection, whether it's the in-dwelling of the Christians, enlightenment for Buddhists, or what have you, the aliens have rendered God impotent in the face of these demons. Grounding for protection, a meditative practice for those who delve into spiritual work, won't work here, as well as anything that is thought to protect people, such as their love of God or Christ, praying, angels, or even baptism. Not only do we not have any defenses against them, but nothing from the spiritual realm has any protection to offer us either, if that is what you believe." Abe's observations silenced the group. After a few minutes, Abe asked, "So, how do you explain tonight's attack?"

John leaned back. "It seems the entity has completely taken over Miranda's id. This is the first time it has appeared as Miranda in this third attack. It first attacked Favian Widener and killed him. Then it attacked Jack, creating the hallucination that it killed his wife. Miranda appeared as herself during the third attack on Grace. That could mean he completed his takeover of her subconscious, and he has full possession of her metaphysical body. In my experience, I have seen detached ids, and they can materialize separately from the physical body. This also means that it can detach itself from Miranda any time it pleases now.

"Now, another thing you should know about ids—they are physically located at the back of the chakras within our energy fields and plugged into the middle of each chakra. You know the expression, 'It's in the back of my mind'? It's actually an accurate statement."

Abe snapped his fingers and pointed to John. "Ah, like the MRI. Okay, I'm with you. That would explain that image. But how did this demon take over Miranda's id?"

"The demon has been able to hitch a ride with her because it occupied the root caused by the death of her parents when she was eleven years old," said Jack. "Based on what the alien-demon shared during our meditative journey, I think each demon is the expert on the misery the trauma creates and has the ability to latch on and take over, then with its substance, suck all the light of the soul from the person, which helps it to take over the energy of our metaphysical substance."

"I think that's a good explanation," John agreed.

Jack nodded. "The root is located in her id, her subconscious. Now, when Miranda tried to kill herself with sleeping pills because of Favian's death, it reinforced that main black root and broke her down enough emotionally where it was able to occupy her entire id. We're lucky it didn't take her over completely because it would possess the ability to harness all of her powers."

"Her powers?" asked Abe skeptically. "What? Is she a magician?"

John chose to overlook what he could have interpreted as an abrasive comment. "Anyone who was able to access these powers was most likely considered a magician hundreds and thousands of years ago. They probably would have considered me a magician with what I can do, or you, having command over your mammoth machine. As people remove their black roots planted into the subconscious from traumatic events and they become self-actualized, humans are supposed to have all sorts of possible powers, such as telekinesis, levitation, psychic abilities, and mind reading. Those would probably have been considered magic as well. All of these are thought to be part of a run-of-the-mill demon's powers when they possess people, but in reality, the demons could know how to tap into humans' natural abilities." John used the break in the conversation to ask, "So, Abe, what did you bring?"

"Oh, yes. We have an alien species to remove from our Miranda. But, I see you have some equipment as well." Abe pointed to the large rectangular object wrapped in brown paper. "Why don't you show me yours, and then I'll show you mine," Abe said with a slight smile.

Choosing to ignore Abe's inappropriate allusion, John nodded and walked over to the corner of the living room where he had placed his things. "Do you have some scissors, Grace?"

Grace nodded. She went to the kitchen, returned with a box cutter and handed it to John. He took the blade and cut open the cardboard.

Jack and Grace looked at the object with interest. "A mirror?" asked Abe.

"These days, most mirrors are coated with aluminum. This old mirror was made of silver, used because of its reflective qualities. My ancestors used silver for protection against evil spirits, and they believed that using silver in mirrors would prevent the mirror from becoming a portal for demonic spirits. Although the science was lacking, I think people used to have knowledge of what worked, and to them, it was common sense. Not everything people did was driven out of superstition. There could have been people, although only a few, who experienced these things and could see it, and they came up with ways to combat the unseen."

"Ah, yes, silver. It makes sense." Abe stood up and looked at the mirror. "You know, science can be used to prove these old wives' tales too. Silver is the most electrically conductive element and the most thermally conductive metal. It's even more conductive than copper, but because of its expense, it's not as widely used as copper. In World War II, silver was used instead of copper for electromagnets because of the copper shortage, arising from its utilization in separating uranium to create our first atomic bombs for the Manhattan Project. Which brings me to what I brought."

He walked over to the door where he had put his things and retrieved a black bag. He put it down on his seat, unzipped it, and pulled out a rod with coils wrapped around it and a handle. "Jack told me that the alien used dark energies to travel the universe in order to arrive at our little planet on the outskirts of the Milky Way.

It's all about electromagnetic radiation. Moreover, when Jack relayed what happened to him in the hospital bathroom and the smell that accompanies the demon, after doing a bit of research on our earthly demons, I concluded that nauseating smell was sulfur in gaseous form. These demons are not only perfectly matched to our metaphysical bodies and our energy centers, but also it's easy for them to assimilate themselves into our bodies because sulfur is a building block of human life and is everywhere in our atmosphere. And since air pollution is rampant, it increases the amount of sulfur, which makes it impossible for us to ward off their entry into our atmosphere. Thus, I brought this little gem. It's an electromagnet used in World War II. It has silver coils wrapped around an iron core."

John nodded. *It's a good thing we have someone like him on our side.* "Yes. I have had personal dealings in combating demons." He waited for the expected shocked expressions. He received them, and then moved on. "One girl who was possessed had a sulfuric smell. I had also met a gentleman who had gotten raped by a group of men. He had a 'pet' in the crawlspace underneath his stairs. He told me that the creature was working with him to avenge him. I thought he was kidding. He was not. When I opened the door, my eyes stung from the sulfuric odor. A red pair of eyes glowed back at me. The body looked like a weird, deformed version of Yoda from *Star Wars*."

Grace's shoulders shook as a shiver traveled up her spine, and her forehead pushed up worry lines. Jack and Abe exchanged wide-eyed looks.

"When I arrived home, I was nauseous and dizzy, like I had been attacked. My ear swelled up instantaneously, and I had to go under a doctor's care to resolve it. What I smelled that day, in addition to meeting a woman who was possessed and had the same smell, it was beyond a sulfuric smell. I had been to hot springs, and you can smell sulfur. When you smell the sulfuric gas emanating off a demon-like creature from the pit of hell, it's like the sulfur becomes something else.

"Here's my theory. Hell creates a different, inter-dimensional version of the sulfur, the reason why it smells hideous. If these beings have been created with sulfur, or if they had acquired the sulfur gas from the earth's atmosphere to enable them to stay put within the earth's atmosphere, it becomes a bastardized version so it could combine with their ethereal form."

Abe's eyes squinted a bit, an indication of his brain working on overtime. John challenged his body of scientific knowledge, but his field was full of doubters, and most probably would have believed John's ear problem caused hallucinations of a demon-like creature living in the man's crawl space. Abe thought it a terrible, tragic mistake to discount the human experience. He had seen this tendency in action. When his mother had gotten sick, the doctor discounted her symptoms until she had a heart attack and died. His defense—because her symptoms didn't display all of the typical male patterns of heart disease, the doctor bypassed all of her complaints and blamed them on anxiety. Abe vowed to never be that scientist who would completely ignore what another human being had to say. John remained lucid throughout the conversation and was able to detect Miranda's "roots," something he shouldn't have been able to do without seeing her MRI and the thermal camera images. Yet, he did do it, helping Abe's impression of John's credibility.

"So, it's still sulfur, but a bastard variant," Abe verified.

John nodded. "I am hoping the scientific foundation you have laid here will hold, even though we are dealing with 'demon sulfur,' or in our case, 'extraterrestrial demon sulfur.' Normally, sulfur interacts with the silver, changing the chemical makeup. Also, both iron and silver are thought to have properties that ward off undesirable supernatural entities."

Abe pointed to John. "Exactly. The electricity amplifies the power of the silver and iron together, sending out electromagnetic radiation containing microwaves and the infrared spectrum. The silver interacts with the sulfur and creates silver sulfide, the black tarnish you see on silver when it has been sitting for a little while. If the demon has any sort of sulfur-containing presence, this silver-encased electromagnet should be able to separate the entity from Miranda's molecular structure and disintegrate it, if it works at all."

"And if the alien doesn't have any sulfur or microwaves left over from the big bang?" Jack asked.

Abe shrugged. "Then we're fucked. All of our efforts will be completely ineffective, and we should bow to our new dark overlords."

John nodded, smiling for the first time since his arrival. "So, we can use the mirror and the electromagnet to draw it out."

Abe rubbed his chin. "Oh, one more thing." He pulled out five small bottles and gave each person one. "This one is for Miranda." He gave Jack the extra bottle.

Jack looked at the label. "Colloidal silver? Doesn't this stuff turn people blue?"

"Yes, when consumed in very large quantities. Just for tonight, no. It will probably stay in our system forever, but one dose shouldn't turn us all into blueberries. If we're right about the chemical makeup of this entity, it will protect us from any nasty, smelly alien-demon from taking over our bodies."

"I have something else to add to our arsenal." John went to the corner of the living room where he had his bag. He pulled out a black, cloth bag. He put on some latex gloves, and from inside the bag, he pulled out a long scroll.

"Wow, that looks, really, really, old," Abe said. "Is that written on papyrus? And that looks a bit like Hebrew. Hmm, and the symbol, the flower of life, right? May I see?"

"I don't want to insult you, but no, I'm not comfortable with anyone else handling this book, and it is Aramaic, a precursor to Modern Greek, Egyptian, Hebrew, Turkish, and Arabic languages. It is over 2,500 years old. And yes, it is written on papyrus, and no, it's actually the fruit of life, which is a symbol hidden inside of the flower of life. Thirteen circles, when joined together in the middle, forms a metatron cube, which contains all of the shapes possible in this physical plane. It is the beginning and synthesis of all life forms here on earth."

"What is the flower of life?" asked Jack.

"It's a symbol found in countless temples, synagogues, and churches thousands of years old, across the world, in nearly every culture, a mystery no one has been able to solve."

"It's beautiful," Grace said. "What in the world is it, and how is this going to help us today?"

John smiled. "This is where we depart from the scientific to the metaphysical. This is the *Book of Chronicles*."

Jack, Abe, and Grace waited for him to continue his explanation.

"The Book of Chronicles is noted in the bible in the story of Ester."

"Ah, yes," said Jack, "the story of how the Jewish holiday Purim came about. Ester, a Jew, married the King of Persia in the fable. The King wrote in his Book of Chronicles every day. Ester didn't reveal her Jewish ancestry until one of the king's henchmen victimized her people because her adoptive father Mordacai pissed him off when he wouldn't bow and tremble in his presence. By then, the king was so taken with her beauty, when Ester informed him of the mistreatment, he punished his soldier and stopped the persecution of the Jews because of his love for Ester."

"But, that is supposed to be a fable," Abe observed.

John shook his head, smiling.

"That's really it? *The Book of Chronicles*? And you have it?" Abe's look of amazement spoke for all of them.

"Yes."

"How, how in the world did you get it?" asked Jack.

"That is a long story."

"How is this incredible book going to help us?"

John paused. "It turns out the Book of Chronicles has great power. When I acquired this book, I traveled to Jerusalem and paid a scholar a great deal to translate every bit of this book. It's more in the way of a book of wisdom of ancient knowledge rather than a book of records as the bible depicts. I brought it here today because it's the one resource I have to help conquer this being."

"Okay, how?" asked Jack.

"Patience," said John. "There are some powerful prayers in here. It was difficult to get an exact translation on some of the words. It took a great deal of time for the scholar to research it. But I need you all to promise that you will not breathe a word to any other living soul that you ever saw this book. Your only protection is to take this knowledge to your grave."

"Protect us from what?" asked Grace.

"This book shouldn't even exist. There are people who don't want it to exist. They have already demonstrated that they are willing to go to any lengths."

"Why do you say that?"

"Because the scholar who translated this book died from unnatural causes." He paused as he allowed the three to process this information. "I wouldn't have brought it if I felt I had any other choice or resource. You need to promise me to forget you ever saw this book. Agreed?"

"Agreed," said Grace. Jack and Abe nodded.

The doorbell rang. "Chinese food." Grace grabbed her wallet and ran to the door.

"I'll help her." Abe ran after her.

Jack smiled. It seemed his friend had a crush. He looked over at John. He had noticed as well. Abe, after insisting on paying for all the food, carried the bags to the kitchen set up the plates. Jack never recalled seeing his friend so taken with a woman.

"This is what it's all about." John sat back down.

"What? Horniness?"

John laughed. "No. Love."

Jack nodded.

John's eyebrows knitted into thought.

"Something troubling you?"

"Miranda's been sleeping all this time?"

"I suppose."

"An attack, then silence. I'm more comfortable with the attack."

Miranda had been sleeping for hours while they'd been plotting. "I think we should try and wake her for dinner."

The men walked down the short hallway. Jack turned on the decorative, tasseled lamp sitting on the end table next to the bed. It gave off a dim light. "Miranda." Jack gently laid his hand on Miranda's shoulder. "Miranda." He shook her shoulder. "Miranda," he said a little louder. He looked at John. "Something's wrong." He turned Miranda on her back and put his fingers on the side of her neck. "She's alive. Miranda!"

"Come on, Miranda, wake up," said John.

Jack looked down at Miranda's hand. She held a prescription bottle. He took his glasses out of his pocket. "Zolpidem. Shit."

Grace and Abe ran in. "What's going on?" asked Grace.

"This," Jack said, giving her the bottle.

"How did she get this? I thought you said the EMTs took all the bottles she had."

"And I checked to make sure she didn't have any pills before we drove here. I had her show me everything, falling short of a strip search. Believe me; I know how to conduct a search."

"Are you telling me that the devil did it? I don't like this," said John.

"That's an understatement," Abe chortled.

"Well, what do we do?" asked Grace. "Do we let her sleep it off?"

"No," John said. "It wants her asleep, and I can guarantee you it's not for a good reason. Another attack is coming, and she is in great peril. We witnessed the entity's progress, and it's finalizing its possession. We should get ready. And hopefully, we're not too late."

26
FIGHT

Miranda awoke with a start. She had trouble moving. When she looked down, a row of ropes bound her to the recliner in Dr. Grace Kelly's living room. Jack sat in front of her, holding onto her bound hands. "Miranda, we have to talk."

She shot him a confused look. Grace, John, and Abe stood behind Jack. "Do I have a choice?"

Jack held up the prescription bottle. "Do you know where this came from?"

Miranda focused her eyes on the bottle. "That's my bottle, but I haven't seen it since, well, you know."

"I know. I saw it too when I found you. Somehow, you had this in your hand when we tried to wake you up. Do you have any idea how it got there?"

Miranda shook her head. "No, I have no idea. You saw. I showed you. I didn't have any pills when I left that hospital, none of the bottles. The hospital kept them all."

Grace, John, and Jack looked at each other.

"You found this in my hand? And that's why you tied me up?"

Jack put his head down and rubbed his head with his hand, then looked at her, attempting to say something, then closed his mouth again.

"What? Why did you tie me up?" Her face flushed. *Oh, God, what happened?*

"Miranda," Grace sat next to her on the other side of the chair, "you somehow had the last sleeping pill, and if you can't explain how you got that pill... and there's something else, too." Grace's expression held the pain of the event.

"Grace was attacked tonight," Jack continued. "We don't blame you for it."

"If you don't blame me, then why did you tie me up?" For a split second, she wondered if she made a fatal error, putting her trust into strangers. Maybe she should have gone home to be with Alison and Steven.

John stepped closer. "The entity appeared as you. It entered the kitchen while you slept on the couch."

"What did you see?"

John was careful to control his facial expression and his tone. "Like we said, we don't blame you. It took a foot-long blade and stuck it right through the seat into Grace's back and through her chest. When the entity disappeared, so did the illusion."

Anger and resolution smoldered in Miranda's eyes. *A year of this crap*. She tired of the entire thing so much, she ached with ridding herself of this alien-demon asshole and getting her old life back. Yet, if it weren't for her problems, Alison wouldn't have remet Dan, and Miranda wouldn't have met Steven. How could her life end without making it through? Wasn't God supposed to have a grand plan for everyone? How could hers involve so much pain? Was God a sadist? Regardless, she couldn't let go of her old life. It could be just an ideal, but she needed it to fuel her drive to the end. "That's it. I've had it. I want it gone. No one wears my face to hurt my friends and gets away with it."

Jack patted her hand. "Good." He and Grace rearranged the furniture in the living room to create an open space around Miranda. John leaned the mirror up on the couch and put the scroll on an end table. Abe plugged in the electromagnet and rested it on the coffee table next to the couch.

"So, what's all this?" Miranda gestured her head toward the items.

"Surprises," said Abe. "And if it's okay with you, I think they should stay that way."

"Understood." Miranda shifted in her seat. "Let's get this done. What do we do first?"

"We're ready to go, right?" John looked to Grace, Abe, and Jack for confirmation. They nodded.

The lights in Grace's apartment flashed. "Here it comes," said Jack.

Abe placed his hand on the back of his friend's arm. "Looks like we might have to go to plan B."

Miranda looked around, her breath coming out in quick spurts. Grace held onto Jack's arm. A sulfuric smell hit Grace's nose, and she coughed.

The demon stood right in front of Miranda. It was the most terrifying thing Grace had ever seen. Not even Jack's detailed description could do it justice. It looked like a giant human, but the evil emanating from its presence overwhelmed her. If absolute darkness had a feeling, this thing would be it. He had a rod in his hand. "Lights out," he growled. He brought the rod down on her head. Miranda passed out.

"No!" cried Grace. She took a step toward Miranda, but Jack held her. Physically, Miranda was fine. The entity cackled a low, rumbling laugh. The lights in the apartment flashed like a strobe and then went dark for five seconds.

Abe, Jack, Grace, and John braced themselves.

The knot in Grace's stomach made her pant, perspiration gathering on her forehead. When the lights flickered on again, Miranda stood next to the chair.

"Neat trick, huh?" Miranda laughed the same low, rumbling laugh of the alien-demon.

John nodded to Abe. "Plan B."

"You don't get it, do you?" she spat. "I wanted you all here together. You think you could defeat *me?*" She laughed again. "Stupid, stupid, stupid. Suckers. All of Miranda's knowledge became my knowledge, and now we can descend like the plague. Humans are a blight upon the world. Before your horrifying deaths, you will pay."

Jack's dread tripled. It didn't matter what they did to save Miranda. All of the preparation meant nothing. Now, they had to fight their way out. For the first time in his entire life, he was unsure he could make it out alive.

The rotten egg smell became overwhelming. A deafening buzz filled the room, the buzzing Miranda had described when she had finally remembered everything. How he regretted not realizing the full magnitude of this little fact, and he was not one to live with regrets. The alien-demons had been accosting her for months on end. John and Grace held their hands to their ears.

Four more demons appeared. Jack couldn't pull his eyes away. The more he peered, the more terror descended on him. He had never seen anything so dark and black. It was like staring into a black hole shaped like a body. As his eyes adjusted, he saw the different levels of blackness, and out of the blackness, the shape of what served as faces, a large mass of writhing strands and roots and nothing consistent in the way of skin. He could see the same lack of skin all along its body and the black, plasma-like, parasitic roots, looking to entwine themselves within an unwilling host. In the chest, black ooze sat where one's heart should be. He looked over at Abe. Abe looked at the demons' faces. His eyes filled with wonderment and fascination.

A force jabbed Grace's stomach. Grace coughed and doubled over. It took every fiber not to vomit. Abe, John, and Jack doubled over as well, groaning. As if they were puppets pulled up by their strings, they all jerked back to the standing position.

"Ha, now it's a party." Miranda clapped. "My friends have arrived. I had to get Miranda to sleep a while so I had time to prepare and take her over. The invasion has begun." The demons dissipated and reappeared in front of Jack, John, Abe, and Grace. She stuck her face into Dr. O'Connor's. "Yes. The devil did it."

Grace struggled to move her arms and legs. Her inner world, the one she worked so hard to build up all of these years and allowed her to help others find peace through her psychological practice began to crumble. Her arms and legs bound. Bound. No. She couldn't. "Jack, I can't move."

Jack tried to move his arms and hands. "Neither can I. John, you?"

"No." John breathed heavily.

"Yep, pretty stuck here," Abe reported.

Miranda laughed. "You humans. Even when you think you have it together, you don't. You carry everything with you, from your birth to your death, which makes all of you," she took her finger and tickled under Jack's chin, "ripe for the picking," she pointed to the alien-demons, "so my brothers can take over. Everything you have been through with Miranda was just a stalling tactic. We now know everything we need in order to enslave your entire species." Miranda's eyes shone as if it were her birthday. "It was the best time ever, seeing you work so hard, struggle, and all for nothing. How does it feel, knowing you are all complete and utter failures, that nothing you did gave you any more control over your destiny, your safety, your fates?" She gazed upon the four, her sadistic, black eyes alight with their misery.

Grace glared at Miranda. John and Jack struggled to move their immobile arms and legs. Abe stood there, conserving his energy.

"Ah, Jack, poor guy, crippled in so many ways," Miranda-alien-demon gloated. "Such pain you go through. Here, let me help you out." She touched him in the middle of his chest. Jack's eyes opened wide, and he cried out. Grace and John struggled to break free from their invisible bonds to no avail. "Poor Favian Widener saw what you would experience tonight, but was powerless to stop it, like all of you are powerless to stop us."

Miranda chuckled as she stood in front of Abe. Abe glared back at her. "Ah, finally, a flash of anger from the emotional retard. Mmmm, I sure do love that anger you humans have," she purred. "The angrier you are, the easier we can take you over. You were right, John. Jack sure is an easy target, isn't he?" Jack cried out in agony, squirming as an unseen force twisted his back from the inside. "Torture is so much fun."

Miranda stepped back in front of Jack and looked straight up at him. "Maybe next time, you'll mind your own fucking business," she hissed.

"Leave him alone. Leave him alone," cried Grace. "Please, Miranda, I know you're in there. Don't let him do this."

Miranda-demon laughed, the low, metallic chuckle of the demon more pronounced. "Miranda is tied up at the moment. Ah, the loss you felt when your mother died." She bent to the side to look into Grace's tormented eyes. She inhaled deeply. "Still so ripe. And what's this?" Grace struggled, trying to move her frozen limbs, a mixture of terror, misery, and anger on her face. "Ah, I can't believe my luck!" Miranda's look was of surprise and delight. "You were raped! And it wasn't one guy." Miranda smirked.

"No!" Grace screamed on the top of her lungs, fighting with every ounce of her being to move. It managed to see in one second the one event she struggled against all of her life. Grace felt her sense of self slip away as she flashed back to that day, the rape, the day that taught her the evil side of the human heart. She struggled all her life to hold a love for humanity, an innocent ideal eradicated when she learned of the whole nature of human beings, always working to recapture that feeling. Sadly, not even the thousands of people she counseled could fully bring her back to her early, childlike view of the world.

Instead, she developed strength and compassion for everyone who suffered. Unfortunately, the realization that all her fears she expressed to John in the kitchen filled her with horror. She let go of having to be in control, for the moment. She just had to make it through this night, if they could possibly find a way, and to tunnel down inside of herself to retain her wholeness.

John and Abe strained against their invisible bonds, glaring at Miranda, helpless as they were forced to watch the unraveling of their friend.

Miranda laughed. "Ah, reliving the nightmare already, I see."

Abe shuddered. Grace's screams intermingled with Jack's, the cries of the deepest human suffering he had ever experienced. Hell had arrived, and they were powerless to stop it.

"Good!" Miranda clapped her hands together as if she just thought of a party game to play. "I know! Why don't we help reenact the whole thing for you, right here? We could use some entertainment for our guests." Miranda flicked her finger, sending Grace into the wall ten feet behind her. The way her arms were pinned up behind her head and one leg lifted off the floor made her body seem contorted and uncomfortable. Miranda flicked another finger.

Grace's muffled cries pierced Abe through and through.

Miranda smiled. "Just like you remember it, isn't it? Have fun!"

Jack's pain and anguish radiated from his core to his guttural shrieks. It was as if a hammer beat every part of his back and neck, his body flinching with every pounding.

Abe and John yelled in protest.

"You will not be here long, I can guarantee you." Abe's voice seethed with rage.

"Aw, what's the matter, Abe? Angry you can't get in on some of that action with your love interest over there?" Miranda gestured her head toward Grace anguished screams. Abe flinched with each cry of misery, his stomach churning.

"Just do it! Go ahead, enter me. Take me over. If we can't do anything about it anyway, then get on with it."

"Oh, so brave! Who knew the nerdy little Jew from Queens had it in him." Miranda's voice dripped with false admiration. "All to save your lady love. It's hard, isn't it? Always misunderstood by everyone, never experiencing that connection you long to feel? Suppressing it all with science? But science can't suck your cock at night, can it? It can't take its warm, soft lips and wet tongue and envelop you, can it?" Miranda leaned into him, speaking in a low, soft, sultry voice next to his ear. Abe recoiled, disgusted, doing his best to move his head away from her hot breath. She stepped back. "A cruel mistress is science. I'll tell you what. If you let my brother use your body, we'll make Grace your subservient slave. How does that sound?" Miranda asked, her tone more appropriate for someone who was trying to decide whether or not to buy a shirt.

"Listen, let Grace, Jack, and John go, and I'll do anything you want. Hell, I'll carry you all around if I have to." Abe smiled, thinking of the colloidal silver distributing throughout his body, hoping beyond all hope the negligible amount of silver the liquid contained was enough to disintegrate these, these...

"Hmm, tempting," Miranda put her pointer finger to her lips and tapped them, "but no. Every human is going to live in the agonizing state you see here." She pointed to Grace and Jack. "All the horror, all the pain, all the fear. My kind will deliver Hell on earth. First, we'll enslave all of you and then torture you. We'll keep you alive so we can keep doing it over and over and over. It's delicious, isn't it? We'll ride you like livestock.

"You, Abraham, will die a lonely death, never having accomplished anything in science, wasting your entire life away, never connecting with another human. You'll be dead for a year before anyone discovers your rotting corpse." Miranda-demon's tone rose to emphasize the last few, cruel words.

Abe's contempt seethed from him. "Don't be so sure."

Miranda glared at Abe. "You are tiresome, aren't you? Why do you think half your friends can't stand you? I think it's time for you to live out one of your fears." Miranda flicked her finger and sent Abe into the wall right next to Grace.

John breathed heavily. Miranda motioned with her finger again. Grace made a gurgling sound and moaned. *God, the pain she's going through.* He heard a zipper and jingling, like someone's pants fell to the floor.

"No! No!" Abe shouted. "Grace, I don't want this. I don't want this. Please, please know I don't want this! I love you! I would never do this to you, not in a million years!"

Miranda-demon waved her hand. "Oh, don't be such a baby! Sure you do. You humans do it all the time. Now your lady love, when she looks at your face, will associate you with the worst day of her pathetic life."

"Leave them alone," John said.

Miranda turned around and took a few steps to face John. John met Miranda's stare.

"Hmm, not nervous. Why is that, Dr. John?"

"Because you don't scare me."

"Oh, and you think you're going to distract me so you can save your friends. You've been watching too many monster movies. Call out to distract the beast. Nice try, but no." Another scream from Grace became muffled as John could only imagine what the demon had Grace do next.

"No!" yelled Abe. "Grace, I would never do this to you."

Miranda turned back to John. "So, you were saying?" Her chilling tone was so casual, as if the discussion was about the weather. "There's nothing human left of Miranda. I will make you watch as I torture the entire human race."

John glared at Miranda.

"Oh, nothing to say now?"

"No. I'm picturing what it will be like when we disintegrate you."

"Oh? And how will you do that?"

John smiled. "It's a surprise."

"No, I'm the one with the surprise." She twisted her hand. Jack's body contorted around. They heard an awful, sickening crack of Jack's bones twisting and shattering inside of him. Jack cried out in agony and then passed in and out of consciousness from a pain so profound, he moaned uncontrollably while unconscious. Miranda seemed delighted when she saw John flinch.

"You have done very well for yourself, haven't you?" She commented as if she hadn't just crippled a man. "You don't have any of those roots. Amazing. We didn't think any human capable of getting rid of the black roots of trauma and misery." Miranda motioned with her finger, and two of the demons materialized in front of John and beat him in the face. He grunted with each blow. Miranda smiled and turned to call over her shoulder. "Hey, having fun yet, Abe? I think you got off easiest out of anyone here, don't you think? Don't worry. You'll learn to love this. When you work for us, you'll have Grace to come home to every night, tied up in a dungeon, her mouth open and waiting just for you. We need someone like you on our team. Your knowledge of the earth is going to be useful to us. You will help us harness that electromagnetic energy so my kind can enter the entire planet all at once. Everything is working out according to plan."

Abe glared at Miranda's back. By then, Grace had succumbed, as though she left and traveled somewhere else while forced to perform movements against her will. Abe could already see the bruises from her attack forming all over her face and back. Indignation and outrage consumed him, but the physiology of the situation forced his body to respond despite the circumstances. His attraction to Grace was not squelched even with the atrocity of the situation.

"Don't worry. You'll stop feeling guilty after a while. Sit back and enjoy it," Miranda called back to Abe.

Abe's face twisted with anger as he was forced to watch the work Grace performed on him, the beating of his new friend, and the crippling of his old friend. The only way he could keep himself from puking was to envision the demons as a pile of black dust. Plus, there had to be a reason to recruit him rather than to make him submit. Why ask him to join rather than strive to fully possess him by force? He must have something they want. Or, they misjudged his character. Or, he was a threat.

"Consider yourself lucky, Dr. John." Miranda-demon had to speak louder over the sound of the beating and screaming. One of his eyes had swollen shut, and his lip felt like a parade float. "I was going to kill you because the knowledge you have is deadly to our kind. But, I do need a plaything to keep around, and it would be much worse for you if we helped you realize your own worse fear. Right? And as you know, you're only a weak human worm. If we keep beating and torturing you, you will eventually break down, new trauma roots will be created, and we will take you over with the rest. I wonder how long you will last. Anyone want to take bets?" She looked around. "No?"

John glowered at Miranda with his open eye.

Miranda smiled back. "This has been so much fun. It's the part I love most. But we do have an invasion to execute."

Miranda motioned with her finger and slammed the writhing Jack up against the wall next to Abe. Jack cried out as his neck hit the wall behind him and cracked.

Miranda giggled. "Ooops, did that hurt? So sorry." She motioned upward and forced Grace up against the wall. Three out of the four shadow demons lined up in front of Abe, Jack, and Grace.

"Open wide," said Miranda-alien-demon with a hint of the alien's voice as an undercurrent to her own. Grace screamed. The writhing tentacles of the shadows inched closer and closer.

Jack hung there, helpless. Abe and John struggled in vain. The demons' tendrils reached out to envelop Jack, Abe, and Grace.

John saw the dark shadows disappear into them, the parasitic tendrils wrapping themselves into each body. He held his breath and waited, hoping the colloidal silver had time to process through part of their bodies.

Suddenly, the pressure on their bodies and limbs released. Jack, Grace, and Abe fell to the ground panting. The blackness left their bodies. A horrible metallic screeching entered their ears. The shadows writhed in pain. Vapors rose from the demons along with a burning smell.

"What is this?" Miranda shouted. "Take them over, you useless pieces of shit."

"The colloidal silver," Abe shouted, smiling. "It worked. It burned them."

John looked over to the radio with his one eye. Not that it surprised him after the night's events, but "Blinded by the Light," Manfred Mann's Earth Band, blared from the speakers.

Miranda stopped, the darkness temporarily leaving her eyes. "Mom? Dad?"

"John, the mirror," Jack shouted over the screeching. "I can't move my legs."

John took the mirror and held it up to Miranda. A human form appeared, the size of a child, completely enveloped in the black, plasma-like ooze. The little girl screamed. Miranda looked at the demon in the mirror encompassing eleven-year-old Miranda. "You're toast." Her green eyes smoldered.

John stood the mirror up against the couch, picked up the scroll, and unrolled it. "Abba, e allaha, kulana it glaga besra, reksa, abba, bi arya, bi ya kulana it, kulana it hesaha seya abba kulana it abba sena peyatayara." A bright light shined from above. "Netara seyazaba dema nesma abba sedaya hetepaya heynaga mesaqa palga sekna terabasny. Zemna mab esanuta misimanu sultana by sedaya kulana it erabagna begaza bys meru. Dema sema syrya heyratu kulana it biyara deha." The fruit of life symbol glowed on the scroll in John's hand and arose from the book, the centers of the thirteen circles coming together to form the metatron cube.

Abe, John, Jack, and Grace watched, transfixed. The metatron glowed with a silver, white light. The shape spun faster and faster until a male figure burst forth from the metatron.

It was the most brilliant, illuminated, and beautiful being Jack had ever witnessed, perfect in every manner. A name appeared, like it was written into his brain—*Metatron*. Metatron held up his arm, and a light burst forth and shot into Miranda's demon, and then the four demons in the room. Miranda's demon-cry sounded like a metallic clicking, releasing its tendrils intertwined into Miranda, freeing little Miranda in the mirror.

"Now is the time to let go of the hurt and pain caused by your parents' death," John commanded over the din. "See the black root releasing its hold." Miranda closed her eyes. Metatron raised his other arm. A beautiful golden light shot into Miranda. John saw the black root lifting away from Miranda's body and dissipating as she filled with the golden light engulfing her from Metatron's palm. Little Miranda in the mirror smiled and absorbed herself back into Miranda's body. Miranda fell to the floor, unconscious.

John smiled. "Good job, Miranda."

Abe managed to collect himself and got Grace to sit up. She shook from cold and adrenaline, her face cut, swollen, and bruised. He rubbed her arms, took off his sweater, and pulled it over her head. He got up and stood behind the mirror with the electromagnet.

"Now, Abe," shouted John.

Abe turned on the electromagnet.

Time suspended. Miranda's demon towered above everyone else in the room. The light from Metatron, amplified with the electromagnet, disappeared into the blackness of the entity. The light illuminated the dark recesses of the alien. The roots sprang forth from the darkness, all writhing in pain.

"Abe, it's working," Jack managed to shout over the whirring of the machine and the screeching of the demons and in between his cries of pain. "Keep it going."

The tendrils in the demon's face writhed. The silver and iron of the electromagnet caused the demon's parasitic tendrils to shrink up into a tight ball, and then drew it in. Smoke filled the air. Miranda's demon disintegrated into a fine powder. The rest of the demons clicked a metallic scream as the electromagnet sucked them in. Abe held the electromagnet and smiled as each plasma-shadow burned. He turned off the machine right before the last one was drawn in.

"What are you doing?" Jack cried.

Abe got up and faced the dark shadow. "You go back and give those assholes a message: your invasion failed. And if we ever see any one of your species here in this world again, we will disintegrate you just like them." He pointed to the pile of smoking, black dust on the floor.

Archangel Metatron released the demon from its hold. It gave a loud, defiant screech and then disappeared up through the ceiling.

John, Jack, Grace, and Abe looked at Archangel Metatron.

Grace could never tire of looking into the angel's eyes. His radiating light appeared holographic. Each particle of his body and each particle of light shimmered with its own illuminated brilliance. He had what appeared to be wings, but they were not bird-like in appearance as they are so often depicted. Golden-silver in color, they left a trail of light when he moved. His beauty was beyond human imagination. He walked over to Grace and put his hand on her forehead. A blissful warmness enveloped her body. When Metatron removed his hand from her forehead, she was asleep. The bruises, welts, and cuts up and down her legs and on her face had disappeared.

Abe ran over to her and touched her cheek. His eyes filled with wonderment. He looked up gratefully at Metatron.

Metatron nodded and walked over to Jack. He reached out and touched his forehead. The same feeling washed over him. The pain disappeared in his back and neck. *Did that just happen? My lifetime of pain and misery vanished?*

Metatron nodded and smiled. *We need you, Jack.*

Metatron walked over to John who was still standing by the mirror. A golden, silvery light enveloped John. The bruises and cuts on his face disappeared.

He walked over to Miranda and touched her in the middle of her chest. Jack could see a golden light come from the tips of Metatron's fingers and enter into Miranda.

Metatron explained to Jack and John, *It's to sew up her aura and chakras, mend them after the removal of the root.*

John watched, amazed, as Metatron sewed up Miranda's metaphysical body. He had seen this process before when he worked with clients, but witnessing it with his own eyes brought this experience to an entirely new level.

Keep up the good work, they all heard from Metatron's voice inside their heads. Archangel Metatron transformed back into the metatron cube, then the fruit of life, and disappeared up into the ceiling. As Metatron left, "Blinded by the Light" finished out on the radio, and the radio turned itself off.

Jack sprung up off the floor. Manfred Mann was certainly correct. They made it through the night. Maybe the song meant something after all.

Jack caught a gleam from the corner of his eye. Leaning up against the couch were five silver, glowing swords.

27
WAR

Abe lifted Grace off the floor and brought her to her bedroom. He placed her on top of her bed and covered her with a blanket folded at the foot. He sat next to her for a while, touching her cheek and stroking her hair, watching her sleep. Her breath was even in her peaceful slumber.

The sunlight peeked in from behind the drapes in the window. Inside of him, he waffled between happiness for everyone's healing and their victory and endless worry. That couldn't have been the last of it. What did the future hold?

Jack tiptoed into the bedroom and observed Abe's troubling thoughts in his expression. He motioned with his head for the two to speak outside her room. Abe nodded, adjusted the blanket up to Grace's chin, and followed Jack out to the living room.

Abe's smile intermingled with tears when he saw his friend walk down the hall like a twenty-five-year old.

When they reached the living room, all traces of the demons and the battle had vanished. Grace's apartment looked exactly as it did before the entire battle had begun, except for the swords lined up on the couch. There weren't even any traces of tarnish on his electromagnet. He looked out the window, appreciating the full view of the colorful sunrise through the open drapes. He took in a deep breath as he beheld the brilliance of the dawn.

Jack placed his hand on the back of his friend's shoulder. Abe looked at him. "How are you holding up?"

Jack smiled. "I'm fine. For the first time in decades, I don't have any pain."

Abe's eyes watered with joy. "Jack, I'm sorry. All these years. I should have let you know how special you are to me."

"Hey, what's this? You saved *all of mankind* from enslavement and you're apologizing? Abe, you are a good man, and I knew it all along. That's why we're friends."

"You seem to be handling this whole thing pretty well." Abe wiped his eyes.

"I've been through this before," said Jack. "It's just another chapter in the book called *The Shit That Happens in Jack Gallagher's Life*".

Abe cracked up laughing. Jack smiled. Familiar with the after-effects of battle, he anticipated Abe's state. When he survived the riot at the prison, he had a few rough days afterward. After the first battle, the rest of life gets easier to handle. "I've been through it, Abe, and I'm here."

Abe's gratitude swelled.

John walked into the living room from the guest bedroom. "Miranda's sleeping. I think she's okay. So," John rubbed his hands together, "who wants a drink?"

Jack and Abe laughed. "I'll have one," said Jack.

Abe nodded and raised his hand.

"I know where Grace keeps the vodka." Jack walked with a spring in his step to the kitchen.

Abe had trouble containing his amazement. "I can't believe he's walking. I never thought I would be so happy for someone. I wasn't even sure he would survive this. Then again, I wasn't sure any of us would."

"Pretty wild, what's happened." John walked over to the couch and picked up one of the swords. They glowed with a white light from within. The handle had crystals encrusted on the hilt: red, orange, yellow, green, blue, indigo, and violet, in order just like the chakras, and a bunch of ornate decorations and symbols, what John surmised to be in the language of the angels. He put the handle into his hand, shifting it in his grasp to get a feel for it. It was so light, he looked like an expert as he sliced the air. The blade left behind a golden-silver-white light trail.

John looked down on the couch and saw a parchment containing calligraphy.

"What is that?" asked Abe.

"It's a note to us. Use these swords when in battle. Forged by Archangel Michael. They will appear when you need them, like a constant friend." He showed Abe the pictures accompanying the text on how to use the swords to maximize their effectiveness.

The swords disappeared. John and Abe looked at each other and shook their heads.

Jack came out with the bottle and glasses. "Anyone mind if it's straight?"

"Mind?" The last several hours had been a bit much on Abe, all topped off with disappearing silver swords. Damn right he needed a drink. Abe reached for the bottle, opened it up, and took several swigs, but choked as it burned his esophagus.

"Whoa, easy there." Jack patted his friend's back.

"I think I'll take mine with ice." Abe gave the bottle back to Jack.

"Okay, ice it is." Jack handed the glasses and bottle to John and went back into the kitchen. John and Abe set the glasses on the table. Jack came out with a bowl of ice and some tongs and put it on the table before he took his seat beside Abe on the couch.

"Am I the only mess here after this thing? You seem to be pretty calm too," Abe remarked to John.

John laughed. "I've seen UFOs, fairies, spirits, ghosts, angels, bigfoot, something that left a three-toed imprint on my property that couldn't be identified, black spirit-deer, a man with horns growing out of his head, someone's pet demon that lived in his crawlspace, and now, spirit swords. It's just another day for me."

"Spirit swords?" Jack asked. John handed him the note from Archangel Metatron. "Where are they now?"

"They disappeared," said Abe.

Jack laughed a little. "Of course they did. You know, yesterday, I wouldn't have believed that statement."

Abe chuckled. "Yeah, tell me about it. I know the alien demon didn't beat me like he did you guys, but I feel like he hurt me most."

Jack nodded. "I know, Abe. I saw it."

John finished taking a sip of his drink. "The thing you have to understand about demons, no matter what planet they're from, they take a little seed of doubt, insecurity, or fear and then amplify it until it seems bigger than yourself—what demons do best. Fears, Abe, often seem a lot bigger than they truly are, and then they capitalize on it."

"But, what he said was true. Half of my friends can't stand me. I have been lonely all my life. If I didn't have science, I would have lost my mind."

Demons take the truth and twist them into something different, for their purpose, until they decimate their target, Jack surmised. "Listen. You should know I have a deep respect for you. You are one of the most interesting and intelligent people I know. I like you very much, and that says a lot because I don't like many people." It pleased Jack when Abe laughed, lightening the mood. "Believe that. And if it bothers you that much, what that smelly piece of shit said to you, then prove him wrong. Besides, your friends love you. I have heard people speak about you in very high regard."

Abe nodded, looking down at his glass. "I really do love Grace. It's not logical, and it's terrifying." He laughed, and Jack and John laughed along with him. "I didn't think love at first sight existed. I convinced myself that attraction could be explained away with the release of the compounds androstenone, androstadienone and androstenol and a woman's fertility cycle. I've never felt a connection with someone like I feel with Grace. It's more than the chemistry. I feel like I've known her for ages, and we picked up right where we left off."

"Yeah, that was obvious from the start," John observed.

"And what do I get? She's forced to do something to me that would remind her of the most traumatic experience of her entire life, so that each time she looks at me, all she can think of is rape and violence."

John swirled the liquid around in his glass. "Abe, what you experienced was brutal and confusing."

"I don't know what I'm complaining about anyway. Grace had it worse than I did."

"It doesn't minimize what happened to you," Jack consoled. "Besides, you have to keep in mind that the demon looked to bring down each of us in the worst way he could to break us." Jack's voice faltered. *Crap. Break was the wrong word to use.*

Abe nodded.

John looked at Jack. "So, Jack, how are you holding up?"

"Can't complain here. Doing better than I have been in years. My wife's years of praying are finally answered. It's a hell of a way to answer them, though."

John nodded. "You still a bit wound up?"

"Sure. I guess everyone is."

"And what else?" John probed.

"I don't know. I feel grateful, so..." Jack put his head in his hand, and his shoulders shook. Abe put his hand on his friend's shoulder. Jack composed himself quickly. "I mean, I don't know what to make out of this. One minute, I'm contemplating life in a wheelchair, if I survive the ordeal, if we aren't enslaved by the demons, and the next minute, I can do cartwheels if I want. I'm convinced I'm in a dream, that I'm going to wake up tomorrow and all the pain will return. Or, the alien-demons will return to cripple me again."

"We've all experienced miracles," John reflected. "You had a miracle happen to you, Jack. And you feel good. Let's take it day by day."

Jack nodded.

"So, how are you doing, John?" Abe asked.

"I'm doing okay, thanks. The demon wasn't able to latch onto any roots. I've been working on my roots for years, so I have a head start. We'll get you up to speed, though." Archangel Metatron healed his wounds, which was great because he didn't have to heal over a fat lip and black eyes. He's had those before. They won't kill you, but they'll be sore for a while. Without any roots of trauma and abuse, he was able to assess situations and emotionally do what was necessary to function in all situations. The demon-aliens were outside their control, and no one was at fault for their invasion. It was a scrap between God and Satan. Sure, he had feelings about having to battle for humans' right to live. Yeah, he felt what every human would feel in a nearly hopeless situation: angry, confused, angry, angry, angry, a little scared, and powerless as two all-powerful entities treated the entire human race as pawns in their age-old squabble. Maybe all of the experiences he had until that point has helped him be the most prepared out of anyone for the struggle for humanity's survival. At that point, he knew exactly what he had to do to process those feelings and get himself ready and to get his new friends ready to fight. When he boarded the plane that day, he had no idea that he would become an essential part of saving all of humanity from destruction. Funny, the little surprises in life.

"I know one thing," said Jack. "I want to process out those metaphysical black roots so these things can never come back to cripple me again. I think it's something we should all do, so we don't have to worry about getting attacked a second time. They might figure out a way around the colloidal silver."

John nodded. "If we tell people about this, no one would believe it, and they know it. That's why they're not hiding anything from us anymore. Once the alien-demon had his plan, he came out of hiding and told you and Miranda about it. Guys, I don't ever recall feeling terror, but even though I don't show it, I'm pretty close. We have to get ready for a full-scale invasion."

"Oh, shit." Abe hit his forehead with his hand. "I fucked up. Oh, God, I'm so sorry." His chest heaved. "I should have burned him up."

"No, Abe." Jack placed his hand on the back of Abe's shoulder. "It doesn't matter. The alien-demon played us all along. He had everything he needed, spending more than a year inside Miranda, learning the way the human body works."

"Absolutely," John agreed. "We got recognition from the source of all creation, Archangel Metatron, and that's astounding, but it doesn't help that we are isolated in our fight, from our colleagues, from the world's governments. It looks like we are responsible for fighting any future invasions."

Jack put up his pointer finger. "Yeah, but the president doesn't have a special spirit sword." Abe and John laughed.

John swigged his drink and poured some more. "I guess we're special, then. I'm going to have to help you guys process your roots. This process isn't instantaneous. It takes many weeks, sometimes years, because the deeper you go, the farther back you go in your memory, the more issues you uncover, even as far back as birth. You'd be surprised what people remember."

"How does this process work?" asked Abe. "I've heard about psychologists being accused of implanting false memories in people. How can you be sure the memories are real?"

"You never suggest," Jack explained. "You always listen, help people figure out for themselves what they experienced. Ask appropriate questions at the right time. It's a skill you develop, like your analytical skills, Abe."

Abe looked at John. "Where do you live? Grace said you flew in?"

"I did," responded John. "But I was thinking I should get an apartment around here."

Abe raised his eyebrows. "Wow, really?"

"Yes. We are the only ones who can ward off an invasion."

Jack shook his head and looked down into his glass. "How in the world are we going to do that?"

John shrugged. "Haven't a clue. But if we don't do it, who else will? Then everything we went through here today will have been in vain."

Jack shuddered. He didn't want them returning and crippling him again. "If you are going to move out here and work on this, I will do everything I can to help."

"Me too," Abe agreed. "Like the demon pointed out, I don't really have a life anyway, and I've been looking for a new hobby."

"Abe," Jack said, "You have a life. A brilliant one."

"Yes, you do," Grace chimed in. Jack and Abe turned around.

"Grace. How are you?" Abe sprung up and ran around the couch and touched her elbow lightly. "Come here. You shouldn't be standing. Sit, sit." He led her around and had her sit down on the sofa between him and Jack.

"No need to fuss, really. I'm fine. Even better now that I know I won't have a ton of cleaning to do after the battle." Grace sat down and looked around her apartment as the men chuckled. Well, she wasn't exactly fine, but she would be. She didn't want to become a victim in everyone else's eyes.

"Grace, really, how are you feeling?" asked Jack. Grace had not shared her background with him.

"I'll have some recovery work to do, but I've been through this before." Grace pushed her lips out. "This doesn't sound good, but since I am among friends... I was drugged and then gang raped in a club. I suppressed the memories at first, but then they resurfaced. I spent many years in recovery. The fact that it happened again didn't put me back to where I was when I was a young woman, but I will need to do some recovery work. It will not be as bad as the first time around. It doesn't sound right, I know, but I can't help the way I feel. Instead of trauma, I feel like a warrior with a task to complete. I can see what it will take to get me back to where I was, and I have no fears or hesitancy in doing it."

Jack knew exactly what she was talking about: the process to ensure that the bad experiences don't overwhelm an entire being and send one into a darkness with no end. The byproduct: a tougher, scarred version of warriors who suffer through the battle of their lives. The alternative: eating a bullet.

Grace rubbed her arms. "Besides, I guess I feel pretty good after all the angel juice. But my God, Jack, you look wonderful."

"I feel great," said Jack. "Better than I have in years, maybe even ever."

Grace smiled. "Thank goodness. I'll bet your wife will be happy."

"She's been praying every day for years. I'll have to say yes to that one." *Life is certainly strange.* It is a rare occurrence when the events of the world, as dark as they are, align the stars to have circumstances culminate in one's favor. *The world has to come to an end in order for me to feel better?* Ridiculous, but true.

"And how about you guys?" She looked at the men.

"Good here," reported John.

"I'm okay," said Abe. "The angel didn't heal me like he healed you guys."

"He healed us physically," said John, "but he wanted us to work through our emotional issues. He can't do that for us." Abe and Jack had a questioning look. "He shared it with me before his departure. If he healed us of everything, he would interfere with our life path, and he's not allowed to do that because it's a pact made between each soul on earth and God."

Jack shook his head. "Jesus, the shit you come up with..."

John laughed. "Yeah, tell me about it."

A pause in the conversation revealed Abe staring at Grace. Grace smiled awkwardly.

Abe cleared his throat. "Sorry."

"Oh, no, it's okay," Grace said.

"Um, you... you look nice in my sweater," he stammered. Grace had on a pair of black stretch pants with the sweater.

"Oh, thanks," said Grace, looking down. "It made me feel better when you put it on, so I didn't want to take it off."

"Keep it," Abe waved his hand. "I have a closet full of them. Uh, not the same exact sweater..." Grace returned his anxious gaze with a compassionate smile. "Yes, well, I wanted to say..." Abe started.

She took the opportunity to speak while he paused to search for the right words. "No need to apologize. You were as much of a victim. But, there's something I learned." Grace took Abe by the hands and looked into his eyes. "There will be a recovery process. You will realize that you have been victimized, but you don't have to continue to be a victim. You will become a survivor. After you live in that realm for a little while, you will understand that you don't have to merely survive, just barely hanging on. You can thrive, living the best, most brilliant, happiest life you can. You will heal into a thriver. That's what we are."

Abe breathed a sigh of relief and touched her cheek as if she were an angel herself. A thriver. He liked that. *What a smart woman.*

"You said something in the midst of our experience together. You said you love me. Did you mean it?"

Abe cleared his throat and looked down, swallowing hard. He grasped her hands and looked her in the eye. "Yes. I meant it. I love you. But, how can you... I mean, could you, with everything that happened..." Abe had never had to express himself like this to anyone and under these circumstances. He really wanted to say, *I love you, but now you will associate me with rape and violence, so is there any chance we could make it work?* Would that be too crass, too honest? Not honest enough? Too soon?

While Abe fumbled over the right words to say, Grace reached out and grabbed his hand. "I think we can try."

A tear descended on Abe's cheek. He nodded and smiled, rubbing at the corner of his eye with the heel of his hand. Grace held onto his other hand.

Jack and John smiled at the couple.

"Here, let me get you some tea." Abe, jumped up. "You sit."

Grace smiled. "No, that's okay. How about getting me a glass so I can raid my liquor cabinet with you guys?"

Abe laughed. "Okay. Stay right here. I'll be right back." He dashed into the kitchen as if he were afraid she would disappear if he didn't arrive back quickly enough.

Grace looked after him as she turned to watch him walk to the kitchen. "He really is sweet, isn't he?"

Jack nodded. "Yes, he is, deep down, once you get past all that knowledge in his head and scientific jargon. That's why we've been friends for so many years."

Grace smiled. "How's Miranda?"

"She's sleeping," said John. "We figured you would sleep more."

Abe arrived from the kitchen. He seemed relieved Grace was still there. "Here's your glass."

"Thanks." She smiled at Abe, and Abe sat beside her. "I thought so too. I had a really deep, peaceful sleep, but wasn't long."

"Why?" asked John.

"I don't know." She poured herself some vodka into her glass. "I awoke and sat straight up in bed. I wasn't sure if it all really happened or if it was some crazy dream. It took me a moment to remember the angel and that we won the battle."

John nodded. "For the moment."

Worry clouded Grace's face. "Do you think they'll come back?"

Jack put his hand on her arm. "Another attack is imminent."

"We better get ready then." Even though they could not take over their body's root system anymore, with the colloidal silver as an effective protection, they proved they were a physical threat to everyone's safety and existence, an idea that would create nightmares for Grace. She pushed it out of her mind for the moment. She had to focus on getting herself on the right path, and then she would be able to deal with the bigger picture.

"We will," said John. "I told Jack and Abe, I'm moving out here to help for a little while, as soon as I can."

"That's great news," said Grace. "And thank you."

"It's our fight, now," said John. "I'm not going to give up after everything we've been through."

"And neither am I."

Everyone turned around. Miranda stood at the entrance of the hallway.

"Thanks, Dr. O'Connor," said Miranda. "I was hoping we would form a team and continue to defend the world from the alien-demons. I learned a lot while I was possessed. They won't stop until every last person on earth is under their control. There's a larger plan at work. It's more than just revenge, more terrifying and insidious. They want to keep us all alive in a state of agony, for as long as they can, entrap us in a state of perpetual terror. For what purpose, I'm not really sure.

"We have to at least try to resist. In order to fight this on our own, we need capital."

"Oh, Miranda," Grace walked over to her and giving her a hug.

Miranda hugged her back, relieved there were no signs of blaming Miranda for being so weak and succumbing to the alien-demon. She worried as she sat in bed that the doctors wouldn't be able to even look at her, or leave her to fight them alone after their ordeal. Her face was synonymous with the demon's, who levied unspeakable horrors against them. How wonderful and skilled they were, and how lucky she was to be in their presence.

She listened to them for a moment before entering the living room. Grace spoke about developing a warrior mindset. Miranda cried for a moment after hearing Grace explain how she became so courageous and strong. Not only that, but they were still all here with her and speaking about staying together to form a team with her. She didn't feel like she deserved it, but she had four people willing to help her defeat an entire army of the alien-demons.

She got up from the floor, wiped her tears, and vowed to become as strong as they were, for them. She had been a passenger in her own healing. Now, she had to step up and become a leader.

Grace motioned to a chair. "I thought you would sleep for a long while."

"I got more sleep than you all did." Miranda sat in one of the chairs around the coffee table.

Grace smiled. "That's true. Would you like a drink?"

"No, I'm fine, thanks." Drinking could leave her vulnerable, something she vowed she would never be again.

"You said you ran through some numbers?" Jack asked.

"Yes. I figured out a way to finance our fight."

John raised his eyebrows. *She's a sharp one.* "Okay, how?"

"I'm going to start a jewelry company. I'm going to sell silver necklaces, bracelets, and earrings with the fruit of life and Metatron symbols. I think for whoever buys it, the silver and the symbols will offer some sort of protection from the demons. I'll finance and run the entire enterprise." The numbers appeared in her head as she sat on the floor listening to them. She had a few thousand dollars in the bank to get things started. When they could manage to get the sales to take off, she would find a factory to manufacture them in bulk. The entire business plan laid itself out in her head for her for the next five years, a talent that had earned her contracts with all the top businesses in their area.

The four paused as they thought about Miranda's idea. Grace and Abe nodded.

"I also thought about how to get the word out, how to spread the knowledge of what we all experienced."

"Okay," said Jack. "How again?"

"One of us writes a controversial book about the experience and claims the entire incident is a true story. Most people probably won't believe us, but at least we'll inform the public. The controversy will spread the knowledge. Plus, we can start an organization where we will share our experience called the World as One."

John and Jack nodded. "I can do the book," John offered. "It's not like I'm not used to the controversy. *Id Speak* caused a stir when it came out."

"I can run the World as One," Grace offered.

"I think those are great ideas," said Abe. "I'll run the technological support for our efforts."

Grace agreed. "The task of defending the planet seemed overwhelming, especially with the finances and getting the word out. Now, it seems within reach."

"Yeah, good job, Miranda," said Jack.

Miranda nodded. "It's my tribute to you, Dr. Gallagher, and to all of you. When I felt the easiest thing for me to do was give up, you didn't give up on me. Now I will fight them to my last breath."

"Since we will be working together, Miss Miranda," Jack smiled, "the first thing you need to do is call me Jack."

Miranda smiled. "Okay, Jack."

"So, how are you going to handle this with your boyfriend and your sister?" asked Jack.

Alison and Steven, ever-present in her thoughts, blissfully unaware that life as they know it will end. How could she tell them? Would they believe her? Would they remember up until the MRI with a bit of prodding? Should she stay together with Steven and put him in constant danger? Maybe she should move away, to Yemen or Tibet or something. Feign a business trip or an international job, pack up the team, and move. It would be safer for her dear loved ones than sticking around. At this point, it was about as safe to be around her as it was being around an armed nuclear bomb. "I don't know yet. On some level, I hope they never remember what I went through."

Jack nodded.

"Thank you. Thank you all again. And thank you to Metatron. These aliens might have entered our world through me, but I will make sure they will be wiped from the face of the earth through me. We are at war."

Miranda's eyes glowed bright green, smoldering with defiance, fueling her next statement where her confidence lacked, unsure she would ever be capable of achieving her new life's dream. "And maybe, one day, I'll save you all, too."

• • •

In the dark recesses in between galaxies, the electromagnetic portal right next to the earth whisked the defeated demon onto the star path leading back to his world, leaving behind his commander and comrades in a pile of black ashes. Lucifer would torture him for their failure. He might have tortured them even if they succeeded.

In a sense, the mission had been an overwhelming success. His commander gathered a detailed account of how to conquer each human on earth.

To his father, though, total success was the only option. Without it, only total failure exists, and because his team was not able to achieve total success, Lucifer would see it as a total failure, and for that, his punishment was eminent.

A hatred for all mankind burned deep within him and a desire for Earth to explode into little tiny pieces. He would endure his punishment to help his kind realize their Father's will and their ultimate desire...

The decimation of the human race.

About the Author

Kirsten has written hundreds of parenting and mental health articles and has edited thousands as an expert mental health professional. She fetched an international award with her first co-authored book, *Farming Industrial Hemp: Not Your Daddy's Tobacco*, which was instrumental in raising awareness of the dangers of growing industrial hemp in unsafe conditions and influencing Congress in growing guidelines for the budding industry. Her foray into fiction includes *Go!*, a short story that was presented to Simon & Schuster as an award in a contest and published in *The Potato Soup Journal* twice, once in 2022 and once in March 2023 in their best-of anthology. She serves as the Vice President of Apex Literary Management, a boutique literary agency, and is the lover of long subtitles.

CONNECT WITH KIRSTEN G. SCHUDER

For a special thank you for reading this book, **sign up for Kirsten's email list** to **receive your free story**, *12 Hours*, based on a true story of Dr. Gallagher's survival of the 12-hour prison riot.

Also, receive news on the publication of the next book in this series, *Inside Dweller: Book II: IN-Vasion*, and many other free stories:

https://kirstenschuder.gr8.com/

Come join the conversation on Medium,
Kirsten’s Short Attention Span
https://medium.com/kirstens-short-attention-span

Connect with Kirsten's on social media:

Pinterest: https://www.pinterest.com/kirstenschudera/
Facebook: https://www.facebook.com/kirsten.schuder/
Twitter: https://twitter.com/KirstenSchuder
Linkedin: www.linkedin.com/in/kirsten-schuder-161a0672

NOTE FROM KIRSTEN G. SCHUDER

Word-of-mouth is crucial for any author to succeed. If you enjoyed *Inside Dweller*, please leave a review online—anywhere you are able. Even if it's just a sentence or two. It would make all the difference and would be very much appreciated.

Thanks!
Kirsten G. Schuder

Made in the USA
Columbia, SC
02 January 2024

29727706R00212